W9-BXL-691

PURSUIT

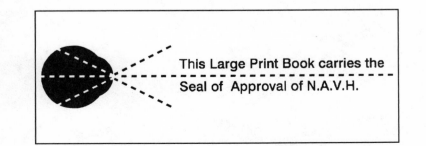

This Large Print Book carries the
Seal of Approval of N.A.V.H.

PURSUIT

KAREN ROBARDS

WHEELER PUBLISHING
A part of Gale, Cengage Learning

Detroit • New York • San Francisco • New Haven, Conn • Waterville, Maine • London

GALE
CENGAGE Learning™

Wheeler Publishing Large Print Hardcover.
The text of this Large Print edition is unabridged.
Other aspects of the book may vary from the original edition.
Set in 16 pt. Plantin.
Printed on permanent paper.

LIBRARY OF CONGRESS CATALOGING-IN-PUBLICATION DATA

Robards, Karen.
    Pursuit / by Karen Robards.
        p. cm. — (Wheeler Publishing large print hardcover)
    ISBN-13: 978-1-59722-889-3 (alk. paper)
    ISBN-10: 1-59722-889-3 (alk. paper)
    1. Women lawyers—Fiction. 2. Traffic accident investigation—Fiction. 3. Presidents' spouses—Crimes against—Fiction. 4. Adultery—Fiction. 5. Conspiracies—Fiction. 6. Washington (D.C.)—Fiction. 7. Large type books. I. Title.
PS3568.O196P87 2009b
813'.54—dc22   2009000207

Published in 2009 in arrangement with G. P. Putnam's Sons, a member of Penguin Group (USA) Inc.

Printed in the United States of America
1 2 3 4 5 6 7 13 12 11 10 09

As always, this is for
Doug, Peter, Chris, and Jack.
with love.

ACKNOWLEDGMENTS

First of all, I want to thank my wonderful editor, Christine Pepe, who has done such a great job with this book. I also want to thank my agent, Robert Gottlieb. More thanks go to Leslie Gelbman, Kara Welsh, and everyone at Signet, and to Stephanie Sorensen in Publicity. Finally, to Ivan Held and the rest of the Putnam family, many thanks for your continued support.

I couldn't do it without any of you!

1

"Is she there? Do you see her?"

As Jessica Ford pushed through the smoked-glass door in front of her, cell phone clamped to her ear, urgency sharpened John Davenport's voice to the point where the alcohol-induced slurring of his words almost disappeared.

"Yes," Jess answered, her hand tightening around the phone as the door swung shut behind her, because the lady was and she did.

On the fringe of a raucous crowd intent on watching a televised basketball game, the First Lady of the United States was sitting alone at a table for two in a dark, secluded corner of the hotel bar, knocking back a shot of some undetermined golden liquid with the stiff wrist and easy gulp of a practiced drinker. Wearing a generic black tracksuit with white stripes down the sides and white running shoes. With her trademark short blond hair tucked up beneath a baseball cap pulled low over her eyes. The sheer unlikelihood of her presence in this mid-priced hotel just a few blocks from the White House at ten minutes past midnight on a Saturday night, plus a strategically placed leafy potted ficus near her elbow, was all that stood between her and a Texas-size scandal.

Jess felt butterflies at the realization.

"Thank God." Davenport's tone was devout. "Tell her . . ."

A cheer from the basketball fans made it impossible for Jess to hear the rest. Grimacing, fearing disaster with every way-too-fast beat of her heart, she hurried toward the corner.

Even knowing what she did, her mind boggled at what she was being asked to do. She was not the First Lady's handler.

"I couldn't hear you. It's kind of crowded in here," Jess said into the phone as the cheering died down.

"Shit." Davenport added a few more choice words under his breath. "Just get her out of there, would you?"

"Yes." Jess had already learned not to say "I'll do my best" to her formidable boss. He would snap that he wasn't paying for her to do her best, he was paying for her to *do it.* End of story. The phone disconnected with a click in her ear. Okay, the problem was now officially hers.

Where the hell is the Secret Service when you need them?

Casting another glance around, she had her answer: Nowhere useful, obviously. There wasn't a black suit in sight.

Davenport had said the First Lady would be alone. Silly of her to have doubted the all-knowing one.

"Mrs. Cooper?" she asked in a low voice as she reached the table, mindful of possible listening ears. Besides the First Lady and the basketball fans, there were only a few other patrons in the small, wood-paneled room. No one seemed even remotely interested in the solitary woman in the corner.

Still, it never paid to take chances. She needed to get her newest problem out of there fast.

The First Lady continued to stare at her now-empty shot glass. If she'd heard Jess speak to her, she gave no indication of it. Clearing her throat, Jess tried again.

"Mrs. Cooper? Mr. Davenport sent me."

That did it. The brim of the baseball cap tilted up. The look Mrs. Cooper gave her was tense, wary.

11

"Who're you?"

Jess attempted a reassuring smile. It felt tight.

"Jessica Ford. I work for Mr. Davenport."

The blue eyes that seemed so soft and gentle on TV and in magazine spreads narrowed. Tonight they were red-rimmed and puffy, devoid of obvious makeup, and hard. The attractive, round-cheeked face was puffy, too, and pale, but still instantly familiar in the way a fuzzy copy of an iconic photograph is familiar. The lines seemed blurred, the angles less defined, the features indistinct, but the subject was definitely recognizable.

It was impossible to miss that Mrs. Cooper had been crying.

They fight a lot. She and David. All you need to do is hold her hand and nod sympathetically until she gets it out of her system, Davenport had said.

David being the President. Of the United States. And before she could get busy with the hand-holding, Jess first had to coax his wife — one of the most recognizable women in the world — out of a packed hotel bar she had no business being in. Without anyone recognizing the icon in their midst. Jess could already almost feel a posse of gossip-hungry reporters panting at her heels.

FIRST LADY FLEES WHITE HOUSE, the headlines would scream.

Oh, jeez. If she screwed this up, she would probably lose her job. For sure, her boss would go crazy. The *world* would go crazy. The image of the weepy, sweats-clad, runaway First Lady would be plastered on every TV screen and on the front page of every newspaper and magazine in the world. The political fallout would be incalculable. The personal fallout would be incalculable. And hers would be the first head on the chopping block.

This was way too much responsibility. Jess felt her palms grow damp. She clasped them in front of her. *Do not wring them.*

She didn't, but she still must have looked less than reassuring because the First Lady's expression turned hostile.

"I don't know you. I want John."

Perfectly manicured pink nails drummed the table. Then Mrs. Cooper's well-tended hand curled around the cell phone lying beside the shot glass. Davenport was the First Lady's old friend and personal lawyer. Jess was a lawyer, too, junior grade, who had been working for the filthy-rich megafirm of Davenport, Kelly, and Bascomb, the most prestigious and powerful of the giant

13

legal firms operating in the shadow of the U.S. Capitol, for just under a year. Although officially known as an associate, Jess sometimes thought her main duty consisted of asking "How high?" when Davenport said "Jump." When Davenport had hired her part-time during her second year at George Mason School of Law, which catered almost equally to older night-schoolers wanting to change careers and hardscrabble kids with crippling student loans and no money, such as herself, Jess had been giddy with excitement over her good fortune. This was her big chance, an opportunity to grab the golden ring for herself and her family, and there was no way she was going to blow it. If she had to work a hundred hours a week, she would work a hundred hours a week. If she had to put up with crap from the Ivy League blue bloods in the corner offices, she would put up with crap. If she had to be more efficient, more knowledgeable, and more determined than everybody else to get where she wanted to go, then that's what she was going to do.

That was the game plan. And so far it was working. She'd been offered a full-time position upon graduation, and she did the prep work on many of Davenport's most important cases. The drudge behind the star, that was her. For now. Not forever.

Jess definitely knew who Annette Cooper was. Not surprisingly, although the First Lady had been in the office a number of times while Jess had been there and Jess had once been sent to hand-deliver some papers to her, Mrs. Cooper didn't remember her.

Wallpaper, that's what I am, she thought as Mrs. Cooper punched a single button on the phone and lifted it to her ear while running suspicious eyes over Jess. Jess took quick mental inventory in conjunction with Mrs. Cooper's sweeping look: twenty-eight years old but younger-looking; chin-length mahogany hair pushed haphazardly behind her ears; square-jawed, even-featured, ivory-skinned face with a hastily applied minimum of makeup imperfectly concealing a scattering of freckles; hazel eyes complete with contacts; five-two, slim, regrettably flat-chested; dressed in her favorite go-to black pantsuit with a black tee and, unfortunately, well-broken-in black sneakers (she usually wore heels when working because she needed the height). She was wearing the sneakers because her new roommate, her college-student sister, Grace, had apparently "borrowed" her good black heels without asking and had scattered the rest of her meager shoe wardrobe around the walk-in closet they now shared.

"You sent a *flunky?*" Mrs. Cooper spoke in an outraged tone into the phone. Davenport presumably had answered. There was a pause, and then Mrs. Cooper swept another condemning look over Jess. "Are you sure? She looks fifteen years old."

Jess tried to shut her ears and keep her face impassive even as she positioned herself between her new charge and one of the couples. Luckily, the noise level in the bar made it extremely unlikely that they could hear a thing.

Jess only wished she were so lucky. That she had not yet succeeded in impressing Mrs. Cooper was excruciatingly clear.

"Not when you do something like send over a teenage stand-in. This is *it,* do you hear? *I mean it.* I need *you.*"

Whether fighting with her husband was a regular feature of Mrs. Cooper's life or not, she sounded both angry and desperate. Her voice was low but increasingly shrill. She blinked rapidly. Her cheeks had flushed a deep, distressed pink.

Uncomfortable, Jess glanced away.

I'm counting on you for this, Davenport had said in the phone call that had interrupted Jess's sleepy viewing of a Lifetime movie from the cozy comfort of her bed and sent her scrambling out of her pj's and into the car he had sent to pick her up. From the way Davenport had slurred his words, it was obvious he'd been imbibing pretty heavily.

In no shape to babysit Annette tonight, was how he had unapologetically put it. *Anyway, I'm not home. It'd take me an hour or more to get there. While you . . .*

Her apartment was maybe ten minutes away.

As she had scrambled into her clothes she'd thought, *This is a chance to get to know the First Lady.* It's inner-circle stuff, the kind of thing that any newbie lawyer would kill for. It could lead to a promotion. It could lead to a whole lot more . . . everything. Responsibility. Prestige. Money. Always, in the end, it came down to money.

The story of her life.

"But I *need* you. This is an *emergency.* Do you hear? This is *it,*" Mrs. Cooper told Davenport again, louder than before, drawing Jess's attention back to her. To Jess's horror, big tears started to leak from the First Lady's eyes and roll down her cheeks. Her face crumpled, her mouth shook, and so did the hand holding the phone. Jess shot a sideways glance at the next table, then tensed at the sound of a footstep behind her. Pivoting, using her body to block the sight line to her illustrious charge as best she could, she confronted a waiter who was clearly intent on checking in with the customer at the corner table.

Yikes.

"I tell you, it's *true*," Mrs. Cooper continued in what was almost a sob, growing louder with every word. Sight lines she could block, Jess thought despairingly. Voices, not so much. "It's a nightmare. You have to help me."

"We don't need anything else, thanks," Jess said brightly to the waiter.

"You sure?" The waiter was maybe mid-twenties, a slight guy with dark hair and eyes. His gaze slid past Jess, seeking Mrs. Cooper, who was — thank God — silent again, apparently listening to Davenport now. Jess could only hope that the woman's head was once again down, with the baseball cap obscuring her face.

Taking a sliding step to the left with the intention of more completely blocking the waiter's view, Jess nodded.

"I'm sure."

"That'll be twelve dollars, then."

Twelve dollars. Okay, Jess, pay the First Lady's bar bill.

Jess opened her shoulder bag, felt around

in the zipper compartment where she kept her money, came up empty, looked down and suffered a split second of horror as she discovered that Grace had "borrowed" her cash along with her shoes. She didn't really want to hand over a credit card, because she had some sort of barely coalescing idea that it would be better if there was no hard evidence that she — and, ergo, Mrs. Cooper — was ever in this bar. Besides, the object was to break land speed records getting the First Lady out of there and waiting for her card to be returned would not facilitate that. Before she could completely panic, she remembered the emergency twenty-dollar bill she kept folded away at the bottom of the zippered compartment of her purse from force of habit now, although it had begun at her mother's insistence when she had gone to her first — and only — high school dance.

Honey, believe me, you don't want to have to count on any man for anything, not even a ride home.

Words to live by, Mom.

Jess handed the twenty over, and the waiter hurried away.

Enjoy the tip. A tinge of regret about forking over money she didn't even owe colored the thought. The whole twenty was gone, of course. Because she couldn't wait for change.

"As quick as you can," Mrs. Cooper said, her tone urgent. "Hurry."

Jess turned back to the table in time to see the phone snap shut. Mrs. Cooper lowered it, holding it clenched tightly in her hand. Then she looked up at Jess. Her jaw was hard and set. Her eyes were still damp, but tears no longer spilled over. Instead, the soft blue glinted with — what? Anger? Determination? Some combination of the two?

"I can't believe that bastard sent you instead of coming himself."

Jess blinked. The reality of the woman in front of her juxtaposed with the First Lady's saccharine image was starting to make her head spin.

"Mr. Davenport was afraid he couldn't get here quickly enough." The calmness of Jess's tone belied the hard knot of tension forming in her stomach. "I brought a car. It's waiting outside. We should go, before . . ."

A small but comprehensive gesture finished her sentence: *before somebody figures out who you are and the shit hits the fan.*

"Don't give me that. He's drunk as a skunk." Mrs. Cooper abruptly stood up, the legs of her chair scraping loudly back over the wood floor. Despite the potentially attention-attracting sound, Jess breathed a silent sigh of relief. It had just occurred to her that if Mrs. Cooper didn't want to move, she had no way of budging her. Tugging the brim of her cap lower over her face, and tucking an envelope-size, absolutely gorgeous, and totally inappropriate crystal-studded evening bag beneath her arm, Mrs. Cooper stepped away from the table. "All right, let's go."

Without another word, braced for the possibility of discovery with each step, Jess turned and led the way to the door. As she skirted their tables, the basketball fans leaped to their feet, cheering in deafening unison and nearly causing her heart to leap out of her chest. She stopped dead. A glance over her shoulder showed her that Mrs. Cooper, likewise clearly startled, had stopped in her tracks as well, her mouth dropping open, her eyes shooting fearfully to the celebrating crowd. But their noisy exuberance had nothing to do with her, and, indeed, the rowdy focus on the TV provided some much-needed cover for their hastily resumed exit. Walking quickly once the initial shock had passed, they made it safely out of the bar without anyone noticing them at all.

At least, so Jess hoped. But with cell phones being as ubiquitous as they were, all it took was one vaguely curious onlooker to snap a picture and . . .

I am so out of my league here.

The dim, old-fashioned lobby was about twenty feet wide and three times that long, with the reception desk and bell stand opposite the bar and an adjacent restaurant that was now closed and dark. Only a single female clerk in a red blazer stood behind the reception counter, talking on the phone and paying no attention to the two women newly emerged from the bar. The bell stand, located a dozen wide marble steps down from the reception desk, at street level, was deserted. A red-jacketed doorman waited beside the triple glass doors, holding one open for — whom? Jess couldn't see who was on the way inside, but someone definitely was, and as a consequence she felt more exposed than ever.

Keep moving.

"This way." Keeping her voice low, she indicated the main entrance with a gesture. Mrs. Cooper nodded and fell in beside her.

Jess was just thankful that Mrs. Cooper finally seemed to be aware of just how vulnerable to discovery she was and how disastrous that discovery could be. Keeping her head down, the woman took care to stay between Jess and the wall. Striding along beside her, Jess held her breath, her heart pounding, her gaze fixed on that open door. *Anyone could walk through it, glance up, and . . .*

Just as they reached the top of the steps, a pair of middle-aged men, low-level executives from the quality of their suits, brushed through the open door one after the other, each dragging his own battered suitcase on wheels, which clattered along behind them like noisy, overweight black dogs.

"Can I take those for you?" the bellman asked. The businessmen brushed him off with curt shakes of the head and began lugging the suitcases up the steps themselves while the doorman, deprived of his hoped-for tip, scowled after them. Hugging the paneled wall on the opposite side of the stairs, Jess and Mrs. Cooper hurried on down. As far as Jess could tell, neither the businessmen nor the doorman even so much as glanced their way.

I'm not qualified for this. Scandal Quashing 101 wasn't even on the course list in law school.

"Where's the car?" On the last step now, Mrs. Cooper looked out at the street through the plate-glass doors that were just ahead. She seemed tense, on edge — just about as tense and on edge as Jess felt.

"Out front." Jess hadn't thought to tell the driver to wait anywhere else. A screwup, probably, she realized now. She probably should have looked for a side entrance, but she had been in such a hurry at the time that she had just told the driver to stop at the entrance and scrambled out. She could only hope that in the end it wouldn't matter.

"We need to hurry. They'll be looking for me."

"Who?" Jess asked before she thought, although the answer was almost instantly clear: most of official Washington. The press corps. Her husband.

"The Secret Service."

Oh, yeah. Them, too. Although, come to think of it, Mrs. Cooper could probably use a bodyguard about now. And I could certainly use some backup.

As she pushed through the thick glass door at the far end of the trio from the one the businessmen had used, the knot in Jess's stomach twisted tighter. For the first time it really dawned on her what she was doing: spiriting away an unprotected, emotionally overwrought, on-the-lam First Lady. *On*

24

Davenport's instructions, she reminded herself, but the sensation that she was getting in way over her head here persisted.

Next time the phone rings at midnight, I don't answer it, she promised herself as the cold, fresh air of the early April night blew her hair back from her face and plastered her jacket against her body. The smell of car exhaust notwithstanding, its briskness was a welcome antidote to the overly warm mustiness of the aging hotel. *You don't have to be at Davenport's beck and call twenty-four hours a day, you know.*

But the sad truth was that she did, if she wanted to keep collecting her nice fat paycheck. Which, thanks to her always-good-for-a-complication family, she now needed more than ever.

"So, where is it?" Mrs. Cooper meant the car. She stopped on the sidewalk beside Jess, who had paused, too, briefly taken aback. The car was not parked where it had been when she had exited it some ten minutes before, which was just to the left of the front entrance, mere steps from where they now looked for it in vain.

Good question, Jess thought as she glanced swiftly around. The white glow of the hotel's marquee was too bright for comfort. She felt like they were standing under a spotlight. Other nearby businesses — a sushi bar, a liquor store, a pharmacy — spilled light out over the sidewalk, too. A steady stream of vehicles cruised the street in both directions, their headlights providing even more illumination. There were people everywhere, strolling the sidewalk, entering and leaving stores, exiting a car that had just parked in front of the sushi bar. Their noise rose over the steady hum of the traffic. Anyone could glance their way and . . .

"Can I get you ladies a cab?" the doorman asked, making Jess jump. He was right at her shoulder, and she hadn't heard him approach at all.

"N-no, we're fine, thanks." With a shake of her head she fobbed him off, then, without thinking about the whole breach of protocol such a gesture probably constituted until it was too late, caught Mrs. Cooper firmly by the arm. Heart thudding, desperately scanning both sides of the street for the errant car, she pulled the First Lady away from the bright lights of the hotel. *Please let it be here some . . . Hallelujah. There it is.* Her breath expelled in a sigh of relief. "The car's right up there."

The black Lincoln that Davenport had sent waited at the end of the line of cars parked bumper to bumper at meters almost to the intersection. It had pulled over to the curb in the no-man's-land between the legally parked cars and the traffic light. Red parking lights glowing at them through the darkness told Jess that the driver had, as instructed, kept the engine running.

"Oh, shit, there's Prescott." Ducking her head, Mrs. Cooper picked up the pace. She moved quickly between Jess and the buildings on her right, her shoulders hunched now as she sought to deflect the casual glances of passersby.

"Who's Prescott?" Voice hushed, Jess cast a hunted look over her shoulder.

"One of my detail."

"Secret Service?" Jess perked up. At least the responsibility for keeping this woman safe would no longer be hers alone. Yes, there he was, a tall, well-built man in a tailored dark suit talking to the doorman in front of the hotel. White shirt, dark tie. Short, neat, dark hair. Handsome, clean-shaven face. Lifting his hand to his mouth to say something into his fist. He might as well have been wearing a flashing neon sign.

Reinforcements at last. Thank God.

"What are you doing?" Mrs. Cooper grabbed her hand when Jess started to wave at Prescott to signal their location.

"You need protection and . . ."

"Protection?" Mrs. Cooper's laugh was bitter. The hand holding Jess's tightened until Jess's fingers hurt. "They're more like wardens." Her eyes blazed into Jess's. "Don't you understand, you stupid little girl? *I'm a fucking prisoner.*" Her gaze shot past Jess's shoulder. *"Get back in the car."*

By this time they had reached the Lincoln. Mrs. Cooper's fierce command was hurled at the driver, a burly redhead in a black chauffeur's uniform who was at that moment coming around the front of the car, presumably to open the door for his passengers.

As she spoke, Mrs. Cooper jerked open the rear passenger door and ducked inside. With one hand on the open door, Jess exchanged glances with the startled driver. He shrugged and obediently reversed directions. Her gaze slid toward the Secret Service agent, who was looking their way.

Jess hesitated. The First Lady was way more upset than a simple fight with her husband should dictate, and . . .

"Get in," Mrs. Cooper barked.

The driver was already sliding behind the wheel.

His eyes fixed on the Lincoln, now clearly suspecting that his principal was inside, the Secret Service agent turned, waved, and started to jog their way.

"*Go. Now,*" Mrs. Cooper shrieked. Jess looked down just in time to watch as the First Lady's hand slapped the back of the front seat hard.

There was no time. The driver put the car in gear. Heart thudding, Jess flung one more doubtful glance back at the man who was now racing toward them. Then, throwing herself into the backseat with the woman she'd been sent to collect, she slammed the door just as the Lincoln screeched away from the curb.

2

The crash scene was horrific. Smoke roiled in thick gray coils from the overturned car. Having blazed so hot that the tires had exploded and the pines in which the vehicle had come to rest had gone up like torches, the fire, courtesy of the multitude of orange-coated firefighters who were still wetting down the surrounding areas, was now out. Shortly after the crash, the flames had blazed so high that he had been able to see the bright red glow from ten miles out as he had raced to the scene. The smell on the wind — Secret Service Agent Mark Ryan didn't want to think about that. It reminded him of charred meat.

Word was, three people had died in the overturned black Lincoln at the bottom of the ravine. Officially, the identities of the dead had not yet been confirmed, but unofficially he knew that one of them was Annette Cooper, the First Lady of the

United States. Mark thought of the thousands of threats against the First Family that poured into the White House monthly, of the hairy foreign tours to hostile regions they'd shepherded the First Lady through, of the dozens of protesters waving signs and shouting slogans at nearly all her official engagements, at the constant threat of the lone nut job of whom they lived in fear because it was the hardest to prepare for, and thus defend against. He thought of the bomb-sniffing dogs and bulletproof limos and rooftop snipers and legions of police and military types and, yes, the best personal protection agency in the world, the U.S. Secret Service, deployed for the First Family's protection everywhere they went.

There was no other security apparatus to equal it anywhere in the world.

And yet the First Lady of the United States had just died in a fiery car crash.

Already, at one-thirty-five a.m. Sunday, a little less than an hour after the crash, the news was starting to reverberate around the world. And all hell was breaking loose.

As the head of her security team, or, as he was officially known, special agent in charge of detail, he was responsible. The unthinkable had happened on his watch. The knowledge rode like a stone in his gut. His throat

31

felt tight, like someone was gripping it hard. He was sweating buckets even though the temperature had dropped during these predawn hours to the mid-forties.

How the hell had it happened?

"Halt! This is a protected area. You'll have to go back."

One of the marines whose unit guarded the site belatedly became aware of Mark's presence as he slid the few remaining feet to the bottom of the steep, brushy slope, and stepped forward to confront him. About a hundred feet beyond the marines, a circle of klieg lights had been set up to illuminate the crash site in a merciless white glow. To Mark's left, at the edge of the flat area at the base of the slope, tall pines swaying in the wind blocked much of the star-studded sky. A rain-swollen creek rushed past, gleaming black through the thicket of tree trunks. It was dark and hazy where he came to an obedient stop just outside the reach of the bright blaze of the rescue lights, and the equally bright blaze of the TV crews setting up shop on the roadway and bridge above. Having already penetrated the first level of protection designed to keep reporters and camera crews and everyone else at bay, Mark had his ID in hand.

"Secret Service." He flashed his gold

shield and was allowed to pass. The final circle of protection, the FBI, swarmed near the car. Over the snap, crackle, and pop of the superheated metal, the hiss of the settling foam, and the *thump-thump-thump* of the helicopters circling overhead, he could hear them shouting at one another through their transmitters. Closer still, a forensics team in orange coveralls was already setting up shop. Clenching his jaw, he picked his way carefully through the knee-high brush, eyeing the flattened bushes and shorn-in-half trees that marked the car's death roll from the highway forty feet above. Finally, his gaze settled on the smoking hulk of the car, which rested on its crushed roof.

Fury, disbelief, shock, all combined to send adrenaline surging through his system. Uselessly. Because it was too late. There was nothing he could do.

What was she doing outside the White House? What was she doing in that fucking car?

A stretcher was being carried up the slope toward one of the half-dozen ambulances that waited, silent but with strobe lights flashing, on the highway above. Mark didn't know the identity of the body-bagged victim, but he knew who it wasn't: Mrs. Cooper was already gone, having been taken away first in the medevac helicopter that had been rushed to the scene. He'd been en route when the word had come that she was dead, killed in the crash, her body so badly burned that she was almost unrecognizable. But he had continued on, driven by a fierce need to see the site of the impossible for himself.

What the hell had gone down here?

When he had left the White House at eleven p.m., just over two and a half hours earlier, the First Lady had only moments before excused herself from a dinner for the president of Chile. Pleading a headache, she stepped into the East Wing private quarters' elevator that would whisk her up to the family residence. He had watched the doors close on the slim figure in the glamorous white evening gown, said a few words to Will Prescott, the agent on post in front of the elevator, and proceeded on down to the Secret Service White House command post in the basement. Once inside, he had spoken briefly with the agents covering the monitors streaming real-time, full-color views of all hallways and rooms except the most private areas of the residence. At the large electronic board that displayed color photos of every member of the White House Secret Service detail, he'd punched a button to transfer his name to the off-duty column. Then he'd glanced at the digitized protectee locator board that tracked each member of the First Family from room to room, and noticed that only Mrs. Cooper was in the residence, and she was in her bedroom.

Safe and secure for one more night. Or so he had thought.

Now she was dead.

What the hell had gone wrong?

"Who the — oh, it's you." The speaker was FBI Special Agent Ted Parks, whom Mark had known for the twelve years he'd been with the Secret Service and disliked for at least half that time. Of average height, wiry and bald as an egg at forty, making him four years Mark's senior, Parks had his hands thrust deep in his trouser pockets as he surveyed the scene. His narrow face looked ghastly in the harsh glare of the rescue lights. Shock or grief, Mark supposed. Annette Cooper had been wildly popular — at least with those who didn't know her personally. "This is un-fucking-believable."

Mark didn't even grunt in reply. He just kept on walking toward the car. The chemical smell of the foam they'd used to put out the flames was almost stronger than the burned smell. Almost.

35

"Hey, sorry about Prescott," Parks called after him.

Prescott. The name hit him like a blow to the stomach. It confirmed something he'd been told but still didn't want to believe: Secret Service Agent Will Prescott, his subordinate and a good guy, had been in that car. Last time Mark had seen him, Prescott was settling in for a long, boring eight-hour shift in front of the elevator. The job was like that: endless hours of routine punctuated by the rare few minutes of excitement. God save them all from those few minutes.

Prescott and the First Lady in a car of unknown origin speeding away from the White House to an unknown destination. What the hell had happened while he'd been picking up his belated dinner at a McDonald's drive-thru and heading home through the Virginia countryside to the house he now shared solely and reluctantly with an emotionally needy cat?

The third victim was reported to be the driver. A professional chauffeur. He'd been IDed, but Mark couldn't remember his name. All he knew at this moment was that whoever the guy was, he had no business driving Annette Cooper. She had official vehicles with highly trained drivers and full-bore protection to take her anywhere she needed to go. No way should she have been in that car.

"I'm sorry, sir. No one's allowed past this point." Another marine blocked his path. Just beyond him, an official barricade of sawhorses and police tape was being set up around the destroyed car. Now that the last of the bodies had been removed, emphasis was shifting to investigating the crash. He stopped, because there was nothing to be gained by going any nearer. He was already so close that he could feel the residual heat of the burned-out wreckage on his face. There was no brush here where the car had landed, and the dry thicket of last year's grass beneath his feet was short. Short and crisp and black because it had been charred in the fire.

"Fucking press." FBI agent Jim Smolski stopped at his elbow, taking a deep drag on a cigarette as he glanced up the slope. Following his gaze, Mark became aware of a TV crew still filming avidly as a contingent of marines herded them back to the narrow blacktop road, where a barricade manned by the Virginia State Police had been set up to contain them. At least half a dozen TV vans were on the scene, unmistakable because of their logos and antennas, and another one, rooftop antenna rotating wildly, arrived even as he watched. A growing throng of reporters crowded the barricade, jockeying for position and attention as they shouted questions down at rescuers.

"Was the First Lady killed instantly?" "Who else was in the car?" "Where was Annette going?" "Where's David?" "Any idea what caused the accident?" "Who was driving?" "Is the President okay?"

Luckily, the questions weren't directed at him. Mark shut the reporters' voices out as he focused on more important matters. Debris was strewn along the path the tumbling car had taken, scattered among the mutilated greenery as if it had been shaken out of a giant salt shaker. A hubcap, bits of taillight, a shoe . . .

His eye was caught by something that glittered silver in the bright beam of the camera crew's retreating light.

"Somebody's going down big-time for this." Smolski cut his eyes toward Mark. "I'm glad I'm not you guys."

Mark's gut tightened.

On my watch.

"I thought you quit smoking." He turned away, the better to pinpoint the location of the silver thing as he spoke. It was lodged in a bush, an uncrushed bush three-quarters of the way up the slope that was about twenty feet to the right of the car's path.

"I started up again."

Mark grimaced. "After this, I might, too."

Walking away from the perimeter that was now almost fully established around the smoking hulk of the car, Mark picked his way up the slope toward the flash of silver. More helicopters circled overhead now, search beams playing down over the wreckage like dueling Jedi light-sabers. Air swirled like a mini-tornado around him as a particularly aggressive chopper swooped in low. Glancing up, Mark saw the familiar NBC peacock logo on its door.

Goddamn vultures.

Without the TV crew's light, the silver thing became almost impossible to see. Mark kept his eyes trained on the bush, which, he saw as he grew closer, was some sort of scrubby evergreen. There was a whole thicket of them, about waist high, with branches like hairy tentacles that swayed in the wind kicked up by the choppers. Up here, courtesy of the snapped-off trees, the scent of pine was strong, reminding him of the Christmas tree–shaped air freshener his now fifteen-year-old daughter Taylor had hung from the rearview mirror of his car when he'd still been a pack-a-day smoker.

When had those become the good old days?

He couldn't see the silver thing anymore: It was too dark. But he remembered where it was. Reaching in among the prickly branches, he touched it almost at once, felt the cold bumpiness of the surface, and instantly suspected what it had to be: the First Lady's elegant evening bag. He had last seen the sparkling bauble clutched in her right hand as the elevator doors had closed on her. Leaving her, as he'd thought, safe and sound for the night.

Wrong again.

Pulling it out, looking down at it, experiencing the weight of it in his hand, he suddenly felt the urge to puke. It drove home with brutal finality the hard truth that the impossible had happened: Annette Cooper was dead.

He glanced back down at the accident scene. Pictures were now being taken of the blackened car from every angle and what looked like survey equipment was being set up to, if his memory of accident investigation techniques served him correctly, measure the distance the car had traveled from the road above before coming to rest on its roof. Several members of the forensic unit were down on all fours to, presumably, take a look at the inside of the car. He opened his mouth to yell at investigators, announcing his find.

Then he looked down at the small, crystal-studded rectangle and shut his mouth again.

After only a split second of indecision, he flipped open the clasp and reached inside. Along with the various assorted cosmetics and small brush she customarily carried, there were a number of credit cards held together by a rubber band and a good-sized roll of cash. As surprising as those items were — the First Lady never paid for anything herself and, therefore, as far as he was aware, never carried credit cards or money — they were not his target. Just as he had been sure it would be, the brown plastic bottle of tablet-style artificial sweetener the First Lady supposedly favored and took with her everywhere was tucked down at the bottom, nestled against the smooth satin lining. Only, as he had learned to his dismay, the pills inside the bottle weren't aspartame. They were painkillers — Vicodin, Percocet, you name it, including, most recently and disastrously, OxyContin, to which Mrs. Cooper was — had been — hopelessly addicted.

Mark's hand closed over the bottle, which he removed and stuffed in his jacket pocket. The pills inside rattled insistently.

Serve and protect.

She was dead, but he meant to do what he still could to honor that vow. No way was he letting that bottle fall into the wrong hands.

"Yo, up here!" he yelled, and as a couple of FBI heads craned his way, he waved at them. Then, realizing that the bright lights blazing in their faces coupled with the darkness of where he stood prevented them from seeing him, he turned to go back down the slope, the purse now ready to be turned over to the investigation.

He'd taken no more than a step when the sound came out of the darkness to his left. It was the merest breath of a whimper. But it caught his attention, stopping him in his tracks. He looked sharply in its direction.

Something lay curled on the ground just beyond the bush where he'd found the purse. He could just make out the dark shape of . . . what?

Frowning, moving cautiously toward it, Mark at last realized what it was and caught his breath.

It was a body. A girl's small, slender body,

lying crumpled and broken among the swaying evergreens.

3

"Lie still. Help's coming."

Those words penetrated the darkness Jess was lost in. It was a horrible darkness, riven with screams and pain and an explosion of hot, leaping flames. Warm, strong fingers touched her neck, her cheek, and she swam even closer to full consciousness.

My God, my God . . .

"I need some help over here! There's an injured woman!"

The shout, uttered in the same deep, drawling male voice that had told her to lie still, sent terror stabbing through her.

No, no . . .

"Shh," she breathed, because that was the best she could do. He was crouched beside her, bending over her, she realized, and realized too in that moment when she saw stars swirling through the ink-black sky beyond the dark shape of his head that her eyes were now open.

Not dead, then.

The reality of his large body looming so close caused her heart to leap. Her stomach cramped with fear. She sucked in air.

The pungent smell of something burning filled her nostrils. It stung her throat, curled down into her lungs.

Please, God, no.

"Hey! We need help!"

"Be quiet," she whispered, clutching desperately at his trouser leg. She tried to make the caution urgent, sharper and louder, but it came out sounding more like a sigh. A deep, pain-wracked sigh. With reason: She hurt. All over.

Cold. So cold. Freezing cold.

"It's gonna be okay. There's an ambulance here."

The man stood up. Her grip on his trouser leg tightened. He'd made no move to hurt her — he couldn't be one of the demonish wraiths from her dream. Could he? Her instincts said no. He felt safe, somehow. Like she could trust him. Her hand made a tight fist around the cloth near where it broke over his shoe. Conviction coalesced inside her: Whatever happened, he mustn't leave her here in the dark alone.

"We had a wreck." The words hurt her throat as they emerged. She remembered it now, the tires screeching, the car skidding then leaving the road. . . .

What car?

Slow-motion flip-flops, end over end . . .

The others. Where were they?

She started to shake.

"Damn it, move your asses! Get a medical crew over here *now!*"

That wasn't a shout, it was a roar. Loud enough to shatter the night. Loud enough to pull her head out of the terrible vision she seemed to be watching from a distance. Loud enough to make her cringe. Loud enough to penetrate the sounds — the deep, rhythmic thumping overhead, the jumble of voices, the clang of metal, the hum of motors, of which she was just becoming fully aware. Loud enough to be heard. Thanks to him, they would know where she was now without any possibility of concealment.

They?

Her pulse pounded. Panic shot through her veins.

Have to escape, have to escape, have to . . .

She was, she realized, curled on her side on damp, cold ground. Her cheek rested on something that both cushioned and prickled — dead grass? Something large and sharp that she guessed had to be a rock jabbed into her hip. Her head felt like it was lower than her legs because she lay twisted like a discarded doll on a hillside. She had only to push herself up and . . .

Gathering all her force, she tried to get to her feet, to scramble away, to run until the darkness swallowed her up and hid her and she was safe once more. Pain shot everywhere, zigzagging along her nerve endings like white-hot lightning bolts, making her want to scream at the intensity of it — only she couldn't. It hurt too much.

I can't move.

The realization stunned her.

Only her head moved, and her arms, with a great deal of effort. Getting them beneath her, she found she could push her torso a few inches from the ground — and that was all. She was trapped, immobilized in her own body. As she fell back, terror turned her insides icy. Her thoughts went fuzzy. All she knew for sure was that she was in pain, quickly intensifying pain. Her ribs, her legs, her head — they all hurt. She couldn't get away. And she was afraid.

I should be dead.

Certainty laced the thought. The crash had been bad. Flying out into darkness, into nothingness, the car rolling over and over, end over end . . . and screams, multiple screams. Soul-shattering screams. She was screaming, too. She could still hear the screaming in her head.

Are the others dead?

That's what she tried to ask him when he crouched beside her again. Either she was making no sense or he didn't hear. She clung to his trouser leg. The material was smooth and cool and sturdy. A lifeline.

"Help's coming. Try not to move."

He must have felt her grip on him, or maybe he sensed her desperation through the darkness, because he patted her hand in clumsy comfort. *If he wanted to hurt you, he's had plenty of time to do it by now.* Instead she felt protected. *Thank God.* Letting go of his trousers, she clutched his hand instead.

Warm, strong fingers . . .

"Don't leave me," she begged, her voice a hoarse, dry rasp in her throat. "They . . . they . . ."

But her mind fogged up again, and all of a sudden she couldn't remember who "they" were. Wasn't even sure she had ever known in the first place.

They?

Dark shapes rushing through the darkness, silhouetted against the flames . . .

"What?" He leaned closer, clearly having heard her voice but not understanding what

48

she was trying to say. "Who are you? Were you in the First Lady's car?"

The First Lady. Annette Cooper. Oh, God, oh, God, oh . . .

She could hear a flurry of movement not too far away: the crunch of dried grass, the shuffle of footsteps, a fragment of conversation. People approaching.

Jess caught her breath. Terror grabbed her heart and squeezed.

"Please . . ." she begged.

"Over here," he called, releasing her hand with a quick compression of her fingers and standing up. Jess guessed that the forest of swaying bushes surrounding her probably blocked her — both of them — from the view of whoever was approaching.

Until now.

Desperation sent her heart pounding against her rib cage like it was trying to beat its way to freedom.

"Gotcha," a man called back.

Her rescuer crouched beside her again. Jess caught his hand.

"The paramedics are almost here," he said before she totally panicked.

Of course. Paramedics were coming. He wouldn't be yelling like that at anyone else.

But her thundering heart wouldn't be calmed.

More footsteps, drawing closer and closer. Rustling branches. Crunching grass. As a spotlight found her in the darkness she couldn't help it: She cringed. Half-blinded, she felt like a small animal in a trap, helpless to save herself. All of a sudden she was ruthlessly exposed, visible to everyone, vulnerable. Her pulse pounded. Her heart raced. Her hand tightened on her rescuer's fingers. He glanced down at her. She saw the dark gleam of his eyes shift so that they were once again focused on her. Though the spotlight was on *her,* the glaring white beam pinioned *her,* the shadows enshrouding him receded slightly so that he was more visible, too. Her vision was all blurry — her contacts, she must have lost them — and he was still mostly in darkness, but she was able to absorb the broad strokes. He was a big guy, wide chest, broad shoulders, thick neck, short, thick, fair hair. White dress shirt, no tie. Black suit coat . . .

One of them.

Recognition flew through her consciousness with the swift, fierce speed of an arrow. She gasped — gasping hurt — and dropped his hand.

"So, what've we got here?" It was a new voice, another man, and, contrary to the terror she'd felt a moment before at the idea of being discovered by anyone else, Jess welcomed it now. Welcomed him. There was safety in numbers — right?

Safety from what?

"She's conscious. She must have been in the car."

He moved back, out of her line of vision, as paramedics bustled around.

"Hi, there, what's your name?" Another man crouched beside her. Fingers found her pulse.

"Jessica." She closed her eyes against the light. "Jessica Ford."

"We're going to take good care of you."

"Get a cervical collar on her," someone else said.

Then she stopped listening, stopped thinking, stopped doing anything, really, except feeling, or trying not to feel, the pain that came in waves. Her attitude was fatalistic: Whatever happened happened, and there was nothing she could do to change any of it now. There were two men, both EMTs, she thought, both seeming dedicated to making sure she would survive. The man who had found her stayed back, mostly just out of her sight, although she caught the occasional glimpse of him with her peripheral vision as the EMTs stabilized her, then loaded her onto the stretcher and carried her up the hill.

"Keep her away from the press." The drawl in his voice was unmistakable. He had found her, and stayed with her. He was with them still, walking near the stretcher. She was afraid of him now. *One of them.* That was the thought that kept darting through her mind. But she couldn't quite justify the fear.

He hadn't hurt her. And he didn't feel like a threat.

But still she was afraid.

Waking up in the ambulance as they were threading an IV into her vein, Jess realized that she must have lost consciousness sometime during the latter part of the ascent.

Not that it mattered. Now that she was out in the open, now that *they* knew where she was, now that she was hurt and helpless and trapped in her own body, there was nothing she could do to help herself even a little bit. Except maybe . . .

"Call my boss." With what she feared were her last few seconds of clarity before sedation claimed her, she summoned every bit of strength and determination left to her and spoke to the paramedic securing the needle to her arm with tape. At first her voice was a mere thread of sound. She strained to make it louder. The paramedic heard, because he met her gaze with a questioning look. "John Davenport. And my mother. The numbers are in my phone. . . ." Which had been in her jacket pocket. She remembered feeling the solid shape of it bumping against her thigh as they put her on the stretcher, but she wasn't wearing the garment now and — there it was, her jacket, in pieces on a shelf; they must have cut it off her. . . . "Which is in my jacket pocket. Over there."

She tried to cut her eyes toward the remnants of her jacket, but already her lids had grown heavy. With a rush of panic so strong it almost countered the effect of whatever drug was now being pumped into her system, she realized she was going under.

Helpless . . .

But there was nothing she could do to save herself. Even as darkness overwhelmed her, even as she sank bonelessly into the void, she found herself back in the speeding black Lincoln as it shot off the roadway, and screams, her own included, once again echoed in her ears.

4

Mark drove straight back to the White House. Although most of the country, and the world, still slept, he knew that the news of Annette Cooper's death would be sweeping through official and unofficial channels like wildfire. Already the Eighteen Acres, as the White House complex was known, was surrounded by an ever-growing crowd of media. The bright glare of klieg lights as various TV stations reported the First Lady's death packed enough kilowattage, he was sure, to be visible from the International Space Station. The guard who waved him through the Northeast Guard Booth was ashen. Mark parked his car, then went straight to the basement, to the Secret Service command center. He was tapping in the six-digit code when the door was jerked open from the inside.

Harris Lowell, the White House chief of staff, stood in the aperture, one hand still on the knob, his expression changing to a glare as he realized who he was looking at. Stocky and florid-faced, with thinning ginger strands of hair arranged in a classic comb-over and bulging blue eyes, the fifty-four-year-old Lowell resembled nothing so much as a bulldog. A bad-tempered bulldog in a two-thousand-dollar pin-striped suit.

"What the hell happened?"

Mark shook his head. "I don't know."

"It's your fucking job to know."

"Something got screwed up."

"Ya think?" Lowell made a sound that could have been a snort or a bitter laugh. Over Lowell's shoulder, Mark could see that the command post was surprisingly full for just past two o'clock in the morning. Of course, the team that was supposed to be guarding the First Lady now had nowhere to be, so they obviously had assembled there. There were others, too, besides his people, some who were supposed to be working that shift, some who he could only assume had been brought in by the news. Some were standing, some were sprawled in chairs watching the monitors that streamed what was, for the time of night, a tremendous amount of activity going on in the halls and rooms they guarded. A few walked around, seemingly aimlessly. All were chalky-faced. All had the stunned looks of disaster victims. All were silent. And all had at least one eye on him and the confrontation taking shape in the doorway.

"The President wants to see you. He wants to ask you some questions." Lowell brushed past him. Mark caught the door before it could close, and held it open while he turned to look at Lowell.

"I don't have any answers for him right now."

"Your funeral." Lowell seemed to realize the infelicitousness of his choice of words, because his expression changed. His cheeks quivered, and the bellicose glare lost a little of its brio. The reality of the First Lady's death was just beginning to sink in for him, too.

Funny how the world can change in an instant.

"Give me a minute, would you?" Mark still felt like he could puke, and he'd had to pull over to pee by the side of the road twice on the ride in, but he was functioning. And he still had a job to do.

"A minute."

Whether it was meant to be or not, Mark chose to take Lowell's growl as assent. Stepping inside the brightly lit room with its windowless, steel-reinforced walls, gleaming silver banks of monitors, computers bristling with state-of-the-art technology, hanging tapestries that concealed safes holding enough hidden weaponry to fend off a small army, and rows of recharging radios, he shut the door firmly behind him. The scent of coffee from the machine in the corner was strong. It made the gorge rise in his throat.

"Is it true about Prescott?"

The question came from the back of the room. Mark looked at the speaker — Susan Wendell, an attractive, thirtysomething blonde who'd had kind of a thing for the single, good-looking Prescott — and nodded curtly. *No good beating around the bush.* Her face tightened. She swallowed once. Other than that, and a certain whiteness around her mouth, she betrayed no sign of emotion.

Secret Service agents don't cry.

With a gesture, Mark gathered his people around him. Not counting himself, there were seven of them on-site: Wendell, Paul Fielding, Steve Matthews, Michael Varney, Spencer Hagan, Janelle Tandy, and Phil Janke. The first three, along with Prescott, had been on duty when he had signed out for the night. The others had apparently come in as word of the tragedy had spread.

"Anybody know why FLOTUS and Prescott were in that car?" Mark's voice was low. No point in airing dirty laundry in front of everybody in the room. There had been a screwup, and he wanted to know the details first. His own ass might be swinging in the wind about now, but he would do what he could to cover his team.

Lowered eyes. A couple of head shakes. Tense expressions all around.

"The first we knew that anything went wrong was when Prescott radioed in," Wendell said. "He said he'd gone with Mrs. Cooper and Folly" — the Coopers' spaniel — "to the Rose Garden, and Mrs. Cooper had gotten out of his sight and he couldn't find her. He was panicking because she'd given him the slip, but it wasn't like she'd been abducted or anything. She hadn't been gone but a few minutes, and we didn't want to make it into a big deal if it wasn't, so we all rushed out and started looking for her. About the time we got the call about the" — her voice faltered — "the crash, we were in the process of setting up a massive search effort." She winced. "Too late."

Mark's shoulders tightened. There was a lot he wanted to say, but it was too early to start the blame game. Hell, ultimately the blame was his, anyway: These were his people. This was his job.

"I want to know how this happened." Mark's voice was grim. "I want to know every single, solitary detail of what went down. Like, yesterday." Glancing around, he jerked his head at Paul Fielding. Like all of them, thirty-nine-year-old Fielding was in excellent physical condition. But at six-two, with his chubby cheeks and mild blue eyes, his balding head and easygoing air, he always made Mark think of Buddha. A blond Buddha bobblehead in a Secret Service suit. At the moment, Fielding was sweating slightly although the room was cool. He knew the feeling; he also knew Fielding, considered him a friend as well as a colleague. More to the point, he trusted Fielding. He and Fielding had gone through the Academy together. Mark's star had risen higher and faster, mainly because he put more into the job. His life, in fact.

Fielding hadn't made that mistake. He was still married to his first wife, and he had kids who loved him.

"When I come back, I want to watch replays of the surveillance tapes from ten p.m. on," he said to Fielding as the man moved to stand beside him. A sharp rap on the vaultlike door behind him made Mark grit his teeth: Lowell, impatient as always. "Not just Mrs. Cooper but everything. I want to see every single move anybody made in or around the residence. Anybody who entered. Anybody who left. Anybody who so much as sneezed in front of the elevator. And I want video from the Rose Garden. And from every exit out of the Eighteen Acres. Every one, you understand? I want to know when she left, I want to know how she left, I want to know who she was with, and *I want to know why she was in that fucking car.*"

Fielding nodded. "You got it."

"You realize we're going to take the heat for this, people. It's imperative we get some answers fast."

Fielding nodded again, along with the rest of them. Mark knew they all understood the point he was making: Not only their asses but the Secret Service's reputation was on the line.

Whatever had occurred to put Mrs. Cooper in that crash, the bottom line was they had failed.

Now that the knowledge had well and truly sunk in, it was starting to eat at him. He felt as jumpy as a frog leg in a frying pan.

Failure is not an option.

Another rap on the door, louder than before.

Fucking Lowell.

"I also want to know everything there is to know about Jessica Ford." Her name had lodged in his memory, along with her bloodied face and small, crumpled form. If he hadn't stumbled across her, would she have lain out there until she died?

More to the point, who was she to Annette Cooper? And what was she doing in that damned car?

Thanks to the press, the world would know the answers soon enough. He wanted to know first.

"Isn't she the survivor?" Wendell, always quicker than the rest, met his gaze with sharpened interest. Ever the professional, she was keeping any personal-level grief she felt at Prescott's passing well hidden.

"Survivor?" Mark frowned.

"That's what they're saying on CNN. That there were four people in the First Lady's car, and one survived."

Mark felt surprised, then felt stupid for feeling surprised. He'd seen the reporters on the scene for himself, seen the trucks and cameras circling the White House. Why hadn't he realized that every tiny detail they could scratch up would be broadcast instantly around the world?

"Jesus." He'd known it, of course, but the

reality was just now hitting home: The scope of this thing was going to be huge. Global. An international convulsion that would play out in the media for days, possibly weeks, maybe even months to come. And everybody in the world who was in the least bit interested was going to know every tiny dredged-up detail about Annette Cooper's life and death — unless some things could be kept hidden. He hoped to God they could be kept hidden. "Yeah, she's the survivor. And I want to know who the hell she is, and what the hell she was doing in that car. In about fifteen minutes, tops."

"I'm on it," Wendell said.

"Okay, everybody keep your mouths shut on this subject until further notice. No talking to anybody — and I mean anybody — outside this group."

With a nod of dismissal, he turned to open the door. Lowell was standing there, hand raised to knock again, glaring at him. Behind him, the long corridor was filling with people. More Secret Service agents coming in, heading for the room he was just exiting. Medical personnel bound for the in-house clinic. FBI agents. Housekeeping staff. Some military types. More than a few were openly weeping. Others were pale, grim. Most looked to be in the first disbelieving stages of shock.

Hell, he was still in that stage himself. But he was being forced out of it fast. Survival mode was kicking in.

"You got no room for error here, Ryan," Lowell warned under his breath as they stepped across the hall to the elevator that would take them up to the family residence. "The President wants an explanation. Where the hell were you guys?"

"I don't know what happened yet. I will."

Lowell grunted. After that they rode up in silence. At its heart, the White House is a vast, impersonal office building with a small, ultra-luxurious hotel inside where the First Family lives. Now he was headed up to the equivalent of the presidential suite. Mark stared at his reflection in the shiny brass wall. For the first time he became aware that he was sweaty and dirty-looking, his jaw dark with stubble, still wearing the black suit he'd worn to work on Saturday — he'd taken off his jacket and tie when he'd gotten home, sat on the couch, clicked on the TV, and been in the middle of eating his Big Mac when he'd gotten the call about the accident, grabbed his jacket again, and headed out — with his white shirt stained and limp and no tie. Not exactly Secret Service regulation. Well, it couldn't be helped, and under the circumstances he guessed it didn't matter.

Right now he had bigger problems than being on the wrong side of the Secret Service dress code.

When the elevator opened, the hush was what he noticed first. It was thick and heavy, palpable as fog. The scent of fresh cut roses from a huge crystal bowl opposite the elevator made the whole place smell like a damned funeral parlor. He tried not to think about that as he followed Lowell into a small anteroom and through the double doors that led to the elegantly furnished foyer of the family residence. Price Ferris of the presidential Secret Service detail met them inside the foyer. They exchanged the briefest of greetings. Beyond Ferris, he could see that the Yellow Oval Room was already full of people. Some important — he spotted popular vice president Sears and his wife and the Secretary of State and his — and some not, like the First Nephew. They were milling around, drinks in hand, talking in near whispers that combined to roll out into the hallway like the steady hum of traffic. The somber mood was palpable from where he stood. Nodding at his fellow agents as he passed them — and getting the distinct feeling from the looks he received

64

in return that he was about to get his balls nailed to the wall — Mark followed Ferris and Lowell down the long hall to the President's bedroom.

And tried to ignore the knots in his gut.

Ferris knocked at the door. Another agent, Donald Petrowski, opened it. Mark followed Lowell into the room.

David Cooper was sprawled on his back on the big mahogany four-poster in the bedroom that had served every president since Calvin Coolidge. He wasn't a big man — maybe five-ten, one sixty-five — but, thanks to the workout room on the third floor, he was exceptionally fit for a fifty-eight-year-old. Mark knew from personal experience on Cooper's security detail that his healthy tan owed more to some kind of spray than to the great outdoors, and his famous mane of silver hair got a little help from the dye bottle, but, hey, the guy had cameras trained on him twenty-four-seven, and in the dog-eat-dog political arena image was important. He and fifty-two-year-old Annette had made an attractive, photogenic, popular couple. With their now grown son and daughter, they had been the picture-perfect all-American family.

Only those closest to them got to see behind the facade. Right about now, Mark found himself wishing he hadn't ever gotten that close.

". . . at Bethesda?" It was the tail end of a question, uttered in a voice that was unmistakably that of the President of the United States.

"That's right."

The reply, Mark saw as he continued on into the room, came from the First Father, Wayne Cooper. The octogenarian Texas oilman stood near the fireplace with another man Mark didn't recognize. Built like the President except for a slight paunch, his hair gone now except for a feathery white fringe, Wayne was a widower who adored his only son. He was also a billionaire, which, to Mark's mind, explained a lot about how that son had made it to the White House. His other child was a thrice-married daughter, Elizabeth, who was pampered and protected but otherwise ignored. All Wayne's hopes and dreams were bound up in his son.

"I told you, I'm not taking any damned pill," the President snapped.

"But sir . . ."

Except for his dinner jacket, David Cooper was still dressed up in the tux he'd worn to wine and dine the president of Chile. His shoes rested on the tufted gold bedspread of a bed that had not yet been turned down.

66

John Downes, the President's personal physician, leaned over him, his back to Mark. Leonard Cowan, his valet, hovered on the far side of the bed, a tray holding what appeared to be the President's favored scotch and soda in his hands.

"Here's Ryan," Lowell announced.

The President sat up. All eyes focused on Mark. All conversation suspended. Taking a deep breath, he felt his jaw tighten and hoped to hell it was the only outward sign of tension they could see.

"God in heaven, you want to tell us how this terrible thing happened?" Wayne Cooper's booming voice was punctuated by an audible clink as he put his glass down on the marble mantel.

"I can't answer that yet, sir."

"Well, by damn . . ."

"Dad, everyone, could you excuse us a minute, please?" His customary courtesy back in place despite the slight wobble that was barely detectable in his voice, David Cooper swung his legs over the side of the bed. His face was haggard, his skin pale, his eyes red. Meeting his gaze, Mark felt the knot in his gut twist tighter.

The zinger was, David Cooper had loved his wife.

My watch.

"Davey . . ." Wayne protested. Anguish over his son's obvious pain quivered in his voice.

"Please," the President said again. Wayne Cooper frowned, but he, like everyone else, slowly filed out. The click of the door closing behind them was loud as a gunshot to Mark's ears.

The President came to his feet. Their eyes met. It was all Mark could do not to flinch at the accusation he saw in the other man's face.

"I trusted you, Mark. You knew what was going on with her. You were supposed to watch her. You were supposed to keep her safe."

Making excuses wasn't his style, so Mark didn't. "I'm sorry, Mr. President."

Cooper took a hasty turn about the room. Watching him, Mark felt a burning inside his chest. He knew what it was like to love a woman who didn't give a shit about you. It hurt like hell. Right at that moment, his sympathies were with David Cooper.

The President stopped in front of him, ran his hands through his hair. "Just tell me this: Was she out there trying to score drugs?"

The million-dollar question.

"I don't know. Maybe." Mark withdrew

the artificial sweetener bottle from his pocket and held it out. "I went to the crash site. This was in her purse. Along with a roll of cash and some credit cards."

Since the First Lady almost never carried cash, the implication was plain: A drug rendezvous was a definite possibility. The credit cards — who the hell knew what was up with the credit cards? He hadn't had time yet to even begin to think that through. Although as far as he knew, drug dealers still didn't accept them.

Sucking in his breath, the President took the bottle and stared down at it. "Damned pills." Then he looked up at Mark. His eyes were dark with pain. "This can never get out. Her reputation . . ." His mouth shook, and then his face crumpled like a collapsing building. "Oh my God, my God, I can't believe this has happened. I can't believe she's dead. *Annette* . . ."

His voice spiraled into a ragged wail. Even as the door burst open and the room filled with people and he was nearly shoved back out into the hall, Mark could not escape the terrible sounds of the President's keening. Again, he felt a stab of guilt.

My watch.

Lowell caught up to him as he headed for the elevator.

"That woman." Falling in beside him, Lowell glanced all around as if to make sure no one was close enough to overhear. "The woman who was in the car. The one who survived."

They were in the foyer now, walking fast past a group of new arrivals being shepherded into the Yellow Oval Room. Mark recognized a famous singer along with some friends of the First Family. Throat tightening, he wondered when the Coopers' two adult children, Laurie Donaldson and Brad Cooper, would arrive.

He really didn't want to be here for that one.

"What about her?" he asked.

"What do you know about her?"

"Nothing except her name. Yet." The implication that he soon would know everything there was to know about Jessica Ford was understood by Lowell, who nodded.

"Yeah, well, we hear that she's a lawyer who works for John Davenport. We're trying to get hold of him now, but he's not at home and he isn't answering his cell phone. The information we have — and it's preliminary, but we think it's good — is that the First Lady called Davenport, and he sent the car."

"Why?" But at least that probably meant Annette Cooper wasn't out there chasing the drugs she was being slowly, forcibly weaned off of after all. Or maybe she was, and Davenport had found out and sent a car and a subordinate to get her off the streets.

"Who the hell knows?" Lowell looked grim. "Look, you go to this Ford woman, and you keep her the hell away from the press. Stay with her until you find out what she knows. And if she knows anything, anything at all, that could in any way be harmful to the First Lady or the President, you get her to keep her damned mouth shut." The glint in Lowell's eyes reminded Mark just how ruthless the Chief of Staff could be. "You fucked up, now you clean up the mess."

Mark's mouth compressed. Then he nodded and stepped into the elevator.

5

Something woke her.

What?

Jess didn't know. All she knew was that she was breathing hard. Feeling weird. And instantly uneasy. Even as her mind came to full awareness her senses were alert, spurred by a kind of edgy sixth sense that told her something was wrong.

Where am I?

Her eyes blinked open on — nothing. A blur of darkness. The feeling of being inside, with four walls around her and a ceiling she could not see not too far above her head.

Cold, so cold.

Biting down on her lower lip, she tried to control the violent shivers that claimed her. She felt groggy, disoriented. As if she were floating, almost. Her head throbbed. Her mouth felt like it was stuffed with cotton balls. Her body was one big dull ache that, paradoxically, did not hurt as much as she knew it should have. She had the feeling that she was alone, although earlier, she was almost certain she had heard her mother's voice. Others she knew, too. Her sister Sarah's, maybe.

There were no voices now. No sounds, except a steady mechanical beeping and a dull hum and the slightest of drawn-out creaks. She didn't know how it was possible that she could be so cold; she seemed to be swaddled to the armpits in layers of cloth. Against her body, the texture of the cloth was tightly woven and smooth, while the cloth her hands, which were on top of the pile, rested on was coarser and fuzzy. That, plus the firm resilience of the surface upon which she lay and the mounded softness beneath her head, led her to conclude that she was in a bed. A sharp, distinctive smell — antiseptic? — defined it further: She was in a bed.

In a hospital.

Annette Cooper. The wreck.

Horror washed over her in an icy wave. Her stomach turned inside out. She felt a surge of dizziness so strong she almost sank back into the blackness again.

Something's wrong.

That was the thought that kept her

present. It was strong enough to beat back the wooziness that threatened to carry her away again.

What?

The darkness was not absolute, she discovered, as her eyes adjusted: There was the faintest of bluish glows to her right. Slowly she turned her head — moving required so much effort — to find that the bluish glow emanated from a cluster of free-standing machines near the bed. One showed what appeared to be a zigzagging line; it was the one producing the steady beep, and she thought it might be a heart monitor. If so, hers seemed to be beating right on track, with a good, steady rhythm. The deep hum seemed to come from somewhere overhead, possibly from the ventilation or heating system. The narrowing crack of light outlining the door beyond the machines pinpointed the source of a creaking sound: Someone was slowly, carefully closing the door to the room where she lay.

Even as she discovered it, the sliver of light disappeared. The faintest of clicks announced that the door was now securely shut. The area behind the instruments had gone completely dark. But a blur of movement in the shadows where the sliver of light had been told her that she was not alone. A cold frizzle of wariness tingled along her spine.

Who?

Her heartbeat quickened as she heard light, quick footsteps. Her eyes widened as someone stepped around the machines. Then she got a blurred look at a tall form in blue scrubs.

A doctor, then. Or a nurse. Someone medical, anyway.

Her breath released in a near-silent whoosh. It was only then that she realized she had been holding it.

Who were you expecting?

"Are you awake?"

The question was soft, so as not to disturb her if the answer was no. Although the darkness coupled with her bad eyesight kept her from getting a good look at him, it was obvious that the speaker was a man. A stranger. Could he see her eyes glinting at him through the darkness? She didn't know. She knew only that the soporific tone of his voice contrasted oddly with his movements, which were swift and sure as he strode toward the head of her bed.

"Yes."

Her voice was a mere thread of sound, creaky and tired. Her mouth was so dry that it was hard to form even that one short word.

Swallowing to moisten her throat, she followed him with her eyes. She wanted to ask for information, for the conditions of the others in the car, but she didn't have the strength. Her tongue felt thick and heavy, and pushing words out past it required more effort than she could summon at the moment.

"Do you remember what happened?"

He took hold of the tall metal pole standing at the head of her bed. When she saw the plastic bag swinging from it, saw the tubing, she realized that it was an IV pole. And she was attached to it, by a long, clear tube that ran down into the back of her hand.

The liquid in the bag was emptying into her vein. Tape on her hand secured the needle in place.

"Wreck," she managed.

"That's right."

He was holding a syringe, she saw, and fiddling with her tubing, right there where it joined the bag.

"What are you doing?"

The vague sense of unease she had felt since opening her eyes intensified. He was lifting the syringe toward the tubing — which, since he was a doctor, shouldn't have alarmed her at all.

But it did.

Why?

"This will help you go back to sleep, sugar. Just close your eyes."

Again with the soft, soothing voice. Her lids drooped as his suggestion tempted her. To just close her eyes and drift into unconsciousness . . . How good would that feel? And how easy would it be to do?

All of a sudden she remembered the nightmare shapes. But they belonged to the wreck. Not the hospital. She'd been found, rescued, and now she was safe. She could sleep if she wanted to.

So tired . . .

The light from the machines cast a blue glow over the floor. Jess found herself noticing it as her eyes drifted downward and he moved again, his feet shuffling in and out of the light. She forced her lids wide open and her gaze up and watched as he tugged impatiently on the tubing.

Despite her best efforts, her lids felt as heavy, as if her lashes were made of concrete. She wanted to close her eyes in the worst way. But still that prickly sense that something was wrong would not leave her.

"Are you . . . a doctor?"

"Mm-hmm."

The tone of the murmur was comforting. The tubing was cooperating now, and he was, she saw, holding a port and positioning the syringe so that he could send its contents down the tubing into her body with a single quick depression of the plunger.

Not good.

The disturbing thought made her frown even as her eyes slid down his body toward the floor again. Where he was standing now, the blue glow spilled over his legs, illuminating them to the knees. The scrubs were too short for him, their legs ending some three inches above the hem of his black pants, black suit pants. Worn over shiny black wing-tip shoes marred by just a few stray bits of . . . what? Her vision was too fuzzy to be certain, but it could have been dead grass.

Prickly grass cushioning her cheek . . .

Jess's heart gave a great leap and her eyes shot wide open. She sucked in air.

"No! No, stop! Wait!"

But he didn't stop. He didn't even glance her way. Instead, his thumb clamped down on the plunger. Jess couldn't see clearly enough to watch it happen, but she imagined liquid shooting out of the needle into the tube that emptied into her vein.

What liquid?

The question exploded in her mind even as she grabbed for the needle in her hand. Her nails scraped at the tape and she yanked at the tube right where it met her tender skin. The needle — no, a small, clear plastic tube — ripped free of her flesh with a sharp, burning sensation that was as nothing compared to the terror rocketing through her veins.

WHAT LIQUID?

"What the . . . ?" The man snatched at the tubing, caught it, and stared at it in stupefaction for a split second as he saw that it swung free.

He dove for her. She screamed. The bed, on wheels that apparently hadn't been locked, careered toward the far wall as his body slammed against it.

His hand, sweaty and warm, clamped around her wrist just as the front-left corner of the bed smacked into the wall and bounced away. As more screams tore out of her throat, she yanked her arm free.

Run.

Every instinct she possessed shrieked it, but to her horror she discovered she couldn't run: Her legs just would not obey her brain's urgent command. Desperate, Jess kicked violently, but the "kick" message somehow got scrambled on its way down to her legs and she ended up bucking on the hospital bed like a landed fish, screaming and fighting him off with flailing blows that missed more than they landed while the bloodied catheter she had torn from her arm swung behind him, spewing tiny drops of a cold viscous liquid that made her shudder with horror when they sprayed over her arm, her neck, her leg.

He'd put something terrible in the bag. . . .

"Shut up, you!" It was a hoarse growl.

The empty syringe came flashing down toward her. With a burst of horror, she saw that he was wielding it like a knife now, meaning to stab her with it. Then a glimmer of light caught it and she realized that it wasn't empty at all, or perhaps it was another, backup syringe, because it was full of liquid. His aim, she realized in that frozen instant in which she watched the clear tube with its glinting needle drive toward her body, was to plunge the needle into her, to release whatever liquid was in that syringe into her flesh directly, and never mind the IV now.

Black shapes circling the flaming car . . .

"No! Help! Help!"

Screaming like a siren, Jess threw herself violently to one side just in the nick of time — and toppled off the side of the bed.

6

Tired to the bone but so wired he couldn't have slept even if he had ignored Lowell and gone home, Mark pushed through the metal door that led from the hospital's emergency staircase to the third floor. According to an ER nurse who had been extraordinarily cooperative from the moment he had flashed his badge — and smile — at her, Jessica Ford had arrived on that floor some fifteen minutes earlier. As they'd talked, he'd seen a plump blond woman the nurse had confidentially identified as Ms. Ford's mother leaning over a desk and filling out paperwork. He wanted to reach Ms. Ford before her mother did, just in case she might be conscious and feeling chatty. He'd chosen to take the stairs rather than the elevator because the press was already on the trail of the story and had gathered in a seething, amorphous, ever-growing pack in the hospital lobby. The difficulty lay in the fact that some of them might recognize him, and then his presence at the hospital would become part of the story, leading to all kinds of speculation. No doubt at some point the harassed-looking security guards would force them outside, but he didn't have the time to wait for that. It was easier to take the stairs and avoid the problem.

If Ms. Ford had anything to say, he wanted to hear it first. There was nothing else he could do for Annette Cooper now except try to keep her all-American-mom image intact.

He pushed the stairwell door shut behind him with an elbow and was striding down the hall toward Ms. Ford's room when a blood-curdling shriek froze him in his tracks.

It was a woman's terrified scream, so shocking in this hushed, overcooled, sterile environment that it made the hairs on the back of his neck spring to attention. A cold, hard fear seized him even as a terrible premonition jolted his world, even as his gaze shot down the long hallway that right-angled out of his sight just beyond the nurses' station.

For as far as he could see, the hall was dim and nearly empty and utterly incompatible with the explosion of sound that filled it as the woman screamed again and again, raw, jagged screams of pure fear that covered the pounding of his heart — and of his footsteps as he catapulted into a dead run.

Jesus Christ, it wasn't possible. . . .

Mark didn't finish the thought as he raced down the hall toward room 337, the room where Ms. Ford had been taken, where he knew with every bit of gut instinct he possessed that she was screaming like a crazy woman now.

Why?

It was useless to speculate. He didn't want to speculate. He wanted the suspicion that oozed like venom through his brain to be wrong.

Passing a frightened-looking nurse who had apparently paused to ring the security button before going to her patient's aid and shoving aside an orderly, Mark burst into Ms. Ford's room with his Glock at the ready and his heart pumping like a six-cylinder engine.

"Freeze!"

As the door bounced open he was through it, assuming firing stance, the echoes of her shrieks ringing in his ears as his eyes scanned the blue-tinged darkness for her — and whoever might be threatening her.

Only she wasn't screaming now. No one

was. Except for the thundering of his pulse in his ears and the *blip-blip-blip* of some damned machine, the room was quiet as a cemetery at midnight.

No one was there.

No one that he could see, anyway.

"Jessica!" he called.

It was a two-person room, complete with two beds and two TVs and a number of chairs and what appeared to be enough medical instruments to keep half the hospital alive. The partially drawn curtain separating the halves of the room fluttered slightly, but despite that small movement, the room did indeed appear empty: Certainly both beds were unoccupied. They were out of place, though, with the nearer one much closer to the door than it should have been and the far one catty-corner against the window wall.

Careful.

His left hand hit the light switch as he advanced into the room on high alert, continuing to scan his surroundings although there wasn't a soul in sight. The sudden brightness made him blink. Including the bathroom, the door of which was ajar, there were only a few places that he couldn't immediately see, which meant there were only a few places for an intruder to hide.

"Jessica?"

Someone had been there, he could sense it, feel the energy of a recent presence. Despite the current silence, there was also no doubt in his mind that he had followed the screams to their source.

So where the hell was she?

"Jessica?"

Coming warily around the foot of the far bed, the one that was pushed out of position, the one with the askew pillows and missing covers that the glowing machines facing it indicated had seen recent use, he found her. Swaddled in blankets, looking small and fragile, she lay facedown on the slick, gray floor, one delicate bare leg and foot curved toward the door, the other concealed by the bedcoverings that were twisted around her. Part of her back was bared, too, by the green hospital gown that imperfectly covered her. Her bare right arm stretched toward the bed. The other must have been tucked up under her body. Her tangled dark brown hair concealed her face, but still he had no doubt that it was her.

"Jessica?"

Mark crouched beside her, cautious still, keeping one eye on his surroundings, not quite ready yet to holster his gun. She was breathing, he saw at a glance, and as far as he could tell had no obvious new injury. There was no pool of blood, no knife protruding from her back, nothing like that. His fingers closed around her wrist: She definitely had a pulse. He could feel it beating fast and strong.

"Jessica, can you hear me?"

Her head moved, and she murmured something that he couldn't understand. She resisted his touch, trying to pull her wrist away, and he let go.

"It's okay. I've got you. You're safe now."

As he glanced swiftly around the apparently empty space around them, suspicion continued to niggle at the edges of his mind. But so far suspicion was all it was; the truth was that he had no idea in hell what had happened to her. Maybe he'd get lucky and find that she'd just fallen out of bed.

He prayed to God that was all it was.

In the circles he moved in, the circles of loosely connected spooks and spies and personal protection officers and government agents who were all to differing degrees ready, willing, and able to do the dirty work of the powerful, the name of the hospital where she had been taken would be common knowledge by now. . . .

Even as that thought arose to bug him, the orderly, several nurses, a couple of security officers, and who knew how many others burst through the door in a big, untidy knot.

"Miss Ford . . ." It was a male voice.

"Oh my God, he's got a gun!" one of the women cried, and then they all practically fell over themselves as they tried to reverse or otherwise get out of harm's way.

"Secret Service." Mark stood up, flashing his badge, and holstered his gun. Reassured, the security guards — a pair of retired cops from the look of them — stopped fumbling with their weapons and the rescue party resumed its mission, crowding around the woman on the floor.

"Miss Ford? What happened?"

One of the nurses, a thirtyish blonde, smoothed the hair back from the patient's face. Mark caught a glimpse of a smooth, white cheek and a full, pale mouth. Her lashes flickered, but there was no reply.

Superfluous now, he stepped back out of the way and set himself the task of discovering what had befallen her. Checking out the bathroom was tops on his list, so that's where he headed.

"She must have tried to get up," another of the nurses said as he came back out of the bathroom, sure now that no one was in there. All he could see of the group huddled over Jessica was the tops of their heads as they crouched around her. Except for the security guards, who were standing back out of the way, frowning as they watched. "Maybe she was trying to get to the bathroom or something. It looks like she's knocked herself out."

"She's catheterized."

"Well, maybe she didn't realize."

"Think she hit her head on a corner of the table?"

"Possible. Or the floor."

"Yup, there's a bump back here. No cut or anything. It's swelling, though."

"Look, she pulled out her IV."

A round of tongue-clucking followed this discovery.

"Help . . ."

Faint and panicky, it was Jessica's voice. Weak as it was, Mark recognized it instantly through the sea of chatter.

Abandoning his quick turn around the perimeter of the room just to see if there could possibly be someone concealed in a corner somewhere that he could have missed — there wasn't — Mark moved in closer to hear what she had to say.

"It's all right, you fell out of bed. We'll just get you back up and . . ."

"There was . . . a man. He tried to put

something in my IV."

A brief silence greeted this. While Mark frowned — this was emphatically not what he wanted to hear — a couple of the nurses exchanged significant looks. It was clear from their expressions that they didn't put much stock in what she was telling them.

"I was in here earlier." The orderly stood up. He was a skinny twentysomething in blue scrubs. Medium brown hair pulled back in a short ponytail. Traces of acne on his chin and cheeks. He held up both hands as if to deflect blame. "But I just checked the fluid level. I didn't put anything in the bag."

"He had . . . a needle. He tried . . . to stab me with it." Jessica's voice was faint and shaky, and it was clear that speaking cost her considerable effort. But the urgency underlying it carried the ring of truth — as far as Mark was concerned, at least.

Shit. Shit, no.

"Well, that settles it. Definitely not me." With a humor-the-poor-fool smile, the orderly shook his head.

"I tried to run — I couldn't move my legs." Jessica's voice was shriller now, and stronger. "Why can't I move my legs?"

Jesus, was she paralyzed?

"You need to try to calm down." The

nurse's tone was soothing. "Can you roll onto this? No?" There was the briefest of pauses and a kind of shuffling sound. "Okay, everyone, one, two, three."

A moment later, Jessica was lifted back onto the bed and positioned so that she lay flat on her back. She was shivering violently, Mark saw, as they straightened out her limbs. The green hospital gown covered her from her neck to mid-thigh. Her legs were slender and pale and well-shaped, and her feet were narrow with unpainted toes.

As the orderly positioned her legs carefully side by side, she lifted her head a few inches off the mattress and looked down at them with obvious horror.

"My legs aren't working."

She sounded frightened. He couldn't blame her.

"Could you look straight at me, please? I need to check your pupils."

The blond nurse leaned over the bed, shining a penlight into each of Jessica's eyes in turn. For a moment Jessica cooperated, seeming bemused as she stared into the light.

"Looks fine," the nurse said.

"I need to sit up." Jessica moved her head restlessly. "Please."

Someone pressed the remote control, and

the head of the bed rose with a whirr until she was in a semireclining position.

"Get her vitals."

The light was withdrawn, the bed rail snapped back into place, and she was situated more comfortably on the bed, the pillows adjusted under her head, the covers smoothed and tucked into place, all in a flurry of organized movements. As they finished, Jessica lay limply back against the big white pillows, looking absolutely exhausted and about as vigorous as a rag doll.

"Why can't I move my legs? Why doesn't anyone care that somebody just attacked me? Are any of you even listening to what I'm saying?" Sounding both frightened and angry, she clenched her fists around folds of the blue blanket as if she was holding on to it for dear life.

As her gaze swept her caretakers, Mark got his first real look at her face: squarish, with a high forehead, high cheekbones, and a determined jaw. A gash over her right eyebrow was closed by a neat line of perhaps six stitches. A purpling bruise darkened on her right cheekbone. Another one angled up her neck to her ear, also on the right side. Otherwise, her skin was white as chalk. A distraught expression widened her eyes. Her hair was chin-length, the color of chocolate syrup, and badly tangled on the right side, where most of her visible injuries were located. He recalled that she had been lying on her right side when he had found her. Disregarding the effects of the crash, he would describe her as kind of cute rather than pretty, not the type to attract looks in a bar or at a party or anywhere else. The generic kid-sister type, which might explain why she also seemed vaguely familiar. Freckles, which made her look way too young to be the lawyer Lowell claimed she was, dusted her nose and cheeks. She looked like a kid, like a teenager. What she definitely did not look like was a junkie, or a drug dealer, or anyone who had dealings with junkies or drug dealers.

So what the hell was she doing with Mrs. Cooper?

"You're not helping yourself by getting hysterical." The oldest of the nurses, the one with the short salt-and-pepper hair, sounded stern as she withdrew a thermometer from Jessica's mouth and looked down at it. "Hopefully, some of this you're experiencing is just the side effects of all the medication you're on."

"My legs?" Jessica's voice cracked.

"You'll have to speak to your doctor about that. I don't want to say anything that might be wrong. But the hallucination is almost certainly from the medication."

"Not a hallucination! *Someone attacked me.*"

It was then that Mark caught a glimpse of her left hand. The back of it was torn and bright red with oozing blood. It took him a second to realize that the wound had resulted from the IV being torn from her flesh. His gaze shifted to the tall silver pole resting cockeyed against the wall between the two beds, where it had clearly been shoved with some force.

If what she claims is true, the evidence to prove it is right there.

"One time when they had me on morphine after surgery I imagined I was surrounded by a pack of wolves," the orderly said. "Scariest thing that ever happened to me."

Mark was on the move. His target was the bag of fluid that still hung from the IV pole. And the tubing that was attached to it. Whatever had happened in that room, those items would tell the tale. But even if she was right on the money and there had been a man in her room — in other words, if an attempt on her life really had been made — he couldn't let anyone outside of their own small group know it. It was something he meant to explore — and deal with, if it proved to be true — privately.

But he didn't think it was true. In his judgment, such a thing was almost impossible.

"Him! It was him!" Jessica's voice, high-pitched and panicky, made him turn his head sharply. She had apparently been giving him a once-over, because her gaze flew up his body to his face even as he looked at her. Luckily, because every eye in the room was instantly trained on him, the bag and tubing were now stowed safely out of sight in his jacket pocket.

She meant him, Mark realized with some surprise. She was staring at him, fear plain in her face.

7

"You're wrong, you know." Keeping his tone deliberately gentle, Mark moved to stand beside the bed, one hand curling around the cold silver bed rail while the other steadied the squishy, half-full bag of fluid stuffed in his pocket. Her eyes were a clear greenish hazel framed by a thick sweep of black lashes, he saw, as they bored into his. Her brows were straight dark brown slashes that at the moment nearly met over her nose because of the intensity of her frown. "It wasn't me. I was outside in the hall heading for your room when I heard you scream. My name's Mark Ryan. I'm a Secret Service agent. I was there at the crash site, remember? I found you."

Her shoulders, which had been rigid with tension, slumped. Her features softened fractionally as some of the fear that had sharpened them seemed to ease. She blinked and collapsed back against the pillows, although her gaze didn't leave his face and she still frowned.

"I remember."

"We all saw him running down the hall while you were screaming," said the nurse who'd been pushing the security button as he had blown past her. She was of Asian descent, with short, smooth hair and a shapely figure. Using a gauze pad, she wiped the blood from Jessica's hand as she spoke. The scent of alcohol hit Mark's nostrils, and he made a face at the strength of it. It had to sting, but if it did she wasn't reacting. The tear wasn't long, and it didn't look deep. But it was jagged and still oozed blood.

For whatever reason, the IV needle had definitely parted from her flesh in a violent fashion.

"Yeah, he couldn't have been in here doing bad things to your IV," the orderly agreed, passing a blue plastic ice pack to the oldest nurse, who with a quiet word to Jessica applied it to the back of her head. "I saw him, too. I think that means he's got a quadruple alibi."

"What made you think it was me?" Mark eyed her curiously. Did he have a twin running around somewhere that he didn't know about? Or had it really been just a hallucination after all, with maybe her subconscious plugging in his face because he had found her and she therefore associated him with the crash?

She didn't answer. Her eyes seemed unfocused suddenly, as if she were no longer really seeing him, although she continued to look right at him. After a long moment she inhaled deeply, then winced as if breathing in like that had hurt. Her eyes regained their awareness, narrowing on his face, and her body tensed. Her hands clenched tight around the blanket she still gripped.

"Mrs. Cooper?" Her voice was scarcely louder than a whisper.

Mark hesitated. His instinct was not to add to her distress by giving her more bad news so soon, but the impression he got was that she knew the answer even as she asked the question. What exactly had she seen? Why was Mrs. Cooper — why were any of them — in that car? He needed to know the answers like yesterday, so backing off was not an option, whether he wanted to or not. This was the perfect opening — his cue to find out how much she knew about the circumstances surrounding the First Lady's death, and to shut her up if the answers weren't what they should be. What she knew would determine what he did about it, of course. Buying her silence was always an option, and pointing out to her how unpleasant things could get for an up-and-coming lawyer who stepped on the toes of some of the most powerful people in the country was the unfortunate corollary to that, the stick to the carrot, as it were. A job, a really good job paying really good money, could be found for her locally or far from Washington, whatever and wherever she wanted. He was in the position to grant her a number of things. All she needed to do was "forget" whatever she knew, if indeed she knew anything at all, and refuse to talk to the press. The Coopers and their loyalists had many ways of rewarding those whom they considered their friends — and just as many ways of punishing their enemies.

Which was the part that was bothering him.

Under the circumstances, though, he really didn't think that was what was going on here. He couldn't believe anybody in the Texas mafia, as the President's mostly homegrown ring of closest advisers was informally known, would resort to trying to have her killed. To conceal the First Lady's drug addiction, which would certainly be embarrassing and hurtful to the family if revealed but would probably, ultimately, win sympathy for the President who had tried to deal with it? Nah. Anyway, at this point, this girl just wasn't a threat: Nobody had a clue whether she was aware of Annette Cooper's problems at all. And even if she was, he was ninety-nine-point-nine percent sure that buying her off would be the solution of choice. The fact that Jessica had thought *he* was her attacker boded well for the hallucination theory. Anyway, Lowell at least hadn't sent anyone to kill her, because if so he wouldn't also have sent Mark to deal with her. As Lowell was well aware, Mark was many things, but he wasn't one to condone a cold-blooded murder, especially when it happened practically under his nose. And he didn't go in for violence against women under any circumstances.

"Could you give us a minute here, please?" he asked, sweeping a meaningful look around the room. The implication was that he simply wanted privacy in which to break the bad news about Mrs. Cooper's death — which in a way he did, although that wasn't all of it, and he didn't think what he had to say was going to come as a surprise to her.

Jessica's eyes widened, and for a moment he thought she meant to protest. Mark realized that she was probably alarmed at the prospect of being left alone with him, which, if she really thought he'd tried to put something in her IV, he could certainly understand.

"You don't have to worry; you're safe with me," he told her in his best reassuring tone, to head her off before she could protest. "I'm on your side. I'm here strictly to make sure you're taken care of."

She looked at him hard, but she didn't object.

"Well . . ." The oldest nurse frowned at him. So did the blond one, looking across the bed at him as, with a loud zip of releasing Velcro, she unwrapped the blood-pressure cuff she had applied to Jessica's arm a moment before. The security guards shuffled uneasily. Mark had the feeling that if he hadn't been Secret Service, there was no way in hell he would have gotten her alone. As it was, though, it was clear that none of them quite had the guts to come right out and say no.

"It's all right." Jessica clenched the matter.

"We'll be right outside the door," the oldest nurse promised. With a glance at Jessica, the blond nurse stepped away from the bed. Then all of them, security guards included, left the room. There was a soft *whoosh* and then a click as the door closed behind them.

Mark looked at Jessica.

"Well?" Her voice was flat. Her eyes held his. She looked small and fragile lying there. She also looked kind of like she'd been hit by a Mack truck, which when he thought about it wasn't too far from what had actually happened to her. Mind-boggling that this nondescript girl, rather than the First Lady of the United States, or fit, strong Will Prescott, or even the adult male driver, had survived. Either she was a lot tougher than she looked or lucky as hell, and he didn't think she was very tough. What surprised him, though, was how calm and in control of herself she seemed. Pretty remarkable, he reckoned, under the circumstances. She had already suffered a lot both physically and emotionally, and she was probably in pain.

But still she had the moxie to scowl at him.

"The First Lady was killed in the crash," he said. There was no way to sugarcoat it, so best just get it out there.

Her eyes flickered, and she glanced down and away. Her lips shook, then firmed, as if she was refusing to let the emotion she was clearly feeling gain the upper hand. She took a breath, carefully shallower than before. Then, as he weighed what to say next, she was suddenly looking straight at him again. Her eyes blazed.

"Where the hell were you?" There was accusation in her voice.

"What?" She'd taken him by surprise. He almost blinked at her.

"I know you — you're the SAIC of the First Lady's security detail. Why weren't you there with her at the hotel? Or why wasn't somebody? Why was she alone? If you'd done what you were supposed to do, none of this would have happened."

"She was at a hotel?"

He latched on to the one piece of solid information and ignored the rest. He had to, because the guilt that her accusation stirred up was something he couldn't deal with right now. The thing that killed him was, she was right. One hundred percent totally correct.

"Isn't it your job to know that?"

Now she was starting to bug him. Whatever he'd been expecting, to have his balls busted by this girl who didn't look much older than his daughter wasn't it.

Anger bubbled. It was fueled by guilt, he knew. Mark told himself to chill.

"What do you know about my job?" He kept his voice even and his gaze level on her face. "For that matter, how do you know who I am?"

She didn't ease up. "I'm an associate with Davenport, Kelly, and Bascomb, Mr. Ryan. Mrs. Cooper has been to our offices on several occasions, and you've been with her. And I've seen you at the White House, when I delivered some papers to her."

It was all Mark could do not to blatantly look her over again, which he figured would not be politic. The thing was, he didn't remember ever seeing her, not in Davenport's office and not in the White House. Not that he meant to say so.

"That's right," he said, as if he recalled the occasions perfectly. "So, would you mind telling me what hotel Mrs. Cooper was in, and what she was doing there?"

"Are you asking out of idle curiosity, or in an official capacity?"

Keep it cool, keep it easy. "Part of my job."

A beat passed. Then she said, almost sulkily, "It was the Harrington. And I have no idea why she was there."

"So why were you there?"

"Mr. Davenport sent me to meet Mrs. Cooper there because he couldn't go himself."

"The First Lady was meeting Davenport at a hotel?"

"In the bar. Apparently, she called him and asked to meet, but he couldn't make it.

He sent me instead."

"Why?" He couldn't fathom a circumstance in which the First Lady's close friend and trusted confidant would need to meet her in a bar, or would send a stranger — and he was as sure as it was possible to be under the circumstances that Mrs. Cooper hadn't known Jessica from Adam before tonight — to meet with her in his stead. Unless, as Lowell had speculated, a drug deal of some sort was involved. Or maybe the heading off of one.

"Because I live close by. Because I could get there quickly. Because Mr. Davenport trusts me."

"Ah." Mark still didn't get it, but why Davenport had sent a subordinate in his place really wasn't the most important point he needed clarity on at the moment, so he let it go. "So you met Mrs. Cooper in a hotel bar. Then what happened?"

"We left."

Mark stifled a glimmer of annoyance. The antagonistic vibes she was sending his way were starting to get old.

"Care to elaborate?"

"We walked out together to the car I had come in — Mr. Davenport had arranged for it — and drove away."

She stopped, closing her eyes. He waited.

Her dark hair fanned out against the pillow as she turned her head away from him, showing glints of red amid the deep brown. Under the unforgiving glow of the harsh overhead lighting, her face looked almost as white as the pillowcase. Taking in just the damage to her that was visible, he felt bad for even questioning her. But time was of the essence here. He might — thank Jesus — be the first, but he wouldn't be the only one to ask all this and more. He had to know what she was going to say.

"So," he finally said when it became clear she wasn't going to resume talking anytime soon, "you and Mrs. Cooper are in the car, it drives away, and . . . ?"

Her head turned back toward him, and her eyes opened again with a slow sweep of thick lashes. It seemed to cost her some effort to focus on his face. "That's the last thing I remember. Getting into the car and pulling away from the hotel."

Mark made his voice even gentler. "What about the crash?"

"I don't remember it. I don't remember anything from the time the car left the hotel until you found me. Nothing. At all."

She said the last "at all" as if for emphasis.

There was a pause as Mark processed that. She'd been through a terrible trauma just hours before. Trauma often erased the events immediately preceding it from the mind, as he knew from experience. Therefore, it made sense that she wouldn't remember, he decided. And it also made things easier.

For him. And for her.

"You said Mrs. Cooper was alone in the bar. You mean really alone? There wasn't a Secret Service agent with her?" He was thinking of Prescott, who had clearly hooked up with the First Lady at some point before the crash.

Jessica shook her head.

"One of our agents, Will Prescott, was killed in the crash along with Mrs. Cooper and the driver. If he wasn't with Mrs. Cooper at the bar, how was it that he was in the car with you all?"

She seemed to think about that.

"I don't know. I don't remember," she said at last. "Wait — he may have been outside in front of the hotel, on the street. When we came out."

"So he joined you in the car."

"I don't know. I remember being in the car with Mrs. Cooper and the driver, and no one else, as we pulled away from the curb. After that — it's a total blank."

Mark decided to let the logistics of Prescott's presence in the car go for the moment, too. She seemed increasingly exhausted, a nurse or anyone else could come in at any moment and interrupt, and he had other, more urgent, fish to fry while the frying was good. Finding out what she knew without letting her in on anything she didn't already know about the First Lady required a delicate balance. Unfortunately, he wasn't sure he was up to it. Even under the best of circumstances, delicacy had never been his strong suit.

"So what did Mrs. Cooper do in the bar? What was she doing? When you got there."

"Finishing her drink. She was alone at a table in the corner. I told her Mr. Davenport had sent me and a car to pick her up. So she left with me."

"Where were you going?"

She hesitated. There was a new tension around her eyes and mouth that made him wonder if she was in pain. He hadn't had that impression before, but he supposed that if she had been on painkillers, they would have been delivered via the IV, which obviously was no longer happening. It wasn't too big a stretch to assume the painkillers she'd already received might be starting to wear off.

"I . . . don't know. I was supposed to call

Mr. Davenport for instructions once I had the First Lady safely in the car. But . . . I can't remember if I did."

"Safely?" The word tugged at him.

She wet her lips. Her eyes opened wide again to focus on him. It seemed to cost her considerable effort just to lift her lids.

"You know, I was only with the First Lady for about ten minutes, tops. At least, that I remember. I walked into the bar, told her Mr. Davenport had sent me to get her, and walked out with her. We got in the car. And that's it. That's everything. That's all I know. I don't remember anything else. So could you please just go away and leave me alone? I'm really not up to this."

He looked at her consideringly. If possible, she was even paler than before, so colorless her skin appeared almost translucent, and the bruises on her face and neck stood out like zebra stripes. She was shivering now, where she hadn't been before, her hands curled into the blanket. He felt a quick stab of compassion. She was injured, perhaps terribly, and she'd survived a gruesome car crash that had left the three others involved dead. He'd gotten the answers he needed from her, or at least most of them. The important one, which was that she knew nothing and remembered little. So probably it was time for him to back off and turn her back over to the medical personnel who were caring for her.

"The President would appreciate it if you didn't talk about his wife or the crash or anything related to any of that to the press." He evoked the power of the office almost reluctantly. He hadn't said anything about the President earlier, in case one of the others in the room at the time later blabbed to the media the details of his visit to Jessica, which, the principles of medical privacy be damned, he figured they were highly likely to do. He didn't want anyone saying that he was at the crash survivor's bedside at the direction of the President until the way the spin on this was going to be handled had been worked out. Maybe they would decide he had rushed to Jessica's bedside at the President's behest, and maybe they would decide he hadn't. Hell, for all he knew he might not even have officially seen her at all. "I recommend . . ."

That was as far as he got. A plump blond woman — Jessica's mother; he recognized her from the lobby and assumed she had finally finished with the hospital admission paperwork — pushed through the door, high heels tapping, be-ringed hands fluttering in agitation as she spoke over her shoulder to the younger, slimmer blond woman following her. They looked enough alike that it was obvious that they were mother and daughter, although one was about fifty and the other was maybe in her mid-twenties. Both were round rather than angular, and tall, with the kind of bleached-out platinum hair that was clearly the result of multiple home dye jobs. The mother wore hers in short curls; the daughter's was shoulder-length with bangs. Both had round, apple-cheeked faces, snub noses, and dark brown eyes that gave the lie to their hair color. Both wore tight jeans and V-neck pullover sweaters. The mother's was baby blue. The daughter's was pink. Neither looked anything at all like Jessica.

"Honey, you're awake." The mother barely glanced at Mark as she rushed, heels clacking, toward her daughter's bedside. "Oh, my goodness, Jess, you just about scared us to death."

"Mom." Jessica's chin wobbled, and Mark realized to his horror that she was going to cry. She looked past her mother at her presumed sister. "Sarah. Guys, I can't move my legs."

"Oh, Jess." The younger woman rushed the bedside, too, and they both leaned over their relative. Mark didn't know if they all engaged in a group hug or what because he was busy backpedaling away from the lovefest just as fast and unobtrusively as he could. "What matters is that you're alive."

"The doctor down in the emergency room said it was probably temporary," her mother soothed. "He said the X-rays didn't show anything, so it's probably just . . ."

The door flew open again as if propelled by great force. Two little towheaded boys, maybe four and six years old, wearing Batman and Incredible Hulk pajamas respectively, tumbled into the room, the older one shoving the younger one so that he nearly fell flat on his face.

"He pushed me!" Recovering his balance, Batman ran toward the sister — Sarah — who had turned upon their entrance. His arms wrapped tight around her legs. "Mom! He pushed me!"

"Is Aunt Jess dead?" Hulk skidded to a halt near the foot of the bed and peered up at Jessica, whose face Mark could no longer see because of the screen provided by her family. "Nah, she's just crying. Why are you crying, Aunt Jess?"

" 'Cause she's hurt her face, stupid. See all the places?"

"Boys," their mother — at least, Mark presumed Sarah was their mother — warned

111

sharply. "Behave."

". . . have anybody to leave them with," another female voice said apologetically, and Mark's gaze swung toward the door. It was opening again. The speaker was talking over her shoulder to someone — the older nurse, Mark saw as they entered one after the other and headed toward the bed. This blonde was a bombshell, slim yet curvy and tall like the other two, with long, straight hair that swung as she walked. Maybe twenty-one or -two, dressed in a killer black miniskirt and heels that made her tanned bare legs look a mile long. She was wearing a jacket, too, a black leather bomber, but Mark barely noticed that. It was all he could do to look away from the legs.

"I'm sorry, but children aren't allowed on this floor." The nurse sounded like she'd said this more than once and was fast running out of patience.

"Their dad's coming for them," Sarah told the nurse. "It'll just be a little while. They'll be real quiet."

"You said you were going to watch TV and go to bed," the bombshell said accusingly to Jessica. "What happened?"

"A lot." Jessica's voice sounded thick. Mark, who still couldn't see her, took this to mean she was still weepy. "I'm so glad to see you guys."

"Believe me, not as glad as we are to see you."

Group hug again, during which the boys, clearly revolted, crawled under Jessica's bed. Nobody except the nurse — who gave them an evil look — paid the slightest attention.

"One of you could wait with the children in the lobby," the nurse suggested, in the kind of stern tone that made it more of an order than a suggestion.

"It's full of reporters," the bombshell said, glancing around at her relatives. "They were taking the kids' pictures. I don't know how the subject came up, but apparently Hunter told them Jess was their aunt. After that, we had to go."

"They were talking 'bout some lady being killed in a car wreck," Hulk said from beneath the bed. "I told 'em my aunt was in a wreck too. Then they just started asking all kinds of questions and taking pictures."

"And Aunt Grace made us leave," Batman chimed in. "I got to push the elevator button, though."

"Oh, no." Their mother voiced the dismay apparent in the faces of everyone Mark could see.

"What could they have said?" Jessica's

mother made an excusing face. "They're just little kids."

"Nobody should say anything to anybody." Jessica's tone was urgent. "Mom, Mrs. Cooper was killed in the wreck."

"Honey, I know. It's a terrible, terrible thing. She seemed like such a nice lady, too."

"I'm just glad it wasn't you," the bombshell said fiercely. "What would we do without you?"

"Well, we'll just get your IV hooked up again." Giving up on banishing the kids, the nurse went for the pole, obviously noticed the missing bag, stopped dead, and frowned. Mark could feel the thing practically burning a hole through his pocket.

"No! No IV!" Jessica protested in agitation. Not that Mark minded, because her reaction distracted the nurse's attention from the missing bag. "Look, I'm a lawyer, and I know I have the right to refuse to have one. And I refuse! Do you hear? I refuse!"

The nurse shook her head at her. "You have to have an IV. Your medications are administered through it and . . ."

"*No.* What part of 'someone just attacked me' did you miss?"

"Wait a minute." Jessica's mother frowned. "Someone *attacked* you?"

"We're sure it was a hallucination brought

114

on by the medication," the nurse said wearily.

"It was *not . . .*"

While the standoff continued, Mark judged his principal perfectly safe for the time being and slipped from the room.

It had to be a hallucination. That was the only thing that made sense. Yes, there were others, known variously as cleaners, plumbers, repairmen, whatever, covert operatives that routinely dealt with problems to the powerful like the one Jessica potentially presented. But to employ them on a woman who might very well know nothing of the First Lady's secrets, who might very well present no problem at all, would be the ultimate in overkill. He'd known the Coopers long, and he knew the Coopers well. They would never be party to such a thing.

But under the circumstances, and just in case, he meant to keep tabs on Jessica until he could be absolutely, positively certain he was right.

Because one thing he'd learned over the years was that you could be absolutely, positively certain you were right about something — and still be dead wrong.

Nodding at the security guards, who still hovered in the hall, he walked over to one of the three pay phones on the wall behind the nurses' station — a phone that he was pretty damned sure wasn't tapped and wouldn't be monitored, because nobody would ever figure on anything sensitive going out over it — and placed a call to Harvey Brooks, a lab guy he knew, all while keeping an eye on the door to room 337.

When that was completed to his satisfaction, he pulled his encrypted phone — which he hadn't used to call Brooks because, cynical bastard that he was, he figured that somewhere in the coils of the government he worked for there was somebody who could break through the encryption at will — out of his pocket and called Lowell.

8

I'm scared.

That was the thought that popped into Jess's brain as her eyes opened, slowly and reluctantly, on what proved to be the shadowy, whisper-quiet world of her hospital room. Like the desperate hand of a drowning person going down for the last time, it shot out of the black void of the already almost forgotten dream she'd been caught up in, breaking the surface of her consciousness and grabbing hold. She blinked, trying to be rid of it, but still it held on.

Oh, God, we've got to get out of here. . . .

That voice, shrill with terror, swirling up out of the darkness, was more residue from the dream. It was a woman's, but it wasn't hers; she didn't recognize it.

Or maybe she did.

As she contemplated that, a cold little frisson of dread made her shiver. Her heart pumped like she had been running for miles.

In self-defense, she dismissed the other swirling images trying to take shape in her mind before they could solidify, and instead focused determinedly on the immediate, on the here and now.

Instinctively, she knew it was safer that way.

The walls were white, the curtains green. They were closed, with slivers of dull light glowing around their edges and, mysteriously, what looked like a stripe of duct tape running down the center line holding them together. The monitoring machines stood silent beside her bed; she hadn't allowed them to be hooked up again because the idea of machines being attached to her body freaked her out now. Her mother stood between her bed and the machines, looking tired and frazzled in the soft, gray shadows of the heavily curtained room as she reached for something on the stand beside the bed. There were bags under her eyes that were not normally there, the creases running from her nose to her mouth and in between her eyebrows seemed deeper than usual, her lipstick had worn off, and her short cap of blond hair was straight and flat, as though it had not seen a curling iron in some time. Judy Ford Turner Whalen always had immaculate makeup and always curled her hair, world without end; for her to have neglected either showed just how extremely stressed out she was.

The phone was ringing. Her mother was reaching for the ringing phone. Probably, Jess decided, the sound was what had awakened her.

Just looking at her mother made her thudding heart start to slow. Judy was many things, not all of them totally positive, but one thing she definitely was was a tigress in defense of her young. No harm could come to her with her mother in the room — no harm that Judy could prevent, anyhow.

The certainty calmed her. Jess took a steadying breath. Whatever had come before or would come after, for now, for this moment in time, in this gloomy cocoon of a room, she was safe.

"Hello," her mother said cautiously into the receiver. It wasn't like her mother to be cautious, so Jess immediately knew something was up. She felt herself tensing again. Their eyes met. It was hard to read the nuances of her mother's expression through the gloom, but Judy's widened eyes and slight smile acknowledged the fact that Jess was awake.

It also made her think that whatever was going down on the phone couldn't be so terribly bad. Judy wouldn't be smiling at her like that if it was anything bad.

"You think I don't know my own sister's voice? This sure as hell is *not* Jessica's Aunt Tammy." Her mother slammed the receiver back down with enough force to make the phone jump. Jess would have jumped, too, if she'd had the strength. She winced instead, which hurt. "Damned reporters."

"Mom?" Jess frowned at her in surprise.

"They've been trying every which-a-way to get information about you," Judy informed her. "Ron" — Sarah's possibly soon-to-be-ex-husband; their separation had led to Sarah, boys in tow, moving back in with Judy three weeks ago, which in turn had led Grace, who had been living with their mother, to flee to Jess's apartment for sanctuary — "couldn't even take the kids to school this morning. There was a TV truck out in front of his house! He had to call the police to run them off."

"A TV truck?" Realization hit Jess like a bucket of cold water to the face. *The wreck . . .* She shivered. Her stomach clenched. "Mrs. Cooper's death is all over the news, isn't it?" It occurred to her that, as someone who had been in the accident and survived, the *only* one who had survived, she was a very obvious focal point for the media. "Are there reporters here at the hospital, too?"

Her mother nodded.

"They've been camped out around the place since before I got here, and it seems like more of 'em just keep coming. It's a nightmare just trying to get to the car. We had to tape the curtains in here closed because one of them got up in a room in the wing across the way and was trying to take pictures of you lying there in that bed through the window. They've even tried to sneak up here a couple of times. If there wasn't security at the door, I don't know what we would have done."

"Security?"

"There's two Secret Service agents outside the door right now. They change shifts every eight hours or so."

Judy's voice was hushed with respect. Jess knew she was impressed that her daughter rated notice from the White House, no matter how horrific the circumstances. To Judy, a president was somebody you saw on TV. The fact that her daughter's job brought her into daily contact with people who knew people in the White House had been a source of tremendous pride. When Jess had told her that her boss was the First Lady's lawyer and personal friend and that she herself had actually been in the same room as the First Lady and been introduced to her by name and shaken her hand and talked to her, Judy's awe had been palpable.

"You're kidding, right?"

But even before Judy shook her head, Jess knew she was not.

Jess wet her lips. The thought of Secret Service agents outside her door made her blood run cold. *Why?* She didn't know, precisely, she realized. The idea of it just made her feel — panicky.

"Can you believe it? The White House sent them. 'Cause they want to help us out until you're back on your feet, they said." Judy's expression changed as she focused on her oldest child. "How you feeling, honey?"

Jess thought about that. She was anxious. She was dizzy. She hurt all over, with special emphasis on her head and ribs. And her back ached, right down at the base of her spine, with a continuous, deep, throbbing pain that had her arching this way and that in a futile effort to relieve it.

"My legs . . ."

Fighting a rush of fear as she remembered how they had refused to work before, she tried to move them.

Her right leg slid sideways maybe a couple

of inches. The toes curled on her left foot. The pain in her back turned excruciating, shooting up her spine, freezing her in place. She grimaced, and would have groaned, except she didn't want to worry her mother.

"When the doctor came in to see you this morning, he said the X-rays didn't show any sign of permanent damage. No fracture or anything like that. He thinks you must have bruised your spine. They've been giving you painkillers, and steroids to help with the swelling, and he said when that goes down you should be able to move better. He said you'll be stiff and sore for a while, but everything'll heal sooner or later. It's just going to take some time."

Hearing that made Jess feel like a humongous stone had just been lifted from her chest.

"Thank God." She took a deep breath. Until that moment she hadn't realized just how frightened she had been that she might have lost the use of her legs for good. If she wasn't going to die or be paralyzed, then she was going to live and eventually be fine, so she might as well get on with it. "I want to sit up."

Her mother nodded and hit the remote. Jess felt the head of the bed slowly rising beneath her.

"How's that?"

"Better."

Filled with renewed determination, gritting her teeth with effort, Jess concentrated on moving her legs. Her right knee rose off the mattress high enough to tent the covers. She was less successful with her left leg but managed to at least shift it sideways. The effort sent another sharp pain shooting up her back and electric tingles coursing down both legs, causing her to squirm in protest, but still she felt a wave of relief. At least that was proof she could move.

"You're doing good," her mother encouraged as Jess, frozen in place now, waited for the pain to recede. Which, somewhat to her surprise, it did.

Breathing easier, she concentrated again, and managed to get her left knee off the mattress, too. Then she cautiously wiggled the toes on both feet and turned her feet from side to side at the ankle. The pain was bad but not nearly as bad as the thought of her legs being paralyzed had been, so she persevered until she was sure everything still worked. Finally, using her hands for leverage, she scooted farther up in the bed until she was propped up against her pillows, and brushed her hair back from her sweaty face with both hands. Moving hurt. So did lifting her arms and scrunching up her face, which she did in reaction to the other pain, but she kept on. She figured that if she did only what didn't hurt, she would basically just lie there and breathe. Shallowly.

"I need a shower."

"How about I get a bowl of water and some soap and you make do with washing your face and hands for now?"

Jess thought about the effort required to move at all, extrapolated that to the far greater effort to get out of bed and somehow make it to the shower, then stand, sit, or lie there beneath the steaming-hot water for long enough to get clean, and made a face. With the best will in the world, she couldn't do it. A bowl of water and some soap was not what she wanted, but clearly it was what she was going to have to settle for.

"Fine," she said with a sigh.

Her mother headed for the bathroom, flipping on the overhead light as she passed the switch. Jess flinched at the unexpected assault of so much brightness. While her eyes were adjusting to the near-blinding fluorescent glow, she cast a quick look at the bedside clock. The numbers were blurry since she wasn't wearing her contacts, but by squinting and tilting her head and shading her eyes with her hands she was able to read them. The time was five-twenty-three, and from the light filtering in around the curtains she knew it wasn't a.m., because at this time of year at almost five-thirty in the morning it would still be dark outside. Therefore, it was late Sunday afternoon; ordinarily, she would be finishing up briefs to be presented in court on Monday. Apparently, whatever they'd put in the shots they'd given her — no way was she ever having another IV for as long as she lived, as she'd finally made crystal clear to the bevy of hospital personnel who had taken turns trying to bully her into it — must have been something potent to make her sleep for a little more than twelve hours. Her mother had said they'd given her painkillers; she was still feeling pain, so they weren't doing so great with that, but at least she'd gotten plenty of sleep.

Her glasses, the ones with the big black frames that she kept as backup to the contacts, rested on the table beside the clock. They were a little fuzzy around the edges but unmistakable, and she guessed that someone — Grace, most likely — must have fetched them from her apartment. Reaching for them greedily, sliding them on and experiencing the instant relief of seeing the world around her in focus again, she noticed something else: the TV remote beside the clock.

The temptation proved irresistible. She didn't want to know, she was better off not knowing, but she couldn't help herself: She picked up the remote, clicked it at the ceiling-mounted TV just beyond the foot of her bed, and . . .

A close-up of Annette Cooper smiling as she shook hands with someone an unseen narrator identified as Chilean president Jorge Peres de Toros blinked to life. The camera pulled back, and Jess saw that the First Lady looked beautiful in a floor-length white evening dress that shimmered with sequins. Her trademark short blond hair gleamed in the light of the overhead chandelier. Her skin was smooth and tan and glowing. Her eyes were bright.

Jess had expected it, of course, when she had turned on the TV. Still, the shock of seeing Annette Cooper was overwhelming. She caught her breath. As agonizing as it was to watch, she couldn't look away as the First Lady said something over her shoulder to her tuxedo-clad husband, who laughed and nodded in response.

". . . such a short time ago Mrs. Cooper was at the President's side as he . . ."

Biting down hard on her lower lip, Jess

changed the channel.

A shot of the White House filled the screen. A crowd, an enormous sea of people that seemed to stretch all the way to the Mall, had gathered around it, and the camera panned dozens upon dozens of weeping faces. It seemed to be a live shot, taken in real time, because the sky that formed the backdrop was streaked with sunset colors of orange and purple and gold, and the White House itself cast a long shadow across the lawn.

". . . thousands gathering in the capital to pay tribute to First Lady Annette Cooper, who this evening is lying in state in the Capitol Rotunda. Mrs. Cooper was killed in a car crash shortly after . . ."

Punching the button with far more force than was necessary now, Jess changed the channel again. She was breathing hard, she realized, and her palms were sweaty. Her stomach churned. She felt gorge backing up in her throat.

It was night, and a car, blackened and crushed and flipped over on its roof, filled the screen.

Jess's eyes widened. She was instantly bathed in cold sweat. The shot seemed to have been taken from above, and it showed the still-smoking undercarriage, the flattened tires, the circle of charred grass in which the vehicle rested, the dozens of fire-fighters and rescue workers and police officers and military personnel and plainclothes investigators moving around the scene. Make and model were impossible to determine because of the car's burned-out state, but she knew instantly that it was the black Lincoln that Davenport had sent her to pick up Mrs. Cooper in. It was a night shot, lit up by big orange klieg lights focused on the scene and the bright beams of spotlights crisscrossing the wreck from above — helicopter searchlights, she realized, and realized, too, that the shot had been taken from a helicopter soon after the accident.

So soon that she might still have been lying semiconscious on the dark slope that fell away from the road on the right side of the shot.

Jess started to shake.

". . . preliminary investigation indicates that the vehicle was traveling at excessive amounts of speed — one estimate suggests as much as ninety miles an hour in a forty-five-mile-an-hour zone — when the driver, identified as Raymond Kenny of Silver Spring, Maryland, who had worked for the company that owned the car, Executive Limo, for fourteen years, lost control and the car went off the side of Brerton Road and rolled down an embankment, killing three of the four people inside, including First Lady Annette Cooper. She was said to be on her way to visit a dying friend at the Sisters of Mercy Hospital in Fredericksburg and . . ."

Dear God.

Closing her eyes, feeling like the world was tipping sideways and she was clinging on by her fingernails in an effort not to fall off, Jess hit the power button, hit it without even consciously making the decision to do so. It was as if her body, reacting in its own defense, just said no to exposure to anything else that might cause her distress. But even with her eyes closed, even with the voices from the television silenced and the screen gone black, it still felt like she was tumbling down into nothingness as images from the accident chased one another through her mind.

9

Speeding through the night, going faster and faster until the rolling hills and dark pastures and a narrow fence line of tall trees outside the window became nothing more than a black blur and her heart was pumping with alarm, feeling a hard jolt that sent the car skidding sideways, the terrible squeal of brakes drowned out after a single terrified moment by screams . . .

"Jess, are you all right?"

Jess opened her eyes. She was drenched in sweat and drawing deep, shuddering breaths, and she realized from her mother's expression that she was probably as pale as a piece of angel food cake.

"She was said to be on her way to visit a dying friend at the Sisters of Mercy Hospital in Fredericksburg . . ." That's what they'd said on TV.

Only it was a lie. They were telling lies.
Why?

"Jess?"

Frowning, Judy walked toward her carrying a blue plastic basin filled with water that sloshed softly with every step, a small unwrapped bar of soap, a blue washrag, and a matching towel.

"Jessica Jane? Do you hear me talking to you?"

It occurred to Jess that she was staring at her mother as if she had been poleaxed. She willed herself to focus.

Think it through later. Shake it off.

"Oh, sorry. I was just . . . I'm fine."

That is, other than the fact that she was dizzy and limp with dread. Which she didn't mean to share with her mother. Which she didn't even totally understand herself. Taking a not-too-deep breath, she fought to get her emotions under control, to seem like her normal self, so her mother wouldn't guess that something was majorly wrong. She didn't know why she felt this was so important, but she did.

Dark figures rushing past her down the slope . . .

Jess realized she was breathing way too fast.

"You don't look fine. You look worse than you did when you were unconscious, for pete's sake."

"I have a little headache."

That was true, as far as it went. Also, her palms were sweaty. Her mouth was dry. Her pulse was racing. Disoriented, that's how she felt. Almost as if she could see — no, she didn't want to see.

Who were the dark figures? Were they even real?

She didn't want to think about it. She didn't want to know.

Her mother's frown deepened. She was looking at her hard.

"Maybe I should call the nurse."

"No. No, don't."

You can't go there now. Snap out of it.

Every instinct Jess possessed screamed that she had to keep her mother — keep her family, keep everyone — from knowing that her memory wasn't totally wiped out where the crash was concerned after all. Instead, it was throwing up weird images like puzzle pieces that didn't quite fit. No, make that terrifying images.

Fire . . . It started as a tiny orange burst and then — boom! — it exploded, pillars of flame enveloping the car, shooting toward the ink-black sky. . . .

Jess closed her eyes. She clenched her fists. She bit down hard on the tip of her tongue. The pain did what it was supposed to do —

it cleared the hideous pictures from her mind.

"Jess?"

Jess opened her eyes. "It's just a headache . . . I'm better now."

"It's been a while since they last gave you anything for pain — maybe we ought to ask for something."

"It's okay. It's gone."

Her mother was still looking at her with concern. Jess took a deep breath and managed a weak smile for her mother as Judy settled the basin on her stomach.

"Thanks." Jess felt limp, as if the pictures in her head had taken a physical toll on her body. "And thanks for staying with me, by the way."

"Are you kidding? It'd take wild horses to get me out of here. After you thought somebody attacked you?" Judy made a *tsk-tsk* noise. "Here, let me help you with that."

"I can manage."

Making a conscious effort to keep her hands steady and her head in the present, Jess summoned another perfunctory smile and tucked her hair behind her ears and dipped the washrag in the warm water.

"Maybe the attack *was* a hallucination." Careful to keep her voice free of any inflection, Jess wrung out the rag without looking at her mother.

The attack was real. It happened.

But even though she was almost completely convinced of it, she didn't say so. After listening to the TV, she was beginning to get her mind around the true enormity of what Annette Cooper's death meant. The global scope of it. The interest in it. And the possible ramifications. Through no fault of her own, she was caught up in a world-class tragedy. As the only living witness, in fact. Not a comfortable spot to be in. And, she was becoming increasingly afraid, not a safe one.

Whatever was going on — and she was almost positive that something she'd really rather not know about was going on — she didn't want to get her mother — her family — involved.

That was the thing about family, she was discovering. Having them, having people you care about, makes you so damned vulnerable.

Annette Cooper fled the White House.

"Whether it was a hallucination or not" — Jess, mindful of her injuries, carefully dabbed at her cheeks and chin, as Judy retrieved a hairbrush from her purse, held it up so Jess could see it, and set it on the bedside table next to the remote — "I'm

135

not leaving this place until you do."

That was her mother — loyal to the bitter end. For better or for worse.

"I love you, Mom." It was something she almost never said anymore. None of them did.

Her mother's face softened. "I love you too, Jessica Rabbit."

It was a nickname from when she'd been a little girl, funny, so her sisters said, because their Jessica was the polar opposite of her cartoon namesake. Not sexy, not a man-eater, just plain, skinny, blind-as-a-bat bookworm Jess.

Thanks for the confidence builder, guys. She could almost hear them answering, *You're welcome, Wabbit.*

"Look what else I've got." The crinkle of tearing plastic wrap was followed by her mother waving a cheap pink toothbrush at her, then placing it and a small tube of Crest beside the hairbrush. "It's been in my purse since the dentist gave it to me."

Jess's eyes lit up. "Fantastic."

Judy poured her a glass of water from the yellow plastic pitcher beside the bed, and Jess quickly brushed her teeth. The minty tang of the toothpaste was so normal, so much a part of her regular, everyday life, that the very ordinariness of it felt special.

She was suddenly, overwhelmingly, thankful to be alive. The idea of never seeing her mother and sisters again, of their grief if she had been killed along with everyone else in that car, made her throat tighten. They were a mess, every single one of them — herself included, she supposed. They could be, and frequently were, a giant pain in her ass. But in the end, she was just now discovering, none of that really mattered.

What mattered was that they were a family.

Annette Cooper had a family, too.

Jess's throat tightened again. Leaning over the basin, she splashed her face, the better to conceal incipient tears, and discovered that in some places her skin was so raw it stung.

Ironically enough, the small discomfort banished the sudden urge to cry.

Mrs. Cooper ran away from the Secret Service agent who came looking for her.

"You've got to be exhausted," Jess said to her mother in an effort to banish the torturous thoughts that just wouldn't stay out of her head. Wiping the water from her eyes, she looked at Judy. Her mother really did look tired. "Have you gotten any sleep at all?"

Judy nodded. "Maddie came in this morning, so I lay down on the other bed and slept while she was here. She and Grace went out about an hour ago to pick up some things from the house." Maddie was Jess's youngest sister, a just-turned-eighteen-year-old high school senior. The previous weekend, Maddie had precipitated a family crisis — and when weren't they ever in some kind of crisis? — by telling Grace, who told Sarah (because Jess was working all weekend and Grace had to tell somebody, and Sarah possessed the closest ear), who told their mother, who then told Jess, that she was pregnant.

At the time, having National Merit Scholarship–winning, valedictorian-candidate Maddie confess that she was pregnant had seemed like the family-size equivalent of an atom bomb.

Now it seemed manageable. A small pothole in the road of life. One of those things that you end up making the best of, maybe even laughing about in twenty years. When the kid-to-be was a beloved member of the family.

Nothing like almost dying to provide a little perspective, Jess reflected with an inner grimace as she worked the soap into bubbly lather, which she then carefully spread over the parts of her face that weren't either stinging or stitched together.

Mrs. Cooper said her Secret Service agents were more like wardens. She was upset, way more upset than she should have been from something as ordinary as a fight with her husband. She was running away.

"I hate for you to stay with me again tonight — you've got to work tomorrow," Jess said. "You'll wear yourself out."

Her mother operated a small day-care center out of her home. Both Maddie and Grace, who was a junior at University of Maryland, worked there part-time. It was her mother's latest moneymaking venture after she lost her job as a shift supervisor at the Red Cross shoe plant three years ago, when Jess had been in her first year of law school and working at Davenport, Kelly, and Bascomb as a research assistant at night. Since then, Judy had been a temp, a waitress, a veterinary assistant, a sales associate at Macy's, and a pizza delivery person, and sometimes two or three at once. None of which, singly or in multiples, paid enough to support her family. Even with Grace and Maddie holding down part-time jobs, and Jess contributing every penny she could, there was never enough. Until Jess had graduated law school and gotten the fat-salaried job with Davenport. With what

139

she was now able to contribute to the family kitty, everyone was comfortable for the first time that Jess could remember.

Do I even still have a job? Probably the last thing I should be worried about now, but . . . I need the money. We *need the money.* She grimaced inwardly. *Face it, doesn't everybody always need the money?*

"We didn't open today, and we're not opening tomorrow. Probably not the rest of the week, either. I called all the parents — they understand. Lots of businesses around here are shut down out of respect for Mrs. Cooper anyway, and they all know that you're my daughter and what happened to you."

It took Jess a second, but then she caught it.

"Is this *Monday?*"

"Sure is. What did you think?"

"I thought it was Sunday." Jess rinsed her face and reached for the brush, which she pulled carefully through her hair: *Ouch.* She'd been out of it for almost forty-eight hours: unbelievable. And oh my God, it was a work day and she'd missed it. The first one ever. Then she remembered, and realized that it was almost certainly *not* a work day. Not for a firm so closely associated with the First Lady. "Has Mr. Davenport called?

Or anyone from work?"

"There were so many calls the hospital switchboard's only been putting family through."

So many calls — because everyone wanted her to talk about the accident.

The panic that had been slowly building just below her precariously maintained calm started to bubble to the surface.

They — she wasn't quite sure who was to blame — had it wrong about where Mrs. Cooper was going when the car crashed. Jess's memory of what had transpired during the accident might be spotty, but her recall of what had happened before was unimpaired. Mrs. Cooper had been running away from the White House, and Davenport had sent Jess and a car to pick her up and take her — somewhere. Those were facts. Admittedly, Jess didn't remember where they were headed, but for sure it wasn't to visit a dying friend in a Fredericksburg hospital. Maybe that was an honest mistake, maybe it was a deliberate lie, or spin, as Davenport would probably put it, but the discrepancy made her uneasy. Couple that with the images in her mind of dark figures rushing down the slope past where she lay and surrounding the burning car, add in Mrs. Cooper's upset and her claim that she was a prisoner in the White House (more facts), as well as the near certainty that she herself had been attacked right here in this very room just hours after the First Lady's death, and what did you get?

Either something really bad — or a whole lot of vivid imagination mixed with a little bit of truth that added up to nothing much at all.

Her imagination had never been that vivid. Therefore, she was going with something really bad.

You gotta tell somebody. You can't keep this to yourself. It's too big — too important.

"Mom, could you get rid of this stuff, please? I'm finished with it."

"You look better." Giving her a critical once-over, her mother gathered up the bedpan and glass, etc., and headed for the bathroom with it. "Still a little the worse for wear, but better."

"Wonderful. Oh, and you might want to wash your face while you're in there. You've got mascara smudges under your eyes."

"Oh, my."

That, Jess figured, had just bought her a good ten minutes. She barely managed to wait until Judy disappeared into the bathroom and closed the door before snatching up the phone by the bed and punching in

Davenport's number — not the office but the private cell phone number he had given her on Saturday night when he had sent her out to retrieve Mrs. Cooper. It was his direct line, the only number, home or office, that wasn't routed through Marian Young, his longtime secretary.

It was recorded in her cell phone's memory, but her cell phone was nowhere in sight. But she remembered it.

Perfectly, as it turned out. Because he answered on the second ring.

10

"Who is this?" Davenport demanded, instead of giving his name or any identifying information. Jess realized that the hospital name and number must have come up on his caller ID, but nothing that would tell him specifically it was her. The thing was, only a few people had this number, which was normally reserved for very special clients like Annette Cooper, so there weren't a whole lot of choices. Unless he'd thought the number had been discovered by the press.

"Jessica Ford, Mr. Davenport."

She heard him catch his breath.

"God in heaven, Jessica, you're a living, breathing miracle. Do you realize that? Do you appreciate it?"

"Yes." Brushing over that impatiently, she spoke in an urgent whisper with one eye on the bathroom door. "Mr. Davenport, listen, I think something may be wrong about this.

For one thing, a man attacked me not long after I was admitted to the hospital. He tried to put something in my IV. I think he might have been trying to kill me. And . . ."

"How did such a terrible accident happen? Annette, everybody else —" Davenport's voice shook as he broke in on her hurried recital. Jess was pretty sure he hadn't listened to a word she had said. Because it was obvious that just like he had been the last time she had talked to him, he'd been drinking pretty heavily. "Well, I'm just glad you're alive. Just so glad. It just seems so impossible. . . ."

He made a choking sound, and Jess realized it was a sob.

"Mr. Davenport. They're saying on TV that Mrs. Cooper was on her way to visit a dying friend and we both know that's not —"

"Wait! Stop!" Davenport's normally deep and authoritative voice was high-pitched and wobbly. "Don't say it. Not anything. Not on the phone. Anybody could be listening."

Jess's heart skipped a beat. Her eyes widened, and she had an absurd impulse to glance around the room even though she absolutely knew it was empty.

"Who? Who do you think is listening?"

"Anybody. Everybody. Bad people."

"Bad people?" Her heart speeded up. It sounded like he harbored some of the same suspicions she did, when what she'd really wanted was for him to tell her that they couldn't possibly, no way, uh-unh, be true.

"The dark forces. They're dangerous, you know."

She was pretty sure the gulping sound she heard was him knocking back another long swallow of whatever it was he was drinking. It certainly wasn't her swallowing. She wasn't that loud.

"I don't know who else to go to with this. You're the only one I can trust and —"

"No, no, no! Not on the phone!"

Jess was feeling desperate. She got the impression that he might hang up on her at any second. "Could we talk in person, then?"

"Maybe." Another gulp. "Yes, that would probably be a good idea."

"Are you at the office? I could come there —" She thought of her physical condition. She was pretty sure she couldn't even walk. "No, on second thought, I can't. Can you come here?"

"No. Not possible. It would cause too much of an uproar. The media's knee-deep around that hospital. They've already traced the car back to me, you know, and they're calling every number they can find for me practically nonstop. If I showed up there they'd jump on me like fleas on a dog, and I'm just not up to dealing with that yet. Anyway, I'm out of town." She heard him take a deep breath. There was a pause before he continued in a voice that suddenly sounded almost normal. "I'll be coming in for Annette's funeral on Thursday. I could meet you Thursday night."

Annette's funeral. Oh, God.

"Where?" She kept her voice carefully steady.

"The condo."

In addition to his elegant Georgetown mansion and sumptuous Virginia estate, Davenport quietly maintained a two-bedroom suite in the Watergate Apartments. He said it was for the overnight use of out-of-town clients, but Jess suspected that he did some personal entertaining of the extramarital sort there as well. Not that it was any of her business. She'd been there twice, both times to drop off paperwork for her boss, once in the evening and once in the early morning before heading to work. The first time, the dining table had been set for two, a bottle of wine or champagne or something had been chilling in an ice bucket beside the table, and fresh flowers perfumed the air.

She had noticed all this accidentally, just from glancing past Davenport as he'd come to the door in his robe. Poker-faced, she'd handed him the documents she'd brought him, turned around, and left.

Because that's what junior lawyers who wanted to rise in the ranks did: exactly what they were told. Without asking any questions.

"You remember where it is?"

"Yes." She noticed that he wasn't mentioning the address, realized it was deliberate, and felt a cold chill. She could almost feel unseen ears listening in.

If she was paranoid, then he was, too. The knowledge was the opposite of comforting.

"I hear you're going to be released from the hospital in the next couple of days. When you get out, that's where you go. You just call the office when the time comes, and I'll send Marian over to get you. You won't be able to go home anyway. There'll be media everywhere. The next few weeks are going to be a damned circus."

It was the first time Jess had really, truly comprehended how much her life had been altered. Reporters would be after her; she couldn't go home. . . .

She had to fight to keep her voice steady.
"All right."

"And Jessica . . ."

"Yes?"

"Anything you may have seen or heard while you were with Annette, just forget it, understand? Forget it."

"Okay."

Then Jess remembered the Secret Service agent talking to the hotel doorman before he spotted them and came running toward the Lincoln: Prescott, that was his name. And she realized that simply forgetting what little she knew wasn't going to wipe the First Lady's trail clean. Not by a long shot. There was that doorman, for instance, and . . .

"They're going to find out she was at the hotel," she warned. "Mrs. Cooper —"

"Don't say another word," he interrupted, his voice suddenly fierce. "Not over the phone. Not anywhere. Not to anybody about anything, do you understand? Not to investigators. Not to the press. Not to your family. Not to *anybody.* Nothing. Say nothing. You don't know anything. You don't remember anything."

"Yes, all right." There was real fear in his voice, she realized. And that scared her worse than almost anything else so far. For

Davenport, the rich and well-connected power player, to be afraid was huge.

Over the phone, she heard the muffled sound of a doorbell.

"Look, somebody's here. I've got to go. I'll be back in D.C. on Thursday. We'll talk then. In the meantime, you just sit tight and *keep your mouth shut.* About everything, and I mean *everything.*"

He disconnected, and not a moment too soon. Jess was in the act of restoring the receiver to its cradle when a quick knock sounded on the door to her room.

In a guilty panic, she dropped the receiver, which fortunately landed on the phone but jangled. Her eyes widened, riveting on the door. Who would knock, instead of just walking in? Not her family, or the nurses . . .

A reporter maybe, having snuck past security? Or somebody else? Somebody sinister . . .

Jess's pulse shot into overdrive.

The knob turned . . .

Her breathing suspended. Her fight-or-flight response kicked in, but unfortunately under the circumstances flight was not an option.

The conclusion she came to as she watched the door start to open made her sick: *Whoever this is, I'm a sitting duck.*

She was just opening her mouth to yell for her mother when Judy walked out of the bathroom.

"Mom . . ." Jess said. Before she could continue, Judy, oblivious to the possibility of any kind of threat, simply caught hold of the edge of the door and pulled it the rest of the way open.

For a moment Judy said nothing, just stood there looking at whoever was on the way in that Jess couldn't quite see. Then she smiled, and Jess's pounding heart began to slow. She took a deep, calming breath. She knew that expression. Whoever was standing there, it was someone Judy knew. Someone she liked. Someone who was welcome.

That's why the name that came out of her mouth shocked Jess so.

"Why, hi there, Mark. Come on in."

Mark Ryan walked into the room. Beyond him, through the open door, Jess got a glimpse of the hospital corridor, a nurse hurrying past, a woman in street clothes walking in the opposite direction, and a huge, bald-headed, dark-suited Secret Service agent leaning against the opposite wall and watching with unsmiling intensity as Ryan entered the room.

An icy little shiver ran over her at the sight.

Were they there to keep people out — or her in?

She didn't want to think about it.

"I've got some information for you." Ryan bestowed an easy smile on her mother. Then his gaze went past Judy to seek out Jess. "You, too, Ms. Ford, since you're awake."

She looked at him warily.

Judy said, "Oh, you can call her Jess. We're not fancy."

Her mother, bless her man-eating little heart, was sucking in her stomach and beaming and fluttering her hands so that her rings flashed and doing everything but batting her lashes at him, which wasn't surprising. Judy had always been an absolute idiot when good-looking men were concerned. And Ryan was nothing if not good-looking. He was in his late thirties, with thick, light brown hair that had probably been white-blond when he was a kid, cut ruthlessly short. His face was lean and angular, with the kind of outdoorsy, baked-in tan that would send a woman racing for the Retin-A before the wrinkles could set in. His brows were sandy above eyes that were a clear ocean blue. His face wasn't perfect: His nose was a little thick. His lips were a little too thin, a little too crooked. There were creases around his eyes, and deeper ones running from his mouth to his nose. But on the plus side, he was a hair north of six-foot-two, with wide shoulders and an athlete's toned physique that the navy suit, white shirt, and navy-striped tie he was wearing served only to emphasize.

Taken all together, it added up to sex on the hoof.

Jess had noticed him the first time he'd walked into Davenport's office at the First Lady's heels. He hadn't spared her so much as a glance.

She had remembered him when he had accompanied Annette Cooper on a second visit. At his request, she had handed him a glass of water, which he had passed on to the First Lady. He had thanked her with a nod and a smile that had sent a disorienting little thrill shooting through her solar plexus clear down to her toes.

By the First Lady's third visit, she had been anticipating seeing him again, even though she would have died before she admitted it to anyone. Standing behind Davenport's desk while Davenport and Mrs. Cooper talked, she had given him a little smile.

He had smiled back with enough charm to make her catch her breath.

On his fourth visit, he had smiled at her as soon as he had walked through the door. Her reaction? Basically, *Be still my heart.*

When Davenport had needed someone to hand-carry some papers over to the White House's East Wing for Mrs. Cooper's signature, she had actually volunteered to go despite a punishing workload that already promised to keep her in the office until after ten that night. Because she had hoped to see Mark Ryan there. Because, much as it irked her now to acknowledge it, she'd been nursing a little bit of a crush — oh, all right, a great big giant crush — on him.

Sure enough, he'd been there, standing right beside the door to the First Lady's office as Jess had approached. It had been obvious from his unsmiling glance, from his brusque tone as he'd asked her business, from his entire demeanor, that he hadn't the slightest clue that he had ever seen her before.

Humiliatingly obvious.

After getting the required signatures from Mrs. Cooper, she had slunk back to her office while vowing never to let herself be so stupid as to have her head turned by a handsome face and a practiced smile again.

And now here she was, stuck in a hospital bed, wearing an ugly green gown that everybody knew meant she was naked underneath, her hair a dirty mess, her face bruised and stitched, which, if you wanted to look on the bright side, at least probably meant that the makeup she wasn't wearing wouldn't have been an improvement anyway.

Wearing the same kind of big black glasses that had led to her high school classmates calling her Four Eyes.

So what? she challenged herself. *Why do you even care?* Then she added firmly, *I don't.*

Ryan had found her lying injured and barely conscious after the crash, and had stayed with her until she'd been loaded into an ambulance. He'd come to the hospital that same night, from all accounts running into her hospital room like the Terminator on a mission to save Sarah Connor. From the way her mother beamed at him now and called him Mark like it was something she was used to doing, Jess assumed he'd been in her room more than once since.

And he still didn't remember her from before. That was all too clear.

Bottom line was, she was getting tired of being wallpaper.

"That okay with you?" He was looking at her, and Jess realized he was referring to her mother's invitation for him to call her *Jess.*

She was tempted to say, "Ms. Ford works," but didn't want to listen to the flack from her mother later.

"Sure."

"I'm Mark."

Well, golly gee. I get to use your first name. What an honor.

"You said you had some information?" She couldn't help it. Her tone was frosty.

The sad thing was, despite everything, she was itching to whip off her glasses, even though she was practically blind without them. She glared at him through the embarrassingly thick lenses as he walked right up to her bedside, with her clueless mother — who'd clearly spent the hours while her injured daughter had been at death's door happily working on making the hunk's acquaintance — sashaying along behind.

Judy only ever wiggled like that in the presence of an attractive man.

Jess gave her a look. *Give it a rest, Mom.*

Judy didn't even notice. She was too busy ogling Ryan's butt.

Ryan asked, "Remember thinking somebody tried to tamper with your IV the night they brought you in here?"

Oh, yeah. "I remember."

"Well, just to be on the safe side, just so we could know for sure what we were dealing with, I took the bag of fluid that was in your room that night and had some lab tests run on it. The results just came back, and it's good news — there was nothing harmful in it at all. Nothing that shouldn't have been in there."

Judy said, "That was so *smart* of you. What a relief."

Jess's lips compressed. She would have glared at her mother if she'd thought Ryan wouldn't have noticed.

"So you're saying I imagined that attack?"

"It's pretty clear it was a hallucination, yes."

"He never actually put anything into the bag itself, you know. He was emptying the syringe into a port in the tubing when I figured out what was going on."

"I remembered you said that, so I had the tubing checked, too. No sign that it had been tampered with. No trace of anything that shouldn't have been in there in the fluid or on the sides of the tubes or on the bag. Absolutely nothing out of the way at all."

Jess didn't say anything for a moment. A million thoughts chased one another through her mind. Chief among them was *It was* not *a hallucination.* Followed closely by

I don't think.

In the end, what it boiled down to was, there were three possibilities: Her instincts to the contrary, it indeed had been just a very real hallucination. Or the lab that had examined the bag and its contents had made a mistake. Or Ryan was lying.

Why would he do that?

Three inches of dark suit pants beneath too-short scrubs. Shiny black shoes in a pool of blue light.

"Isn't that wonderful?" Judy enthused, giving her daughter a look that meant *Be enthusiastic or die.* "We don't have to be afraid somebody was trying to kill you anymore."

"Oh, yay," Jess said.

"I just thought knowing that might make you sleep a little easier." Ryan smiled at her. The same charming, eye-crinkling, you're-somebody-special smile he had used on her in Davenport's office weeks before. That she, to her everlasting shame, had believed was actually genuine and meant for her.

She did not smile back, and pretended not to notice that her mother was practically salivating over the man.

Who wears dark suits and shiny black shoes? Who had Mrs. Cooper described as being more like wardens than protectors?

158

Who was now parked outside her door giving her the willies with the knowledge that she couldn't go anywhere without their knowledge?

Secret Service agents.

"It will," she said.

Like she believed him. Like she trusted him.

She didn't. Not for a minute. Maybe he was telling the truth, and maybe he wasn't. Maybe he'd had that bag tested, and maybe he hadn't. Maybe he was her friend — and maybe he was her enemy.

He was a Secret Service agent, too.

If the Secret Service was somehow involved in this — and she still couldn't quite get her mind around what she thought "this" was — he was very likely involved, too.

In Mrs. Cooper's death.

Jess felt as though a giant hand had just grabbed her heart and squeezed. *There. That's what you've been pussyfooting around.* She suspected . . . that it wasn't an accident at all.

Oh, God, I can't think about this now.

Too late: Her heart picked up the pace. Her mouth went dry. She only hoped that none of what she was trying not to think about was showing on her face.

Because Ryan was watching her. Carefully. Like he was trying to read her mind. His baby blues bored into her eyes like information-seeking tractor beams.

For the first time in her life, Jess found herself thankful for her glasses. Superman himself with his X-ray vision couldn't read much through *her* lenses.

"You doin' okay?" Ryan asked in a confidential tone, as if the question was for her ears alone and her mother wasn't even in the room. That southern drawl of his — she wouldn't be surprised to learn he practiced it just to make it sexier — was more pronounced than usual. It was *intimate.* Just like his smile. Which he probably practiced, too.

"I'll live."

Giving her a hard sideways glance that was mom code for *What's the matter with you?* her mother added, "She's doing so well; the doctor who came in this morning said they'll probably release her in the next couple of days. He said all she needs now is some time to heal, and maybe some rehab. Because she's still having trouble with her legs, you know. And . . . other things. And she's in some pain."

Mo-ther. Do you always have to tell everybody everything you know? Answer, arrived

160

at with silent, groaning resignation: *Yes, you do.*

"I'm sorry to hear she's in pain. But I'm glad she's doing so well otherwise." Ryan flashed one of those smiles at Judy, then looked again at Jess, who gave him a quick little — grim — smile of her own. "You remembering any more about what happened? About the crash?"

His voice was gentle. His eyes were sharp.

Dream on, pretty boy. That stupid I'm not.

Jess shook her head. "Where the accident's concerned, my mind's a complete blank."

"And let's hope it stays that way." Judy shuddered and shook her head. "Why on earth would you even want to remember? It's just so horrible I hate thinking about it. You're better off not having any kind of images of it in your head, honey. Just let it go."

"Yes, Mother." Jess's tone was so sweetly obedient that Judy gave her another of those hard looks. Okay, so she was going to hear it from her mother later. It was worth it.

"If it does start coming back to you, I hope you'll let me know. We're still trying to figure out exactly what happened. And the press — well, they'll make your life hell if you let them. Better to let any new information come out through official channels."

She knew what he meant: *official channels like him.*

"You'll be the first person I tell if I remember anything," she promised. *Liar, liar, pants on fire.*

"I know it's early days to be talking about this, but the Cooper family wants to . . ." he began, but then the door opened without warning and he broke off. Which was too bad: Jess would have been interested in hearing his version of what the Cooper family wanted just so that she could be sure to avoid it.

11

"Jess, you're awake," Grace said happily as she entered. She was carrying a pizza and looking hot, as usual, in jeans, boots, and her favorite black leather motorcycle jacket. Behind her, Maddie had an arm wrapped around a brown paper bag. Her other arm hung by her side, weighted down by the big red plastic tote bag her mother had used for her beauty essentials for as long as Jess could remember. Despite everything, the sight wrung a slight smile out of Jess.

What was the first sure sign I was going to live? My mom had her beauty bag brought to the hospital.

"Hey, guys," Jess said.

"Hi, Jess. Hi, Mark." Grace, who liked good-looking men every bit as much as Judy did, smiled at Ryan as she put the pizza box down on the empty extra bed. Men fell for Grace by the boatload and always had, but Ryan's answering smile was no different than the one he'd bestowed on Judy — or, for that matter, Jess.

In other words, it dazzled with practiced charm. Grace's animated expression made it clear that despite her umpteen past and present boyfriends, she was no more immune than the rest of them.

What Ryan's reaction was to Grace Jess couldn't tell. The eyes behind the smile were unreadable.

"You would not believe how bad it is out there. They know who we are now — we practically had to fight our way through." Grace tossed her hair — for Ryan's benefit, Jess knew — and opened the pizza box.

"Who are you talking about?" Jess asked.

"The press. They're, like, lying in wait out there in the parking lot. They keep asking us how you're doing, and who's called, and if you've said anything about the accident. Of course, we don't tell them anything." She cast Ryan a smiling glance. He acknowledged it with another slight smile of his own, which Jess interpreted to mean her family was keeping silent on his orders. Grace's gaze shifted back to Jess. "Oh, and I ran into Bruce Minsky and he asked me to give him a call and let him know when he can stop by the hospital to see you. He said he'd been trying to call you here in the room and on your cell, too, but not getting any answer. Which, after I told him you've been unconscious, he perfectly understood, of course."

Bruce Minsky was a junior accountant employed by the giant accounting firm that did work for Davenport, Kelly, and Bascomb. He and Jess had been on exactly four dates, three for coffee and once for dinner — actually, fish sandwiches eaten at her apartment while they went over some financial records for a case Davenport wanted Bruce's boss to testify about. Bruce seemed smitten. Jess was less so. Probably because they were so much alike. Both nose-to-the-grindstone types. Both total straight arrows. Both a little uncomfortable with the opposite sex. When the two of them got together, it was, in her opinion, kind of like a geek-o-rama.

"I don't want visitors. And I don't know where my phone is."

"But Bruce is so cute. With those little glasses and all."

Jess started to make a face at her sister, but it hurt too much. Which was probably just as well. Ignoring her was the dignified thing to do. And the only thing that worked in the long run.

"I told Grace we should try to sneak in

165

through one of the side doors, but she wouldn't do it." Maddie plopped the grocery sack on the bed beside the pizza box and started rummaging through it. "I think she just likes being on TV."

"You can get on TV by just walking into the hospital?" Jess asked, bemused, as Maddie pulled out a package of paper plates.

Grace nodded. "You won't believe how huge this is. The whole city — the whole country — the whole world, even, probably — is practically shut down. Actually, you're lucky you're in the hospital so you don't have to deal with it. You're the one they really want to talk to. You're the survivor."

"Grace, don't worry your sister." Judy's tone was stern.

Mother and third-oldest daughter exchanged a look. Jess was left wondering what wasn't being said. She decided she didn't want to know.

"Anyway, we brought dinner." Sliding a slice of pizza onto a paper plate, Grace advanced on Jess's bed with it. "Your favorite: thin-crust pepperoni."

The smell reached Jess's nostrils, and she felt the faintest stirring in her stomach: hunger.

It felt good to be hungry. The last time she had been hungry was around eight on

Saturday, when she'd made a grilled cheese sandwich while she'd read over some back cases in hopes of finding additional support for a position Davenport, Kelly, and Bascomb had taken on a pleading that had been overturned on appeal.

Just hours before the crash.

"I have Cherry Coke," Maddie added.

Her youngest sister was nowhere near as head-turningly beautiful as Grace, but Maddie was still very pretty in her own quieter way, with delicate features and a fresh-scrubbed look that didn't depend on makeup for its allure. Her natural dark-blond hair was pushed back from her face by a narrow purple headband so that it fell straight and shining to her shoulders, and her school uniform of white shirt, navy blazer, and khaki skirt looked almost stylish on her slender figure. She stood five-foot-six in her white ankle socks and sneakers. She looked like what she was, a wholesome, high-achieving, all-American high school girl with a bright future.

Jess had spent the entire previous week sick to her stomach at the thought that Maddie was pregnant. But now she was just glad to see her sister.

"Thanks," Jess said.

She smiled at Maddie, who was heading

toward her with the can of soda extended temptingly. The Cherry Coke had been purchased especially for her and was a peace offering, she knew, because Maddie was the only one who knew she liked it. Last summer, with Judy tied down by the day care and unable to get away, she and Maddie had discovered it together when Jess, on her precious one week of vacation before starting full-time at Davenport, Kelly, and Bascomb, had driven her around the Northeast on a whirlwind tour of possible colleges — colleges that Jess hoped and prayed Maddie would get a scholarship to. They'd been full of big plans for Maddie's future — or at least, as Jess had realized when she thought back over it, she had been full of big plans for Maddie's future. Maddie really hadn't said much. The last time Jess and Maddie had been together, it had been over at Judy's house the weekend before the crash and the whole family had ended up shouting at one another over the ramifications of Maddie's pregnancy. Maddie had capped off the festivities by running from the house in a flood of tears. Then she'd spent the following week shacked up with the twenty-year-old auto-mechanic boyfriend no one had even known she had. She'd been with him the night of the crash, too, as it had turned out, and thus had been the last of the family to find out what had happened to Jess.

But that was then. This was now.

"You're welcome." Maddie handed the soda to Jess. Jess's slice of pizza already waited on the table beside the bed, courtesy of Grace. "There's plenty," Maddie added, smiling shyly at Ryan. "Just help yourself."

Jesus, he'd charmed her, too.

Ryan shook his head.

"Thanks, but I've got to go." He looked at Jess. "If you remember anything, or you need anything . . ."

"I'll be sure to let you know."

"Your mother has my number."

Jess nodded.

"I don't know if you should be eating pizza and a Cherry Coke just yet," Judy worried aloud, frowning at Jess as she carried her own slice of pizza toward the chair in the corner and sat down. "We should probably ask one of the nurses first."

"I'll be fine, Mom."

Judy frowned still, but her gaze left her daughter to follow Ryan as he headed toward the door.

"Bye, Mark."

"Bye, Mark," Grace and Maddie chorused.

He responded with a wave as he left the room.

"Yum," Grace said as the door clicked shut and she plopped down on the corner of Jess's bed. From her tone, she wasn't referring to the pizza she was nibbling on. "I could eat him for supper."

"He's too old for you," Judy said reprovingly.

Grace snorted. "Well, I hate to be the one to break this to you, but he's too young for you."

"Then it's a good thing I'm not interested in him, isn't it?" Judy bit into her pizza with dignity. "I'm just real grateful to him for everything he's done for Jess." Her gaze shifted to her oldest daughter. "Not that you seem to be very grateful yourself. You were downright snippy, missy."

Jess chose that moment to pick up her slice of pizza and take a cautious bite. Since she couldn't tell her mother the truth, the best thing would be not to tell her anything at all. And she couldn't talk with her mouth full, could she?

"You know, I think he likes you," Grace said to Jess. "He's been coming by to see you a lot."

Yes, because he's scared to death I'm going to remember something about the ac-

cident and tell somebody.

Right out of nowhere, that was the thought that popped into Jess's head.

It was followed almost immediately by another: *What happens if I do remember something? What if it's bad? As in, it provides evidence that Mrs. Cooper's accident was no accident?*

Jess felt cold sweat prickle to life around her hairline at the thought.

There it was again, that thing she hadn't wanted to face.

I don't think it was an accident.

She swallowed convulsively, and the tiny bit of pizza she was chewing caught in her throat and nearly choked her. It was suddenly as tasteless as a mouthful of rocks, and as hard to get down.

Now that the thought had taken form and shape in her mind, it was impossible to dislodge.

She couldn't prove it, of course. And she didn't want to. Didn't even want to have the idea taking root like an impossible-to-eradicate weed in her mind.

Because she knew what would happen if she did remember something that blew the whole accident scenario out of the water, knew it with the kind of conviction that no amount of evidence to the contrary was ever going to be able to change.

If I remember, they'll kill me.

12

He'd told the truth.

At least, every word he'd said had been the truth.

That was the same thing, wasn't it?

No. Hell, no. Mark knew that was the answer even as he asked himself the question. What he'd said, while absolutely factual, was actually a pathetic lie.

And the need to tell such a lie was still worrying him.

The lab results had come back clean, just as he'd said. Everything that had been tested had checked out perfectly. There had been no traces of anything that shouldn't have been in that IV bag anywhere on it or in it. Nothing that shouldn't have been there in the tubing, either.

As for the catheter, the soft little tube that had actually delivered the contents of the IV into her vein, it was missing by the time the apparatus got to the lab and Brooks got his hands on it.

Given the chain of custody, it almost certainly hadn't been attached when he'd stowed the bag in his pocket. Because if it had become dislodged in his pocket, or in the transfer to Brooks — who had been horrified by Mark's less-than-protocol handling of the evidence and had promptly plastic-bagged everything — in the grocery store parking lot where they had agreed to meet, one of them would have found it.

Yep, everything had been clean. Every test Brooks had run had revealed nothing except the standard saline solution.

Which was the problem.

Mark had obtained Jessica's medical file. The one that started with her arrival in the emergency room, where the IV line had been placed.

According to the file, there was a whole raft of medications that should have been in that IV fluid.

They weren't there.

None of them. Not one. No trace.

Just plain old saline solution. Generic. Standard.

No trace of her blood or DNA on the tubing, although usually when an IV was inserted there was a little bit of a backflow as the nurse made sure she or he had a vein.

Not in this case. Nada.

No catheter, either. Nothing at all to connect the unit to her.

If the thing had ever been used, Brooks said he couldn't tell it.

Which meant what, exactly?

That the IV unit he'd removed from her room and had tested was not the one that had been used on Jessica Ford.

There were other possibilities, of course, because there were always other possibilities, but in this case they were so convoluted he got a headache trying to work them all out. The bottom line was, the most likely explanation under the circumstances was that the IV units had been switched, probably in the brief period that had elapsed from the time she had pulled it from her arm to the time he'd burst into the room.

Which meant she almost certainly had been attacked right there under his nose in her hospital room, just as she had claimed.

And the attacker, upon realizing that he'd failed in his objective, which Mark was going to assume was Jess's murder, knew that the doctored bag could provide solid evidence of what had gone down, grabbed the incriminating IV bag, put up a fresh one, which he would have brought with him for just that purpose, and somehow made it out of the room without being seen by him or anyone else.

Mark tried for what must have been the hundredth time to visualize the room as it had looked when he had barreled into it. He'd been on high alert, looking all around, ready to take down an intruder — but in thinking back on it, the room never quite became clear to him. He remembered it being filled with shadows and distracting things, including a dividing curtain that swayed in the breeze of the opened door, a bed that moved as he went past it, and that damned open bathroom door.

At the time his primary focus had been on locating Jess.

Someone could have slipped out.

While he'd knelt beside her. No, wait, wouldn't the hospital personnel racing toward the room have noticed someone coming out the door? So the next window of opportunity would have been in the mass confusion after everyone else had arrived in the room.

The simple thing to do, of course, would be to check the security tapes and see who was in the vicinity around the time of the attack who shouldn't have been there. There were two cameras in each corridor, filming everything that went down in them. Spotting a suspicious individual should have been a piece of cake.

But the cameras for the third floor had mysteriously turned up without film in them, an oversight on the security staff's part — or something more ominous?

Mark's vote went to something more ominous.

"Goddamn it, Lowell, don't tell me nothing went down in that hospital."

Despite the accusation in it, Mark's voice was hushed as he slid into the red vinyl corner booth where the Chief of Staff was already sipping a cup of coffee while he looked over the menu.

They were meeting at the IHOP on the fringes of Anacostia, a troubled D.C. neighborhood where the press would not expect anybody to turn up.

"God Almighty, are you still going on about that?" Lowell shook his head in disgust. "I already told you, whatever did or did not happen there had nothing in the world to do with us."

Mark's eyes narrowed as they fastened on Lowell, but before he could reply he saw the waitress, a tiny gray-haired grandma-type in IHOP's trademark uniform and sensible shoes, bearing down on them. Only three of the other booths were occupied.

Two guys who looked like truckers plowed through an enormous breakfast in one, an AARP-type couple who probably went with the RV parked outside nibbled doughnuts and read the paper in another, and the third was occupied by an old street guy with grimy fingers nursing a cup of coffee.

"Can I get you some coffee?" the waitress asked. When they nodded, she poured each a cup.

Caffeine was something he desperately needed at the moment. He had spent most of the previous night at Quantico, where the death car, as the press were now calling it, had been taken via flatbed truck after the accident and where it was now being held in a warehouse to keep the telephoto lenses of the press from getting any more ghoulish shots of it. Officially, he didn't have clearance to look at it, but unofficially he had friends in the Bureau who gave him access to the car and to the files that went with it. The official cause of the crash — an over-correction made at a high rate of speed, possibly because of an animal of some sort on the road, although that last was pure speculation — had already been determined. It had been trumpeted all over the world, and given that the world supposed Mrs. Cooper to have been rushing to a dying friend's bedside when the crash occurred, it even made sense.

Since Mark had been around when that particular bit of spin had been decided on (because Mrs. Cooper did indeed have a friend in the named hospital that night), he knew damned well it wasn't true. Which once again begged the question: What the hell had the First Lady of the United States been doing in that car?

Mark knew that he would never pass another peaceful night until he had the answer.

The waitress left. Mark fixed Lowell with a grim look.

"Jessica Ford doesn't know squat about the First Lady's habits, and doesn't remember anything about the accident. Nothing, you understand? She's no threat to anybody. I want to make that crystal clear."

Lowell took another sip of coffee and met his gaze over the rim of the cup.

"You sure about that?"

The waitress returned, asking if they were ready to order.

"I'm ready," Lowell said, and told her what he wanted.

For the sake of not attracting attention, or at least Mark assumed that was his motive, Lowell had clapped an Orioles cap on his head, and removed his expensive suit jacket. His blue shirt and rep tie were generic enough in appearance to go unnoticed. Mark was similarly attired, minus the baseball cap, although his white shirt and gray tie were genuinely generic, bought on sale at Macy's. Lowell's round, ruddy face was well known in government and political circles but unlikely to be recognized here. Unless they were very unlucky, knowledge of this meeting would stay between the two of them, which was how they both wanted it.

The waitress looked at Mark.

"You?"

He ordered, too, bacon and eggs and toast and orange juice. He figured he needed the energy. Just like he hadn't been sleeping, he hadn't been eating well since the crash. His stomach was too tense; he felt like if he swallowed more than a few bites, it would come right back up.

It didn't help that everywhere he looked, from TV to the front page of newspapers and magazines to black-bordered "in memoriam" billboards looking down over the expressways, he saw Annette Cooper's face.

My watch. He couldn't get the guilt out of his system.

The waitress left.

He eyeballed Lowell.

"Yeah, I'm sure."

"Really? Then why did she call Davenport last night and tell him she thinks there's something wrong with what's being said about the accident?"

Mark blinked. He didn't know why he was surprised, but he was. He knew how this worked: broken legs and arms, burglarized offices, "accidental" fires — those were all in a day's work in the high-stakes world of politics. An illegal wiretap or two was hardly even worthy of mention.

"You monitoring her phone calls?" He kept his voice carefully even.

"What do you think? Of course we are. The funeral's in two days' time, and nobody wants any kind of crap about Mrs. Cooper getting out to spoil it. The lady — and the family — deserves to be allowed to rest in peace."

Mark couldn't argue with that. But he sure as hell could raise a stink over the method of containment he was becoming increasingly convinced someone had tried to employ. He decided to call Lowell's bluff and see what reaction he got.

"So somebody did try to kill Jessica Ford that night in the hospital."

"No. Hell, no." Lowell glared at him. "I

already said that, all right? As far as I know, nobody did anything to little Miss What's-her-name in the hospital or anywhere else. What do you think I am?"

While Mark debated about whether or not to tell him, the waitress arrived, bringing their food. She slapped it down in front of them, asked if she could get them anything else, and took herself off when they declined.

"You get the word out to whoever's interested that Jessica Ford is not a threat," Mark said. The thing was, Mark knew that Lowell might be telling the absolute truth and still somebody in the big, amorphous, interconnected circles of shadow people who protected the President and his family might have targeted her in the panic following the First Lady's death. "I'm taking care of it. You tell them that."

"I tell you what you need to do." Lowell dumped ketchup on his eggs. Mark had to look away. His stomach was bothering him again, knotted so tight he knew he wouldn't be able to choke down so much as a bite of the triangle of buttered toast he'd picked up. He put it back down on the plate without even making the attempt. "You need to get her to sign a secrecy agreement — offer her whatever money you have to —

and get her the hell out of town until this blows over. I've checked into her background — she doesn't have a pot to piss in, and never has. Comes from nothing. She'll be glad to get the money. And to keep her mouth shut for it."

"The problem with a secrecy agreement," Mark pointed out in measured tones, "is that it exists. If she doesn't know anything, it clues her in that there just might be something to know. And if it somehow goes public, it makes it look like there's a conspiracy. Like somebody has something to hide."

"Hell, we do have something to hide. There's no reason in the world for anybody to know that Mrs. Cooper had a problem, or that she was out there trying to score drugs when she died."

"You sure that's what she was doing?"

"It's looking like it. Why else would she sneak off like that? With that amount of money in her purse?" Lowell shoveled down his doctored eggs with enthusiasm. Watching was making even the coffee turn sour in Mark's stomach.

"I don't know."

There was a lot he didn't know, Mark reflected — like what state Mrs. Cooper had been in when she left the residence that

183

night, or if anybody besides Prescott had been with her when she'd headed out to the Rose Garden. One reason he was having so much trouble figuring out those things was that he'd been put on official leave: Just as he had suspected, his had been the first head on the chopping block. He was still on the payroll, still in the loop; he was still working, as was evidenced by his careful coordination of the babysitting of Jess Ford. But all that was on the QT, at the behest of Lowell and the rest of the President's inner circle. Because they knew he was loyal, knew he'd keep his mouth shut, knew he'd get the job done for them. For the record, though, he was in deep shit, complete with all the media finger-pointing that came with it. The worst thing about it was being denied access to the very things he needed to use to get answers. Answers to the questions about that night that were eating him up. The White House surveillance tapes, for example, were not available to him; they'd been turned over to the investigative arm of the Secret Service. Between them and the FBI, the crash probe was being conducted at the highest levels, as his boss had assured him when he'd pressed for access. Lowell had refused to intervene.

Your job is to handle the survivor, Lowell

had said. *Let the trained investigators handle the investigation.*

The trained investigators who didn't know anything about Mrs. Cooper, and thus had no clue what to be on the lookout for. Which, maybe, was the point.

Or maybe he was just growing increasingly suspicious with age. And experience.

"So what do you suggest?" Lowell stabbed a sausage link with his fork and took a huge bite.

"We pay her off, but we channel the money through someone else. If it comes from us, she's immediately suspicious about why, right? What we don't want is for her to start asking herself that. We just want her to take the money, keep her mouth shut, and fade out of the picture."

"Amen to that. You sure you can fix it?"

"I'm sure."

"So we're good?" Lowell polished off the last of his meal and took a quick last swallow of coffee as he stood up.

Mark looked up at him. "As long as nothing else happens to Miss Ford."

"Nothing *did* happen to her."

The waitress had seen Lowell stand up and was heading their way with the check. Mark stood up, too, his stomach as tight as a clenched fist, his breakfast uneaten. What

185

he needed, and he hated to admit it, was a cigarette. He'd quit four years ago, gone cold turkey since, and now he was craving nicotine in the worst way.

The truth was, as he'd discovered about himself before, he really didn't handle stress all that well.

"Was there something the matter with the food?" the waitress asked as she handed him the bill. Lowell was already on his way out the door. Mark understood: Mark had requested the meeting, so breakfast was on him.

"Turns out I wasn't hungry after all." Mark put a couple of twenties down on the table, more than enough to cover the food and a tip, and followed Lowell.

Who was already gone.

Funny, he reflected as he pushed through the door into the gray bleakness of a cold April dawn and felt the chill of the rushing wind bite into him, he didn't feel any better about things now than he had before the meeting.

The day was just getting started, and it was already on its way downhill. And he still had Prescott's funeral to attend.

13

In the end, avoiding the media had been surprisingly easy, Jess reflected as she looked out the concave glass window of the helicopter that was at that moment carrying her toward D.C. Avoiding Mark Ryan, who'd been hovering around her and her family like a hungry bat with a cluster of mosquitoes in its sights, had been equally simple: She'd simply waited to go until he wasn't around. Leaving the hospital by helicopter had worked like a charm; apparently, no one had expected it. Of course, it also helped that her exodus had been carefully timed to coincide with Annette Cooper's funeral service.

The thought made her queasy. Or maybe it was the motion of the helicopter, swooping up and down like a hawk riding the gusting air currents as they followed the twisty path of the Potomac past Reagan National Airport and into D.C. As Davenport's assistant, Jess was no stranger to helicopters, but seeing the Capitol laid out before her like a sparkling miniature village was something that never failed to awe her.

Even today.

"Mr. Davenport wants you to feel free to use the condo for as long as you need to. He anticipates that it will be for at least several weeks," Marian said.

"That's nice of him."

Davenport's longtime personal secretary was buckled into the cushy leather seat next to Jess. She was sixty-one, unmarried, and totally devoted to Davenport and, to a lesser extent, the firm. Tall, lean, and elegant, with coarse iron-gray hair that she wore in an elaborate chignon, she was dressed in a pale gray skirt suit and a lavender blouse. Her features were strong rather than attractive, her makeup was minimal but well done, and she was very good at blending into the woodwork until Davenport needed her.

Which he constantly did. As far as everything that wasn't connected to legal research (Jess's department) was concerned, Marian was Davenport's right hand. She knew him better than his young third wife, sent the gifts, made the reservations, fielded his phone calls, set up his meetings, and then sat in on them taking notes. If Davenport had a secret that Marian didn't know, Jess would be surprised. No, she would be shocked. But Marian kept Davenport's secrets, too.

Besides the pilot, who was sitting up front and was separated from the passenger compartment by a partition, she and Jess were alone in the helicopter. According to Marian, Davenport had decided that the fewer people who knew where they were going today, the better.

The safer. But Jess filled that in for herself.

The million-dollar question was, did Marian know what was going on? That Davenport was afraid of something concerning Annette Cooper's death, concerning the crash? Or was this one secret Davenport had kept from her?

Jess didn't know, and she couldn't ask. She wasn't going to say a word on the subject to anyone until after she had talked to her boss.

Davenport would know what to do, where to go with her suspicions, to whom it was safe to tell them. Because right now, she didn't feel like she could trust anybody else.

Not the cops, not the FBI, and certainly not the Secret Service, all of which had sent representatives to question her about the crash once they learned she was conscious and coherent. She had said the same thing to each of them: *I don't remember.*

They had gone away.

She had been on pins and needles, fearing they would come back. Which was why she'd been so glad to leave today, twenty-four hours ahead of schedule.

The Secret Service agents outside her room, all of whom had become accustomed to her comings and goings inside the hospital over the last few days as she'd suffered through more tests and X-rays and treatments and had worked with physical therapists to regain her mobility, had followed her at a discreet distance as she'd headed for the elevator some thirty minutes earlier. Their faces were vaguely familiar because they'd been around, but she didn't know either of them and they didn't know her in any kind of personal way, which made telling them that she needed a few minutes alone with her companion — Marian — and then closing the elevator doors in their faces all the easier. After that, it was a piece of cake: a trip up to the hospital's helipad, bundling into the chopper, and taking off. She was free.

Just like that. After tossing and turning through a sleepless night and then suffering butterfly-inducing anticipation all morning, the ease of her escape — because that was how she thought of it — was almost anticlimactic.

Maybe Ryan wasn't at the hospital because he was attending Mrs. Cooper's funeral. If he'd been there, she had a feeling that getting away wouldn't have been quite so simple.

She hadn't even told her mother and sisters where she was going. Just that her boss was sending someone for her, and she would be staying in one of his houses for a while until media interest died down. Grace had packed her a suitcase and brought it to the hospital that morning. Jess had parted from her and Judy and Sarah and Maddie with a round of weepy hugs. Judy had wanted her to come home with them, but Jess, with Marian backing her up, had been adamant: Davenport was a pro at handling crises of all sorts, and she would do what he wanted her to do. Reluctantly, Judy saw the sense of that: Like the hospital, her house and Jess's apartment were still under siege, and some reporters had even started waving fat checks around in hope of procuring an interview.

"I'll be fine. I'll call you," she promised her mother. The truth was, she was desperate to get away from them, terrified that somehow what she knew, or suspected, would be conveyed to them and then they would be in danger, too. Or maybe they didn't even have to really know or suspect anything. Maybe just being in her vicinity was enough to make them targets.

And maybe she was just totally paranoid, too.

But she didn't think so.

"Mr. Davenport wanted me to assure you that you're still drawing your salary, by the way," Marian said. "I made the arrangements for it to be direct-deposited into your account yesterday. It will continue until you're able to come back to work. And he said to tell you that you'll be getting a large settlement soon."

Jess couldn't help it. Even under the circumstances, the prospect of obtaining a substantial amount of money made her heartbeat quicken. It was a result, she was sure, of having spent almost her whole life never being sure that she and her family would have enough groceries to last out the week, or a roof over their heads from month to month.

Lifting her eyebrows with what she hoped looked like only polite interest, she said, "A large settlement?"

Marian looked impatient. "You were badly

injured in a car wreck. The limousine company and its driver are liable, among others. Ordinarily it would take months, possibly years, to negotiate just compensation. Given the circumstances, though, Mr. Davenport was able to do very nicely for you. All you have to do is sign the papers."

Clearly, working around lawyers for so many years had an effect on people, because Marian was sounding like one herself.

"What papers?" If Jess's tone was faintly wary, well, she guessed she had reason. One thing she had learned for sure over the years was that if it sounded too good to be true, it usually was. "And how large a settlement are we talking about?"

"Mr. Davenport will explain. He'll go over everything with you when you talk to him later."

Fair enough. "What time is he coming?"

The look Marian gave her was withering. "When it's convenient for him."

"I'll be sure and be ready, then." If there was a smidgen of dryness to her tone, Marian didn't appear to notice.

The two of them were publicly cordial, but they were not friends. Jess sometimes wondered if Marian, jealous of her own position in Davenport's life, didn't resent Davenport's increasing reliance on Jess.

193

Jess said nothing else, and the conversation ended. Her gaze drifted down to the scene below. For the first time in her memory, nothing was moving on the Beltway or 295 or any of the other arteries into and around the city. Cars had pulled over to the side of the roads; the expressways were clear. Seeing the flashing blue and red strobe lights at the entrance ramps, Jess realized that police had them blocked off. Instead of cars, D.C.'s center was filled with people. Hordes of them, tens of thousands of them, stretching from the Lincoln Memorial to Capitol Hill in a near-solid carpet, massing in Constitution Gardens, surrounding the Vietnam Veterans Memorial and the White House and the Washington Monument, crowding around the Tidal Basin and the Reflecting Pool and filling the Mall, filling the downtown, filling the whole of D.C. for as far as she could see, packing the streets and the public spaces so that everywhere you looked they were all you saw, eclipsing the buildings and monuments, the variegated colors of their clothing putting to shame even the intense pinks of the cherry blossoms for which D.C. was famous.

She remembered that Congress had declared today a national day of mourning.

A motorcade, composed of vehicles that

from this height appeared no bigger than the Hot Wheels cars her nephews loved, caught her eye. It moved slowly down Constitution Avenue. From the tiny flags flying on the lead cars and the number of long black vehicles involved, Jess knew what it had to be: Mrs. Cooper's funeral cortege transporting her body from the Capitol Rotunda, where it had been lying in state, to the National Cathedral for her funeral service.

Of course. It was just after one-thirty. The funeral was scheduled to begin precisely at two p.m. The dolorous tolling of church bells all over the city — that was the sound that was barely audible over the thumping of the helicopter's rotors; she only just identified it — rang out in long peals of collective grief.

Throat suddenly tight, Jess leaned back in her seat, unable to watch further. Remembering the sweats-clad woman who'd done shots in the bar, who had been obviously frightened of something but was nevertheless determined to escape, whose arm she had taken and flight she had so disastrously shared, she ached inside. Closing her eyes, she said a silent prayer for the souls of Annette Cooper, and the Secret Service agent and the driver who had died with her.

Then she added her own fervent thanks for being allowed to live.

When she opened her eyes, it was to discover that Marian was watching her, a sour twist to her mouth.

"Mr. Davenport is sick with grief about this." Marian clasped her hands tightly in her lap. "He seems to feel that if he'd gone himself that night instead of sending you, Mrs. Cooper wouldn't be dead now."

The unspoken subtext was that she'd screwed up. The hard gleam in Marian's eyes made the message unmistakable. Did Davenport share Marian's view? Jess hadn't thought of that. But her conscience was clear. Whatever had happened, she knew in her heart she could not have prevented it. She was as much a victim of the accident as the other three. The only difference was that she had survived.

So far.

That thought made her go cold all over. She tried to ignore it.

"If Mr. Davenport had gone that night instead of me," Jess pointed out, "he might very well be dead now, too."

That shut Marian up, just as Jess had intended. The other woman pressed her lips together and stared straight ahead.

Instead of looking down again, Jess carefully concentrated on the bright blue sky and cottony white clouds all around them. Though crisp, it was a bright, sunny spring day, with a brisk wind that blew the clouds around like feathers. The air, as she knew from her quick journey across the hospital rooftop to the helicopter, smelled sweet and fresh with scents of new grass and blossoming baby leaves and just-blooming flowers.

The day was too beautiful for a funeral.

Her phone began to ring. Jess's eyes widened. The sound was so *normal,* so much a part of her ordinary, everyday existence before the accident, that in the context of what was happening to her now it was almost bizarre. It took her a second to realize what it was, and then she unzipped her purse, which the hospital had given to her mother along with a bundle containing the now-ruined clothes she had been wearing when the accident had occurred. Judy had brought the purse to the hospital that morning in anticipation of Jess's departure later in the day. Fishing her phone out, she saw the number and name on her caller ID: Laura Ogilvy, one of her lawyer friends from work. No doubt calling to ask how she was and to glean all the gossip she could.

A glance at Marian, who looked on with way too much interest, made her initial reaction certain: She wasn't going to take the call.

"You're not going to answer?" Marian asked with disapproval when the call went over to voice mail to join the other forty-seven messages she had waiting.

"My battery's low. Anyway, I don't really feel like talking right now."

Which was the truth: She didn't. She was physically much stronger, although the outward signs of her injuries — the bruises, the stitches — were still apparent. Face it: Mentally, she was all over the place. She knew what she knew, she suspected what she suspected.

And she remembered . . . more than she wanted to.

The Watergate complex, famous for its explosion into the national conversation when it was the site of the notorious burglary that had torpedoed Richard Nixon's presidency, was actually a semicircular grouping of upscale skyscrapers overlooking the Potomac that housed a hotel, apartments, and condominiums along with a variety of pricey restaurants and shops. As the helicopter set down atop one gleaming silver tower, Jess got a glimpse of a sparkling fountain set in a green lawn surrounded by neatly clipped hedges in a courtyard below.

Then the runners settled, the motor was cut, and the rotors slowed. Jess unbuckled her seat belt just as the pilot opened the door.

He lifted the wheelchair from the cabin. Marian got out first, and Jess followed, climbing down into a cold, stiff wind that belied the day's sunny brightness. Her back ached with every movement, and she was stiff as cheap new jeans, but she was able to walk the few steps to the wheelchair, which the pilot held for her, without feeling like she was going to collapse. Still, she sank into it thankfully, and was glad that it was motorized so that she could get to the elevator without relying on Marian's help. The other woman's expression was unyielding as she carried Jess's suitcase.

It took just a few minutes to reach the apartment.

"Now that we're here, I can tell you that Mr. Davenport will be busy for the rest of the afternoon. He'll call me with further instructions sometime after six."

Marian spoke behind her as Jess rolled across the spacious, gray-carpeted living room with its white leather couches and chairs and black Lucite tables toward the big picture window. Jess noticed that she was careful to subtly stress the *me* in that last sentence, thus confirming her impression that in Marian's own mind at least, the woman was battling to retain the supremacy of her position in Davenport's life.

Jess just nodded in reply. They were on the twelfth floor, so she had a panoramic view of the Georgetown Channel of the Potomac curving around Roosevelt Island below. There were no boats on the river below her, not even the big commercial barges that seemed to run continuously, and even as she wondered at it, it hit her that it was because the entire country, and especially D.C., was shut down in a paroxysm of grief over the terrible tragedy that was reaching its culmination at that exact moment.

Marian sank down on the couch and flipped on the TV.

The slow, sad notes of a military dirge caught Jess by surprise. She turned around. Her gaze was riveted by the pale stone and soaring Gothic arches of the National Cathedral filling the big TV. Her breathing suspended, her hands clamped around the edges of the wheelchair's arms, and her throat threatened to close up.

She was watching the event live.

A military honor guard carried a flower-draped coffin up the wide front steps.

Marines in dress blues stood at attention on either side. Behind the coffin came the President of the United States, his face as white and still as if it had been carved from marble, his two adult children and their families close behind him. They were followed by Wayne Cooper, the President's father; his sister, Elizabeth; and a gaggle of other family members Jess didn't recognize. A contingent of Secret Service agents glancing cautiously from side to side and receiving instructions via earbuds formed a moving wall of protection that fanned out on either side of the family party and brought up the rear. The hearse and the long black motorcade surrounding it waited at the curb. In the opposite lane from the motorcade, boxy white news vans with satellite feeds formed a nucleus around which a heaving mass of reporters, held at bay by stern-faced lines of uniformed cops manning sawhorse barriers, narrated the proceedings for their various audiences. Other than the motorcade and the media, the street was empty, obviously having been cleared in anticipation of the arrival and eventual departure of the funeral cortege. Hundreds of mourners lined the sidewalk across the street from the cathedral, pressing up against more sawhorses controlled by more somber-looking cops. The camera panned the crowd, and suddenly thousands of ordinary citizens, dressed in everything from jeans and sweatshirts to business suits to the ethnic attire of many cultures, packed the shot for as far as the eye could see.

". . . sensational story reaches its tragic culmination now, as the First Lady of the United States is carried in her coffin into the National Cathedral. Annette Wiley Cooper first appeared on the national scene five years ago, when her husband became Vice President upon the death of then Vice President Thomas Haynes. This past November, David Cooper won the presidency, and in the brief months since his inauguration, Annette Cooper cemented her hold on the affection of a nation. The causes close to her heart were education and literacy, and . . ."

"Mr. Davenport is there in the cathedral, you know." Marian cast an evil look Jess's way as she spoke over the TV. "I was invited to attend, too, but he asked me to stay with you instead."

"I'm sorry you had to miss it." Jess's careful politeness was an attempt to neutralize Marian's barely veiled venom. She didn't think it worked, but at least the other woman shifted her gaze back to the TV.

Jess did, too, to find that on the screen now it was night, with the flashing strobe lights of an ambulance painting bright bursts of blue and red across the small, dark-haired figure on a stretcher that was being loaded into its open back.

With a shock Jess realized she was looking at a taped shot that had been filmed in the immediate aftermath of the crash, and that the victim on the stretcher was her.

She swallowed hard.

". . . sole survivor of the accident, attorney Jessica Ford. So far investigators say she has been unable to remember any of the details of what happened that night, although it is believed that she was accompanying Mrs. Cooper on her doomed dash to the hospital at the request of Mrs. Cooper's longtime friend and personal lawyer, and Miss Ford's boss, John Davenport, who sent the car. . . ."

Suddenly Jess found herself watching another taped shot, of Davenport walking up the steps of the National Cathedral with his tall, blond, ex-model wife, Brianna, at his side. Fit and trim at fifty-eight, with thinning white hair and a thick white mustache set off by a tan that Jess knew was carefully maintained, he looked nothing if not distinguished. Both he and his wife, with whom he had two young children, were clad in black, both wore sunglasses, and both emanated Washington-insider glamour. It was clear that the scene had taken place only a short time ago, while the mourners filed into the church prior to the casket's arrival.

"I hate to interrupt, but they're getting ready to take Mrs. Cooper inside now." Katie Couric broke in on the reporter's recitation, and the shot turned live again as the coffin was carried into the sanctuary to the strains of *Ruffles and Flourishes*. Still walking behind it, President David Cooper bowed his head. One on either side of him now, his children clasped his hands.

Jess couldn't watch any longer. Chest tight, throat burning, she thought of Annette Cooper as she had last seen her and felt a dreadful, tearing grief for the woman and her family. Tears springing to her eyes, she fled to the nearest bedroom.

And cried until she had no more tears left to shed.

She wasn't prone to crying. In fact, she almost never cried. She was the stoic, practical oldest child who kept her head in any crisis and who everyone looked to for a solution to any problem. Ms. Fix-it, her mother called her. But since the accident —

well, *Cry Me a River* wasn't only the title to a song.

By the time she emerged into the living room again, it was nearly nine p.m. She had slept, been awakened by Marian with the news that Davenport would be there at nine, refused an offer of carryout for supper, then slept some more. Finally she had gotten up, taken a long shower, and dressed in anticipation of the meeting with Davenport. Restoring her glasses to her purse, she popped in a new pair of contacts for the first time since the accident. She blow-dried her hair into its usual no-nonsense style, and did what she could with what little makeup she possessed to cover the now yellowing bruises. Fortunately, Grace had packed one of her favorite work outfits, a black Armani skirt suit that she'd gotten on major sale at Filene's Basement and wore with a white silk blouse, which, since Jess kept the entire outfit on a single hanger in her closet, her sister had included. Her good black heels, the expensive ones Grace had borrowed, were in there, too, and Jess had to fight off an instant, automatic flashback to last Saturday night as she slid her feet into them. Her favorite old sneakers, just like the ruined clothes she'd been wearing at the time of the crash, were presumably in the bundle that had been given to her mother. She had worn brand-new sneakers with a sweatsuit in the helicopter earlier, fearing that any departure from what she normally wore around the hospital would alert the Secret Service agents outside her room to her pending escape. But tonight, because she was meeting Davenport, she dressed as she would for work; looking professional was part of getting ahead.

The TV was still on when Jess rolled into the living room. So was a lamp beside the couch. The rest of the apartment was dark. The curtains were closed. Marian sat in a corner of the couch, her jacket discarded so that she wore only her lavender blouse and gray skirt, shoes off, slender legs drawn up beside her, the remote control in her hand.

Home movies of Annette Cooper growing up were playing on the screen. Jess took one look and refused to look again.

"Have you heard from Mr. Davenport?" she asked. It was obvious that he was not yet there.

Marian nodded and stood up, clicking the remote to turn off the TV.

"He asked me to bring you to meet him. Your appointment is at nine-thirty sharp." Marian stuck her feet in her shoes as she spoke, then pulled on her suit jacket.

Jess frowned. "Where are we going?"

Marian scooped up a set of keys from the bowl on the coffee table and headed toward the door. Jess turned — she was getting really good at working the wheelchair — to keep her in sight.

"*We* aren't going anywhere." There was an unmistakable edge of bitterness to Marian's voice. Her eyes were cold as they raked Jess. "He wants to meet with *you.* On your own. Tonight, I'm just your driver."

"Oh." Jess wasn't sure she liked the idea of that. Just the thought of getting in a car again gave her the willies. Kaleidoscopic memories of the accident crowded in on her without warning, and a shiver of dread slid over her skin. Then she gritted her teeth and forced them away. She couldn't spend the rest of her life afraid to ride in cars, for goodness' sake. This had to be overcome, and now was the time to start. Still, the sense of discomfort persisted. She didn't even know for certain that this arrangement had been made by Davenport. Maybe Marian had come up with it on her own, as part of a plot to eliminate someone she seemed to persist in seeing as her rival.

Now you really are getting paranoid, Jess scolded herself. If she had to trust somebody, and she did have to, because this was way too big to deal with on her own, then that somebody would be Davenport. And if there was anything that was certain in life, it was that Marian was absolutely loyal to him.

In other words, Marian would connive in Jess's murder only if Davenport asked her to.

Comforting thought.

"So are you coming?" Holding the door open, Marian looked back at her with obvious impatience.

Jess put the wheelchair in motion. "Right behind you."

They didn't speak again until they were in the elevator, heading down to the parking garage. Marian stood stiffly beside her, her arms folded over her chest, her attention focused on the door in front of her, refusing to look at Jess.

"So I'm meeting with Mr. Davenport where?" Jess tried rephrasing her earlier question. She was growing increasingly nervous, and a little conversation would be nice to keep the bad thoughts at bay.

"What, don't you like surprises? Wait and see." The nastiness in Marian's tone was unmistakable now. The glance she shot Jess was openly unfriendly.

Okay, the hostility was getting old. "Tell

me something, Marian: What did I ever do to make you dislike me?"

Marian stiffened.

"You think you're more important to him than I am because you're a lawyer, don't you? Well, you're not. He only hired you out of that nothing law school you went to because you're a little worker bee who'll do the drudge work none of the other associates want to do."

There was a reason why one of the first things they taught you in law school was to never ask a question unless you're sure you want to hear the answer. Now the other woman's enmity, instead of being hidden, was right out there in the open.

"You know what? I'm fine with that," Jess said. And she was. She'd known all along what her role in the firm was. And she also knew that she was determined to work hard enough to rise above it.

Marian snorted. The elevator stopped and they got out.

The drive into the heart of the city was brief, uneventful, and largely silent. Traffic was heavy now that the funeral was over and the masses of people who'd poured into D.C. to mourn had started moving around, heading for places to eat, places to sleep. Likewise the sidewalks were packed, and the parks, and just about every available space where people could crash. Flags at every public building hung at half-mast. Funeral wreaths, black ribbons, and every imaginable religious symbol from crosses made out of twigs to carved-soap Buddhas adorned trees and lampposts and mailboxes by the hundreds. Other than that, D.C. was its vibrant self, alive again with light and sound and movement and the smells of food and car exhaust and the water surrounding the city.

Jess figured out where they were going only minutes before Marian drove into the parking garage at the side of the building that served the law offices of Davenport, Kelly, and Bascomb. There was no attendant on duty, so she used her pass card to get in, then drove straight to the elevator that was available only to building employees who had a special key.

Jess was too junior to have one.

"Mr. Davenport said you were to meet him in his office." Marian handed over the key. "I'll be down here waiting when you're ready to leave."

14

An office skyscraper at night is just naturally spooky, Jess decided as she rode the elevator up to the twentieth floor, the highest of the four floors that the law firm she worked for occupied — the floor that, naturally, contained Davenport's expansive private office, along with the expansive private offices of the firm's other partners and the less expansive but still impressive offices of a select few top associates. Jess's closet — which was how she thought of her own tiny, interior private office — was on the seventeenth floor, the firm's very lowest level. Just like she herself was at the firm's lowest level.

Down at street level, the building was brightly lit. Its impressive two-story bronze-and-glass entrance would be staffed by a doorman or two, who could summon security at the touch of a button. On the same block, retailers such as Burberry and Brooks Brothers drew window shoppers who then went on to dine at such fashionable eateries as Michael's or The Inn at Farragut Park. Up here, the long halls were dimly lit and deserted, so deserted that the hum of the wheelchair's motor seemed to echo off the faux-finished tortoiseshell walls and the slick marble floors. The offices and conference rooms lining either side of the halls were dark. Their doors were closed and locked. Usually a few gung-ho souls — herself included — would be still working at this hour, and the janitorial staff was always around, cleaning floors and bathrooms and the like, and thus there would be light and sound and the impression of energy and warmth. But on this particular Thursday, this National Day of Mourning when the First Lady had been laid to rest, nobody was at work. The halls felt empty and cold.

Davenport's office was at the front of the building overlooking Connecticut Avenue. The private elevator that connected directly to the parking garage was at the rear. Therefore, it required a journey of several anxiety-compounding minutes to reach her target. Using the wheelchair felt odd, but since as recently as this morning her legs had threatened to give out on her when she had done no more than walk to the bathroom and back on her own, she was afraid that walking all the way from the elevator to Davenport's office and back would be more than she could handle. Plus, he never asked junior associates to sit down in his presence, and she was sure she couldn't stand for any extended period. Of course, under the circumstances, she *could* sit down, and of course he wouldn't mind, but . . . it was less complicated all around to use the wheelchair.

Jess's palms grew damp as she turned the final corner and found herself in the last of the long halls that ended at Davenport's office. This one was wide as well as long, with a deep gold carpet running down the center. The ceiling was high and coffered, and the walls were lined with huge, expensive modern paintings that filled the space between discreet mahogany doors with their polished brass plates announcing the names of the favored associates who occupied them. Behind Jess was a bank of gleaming brass client elevators that connected to the lobby. In front of her, at the far end of the hall, was a reception area where supplicants — no, make that clients — waited to see Davenport himself, and a long mahogany desk where receptionists Denise Caple and JoAnne Subtelny politely repelled all but the favored few with automatic access or coveted appointments to see the great man. To the right was Marian's office.

Jess paused at the top of the hallway to take a long, wary look.

No one was there. The desks, the offices, the halls — the whole damned place — took on a completely different atmosphere when no people were around. The silence was absolute.

Okay, stop it. You're creeping yourself out.

She started moving again.

Jess had almost reached the reception desk when she saw that Davenport's door was ajar. Just a few inches, enough so that she could see that the office itself was dark inside.

Not good.

She let up on the wheelchair's controls. The thing stopped cold. She looked at that open door for a minute, considered the possibilities, weighed her options.

Her heart, which was already beating faster than normal, picked up the pace again. Her breathing quickened, too.

"Jessica?"

Jess almost jumped at the sheer unexpectedness of it. But the voice was Davenport's. No doubt about that, even if it was muffled a bit.

He was talking to her through the intercom on the reception desk, of course. Which meant that he was at his desk. That's where his end of the intercom was, and he had a little monitor on the credenza to his left, which, when turned on, allowed him to view the reception area.

Her shoulders slumped with relief. Then she realized that if he was talking to her, he could see her, and she sat taller in the chair and put her game face on.

"Hello, Mr. Davenport."

"Come on in."

Yeah, okay. Just as soon as my insides stop shaking.

Taking a deep breath, she rolled forward again, skirting the reception desk, pushing the door to his office open wide enough so that the wheelchair could get through.

His office was really a two-room suite with an opulently furnished sitting room complete with twin couches, a quartet of chairs, a wet bar, and all kinds of impressive accoutrements. That was the room she found herself in. The lights were off and the thick drapes were tightly drawn, which was why it had appeared dark from the hallway. To the left were doors leading into Davenport's private bathroom and a small kitchenette. To the right, an open door led into his actual office. Light streamed through its door, although not the bright light of artificial lighting. As she reached it and entered the huge corner office, Jess saw why.

All the lights were off, but the curtains were open to the max. Both outer walls were floor-to-ceiling windows, and the luminescence from the thousands of sparkling lights that lit up the city like a Christmas tree at night was bright enough to cast a lovely, otherworldly radiance over the entire office. Jess stopped abruptly, able for the moment to do nothing but absorb the breathtaking view. There was the glowing dome of the Capitol, the shining white obelisk of the Washington Monument, the White House itself. Then her attention was drawn by a movement inside the office to her left, and she realized there was someone behind the desk. Davenport, of course. Silhouetted against the background of the luminous windows, the desk appeared as no more than a long, black rectangle. Seated behind it, Davenport himself was a silhouette against the city he loved so much.

A sudden prickling at the back of her neck, as if her instincts were alerting her to another, unseen presence, made her catch her breath. The sensation was so strong that she felt compelled to glance behind her into the dark sitting room and then around the office to make sure they were completely alone.

They were. At least, as far as she could tell.

Still she felt tense. Uneasy.

"Drink?" Davenport turned on his desk lamp. Now she could see him properly — a big man sitting in a big chair behind a big desk. His always perfectly groomed white hair was disheveled, as though he had run his hands through it more than once. He wore a white shirt and solid black tie, probably the same ones he had worn to the funeral earlier, only now the shirt was rumpled and unbuttoned at the neck, and the tie was askew. She could also see the empty glass on his desk, and the bottle of Chivas he held up invitingly.

"No, thanks."

He tipped the bottle, poured some into the glass. Jess could tell — from many things, like the slight unsteadiness of his hand, the ruddiness of his face, the twitch in his cheek near his mouth — that he'd been drinking before she got there. Heavily, she feared. The bottle was more than half empty, and there was whisky residue already in the glass when he started to pour. A small puddle of liquid around the glass gleamed in the yellowish lamplight.

"I don't think Mrs. Cooper's death was an accident."

There it was; she'd put it right out there on the table before she could lose her nerve, have second thoughts, chicken out, however you wanted to put it.

He heard her; she could tell he did because his eyes narrowed and he frowned a little. But he barely checked in the act of swallowing about half the glass of booze.

"She had problems, Annette."

As he spoke he lowered the glass, swirling the golden liquid that remained in it and watching it as it sloshed against the sides, then looked at Jess sadly. She sat just outside the circle of light cast by the lamp, probably about twelve feet from the desk, not having moved since she'd been stopped upon entering by the sheer beauty of the view. On the wall behind her and to her left, surrounding the door to the sitting room, were the custom-built floor-to-ceiling bookcases that held everything from his law books to photos of Brianna and their children, taken on the previous summer's safari in Kenya. To her right the wall was covered with pictures of Davenport with nearly every VIP who had passed through D.C. during the last fifteen years, including this

President and his two predecessors.

As Jess had already learned under his tutelage, impressing clients was the name of the game. And that wall was very impressive.

"As soon as I spoke to her at the hotel, I could see that she was upset, even frightened. She ran from her Secret Service detail. She told me she was, to use her exact words, a 'fucking prisoner.' " Talking fast, Jess ticked off the points she wanted to make in chronological order. "She —"

"I should have taken her seriously," he interrupted, shaking his head. "But she wasn't happy. Never happy. Fighting with David all the time. All the other things. The last few months, she just bitched and bitched and bitched. I just thought it was more of the same."

If he wasn't already drunk, he was close, Jess realized with a sinking sensation in the pit of her stomach. She wasn't entirely sure that what she was saying was even registering with him.

"Mr. Davenport. I think Mrs. Cooper may have been murdered," she tried again, spelling it out as plainly as she could in case he wasn't getting the point.

He downed the rest of the Chivas in his glass.

"Doesn't matter." Then he slammed the glass back down on the desk hard enough so that Jess jumped. "None of it matters anymore. God, I hate that 'dust to dust, ashes to ashes' crap. Who the hell" — his voice cracked — "who the hell wants to be dirt?"

He's losing it. The thought was terrifying.

"I think whoever did it also tried to kill me in the hospital." To hell with what Ryan had said about the tests on the IV equipment coming up negative. Either he was lying or the tests were wrong, because she knew she wasn't. Desperation made Jess lean forward as she tried to hammer her point home; she gripped the wheelchair arms tightly. Her eyes fought to hold his, hoping to keep his attention focused on what she was telling him rather than whatever inner demons he was currently battling. "I think they're trying to cover up what they did to Mrs. Cooper. They tried to kill me because they're afraid I'll remember something."

"I told you to keep quiet, didn't I?" He poured more whisky into his glass. Jess watched with dismay.

"I have kept quiet. All I've said to anybody is that I don't remember. But that isn't entirely true. I do remember some —"

He broke in on her before she could finish. "She wanted me. She said, 'I need you, John.' And this time she did. She really did. And I didn't go. I was tired of dealing with her, to tell you the truth. So I sent you."

He chugged from the glass. It was such an inelegant gesture, complete with gurgling sounds as he sucked the booze down, that Jess's eyes widened as she watched. In all the time she had known Davenport, she had never seen him behave like anything other than a very cultured gentleman. He was either far more drunk than she had supposed or in far worse emotional straits.

She continued doggedly, "Somebody was chasing us. Another car. I remember that, and —"

"I tried to protect you. I tried. I did. You can't say I didn't." He drank more whisky, drank it so fast that when he set the glass down again his mustache was wet and a little golden rivulet trickled from one corner of his mouth. He wiped his mouth on his sleeve. "I tried to help Annette, too. I always listened to her. I always advised her to the best of my ability. One time, one time only, she calls me and I don't go running to her as fast as I can. And now she's dead. Dead. Annette. My old friend Annette."

His mouth shook. Jess realized that tears

221

were seeping from his eyes. She sat bolt upright in the wheelchair now, watching him with dismay. This meeting in which she had put so much stock, in which she had planned to tell everything she knew and thus place the whole nightmare in his hands, letting this far more experienced, connected, respected lawyer deal with the mess he had gotten her into in the first place, was turning into a debacle.

Desperate, she tried one more time to get through to him.

"Mr. Davenport, please, I know you're grieving, but this can't wait. I came to you tonight because I don't know who else to tell these things to. I can't go to the Secret Service — I think the man who attacked me in the hospital might have been a Secret Service agent. And Mrs. Cooper was running from her own Secret Service detail when she died. And . . . and . . . I just don't think it's safe. Which means I can't go to the FBI or the local police or any other kind of law-enforcement agency, either, because they all know each other. They all stick up for each other. They all talk. Somebody will tell somebody, and then whoever is behind this will find out that I've remembered something and they'll kill me. And I can't just keep quiet because it's *murder,* the murder of the First Lady of the United States and two other people, and anyway, I don't think just keeping quiet is going to help, because they're afraid I might remember something that will incriminate them and they're going to kill me anyway just on the off chance. You know those 'dark forces' you warned me about? I think it's somebody in the government. I don't see —"

"No, you don't," Davenport interrupted fiercely, his voice thick, his eyes wet. Tears trickled down his cheeks. "You don't see anything. You haven't had time to get married or have kids or build any kind of career that matters, any kind of legacy. You don't know anything about power, about actions and consequences. You don't know anything about how things work, or the kinds of things people sometimes have to do."

He sobbed, then clamped his lips tightly together as if ashamed that the sound had escaped through them.

Jess stared at him, appalled.

"You're right, I don't." She worked to keep her voice very, very steady. If he wouldn't — or couldn't — help her, what would she do? Her stomach twisted at the thought. If she was right about what she suspected — and she was almost sure she was — the perpetrators would hunt her down and kill her without compunction. They were big and bad and relentless, and in the end she would have nowhere to go, nowhere to hide. "But I know I'm in danger, and I'm pretty sure so do you. You obviously think something's wrong about Mrs. Cooper's death, too. So who do we contact? Who do we tell? *We've got to tell someone that she was murdered.*"

Panic curled through her insides as she searched his face. If there was anything there except sodden grief, she couldn't see it.

"I always thought I was a brave man." His eyes dropped away from hers as he poured the last of the Chivas into his glass. "Now I know I'm not. I'm a coward. A *damned* coward."

He picked up the glass and drank thirstily, noisily. When he set the glass down, his mustache was wet, and he swiped his arm across his mouth again.

Jess watched despairingly.

"Maybe you could go directly to the President," she suggested. "Tell him."

He made a sound that might have been a scornful laugh. It was only then, as she tried to figure out what that laugh meant, that it occurred to her that if, indeed, the Secret Service was involved, then the President himself might very well be, too.

Because who else did the Secret Service take orders from?

"There has to be somebody we can tell," she said. "Somebody who can launch an investigation and . . ."

Her voice trailed off as he swallowed the last of his whisky.

The press, she thought, as she frantically sought some other way to get what she knew and remembered and suspected out there and thus do her moral duty and also, she hoped, remove any motive for anyone to kill her at the same time. She would go to the media and tell them everything. It was obvious Davenport wasn't going to be able to help her; even if he wanted to — maybe when he was sober and in a different frame of mind — it might be too late.

By that time, the dark forces might already have found her and shut her up permanently, with no possibility of mistake.

Maybe they'd just been waiting for her to get out of the hospital before they tried again.

Jess's heartbeat quickened at the thought.

Maybe the Secret Service wasn't involved in this after all. Maybe they had been all that was keeping her safe. And she'd just run away from them. . . .

A slithering sound caught her attention. Frowning as she tried to figure out what it was, she realized after a couple of seconds that Davenport had just opened one of his top desk drawers.

"This is the only thing I can do." Davenport stood up, swaying a little on his feet. "This is the only thing left for me. I have to save what I can for my kids."

Jess had only just registered that he was holding a gun in his hand when he whispered, "God forgive me."

Jess's eyes widened. Her stomach contracted. Her heart leaped.

"Mr. Davenport . . ."

Hand shaking visibly, he pointed the gun at her and fired.

15

Three things happened simultaneously.

There was a tremendous *bang,* and the bullet passed so close to her left cheek that she could feel it brush past.

She screamed, throwing herself from the chair.

And something hit her in the back with the force of a freight train. Still screaming, she landed facedown on the antique Oriental rug that covered the center of the floor as an enormous weight smashed violently to earth on top of her, stopping her forward momentum dead, crushing her, forcing the air from her lungs.

It hurt so much that she went dizzy with it.

"Davenport! Drop it!"

The shout sounded almost in her ear. She understood in that split second that what lay atop her was a man, a man who had dived on her hopefully with the intent of saving her life, and then another shot exploded, the sound muffled this time by the bulk of the man whose body covered hers. It was followed almost instantaneously by the sound of shattering glass, then a shower of almost musical notes as if it were suddenly raining tinkling wind chimes.

Cringing, wheezing as she fought to draw air into her flattened lungs, tucking her chin into her chest and wrapping her arms around her head, Jess tried to become one with the carpet, overwhelmingly grateful for the body atop hers. Terror turned her blood to ice as every nerve ending she possessed went wild in anticipation of the impact of a bullet — the next bullet — that would hit her protector's body and even, possibly, tear through it into her own shrinking flesh.

"Jesus God," the man on top of her said. His tone made it a prayer.

There was no other sound. No more bullets. No more wind chimes. No more voices. Nothing.

Just the pounding of her own heart in her ears.

"You okay?" the man asked as he rolled off her.

Jess barely even had to look at him to know who he was: Ryan. She realized that some part of her had recognized him as soon as he spoke. Much as she hated to admit it even to herself, she would now know his deep, drawling voice anywhere. For just a moment he lay on his side on the carpet facing her, looking her over carefully, his face hard, his normally light eyes dark with some emotion she couldn't put a name to.

He was holding a gun, a big black pistol, in his right hand. It was, she was relieved beyond words to see, not pointed at her.

She realized that in that case she was profoundly thankful to see him.

Their gazes met. She sucked in air.

"Fine," she wheezed.

A corner of his mouth twisted up in the smallest of involuntary smiles. "Good to know."

Then, in a horrifying instant of clarity, she realized if he was facing her that meant his back was turned to the source of the danger.

Her eyes widened. "Mr. Davenport . . ."

Fear sharpened her voice. Her gaze flew past Ryan toward the desk, toward the place where Davenport had so unbelievably stood up and pointed a gun at her, shot at her, terrified of what she might see, what might be happening at that very second, only to find that she couldn't see Davenport anywhere. Had Ryan fired that second shot, then, and had Davenport been hit by it and taken down?

"He's gone."

Ryan rolled to his feet with surprising grace for such a big man. He seemed slightly out of breath, which, as a matter of fact, she was herself. He was wearing a black suit and tie with a white shirt, as if he, too, was still dressed for Annette Cooper's funeral, and he looked much better than any man who had just thrown himself into the line of fire to save another's life had any right to. He kept the pistol at his side and pointed down.

"Gone?" Jess frowned in incomprehension.

"He shot out the window. Then he jumped." Ryan spoke over his shoulder as he walked across the room and looked down.

Horror hit Jess like a blow to the chest. "Oh my God."

Pushing herself up into a sitting position, she stared at the far wall where Ryan stood looking down, where, she realized with a combination of disbelief and shock, only a few shards of glass continued to cling to the metal frame. Otherwise, the window was gone. The office was open to the night. The roar she heard wasn't in her ears at all but was some combination of wind, traffic, and shouts and screams from the people below. Fresh air blew in, sharp and clean-smelling, lifting the edges of the heavy curtains, sending some of the papers on Davenport's desk swirling out and skyward on an upward spiral like dueling kites.

"Can you get up?" His voice surprisingly gentle, Ryan came back from the edge and held a hand out to her. "We need to get out of here. Right now. Security will be on the way. And the police. And there might be — hell, who knows. Somebody else."

"Mr. Davenport tried to kill me."

"Yeah, I caught that."

Jess was still stunned, but fear made her move. She put her hand in his and let him pull her to her feet. As she straightened, a sharp pain in her back caused her to wince, and she realized she was shaking all over. His eyes slid over her again to check for a new injury. Except for a laddered stocking and a scraped knee, she was okay.

He dropped her hand. "Where's that damned chair?"

It was on its side a few feet away.

"He killed himself." Okay, that was obvious, which made it a stupid thing to say. But she was feeling stupid or, rather, stupefied, as she stared out at the star-studded night where all of D.C. continued to glow while Davenport had just died in its midst. She had to be in the early stages of shock. Her heart palpitated. She was finding it hard to breathe. She took a halting step forward, then another and another, drawn by an almost irresistible urge to look down into that black void. Impossible to believe that Davenport had just stepped out the window, fallen twenty stories, and was now lying broken and bloodied on the sidewalk below.

"Trust me, you don't want to do that." Ryan caught her by the arm before she reached the edge. "Sit down."

Having fetched the chair, Ryan practically pushed Jess into it and thrust her purse into her lap. She shivered and swallowed hard.

"Don't freak out on me. We don't have that kind of time."

"I'm not freaking out." Her voice was surprisingly steady. "What are you doing here, anyway?"

"You mean besides saving your life? That's something we probably need to talk about. You want to settle in for a chat now or you want to get the hell out of here?"

By way of a reply, she shot him a withering look.

"Then let's go."

He headed toward the door as he spoke. Her hand moved to the controls, turning the chair to face the door, leaving Davenport and everything she thought she had known about him behind. The whirr of the motor sounded as loud as a jet engine to her ears, but she knew that was just because she was so on edge she was ready to jump out of her skin.

"You all set?" Weapon in hand, he stuck his head inside the dark sitting room and looked cautiously all around.

"Yes." She rolled to join him.

"Kick that thing into high gear. We need to *move*. And stay close."

He kept in front of her, his pistol at the ready, moving fast but cautiously toward the hall, glancing back to make sure she was keeping up. With one last disbelieving look at the open air panel that just minutes ago had been the front wall of Davenport's office, Jess rolled into the thick, gray shadows of the sitting room, following Ryan as closely as she could.

That sense she'd had of someone behind her when she'd entered Davenport's office — it almost certainly had to have been Ryan.

She'd already come close to dying tonight. That made it twice in a week. What was it they said about the third time being a charm?

"Can't you speed that thing up?" Ryan frowned at her over his shoulder as they emerged into the relative brightness of the reception area.

"If I could, I would."

They passed the reception desk. She rolled down the center hall, going as fast as she could, putting the pedal to the metal in wheelchair terms, while a fast walk was all that was required for Ryan to keep pace with her. The fact that Davenport was dead and had tried to kill her was more than Jess could take in for the moment. She did her best to push all thoughts of what had just occurred out of her head. Just getting out of there had to be her first priority. The dim lighting, the closed doors on either side, the enormous paintings with their abstract slashes of black — everything felt different now. Her workplace had suddenly become a place of fear. So had the rest of the world.

A bullet could come out of nowhere. . . .

"Security's probably watching us right now." It came out in a horrified exclamation as Jess suddenly remembered the building's elaborate camera system. Heart in her throat, she searched wide-eyed for any cameras protruding from the ceiling.

"Davenport knew you were coming, right?"

"Yes."

"Believe me, when somebody gets around to checking they'll find the cameras up here aren't working for some reason or another."

Jess blinked. *Right.* Davenport would have made preparations. He had planned this. He had told her to come up here planning to kill her.

Davenport's first shot had missed, but if they'd been alone, a second one almost certainly wouldn't have, because after throwing herself out of the chair she had just run out of options. If it hadn't been for the man striding along beside her, she would be dead right now. She looked up at him. He was eye candy as always, but that wasn't what she cared about right then. His jaw was taut, his mouth grim. He scanned the area ahead of them with cold precision. He held the gun like he knew what to do with it, which of course he did. He looked like somebody who could be counted on to keep them both alive.

"I have a key to the private elevator," she told him. "That's how I came up."

"The problem with elevators is that if anybody figures out you're in one, they can trap you in it."

As they reached the end of the hall, Jess was still digesting the mind-boggling thought that somebody might want to trap her in an elevator. Something, a sound, an instinct, pulled her gaze to the elevator bank with its gleaming brass doors. And the numbers above it. One was lit up. The car on the left was on the second floor, no, now the third. It was on its way up.

One look, and she thought her heart might leap right out of her chest.

"Ah, shit." Ryan saw it, too. "Okay, stop."

"What?"

He shoved his pistol into its holster and, when she didn't immediately do what he told her, grabbed the handles at the back of her chair to stop her himself.

"This thing is too damned slow. We've got to *go.* Here, put your arms around my neck."

Jess realized he meant to pick her up at just about the time he scooped her out of the chair. She barely managed to hang on to her purse as she was swung up into his arms.

"What? What are you doing?"

"Picking up the pace."

He was already running with her, racing down the hall away from whoever was coming up on that elevator, heading toward the north end of the building, where she had come up in the private elevator. She wrapped her arms around his neck and held on for dear life. His arms were hard with muscle and strong around her, and he was carrying her in the most comfortable way possible for her, high and close against his chest as one would carry a cherished child. She guessed that he was mindful of her injury and didn't want to hurt her, and she appreciated that.

Still, comfortable this was not. She was bouncing all over the place.

"If you don't want to use the elevator, how do you suggest we get out of here?" she gasped out.

"The stairs."

"Stairs?"

"Yep."

"They'll be here soon," she warned. She knew from experience that the elevators in the building were fast.

"Figured." He was running flat out, his hard-soled shoes pounding on the slick marble floor.

"They'll see the wheelchair."

"Can't help it."

Seconds later they had nearly reached the end of the long hall. It was a good distance from where whoever was coming up on the elevator would emerge but still within their sight if they looked left.

A tiny *ping* sounded in the distance.

"They're here," she whispered in a panic.

"Hang on."

Another bound, and he skidded to a stop in front of the door marked EMERGENCY EXIT. Jess felt one arm shift as he grabbed the knob and jerked the metal door open. Then they were through, and he was holding her tight again. The narrow chute of steel-reinforced concrete had been designed to be fire- and blast-proof, but it looked surprisingly low-tech, beige walls and gray metal stairs with iron-bar railings. Jess could do nothing but hold on tight as Ryan clattered down the stairs with her.

"If you're . . . heading toward the parking garage, you should know that there's somebody down there . . . waiting for me. At street level. Near the private elevator, which means . . . near the building." The ride had just gotten a whole lot rougher, which was why she was talking in bursts. Her grip on him tightened exponentially as her fear of falling or being dropped skyrocketed.

"Who?"

"Davenport's secretary, Marian Young. She drove me here." Jess suddenly felt sick. Had Marian known what Davenport intended? Maybe, but she didn't think so. On the other hand, before tonight she would never have believed that Davenport might try to kill her, either.

"She alone?"

"She was when I left her."

"Okay."

His replies were clipped and brief for good reason. He was in great shape, there was no doubt about that. But she could feel his body heat increasing with each flight of stairs. By the time he burst out through another exit door onto the second floor of the parking garage, he was practically panting.

The scream of sirens hit her even before the door closed behind them, proof that the stairwell was soundproof as well as everything-else-proof. The flashing lights of some kind of an emergency vehicle burst through the large rectangular openings in the top half of the concrete walls to carom around the parking garage in disorienting bursts of blue. She could hear shouts, jumbled voices, the sounds of a crowd on the street just below.

That was good, right? Because there was safety in numbers, and all that?

But as far as she could tell, this level of the parking garage was deserted. If anybody wanted to attack them, this was the place. The walls were gray, the floor was gray, the high, concrete-beamed ceiling was gray. The lights set deep into the ceiling provided circles of distilled illumination in the areas directly below them and cast the rest of the vast space into shadow. Add in the revolving emergency lights, and it became almost mind-blowingly psychedelic. Jess thought they were alone, that no one was following them, but given the constantly changing nature of their surroundings, it was impossible to be sure.

"Do you have a car?" Her narrowed eyes continually scanned the shadows behind him, just in case.

"Across the street."

She realized that he was heading toward the door at the far end of the garage. One flight down, and another door just like it would open onto Connecticut Avenue, at the opposite end of the garage from where Marian was parked. Jess felt a quick welling of pity as she pictured the other woman waiting in her car for Jess to reappear, with no idea that her world had just been smashed to smithereens. Marian would be sick with grief when she found out that Davenport was dead.

Ryan pulled open another door, and then

they were in another stairwell, going down.

When he reached the bottom one short flight later, he pushed open the door. They had to cover only a few more yards through a shadowy corner of the garage before exiting through the door out into the street.

"Maybe we should go tell Marian what happened." She spoke practically in his ear, her voice hushed.

"Yeah. No."

He said it like that was that. Like it was entirely his decision to make. Which, since he was the legs of the operation at the moment, she guessed it was.

Her eyes straining through the darkness, she searched for Marian's car. There were a couple of others, parked and left for the night or however long — but, yes, there it was, right where Jess had gotten out, waiting beneath the neon elevator sign which shed just the tiniest amount of light on the Volvo's navy blue roof. All the lights inside and outside the car were off, but the elevator light above illuminated the interior just a little bit. Jess frowned. She couldn't see Marian. In fact, if Jess hadn't known better, she would have sworn the car was empty.

She was still craning her neck toward it when Ryan shouldered through the door to the street.

They emerged into a growing, jostling crowd, with people packed together on the sidewalk. Most people were barely moving. They were gawking. At something lying in the street.

Jess felt her stomach turn inside out. She couldn't see anything, which was probably a good thing, but she knew what they had to be looking at. Multiple sirens, most still at a distance, filled the air, drowning out the noise of the crowd. About five blocks down, Jess saw the flashing lights of an ambulance as it fought to reach the scene.

"You can put me down now. I couldn't manage the stairs, but this is flat," she whispered in Ryan's ear. Her voice took on an urgent undertone as she noticed a few glances directed their way. "We're starting to attract attention."

Ryan grunted in acknowledgment and set her on her feet, keeping a hard arm around her waist for support. Her legs felt rubbery, but she gritted her teeth and wrapped her arm around him and started walking when he did, responding to his assessing glance with a nod that said she was all right. Using his shoulder as a buffer, taking her with him, he wove through the crowd clogging the sidewalk with single-minded purpose. Against her body, she could feel the solid strength and heat of him.

"Duck your face down. I don't want anybody getting a good look at you."

Of course. She'd been plastered all over TV. People might recognize her. She had forgotten that. It occurred to Jess in a lightning burst of awareness that if she still harbored any doubts about Ryan and his intentions toward her, this was her moment to scream some variation of "This man is not my daddy!" and enlist the power of the many people surrounding them to get away.

The question boiled down to this: Was she safer with him or without him?

On the negative side, he was a Secret Service agent. And she was pretty sure he'd lied about having tests done on her IV.

But then he'd saved her life tonight, and in the hospital. He was a trained protection officer with a gun.

She was pretty sure he didn't want to kill her, or want anyone else to kill her. Otherwise, she'd be dead.

So she was going with, *with.*

Shaking her head so that her hair covered most of her face, she lowered her head so that she was looking at the ground.

"Careful of the curb," he warned in an undertone.

Then they stepped off the sidewalk and

into the street, heading, she assumed, toward wherever he had left his car, dodging the vehicles that were still trying to force their way past and that would occasionally shoot free of the congestion like a cork from a champagne bottle.

The view was better as they crossed the street, because the bulk of the crowd stayed on the sidewalk. For the moment only a single police car was on the scene. The two officers were out of the car. One was trying single-handedly to redirect the honking traffic that was already backed up for blocks. The other was standing in the street, looking down.

Jess couldn't help it. She followed his gaze. She caught just a glimpse of black dress pants and a white shirt, realized that it was Davenport lying sprawled on his stomach on the pavement, felt the gorge rise in her throat, and hastily looked away.

She was suddenly breathing hard. Her pulse pounded in her ears. She felt light-headed, woozy — and then she saw Marian.

Unmistakable with her upswept hair and gray suit, the woman burst through the crowd about two hundred feet away.

"John!" Marian screamed. Her face twisted into a mask of hysterical grief, she ran frantically into the street toward Davenport's body.

In the space of a heartbeat, Jess saw what was about to happen but was helpless to do anything about it.

A small tan car shot past the cop trying to stop traffic and hit Marian dead-on. She flew up in the air, slammed back down on the car's roof, and then was thrown to the ground as the car streaked away.

16

"Marian!" Jess shrieked, pulling away from Ryan. Horror grabbed her heart like a fist and squeezed.

A couple of heads turned in her direction.

"Shut up," Ryan growled, tightening his grip on her at the same time as he quickened his step. "Jesus, don't draw attention to yourself."

Jess didn't fight him, but she couldn't look away. Other people in the crowd were gasping, yelling, surging forward, crowding around the accident site. The cops abandoned what they were doing to run toward where Marian now lay crumpled in the street. One knelt beside her while the other held back traffic, which had now ground to a total halt because the street was completely, hideously blocked. Jess had eyes for nothing but Marian. The woman lay unmoving, her left leg bent at an unnatural angle. A pool of dark liquid was forming beneath her head.

Blood, black as oil as the streetlights hit it.

"I got the license plate number!" a man shouted, elbowing his way through the crowd toward the cops.

"Let the ambulance through!" someone else cried.

"Keep your head down." Ryan pulled her up on the curb with him just as the ambulance rolled past. Behind it came two more police cars, strobe lights flashing, sirens screaming a warning into the night as cars nudged onto the sidewalk and wedged into a single lane to let them pass.

"Oh my God." Jess could hardly talk. Her teeth chattered. Her breathing was suddenly way too fast and shallow. "I've got to go to her."

"Like hell." There was a brutal edge to Ryan's voice that she had never heard in it before. With his arm clamped around her, he shouldered deep into the crowd, clearly intent on putting as much distance between them and the accident as he could. Suddenly, Jess could see nothing but a forest of people. "Anyway, there's nothing you can do."

His arm was like iron around her now, as though he feared she might struggle to escape. She didn't. Too many terrible things had happened too quickly, and all she knew for sure was that she was afraid. They were on the edges of the crowd now, and he was moving faster, propelling her with him as he plunged past others rushing toward the scene, leaving it behind as quickly as he could. More police cars slowly forced their way through the stopped traffic. Cars moved aside to let them pass.

It started to rain, a slow sprinkle that hit her exposed skin like cold tears.

"The car just drove away." Scarcely able to believe what she had just witnessed, Jess looked back, tried to see what was going on with Marian but could not. "It just hit her and drove away."

"That's what it did, all right."

Jess's heart clutched. Her head was up now, and he wasn't saying anything about it, so she guessed it was safe enough. The rain was making her blink in an effort to keep it out of her eyes. "Do you think she's — dead?"

"Hard to say. Believe me, everything that can be done for her is being done."

They rounded a corner into near darkness. The wind caught her hair, whipping it back, driving a cold drizzle against her skin. The smell of booze and garbage mixed with the wet-earth scent of the rain. Jess realized that they had left the crowd behind. The thought scared her. Shivering, she looked carefully all around. Tall buildings rose up on either side; they were in an alley now. A starless and rainy alley lined with trash cans and Dumpsters and mounds of things she preferred not to think about. Rows of dark windows looked down on them like sightless eyes.

Ducking her head against the rain, Jess instinctively leaned closer into Ryan, taking comfort from the solid warmth of his body. Watching what had happened to Marian had stripped the last of her illusions from her. This was big, it was real, and it was not going away. She felt exposed, like danger was closing in from all sides.

Like there was nowhere left that was safe.

Could someone be following us even now?

She looked fearfully back. A white plastic grocery bag tumbling toward them like a pale ghost in the wind made her jump. A sound — a rattle — rain on the trash-can lids, maybe — made her catch her breath. At the mouth of the alley, the flashing blue lights from the rescue vehicles pulsed, giving weird life to everything they touched.

Then the alley opened up, and they turned right into a parking lot filled with vehicles.

There were lights, two tall halogen lamps at either end that emitted a foggy yellow glow, and row upon row of cars. *It would be easy for someone to hide.* Jess's heartbeat quickened, but before she could look around more than once he stopped beside a small, dark-colored RAV4, said, "Hang on a minute," and pressed the button to unlock the doors. Then he opened the passenger door and bundled her inside. A moment or so later he slid in behind the wheel.

As soon as he was inside, he locked the doors. The click as he did so was enough to make her jump. Even as she realized what the sound was, Jess wondered if he feared being followed as much as she did.

"Was that an accident?" Jess burst out, still looking warily all around as he started the car. She was wet, cold, and shaking like a leaf, and she folded her arms over her chest for warmth. The parking lot was filled with shapes and shadows, and she was on pins and needles in case someone should suddenly spring at them out of the darkness. "That wasn't an accident, was it?"

"I don't know. Maybe."

He backed the car out in a fast swoop, then shifted into drive. A moment later they pulled out onto M Street. Jess felt a little safer because they were now moving targets.

"Put your seat belt on."

He was wearing his, she saw. Hands trembling, Jess did as she was told.

"Where are we going?"

He glanced at her. "My house. It's just outside of Dale City. You can stay there until we get this thing figured out."

Jess wasn't in any state of mind to argue. Without a better suggestion, she didn't even bother to reply.

As a result of what was happening on Connecticut Avenue, traffic was already clogging up throughout downtown. He headed away from the congestion, driving fast but not too fast, making good time through the interconnected grid of streets, glancing just a little too often in his rearview mirror for her to think they were now safe. Rain fell steadily, and the constant rhythm of the windshield wipers provided a numbing counterpoint to the swish of the tires on wet pavement. She was shivering, which, she suspected, had very little to do with the fact that she was cold and wet and had a whole lot to do with the fact that she had just witnessed two violent deaths and nearly suffered one herself. He must have noticed because he cranked the heat. A moment later, the smell of damp clothes circulated throughout the car.

"Why would Mr. Davenport try to kill me? Why would he kill himself?" The questions that had been tumbling through her mind spilled over as he braked for a red light. "If there was anybody I thought I could trust, it was him."

"Babe, outside of your family, I'd say there's nobody you ought to be trusting right about now." He gave her a quick, grim smile. "Except me, of course."

Jess looked at him and frowned. Some of the shock was receding, and her brain was slowly regaining its ability to function. *Okay, time to focus here.* Before she fell hook, line, and sinker for the whole "trust me" thing, he had some explaining to do.

Her eyes narrowed at him. "About that. What were you doing in Mr. Davenport's office again?"

"Let's just say I was monitoring the situation."

"Situation?"

"Yeah."

"You know, I don't mean to be ungrateful or anything, but I think I'm going to need a little bit more of an explanation than that."

The light turned green, he accelerated and turned left, and they joined a long line of cars heading up onto the Beltway.

"Just out of curiosity, what happens if you

don't like what you hear?"

Good question. Jess was already asking herself that. She was in his car traveling at around seventy miles an hour on an expressway filled with other cars going equally fast. They were alone. He was a highly trained federal agent; she was a highly trained lawyer. He was big, she was small. Plus, he had a gun. If it came down to a fight for her life, she didn't like her chances.

She made a face. "I'll cross that bridge when I come to it, I guess."

He laughed, a small, amused sound that went a long way toward making her feel safer, and shot a look at her.

"I was following you, okay? To make sure you were safe. Which obviously you weren't."

Jess frowned. "How did you even know where I was? I deliberately left the hospital when you weren't around. No one outside Mr. Davenport and Marian was even supposed to know where I was going."

"Piece of cake."

Now that Jess thought about it — Davenport's secretary, Davenport's helicopter, probably easy enough to find out where the helicopter had landed — she guessed it was, and felt stupid for feeling as safe as she had in the condo. Ryan — and no telling who else — had known where she was all along. What was the word she wanted to apply to herself? *Oh, yeah: thick.*

"So how did you get into the building?"

"I'm good at things like that."

"Up to the twentieth floor?"

"Those damned stairs. I watched you roll into Davenport's office, and I followed you."

"You heard everything I said to him." Jess had only just realized that. Quickly she reviewed the conversation in her mind and stiffened with alarm.

"Pretty much, yeah."

He knew — and he hadn't killed her. Or let Davenport kill her, which would have been way too easy. That had to weigh heavily on the *trust him* side.

"I don't think Mrs. Cooper's death was an accident." She threw it out there like a challenge.

"So I heard you tell Davenport. You want to tell me why?"

Jess wrapped her arms tighter around herself. Despite the blasting heat, she was bone cold. It was all she could do to keep her teeth from chattering.

"She was running away from something. She was nervous, afraid, even." If Jess hesitated, it was because she suddenly remembered once again that he was a Secret

Service agent. And a lot of the evidence that she'd pieced together in her mind pointed to Secret Service involvement in Mrs. Cooper's death and in the subsequent attack on Jess in the hospital, which Ryan had almost certainly lied about. And in Davenport's suicide? She didn't see how the Secret Service could have orchestrated that, but she was starting to feel that anything was possible. And what about Marian? An accident, or something far more sinister? At this point, she just didn't know, but she was prepared to assume the worst. "She tried to get away from the agent — Prescott — who was chasing her, but he caught up with us at the corner and managed to jump into the car."

She paused, watching him for a reaction. There was none. His face was impassive. His eyes stayed on the road. A semi rolled past on the right, rattling the SUV. He eased into the lane behind it.

"Go on," he said.

She took a deep breath. "That put him in the front passenger seat, with me behind him and Mrs. Cooper behind the driver. Mrs. Cooper was screaming at him, telling him to get out, to not call anybody, that what she did was none of his business. He told her that if she wanted to go somewhere, she was going to have to take him, too, or he would call backup to come and collect her and take her back to the White House whether she wanted to go or not. He said he was just staying with her to keep her safe, and they kind of agreed that as long as he didn't call anybody or interfere with her, he could do that. And so she calmed down. Then we got off 95 onto this two-lane road, and she was making phone calls until she lost the signal. So she got mad and threw the phone, which ended under the front passenger seat down by my feet. She wanted me to get it, and I had to unbuckle my seat belt and slide down into the footwell and stick my hand way up under the seat to try to find it. So I was doing that when headlights from behind us flashed through the car. I don't know what happened next — I was down on the floor — but Mrs. Cooper screamed, 'We've got to get out of here,' and then she yelled something at Prescott — something like, 'You called them, you bastard,' something like that. He was swearing that he didn't while she was screaming at the driver to go faster, and the driver did. He booked it, started speeding up, and then we were just flying. I managed to get back in my seat and was grabbing for my seat belt when something slammed into the back of the car. It felt like something hit us; it was this tremendous jolt, but I could still see the other car's headlights, and they were close but not close enough, you know? So I don't know what it could have been. But like I said, we were going really fast, and there was this jolt, and the back end of the car slewed around like we were on ice, and I think the driver hit the brakes — and the car just shot off the road. I remember . . . I remember . . ."

Jess broke off, shuddering, as a slide show of terrible images flashed one after the other through her mind. Trying to make sense of them, trying to sort them out, she stared silently out through the windshield at the now pouring rain. They were on the bridge, she could see the lights reflected in the black waters of the Potomac beneath them, and the sound of the tires changed subtly to reflect the fact that the surface they gripped had changed. It only occurred to her that they were probably going to be following the exact same route the car Davenport had sent had taken that night when she saw the big green sign for I-95 flash past overhead. She was still absorbing the implications of that when the RAV4 trailed the semi down the ramp onto 95. The sudden sense of déjà vu was so strong she felt light-headed.

"You gonna tell me the rest, or am I supposed to try to guess?" Ryan's voice snapped her back to the present.

Swallowing hard, Jess looked at him. The tall lights illuminating the spaghetti-like junction with I-95 shone brightly inside the car, and headlights from cars going in the opposite direction slashed directly across his face. Internally, she juggled seared-into-her-psyche images of the sexy Fed who hadn't known she was alive despite her cringe-worthy efforts at getting him to notice her against what she now knew of him. His face was shiny and damp, his hair and clothes were wet, he had tired lines around his eyes and mouth, and he managed to look hot anyway. But he also looked tough, competent, and, yes, dammit, trustworthy.

She was going to trust him. God help her if she was wrong.

Taking a deep breath, she continued.

"We were all screaming, and the car just started flipping over, and then all of a sudden I was out of the car, sailing through the air kind of doing somersaults, but I could still see the car rolling down the hill and I realized I must have been thrown clear. Then I hit and . . ."

"You blacked out?" he supplied when she

hesitated.

She nodded, relieved to have been offered such an easy out. "Yes."

"So that's it?"

Wetting her lips, she shot him a wary glance. Her mouth had gone dry. This was the part that frightened her the most. It was also the part that she most needed to tell.

"Jess?" he prompted. Something in her silence must have told him there was more.

I could always say, "Then I woke up and you were leaning over me." It would be so easy. She was tempted. Then she shook her head at herself. *No, finish it.*

"Okay." She swallowed. "I did black out, but not for long. I remember opening my eyes and thinking how dark the night was, and wondering what I was doing lying outside where I could see the stars, and why I hurt so much. Then I saw these small, round lights coming down the hill. Flashlights, I realized. There had to be people carrying them. I tried to call out to the people with the flashlights — I knew something was wrong by that time, knew I needed help — but I guess the breath had been knocked out of me because I couldn't make a sound. I lay there gasping for air, watching these dark figures holding flashlights rushing — they were moving as fast as they could with the ground so steep — past me down the hill. And then I realized that somebody was screaming. I hadn't noticed it before, maybe because my ears were ringing. I don't know."

Closing her eyes as the memory took on life in her mind, she raised her hands to her temples, where her pulse pounded ferociously. She had to remind herself to breathe, and deliberately took in a couple of slow, careful sips of air.

Still, she could almost hear the screaming. "Jess?"

Once again, his voice brought her out of it.

Her eyes opened. Her hands dropped to twine in her lap. Unable to look at him, she stared out through the windshield without seeing anything of the closed-for-the-night strip malls and car repair shops and apartment complexes they passed.

"I looked down, toward where the screaming was coming from, and I saw the car. One of the headlights still worked, kind of marking where it was, so I saw it as soon as I looked, lying on its roof with its tires still spinning." She swallowed. "The people with the flashlights reached it right about then. They shined their lights on it. Someone . . . someone was moving inside, trying to get out. And there was still that screaming."

Her fists clenched. Her eyes slid toward him. He glanced her way at the same time, and for the briefest of moments their gazes met. His expression was impossible to read.

Get it out there. All of it.

He was watching the road again. Her eyes stayed glued to his face. She took a steadying breath.

"There was this small burst of flame. Just a little *poof.* About the size of a tiki torch, or something like that. It burned for a couple of seconds — I watched it. And then the whole car just exploded into flames." Her heart clutched as she remembered. "Everybody was still inside. The people with the flashlights didn't even try to get anybody out. They stood there and watched it burn. The screaming . . . it got worse, and then it stopped." By then, she was having so much trouble getting the words out through her dry throat that her voice was scarcely more than a hoarse whisper. "I'm almost sure it was a woman screaming. I'm almost sure it was Mrs. Cooper I heard."

A violent shudder wracked her. The others had burned alive. That was the knowledge that she had to share, that was the knowledge that she couldn't live with. The horror of it made her sick, made her want to vomit, made her want to push it out of her mind forever and never think of it again. Everything seemed to spin. Dropping her head back against the headrest, she closed her eyes, wrapped her arms around herself for warmth, and breathed.

In, out. In, out. Slow and steady, not too deep.

"Okay, hang on." The car seemed to slow, and then there was a bump, and then they rolled forward for a minute before stopping altogether.

Jess opened her eyes. She was still nauseated, still light-headed, still haunted by the images she couldn't shake. Bright light bathed the inside of the vehicle now, and she saw they were at a McDonald's. In the drive-thru line, to be precise. Just as she made the connection, a tinny voice came over the intercom asking to take their order.

"You drink coffee?" Ryan asked.

Jess nodded.

"Two large coffees. Cream and lots of sugar." He glanced at Jess again. "You had supper?"

Jess shook her head.

"You like hamburgers? Big Macs? What?"

Actually, she wasn't a real big fan of McDonald's. But she felt so bad, so weak and shaky and drained, that she was willing to try anything that might make her feel a little more normal.

"A hamburger," she said. "Plain."

He repeated her order into the intercom, added a Big Mac and two large fries, and rolled on around to the pick-up window. Moments later a white bag was passed through the driver's-side window, along with two coffees in foam cups.

He didn't stop, just took the food and pulled back onto the road, and Jess was glad. Everything around the McDonald's was closed, and even though the surrounding parking lots and businesses had their night lighting on, she still felt exposed. Somebody could be following them. Somebody could be watching them. Somebody could be just waiting for a chance.

To do what? To kill her, Jess thought, and shivered.

Clearly hungry, Ryan ate while he drove, taking big bites out of his sandwich and shoveling in fries by the bunch. Jess couldn't choke down more than a couple of bites of her hamburger and she flat-out couldn't stomach the fries, but the coffee helped. She was still nursing it, savoring each hot, sweet sip, when he finished his meal, passed her the trash so that she could stuff it down in

the bag with her own, then shot her an assessing look.

"Better?" he asked.

"Better," she agreed.

"You feel like talking any more?"

Actually, she didn't. She never wanted to
speak of it again. She never wanted to think
about it again. She just wanted it all to go
away.

Not gonna happen.

She faced the bitter truth. And she looked
out at the road unspooling before them, at
the rolling hills and fields that were cloaked
in darkness now, and tried not to remember
the last time she had driven this way.

"I guess," she said.

"You were pretty woozy when I found you
on that hillside, you know. Are you sure you
actually saw everything you just described
to me? I'm asking if you're positive it really
happened, or if there's any possibility that
you could have imagined or dreamed some
of it?"

Suddenly the few bites of hamburger Jess
had managed to get down felt like billiard
balls in her stomach.

"Like the attack in the hospital, you
mean?" Sarcasm laced the question.

He didn't so much as twitch an eyelash.
"Yeah, like that."

Jess let it go for the moment. "I can't be totally sure, of course, because I was in a terrible accident and I did get knocked unconscious." She reasoned it out for him just as she had for herself when the memories had first come flooding back, and she had hoped and prayed they *were* just a really bad dream. "But I am as certain as it is possible to be that they're real."

"You think that the car you were riding in was struck by something unspecified and forced off the road, and then unknown subjects with flashlights, presumably from the car behind you, ran down the hillside past you, surrounded the crashed car with at least one screaming survivor still inside it, and either set it on fire or watched it burn without doing anything to help?"

Jess clenched her fists and tried not to let the memories in again. "Yes. That's exactly what I think."

"Then you were attacked later that same night in the hospital by someone who presumably had not realized you had been thrown clear of the car at the time and wanted to silence the only living witness to the murder of the First Lady?"

"Yes," she said again. Then she took a deep breath and looked at him steadily. "You were lying about the tests on the IV equipment coming back negative, weren't you?"

"Nah."

Jess felt herself tensing. "I know I did not imagine that. I —"

"Hold on a minute." He glanced at her. "I did not lie. I told you the truth. But what I didn't tell you was that the equipment tested negative for everything except standard saline solution. None of the medications that should have been in there according to your chart were there. Which means that either the tests were wrong or somebody switched the bags."

Jess felt a thrill of horror at having her suspicions confirmed, followed by a rush of indignation.

"So you knew I was telling the truth. You knew somebody attacked me. Is that why you were following me?"

He didn't reply. They had reached Dale City by that time, and traffic had picked up again. She allowed him a few minutes of concentration time as he drove past exits for the Potomac Hills Mall, which Jess knew from her own personal shopping experiences was the second-largest outlet mall in northern Virginia, and the Waterworks Water Park. But when they pulled off onto the exit for Clearbrook, stopped at an intersection that boasted a 7-Eleven and a liquor store, then turned onto a two-lane road devoid of traffic and he still didn't answer, she narrowed her eyes at him.

"That's why you followed me to Davenport's office, isn't it? Because you knew I'd told the truth about what had happened in the hospital." The headlights swept over a strip of golden, waist-high grass. Ahead the road gleamed pale, curving away into the night.

He glanced her way. He still looked abstracted, as though he was having a hard time leaving behind whatever thoughts occupied him.

"I followed you as a precaution," he said at last. "Just to make sure you were all right."

Before she could reply he hit the brakes, pausing briefly before continuing through an intersection onto a narrow asphalt lane. It was only then, as the tires swooshed over the smooth ebony surface and her attention shifted to her surroundings, that Jess realized they had well and truly left Dale City behind. Thanks to the still-falling rain, the night was dark as pitch. Woods crowded in close, and the headlights flashed past what seemed like an endless stockade of enormous trees on both sides. She was just opening her mouth to ask where they were when he turned into a driveway and a two-story house came into view. It was a clapboard farmhouse, painted dark gray with white trim. It had an outbuilding off to the side.

His house. Of course, this had to be his house.

There was not a single light on in the place.

It occurred to her that, aside from the RAV4's headlights, there was not a single light in sight.

This was not a neighborhood. There were no other houses around, no other buildings of any description that she could see. Just dark, dark, and more dark.

Apprehension tightened her muscles. Her pulse quickened. She sat up a little straighter, looking all around.

"Is this your . . . ?" she was asking just for clarification as he braked in the small paved area to the right of the house. That was as far as she got because, just as he slid the transmission into park and killed the headlights, she caught a glimpse of two tall figures stepping out from behind the outbuilding and moving swiftly toward them.

That was when she quit talking, because fear closed her throat.

17

"Yo," Mark called out to Wendell and Fielding as he stepped out of the SUV. They replied in kind. Mark immediately started breathing easier. With what had gone down with Davenport and his secretary, it was clear that the situation was out of control. At least, out of his control. He had no doubt that somebody was pulling the strings. He just wasn't sure who it was yet, or exactly what was going on. And while he found out, he meant to do what he had to do to keep Jess alive and well. Thus he'd texted Fielding as soon as he had put Jess in the RAV4 and before he had gotten in himself, and told him to round up Wendell and Matthews and meet him at his house. They were pulling bodyguard duty for the next few hours, or until he figured something else out, whichever came first.

If Davenport had been coerced by some means or another to first kill Jess and then commit suicide, as Mark suspected, and his secretary had then been run down by a vehicle that, he was almost certain, would turn out to be stolen, then the safest thing was to assume he was dealing with a sophisticated assassin or team of assassins operating under a scorched-earth policy.

One who either had orchestrated the murder of the First Lady, as Jess suspected, or was pulling cleanup duty in the aftermath of her death. Either way, it didn't bode well for Jess.

The thing that was proving the biggest obstacle for him in believing that the First Lady was murdered was motive. Annette Cooper's drug addiction was a problem but not a killing one. First, the President and his people had already put a plan in place to handle it. Second, no one outside a tight little circle knew about it. Third, other politicians and their spouses had confessed to various drug-related problems in the past, and the fall-out had not been catastrophic. In fact, in the case of spouses in particular, it had even made them seem more sympathetic to the public.

If the First Lady had been murdered, there had to be another reason, a motive he was missing or knew nothing about. Alternatively, the whole thing, from Annette Cooper's fleeing the White House to her death to the purported attack on Jess in the hospital to Davenport's attempt to kill Jess and subsequent suicide to what happened to Marian Young, was all a series of unfortunate events that had occurred one after the other like falling dominoes. Connected but not premeditated, as it were. Kind of like a butterfly's wings causing a hurricane halfway around the world.

Yeah, Mark concluded reluctantly, and he believed in Santa Claus, too.

"That the survivor?" Meeting him at the front of the car, Wendell nodded toward Jess, who appeared as just a small, dark shape huddled in his front passenger seat.

"Yeah." Mark walked around the car and opened her door. He meant to reach in for her, but she was already sliding her legs out. The rain had lightened up, and the cold sprinkle that was currently falling was barely heavy enough to be felt. He ignored it, and apparently she was planning to as well, because she made no effort to shield her head from the drizzle as it emerged next.

"I take it you know these people."

It was too dark to see her expression, but her voice had an edge to it. Having strangers pop up unexpectedly had probably scared her.

"Yeah. I guess I should have given you a heads-up."

"That would have been nice."

Her shoes — black high heels, which seemed an idiotic choice for a woman who was having trouble walking — made a gritty sound as they planted on the rough concrete of his parking area. He leaned in to help her out, but she shook her head at him.

"I can manage."

As if to prove it, she stood up, one hand holding on to the door for balance.

"Okay." He stepped back, willing to let her do her thing. Wendell and Fielding immediately closed in, providing a human barrier between her and anyone who might be out there watching.

If this was scorched earth, a sniper's bullet was always a possibility. Although he didn't mean to tell Jess that. No need to scare her unnecessarily.

"Jessica Ford," he said to Wendell and Fielding by way of an introduction. He looked at Jess. "Susan Wendell and Paul Fielding, Secret Service."

"Nice to meet you," Fielding said.

Wendell, as befitted her more taciturn nature, merely nodded. Jess nodded back. The five-eleven Wendell towered over her even in the no-nonsense flats Wendell favored. And with Fielding and himself rounding out the group, Jess made him think of a sapling in the midst of a stand of oaks.

He felt a sudden surge of protectiveness toward her. She was under his wing now, and he meant to see to it that she got out of this in one piece, whatever it took.

"Where's Matthews?" he asked.

By this time, Jess had let go of the door and was walking with slow, careful steps toward the house. Mark stayed close, ready to catch her if she needed catching. She didn't so much as glance his way. Yeah, she was ticked.

Women.

"Checking the perimeter," Fielding replied.

Mark unlocked the side door, pushed it open, and stood back for Jess to precede him into the house. There was only one small step onto the stoop, and then another into the house itself, and she managed both with no apparent difficulty. He followed her inside, flipping on the switch beside the door as he passed it so that warm yellow light suffused the kitchen from the old-fashioned fixtures overhead. Wendell and Fielding entered behind him, and he shut and locked the door.

Like all his locks, it was a good one: a

nearly unbreachable deadbolt. It was the most up-to-date thing in the kitchen. Everything else, the harvest-gold appliances, the faux-wood floor, the fruit-print wallpaper, the red-and-gold-checked curtains, was left over from the previous owner. He'd thought about remodeling it a couple of times but didn't see the need. He almost never cooked, and he was hardly ever home. Even when Taylor stayed with him, they mostly ate out.

He turned to discover Jess, with one hand leaning against the round oak table in the center of the room, looking big-eyed and pale and sort of like a half-drowned kitten as she gave comparative rottweilers Wendell and Fielding a once-over.

"So what's the plan?" she asked, her eyes sliding to meet his. He was, he realized, beginning to know her well enough to detect, beyond her annoyance at him, an edge of wariness in her expression. *Well, fair enough.* After all she'd been through over the last few days, she had every reason in the world to be wary. And Wendell, with her slicked-back blond hair, chiseled, square-jawed face, and tall, athletic figure encased in a snug black pantsuit, and Fielding, in a navy suit, his cherubic cheeks notwithstanding, were a formidable-looking pair based on size alone. Add in the fact that Wendell was standing in such a way as to reveal part of the holstered gun at her waist, and he could see why Jess might be intimidated by them.

She was a very small woman, after all. Even in her power suit and high heels, which she must have donned in honor of her meeting with Davenport, it was hard to remember that she was twenty-eight years old.

"We hole up here, get some sleep, try to work out what's going on," he told her. "The key is, we've got enough firepower now to keep you safe from whatever while we figure this thing out."

Fielding and Wendell both nodded in agreement. There was the faintest of crackles, and Wendell seemed to listen intently. Then she said something into her sleeve.

"Matthews says the perimeter is clear. He's on his way in," she announced, and Mark nodded.

"Could I talk to you, Ryan?" Jess asked, straightening away from the table.

Clearly, she meant alone.

"Sure. Make yourselves at home, guys," he said to the others, both of whom had been to his house before on social occasions and both of whom also knew exactly why they were there: to keep Jess alive. With a gesture, he indicated to Jess that she should precede him through the rectangular doorway that led into the dining room. Like the other rooms in the Victorian-era farmhouse, it was smallish and square, finding its charm in narrow mullioned windows and high ceilings. He never used the dining room, either, which was why there were cobwebs in the corners and a fine layer of dust on the table, so he followed Jess on into the living room, which was comfortably furnished with a big flat-screen TV, a big couch, and two overstuffed chairs. The curtains were drawn. The door — the front door to the house, the second of three entrances that included a door in the basement — was closed and locked. To the right, just beyond the entrance to the dining room, were stairs to the second floor.

Only the faintest amount of light from the kitchen penetrated here. Mark bent and turned on a lamp.

As the small pool of light enveloped her, Zoey, the orange tabby cat, looked up from where she had been napping in a corner of the couch, meowed a greeting, and stood up, stretching and kneading the brown leather that was ragged with her claw marks.

A few feet ahead of him, Jess jumped like

she'd been shot and whirled to face him, catching the back of the nearest recliner for balance when the sudden movement was almost too much for her.

"What . . . ?" she gasped.

Mark realized that Zoey's small sounds had spooked her, and he had to smile. He gestured at Zoey, who headed his way as usual, finally balancing on the rolled arm of the couch as she butted her head against his thigh, wanting attention.

The cat operated under the delusion that she was his.

"You have a cat?" Jess looked at him with obvious surprise.

He scratched behind Zoey's ears. True to form, the cat started purring and shredding leather at the same time. The sad thing was, when he'd bought the couch he'd paid a lot for it because he had expected it to last forever.

"She belongs to my daughter."

"You have a daughter?"

He nodded. "Taylor. She's fifteen. She's not here right now. She lives with my ex-wife in McLean. I get to keep my daughter's cat because her mother has allergies."

Or so Heather claimed. The truth was that Heather didn't want a cat in her house — a McMansion she shared with her banker third husband and Taylor — clawing her furniture and shedding on her rugs. So when soft-touch Mark hadn't had the heart to make Taylor return the kitten she'd brought home from a neighbor's one sunny Saturday two summers ago, he got sole custody. Of the cat, not the kid.

Which worked. At least it gave Taylor a reason to want to come and visit. With her busy social life, she was ducking out of their weekends more and more. Who needs a dad when you've got the mall?

For a moment Jess looked like she wanted to ask more questions. Then she frowned, straightened away from the chair, and looked past him toward the dining room.

Mark realized that she was checking to see if Wendell or Fielding were in sight.

He quit scratching the cat and immediately moved away from the couch, thus evading Zoey's attempt to climb him like a tree. Stopping just a short distance from Jess, he stuck his hands in his pockets and met her gaze. "So what did you want to talk to me about?"

Jess looked tense all over again. Reaching out, she caught his arm, pulling him closer.

"Why did you call them?"

He realized she was referring to Fielding and company. Her voice was scarcely louder than a whisper. The top of her head barely reached his shoulder, so he had to tilt his head toward her just to hear her properly.

"Because I need backup. I can protect you from a lone killer, maybe even two — as long as I'm awake. But I have to sleep. And what if there are more than two? What if they take me by surprise?" He watched her brows fold into a forbidding V above her eyes and added, "Hey, it's your ass I'm thinking of here."

"Nobody knows where we are." Even as she said it, she looked unsure. Then she looked waspish. "Or at least, they didn't until you called in the cavalry in there."

His eyes narrowed at her. "We could have been followed. I — or we — could have been caught on video somewhere in or around that building. I was keeping an eye on you while you were in the hospital, so somebody could make a good guess as to where you are from that. Let me put it to you this way: I wouldn't have brought you here unless I knew I had the personnel in place to keep you safe."

Her lips compressed. "Yeah, well, who keeps me safe from your 'personnel'?"

"What?"

"You heard me."

"That's ridiculous."

"Is it?"

There was a commotion in the kitchen. Mark frowned, glancing around, only to feel the flare-up of reflexive adrenaline caused by the sudden noise die down as he heard Matthews say, "So what's up with this chick again?"

Wendell replied — he recognized her voice — but in too low a tone for him to make out the words.

Clearly, Matthews had been admitted to the kitchen. Nothing any more alarming than that. He looked back at Jess.

She started talking at him before he could so much as get his mouth open to attempt to reassure her some more.

"Do not tell those people what I told you. About the wreck. About what I remember. Any of it." It was a low but fierce command. Her eyes — looking more green than hazel at the moment, thanks to, he supposed, some combination of the dim lighting in his living room and how mad she was — blazed up into his.

They were really pretty eyes, he registered. Feminine, flirty eyes. Or at least, they would be if they weren't glaring at him.

"I wasn't going to." His tone was mild. She was scared, and with good reason, so he wanted to be sensitive to that. "Look, you're safe here. You don't have to worry about anything. I'll take care of this."

She looked skeptical.

"Ryan?" Wendell called from the kitchen before Jess could say whatever it was she looked like she wanted to say. "We're not doing you a whole lot of good stuck here in a clump in the kitchen. We need to spread out."

She was right, he knew.

"We good?" he asked Jess.

"Oh, yeah."

She didn't mean it, which her sarcastic tone made clear. Too bad. He was taking her response at face value anyway. The bottom line was, he didn't have time for this right now. Keeping her alive was his number one priority. Keeping her happy fell further down the list.

"We're done here," he called back. "Come on in."

Jess's glare got downright ferocious.

"I don't remember anything after the car pulled away from the hotel," she hissed as footsteps headed their way. Her hand tightened on his arm. If she'd been any bigger, her grip might actually have hurt. "You got that? Nothing. That's what you tell them."

"Jess . . ."

"Got it?"

With what he considered a truly heroic effort, he managed not to roll his eyes. "Fine. I got it."

Her hand dropped away from his arm. Her expression changed as if by magic, the frown vanishing, the tension transforming itself into vaguely pleasant nothingness.

Wendell walked into the living room right on cue, followed by Matthews, who was about six-one with medium brown hair, wearing a dark suit like the rest of them. Typical Secret Service agent. Mark nodded at him, introduced him to Jess. Perfunctory greetings were exchanged.

"Do you think I could take a shower?" Jess's tone was considerably sweeter now as she looked at him. "And maybe get some dry clothes?"

He remembered that she was wet. And had been shivering. And had had a hell of a bad day. All things considered, she was hanging in pretty well. Actually, damned well.

"There's a bathroom and bedroom upstairs you can use," he told her, even as he watched Matthews go over and test the front door, then push the curtain aside to take a peek out the window.

Wendell settled down in one of the chairs, her eyes on Jess as she headed for the stairs.

Jess's back, which was turned to them, was ramrod straight. Her head was held high. She walked slowly, but her gait was surprisingly steady under the circumstances. He was guessing that it cost her to keep it that way.

"You have an alarm system?" Matthews turned away from the window, attracting his attention. Mark caught just a glimpse of the obsidian blackness beyond the glass. At just after eleven p.m., there was still a lot of night to go. A lot of hours in which anything could happen. The thought made him antsy.

"No," he answered.

"That would be us." Wendell's voice was dry.

"Any other means of egress?" Matthews asked.

"Basement door."

Matthews said something back, but Mark missed it, following Jess with his body as well as his eyes now over to the stairs, which were narrow and steep. Mark came up behind her as she paused with one hand on the newel post before attempting the ascent.

"Want some help?" he asked in her ear.

She shook her head, didn't give him so much as a glance. "Nope."

Okay, she was clearly still feeling waspish. Squaring her shoulders, she started to climb. Mark stayed where he was in case he was needed, watching her plant one foot after the other on the treads with steely determination. The effort it cost her was apparent in her tight grip on the handrail and her slight hesitation between each step. His instinct was to run up behind her, pick her up despite what he was sure would be her protests, and carry her to the top of the steps, but he resisted. She would be angry. And embarrassed. While he didn't mind making her angry — she was cute when she was angry — he didn't like the idea of embarrassing her in front of the others.

But his eyes never left her.

Despite the business-like suit, she looked delicate. Fragile even.

Narrow shoulders, tiny waist, slim calves above the idiotic high heels.

The thing that struck him most though, hit him as kind of a revelation.

She had a nice ass.

High and tight and round as a basketball. With just enough of a feminine sway as she climbed the stairs to really catch his attention.

Sexy.

That was the thought that was ping-ponging through his surprised brain when Fielding walked into the room and said,

"So, Ryan, you want to give us an overview of what's happened?"

"Yeah," Mark answered, even as Jess paused and stiffened. What was going through her head was as plain as if she had turned around and yelled it at him: *Don't tell them what I told you.* Which he had no intention of doing, if for no other reason than she'd asked him not to. Anyway, he believed in erring on the side of caution. He trusted these guys, but . . .

There was always a *but.* Always.

"Bathroom's first door on the right," he called up to Jess. "You can use the bedroom beside it."

"Great. Thanks." She started moving again, still without looking at him. In female-speak, this meant he was still in the doghouse with her, as he knew from long and sometimes bitter experience with the species. "I should be down in a little while."

"Don't come back down. Go to bed. Try to sleep. Unless something changes, we're fixed here until at least morning."

"All right. Good night, then."

Mark didn't realize he was still watching her until she gained the top of the stairs and walked out of sight, still without so much as a glance over her shoulder. Then, collecting himself, he turned to find three pairs of eyes looking at him. Wendell's, at least, were bright with speculation. He wondered if she was just more observant than the others, or if there really was such a thing as feminine intuition and if he was witnessing it at work. Frowning, hoping his little mental digression on the state of Jess's posterior had not been obvious, he moved back into the center of his living room and put Jess out of his mind. With Zoey weaving in and out around his ankles, he got back to business, giving them a carefully edited account of the evening's events. They listened intently, which was what he expected. As part of the team that had been on duty that fateful Saturday night, Wendell, Fielding, and Matthews had all suffered in the backlash of the tragedy, remanded to desk duty by the director for the duration of the investigation. Above and beyond providing firepower if needed, they were thus more than ready, willing, and able to help him try to figure this thing out.

They were eager. Their careers had been damaged, too.

"Wendell, I need you to check on Marian Young's condition," he concluded, looking at her as she sprawled out in the chair. *Ladylike* was not in Wendell's vocabulary, and he kind of liked that about her.

"Will do, boss." She got to her feet, running her hands over her hair, and headed for the kitchen, presumably to make the necessary calls.

"If somebody really wants to kill her" — Fielding straightened away from the wall he'd been leaning against and jerked his head upward to indicate Jess — "she's not going to be hard to find. It's kind of an open secret in the Service that you've been keeping an eye on her."

"Fielding's got a point." Matthews rose from the couch. "This house is bound to be a target."

"That's why you're here," Mark said. "Tomorrow we'll move her. We just need to keep her safe for tonight."

"No worries, then." Fielding grinned and patted the Glock holstered at his waist. "Bring it on. I even brought an extra clip."

That was actually pretty funny, considering that Fielding was notorious for running short on ammunition during training exercises.

"Marian Young's dead," Wendell announced, returning from the kitchen. "Arrived DOA at University Hospital."

The tension immediately ratcheted up again.

■ ■ ■ ■

Just because he was a suspicious bastard at heart, Mark waited until he was alone to make a quick phone call. It was to a friend at the FBI; it was made on Wendell's phone, which he filched from her pocket when she removed her jacket and hung it in the hall closet (he didn't want to use his in case it was being monitored, and he figured Wendell wasn't likely to check her own outgoing call history anytime soon); and his request was quick and to the point: He wanted somebody to check the rear of the burned-out Lincoln for any kind of collision or other damage that might have forced it off the road.

That done, he returned the phone to Wendell's pocket. Grabbing a bottle of water out of the refrigerator, he exchanged a few words with Wendell and headed upstairs.

There was one more quick question he needed to ask Jess before she went to sleep.

18

She was shivering when she stepped into the shower, from fear and delayed reaction and God knew what else. Plus, her back ached. Her legs ached. Her head pounded. Collapsing where she stood was starting to feel like a real possibility.

Only she wasn't going to let that happen. If ever there was a time to be strong, this was it. Gritting her teeth, she turned on the taps and stepped under the spray.

What she wanted more than anything in the world was just to be able to go home. To take a shower in her own bathroom, crawl into her own bed, and pretend that none of this had ever happened.

If she could only turn the clock back to last Saturday night, she would never, ever, in a million years have picked up that phone.

But she couldn't turn back time, she had picked up that phone, and here she was.

Taking a shower in the bathroom of a

hunky Secret Service agent she wasn't even sure she could trust.

While jumping at every stray flutter of the shower curtain or unexpected sound in mortal terror that somebody might be trying to kill her again.

Besides Ryan, there were three other Secret Service agents downstairs. Which, on the face of it, might seem like a good thing. Jess was unconvinced. Maybe these three were, as Ryan seemed to think, good Secret Service agents.

And maybe they weren't.

And that didn't even factor in Secret Service agent number four, Ryan himself. *He* didn't want to kill her, she was almost sure.

So why, in that case, hadn't she told him that she suspected the Secret Service itself was involved in this?

The answer was dismally apparent: She might trust Ryan, but not enough. She still harbored that wiggly little smidgen of doubt where he was concerned. Maybe he was just pretending to help her while setting her up for something big; maybe, if he knew she suspected the Secret Service was part of what had happened, he would stop pretending and get on with the something big, which presumably would include her death.

You're paranoiding yourself out here.

She was so tired that trying to figure anything out was useless, so she quit. In an attempt to empty her mind, she deliberately focused on the here and now. The hot water helped, chasing away the shivers and calming the worst of her nerves. In fact, it felt better to Jess than anything had in ages. She stayed under the steaming cascade for a long time, washing her hair, soaping herself from head to toe, then letting the hot water run over her until the worst of the stiffness in her back and legs had washed away.

Two pain pills from the prescription that had been given to her in the hospital, which was now in a small bottle in her purse, taken before she had gotten into the shower and finally kicking in, helped, too.

When she got out at last, she wrapped herself in a threadbare orange towel from the linen closet beside the sink, wrapped another around her hair, then wiped the worst of the steam off the mirror. Having taken her contacts out pre-shower, her reflection was pleasantly blurry. Fishing her glasses out of her purse, she put them on and immediately made a face at herself as she came into focus.

Still the same old ordinary four-eyed Jess, plus a few yellowing bruises and a line of stitches above her eye.

What, had she been hoping for something different?

If she was, it was because of Ryan, and that could stop right now. She wasn't dumb enough to start fantasizing about him again, even if she did get a little thrill from just remembering what it felt like to be held against that big, strong, muscular chest in those big, strong, muscular arms.

He was holding you in his arms because somebody's trying to kill you, fool.

The thought served as a figurative slap in the face. She kicked Ryan out of her head. She needed to try to come up with a plan to survive, not moon over some hot guy.

Maybe I should just tell everything to the media and get it all out there. If everybody knew what I know, no one would have any reason to want to kill me. Would they?

Unwrapping the towel from her head, Jess turned that thought over in her mind and arrived at no definitive solution. Like everything else, the matter was best left to be mulled when she wasn't so tired. Accordingly, she put her efforts into getting ready for bed. The bathroom was clearly used frequently by a female, most likely his daughter. There was a hair dryer in the closet beside the sink and she got it out, retrieved a brush from her purse, and started blow-drying her hair. The process was short and simple, a blast of hot air here, a few twirls of the brush there, and it was done: presto, chin-length bob. Then she brushed her teeth with the travel toothbrush she always carried in her purse and some of Ryan's Crest toothpaste, applied a little cherry ChapStick, rubbed on a little lotion, rinsed out her undies, wrapped them in a towel and tucked them under her arm along with her suit to be hung in the bedroom to dry, and headed out the door.

The hall was dark. The only illumination was a yellowish glow from the living room below. She could hear people talking — the Secret Service on the job. The thought made her shiver. Fortunately, the door to the bedroom was only a yard or so to the left. Too bad she hadn't thought to leave on the light.

"Hey."

Coming unexpectedly out of the dark just as soon as she walked into the bedroom, Ryan's voice made her jump. Luckily, she recognized the deep, drawling timbre of it before her body could go into full crisis mode. She recognized him, too, in the solid long shape sprawled out on the still-made bed.

"What are you doing in here?" She glared at him, which was, of course, a waste of a good glare because he couldn't see it properly. He reached out a long arm and switched on the lamp beside the bed, revealing the boxy bedroom with the headboardless double bed pushed into the corner beside the single, heavily curtained window.

Then the glare worked.

"Waiting for you. Look, I brought you some water." He held up an unopened plastic bottle, then put it back down on the bedside table. He'd lost his jacket, and his shoes, and his white shirt had come untucked. The sleeves were rolled up almost to his elbows. "And some pj's."

He got to his feet as she eyed the new-looking pink flannel pajamas that lay across the foot of the bed. They had a high neckline and a ruffle down the front, and were covered with dancing black poodles. In tutus.

These had to be his daughter's, although they were awfully childish for a fifteen-year-old.

"I'm not sure your daughter would like me wearing her pajamas."

"Don't worry about it. She's never worn them. I bought them for her for Christmas, and she took one look and practically gagged. She made it pretty clear she'll never wear them in this lifetime."

The man was clearly clueless. His daughter's bedroom was just across the hall, and the door was open. Unlike the rest of the house, which was done in soothing if uninspired earth tones, it was painted deep purple and decorated with Day-Glo band posters taped to the wall. Having glimpsed that, and the picture on the living-room mantel of the pretty blond girl on horseback wearing jeans and a black skull-and-bones tee, Jess could see how the pink pajamas might not be quite to the teen's taste.

"Well, thank you." She stepped aside in clear indication that he was now free to leave the room.

He didn't move. "I actually had a reason for coming in here other than pj's and water."

"What?" If her tone was a little abrupt, it was because she was feeling distinctly uncomfortable. Just as she had finished taking in the full glory of the pink pajamas, it had hit her with all the force of a two-by-four between the eyes that she was wearing an orange towel. Period. A skimpy orange towel that covered all the pertinent parts but left her shoulders and most of her legs bare.

The thing was, he'd noticed. That's what had alerted her, the way his expression had changed. He had blatantly checked her out, his eyes sliding over her, while he had thought she was busy examining the pajamas. She'd caught the whole long look out of the corner of her eye. It was an entirely masculine look, an unmistakably sexy look, and her heart was beating faster as a result. Now, as their gazes met, she curled a hand around the top of the towel right where it overlapped between her breasts, just to make sure that the flimsy thing stayed where it was supposed to.

Jeez, am I blushing?

It was then, as she frowned in pure flustered self-defense at the hard, handsome face that was in such perfect focus that she could see every tiny line around his eyes and bristle in the stubble darkening his cheeks and chin, that she remembered she was wearing her glasses. That was worse by far than being caught in a towel. It was all she could do not to whip them off.

Don't be a complete idiot. This is not about you and him. It's about . . .

"Close the door," he directed in a low voice.

She couldn't help it. Her eyes widened a little on his face. Her mouth went dry, and her pulse picked up the pace. If naughty thoughts sprang instantly into her mind, it wasn't because she thought they were going to leap into bed the moment she complied. It was, rather, because the room was small and he was close and she was next to naked.

And she'd had dreams like this. Actually, too many to count.

How embarrassing is that?

"Why?"

"Because I don't want anyone else overhearing this conversation."

Okay, then. She was so near to the door that all she had to do was reach out and close it, which she did.

Suddenly, the room seemed even smaller.

"So, what?" she asked defensively, pressing the top of the towel more firmly against her chest.

"First off, Marian Young's dead. I'm sorry."

Her heart gave a sad little thump, even though the news wasn't a surprise. Jess realized she'd known it all along.

"Poor Marian. She didn't deserve that."

"Nobody deserves that." His expression changed subtly, his eyes narrowing, his mouth tightening, and Jess realized that the face she was now looking at belonged to the Fed. "I've got a question for you: Where were you going? In the car that night, you and the First Lady and the others?"

"What?" Given the change of subject, the question took her a moment to process.

"You told me that Davenport was going to call and tell you where the First Lady was going once you got in the car. Did he call? Where were you going?"

It took her a moment to remember.

"Mr. Davenport didn't call. He was drinking that night, just like he was drinking earlier, and he didn't want to deal with Mrs. Cooper. It was Marian who called. She called the driver directly, and then she called Mrs. Cooper, which made Mrs. Cooper furious, because she didn't like dealing with a secretary. She wanted to talk to Mr. Davenport. Presumably, Marian told the driver where we were going. I'm pretty sure she told Mrs. Cooper, too, because Mrs. Cooper was trying to call somebody to make sure all the arrangements had been made when she couldn't get a signal and got mad and threw her phone. But I don't know who that somebody was, and I don't know where we were going."

Ryan frowned at her for a moment, his expression thoughtful. He was so near she could have closed the distance between them in a single step.

Not that she wanted to, of course, or was even thinking about doing anything like that.

Anyway, he now appeared about as aware that she was nearly naked as he did that she was wearing glasses. Which was to say not at all.

Wallpaper, that's what she was once again. Which was probably a good thing, even though it might not feel like it at the moment.

"The First Lady never said a name?"

"Nope."

"Didn't say anything about what she planned to do when she got there?"

"Nope."

"You sure? She must have said something that would provide some kind of clue."

"Not that I can remember."

"You're not being much help here."

"I can't tell you what I don't know."

"You know, to end this thing and get you back to your normal life, we've first got to figure out what exactly is happening."

"Actually," Jess said, "I may have thought of another way to get myself out of this."

"Such as?"

"What if I went to the media? I know a reporter who works at the *Post.* What if I contacted him and told him everything I know and he published it? Or what if I went on TV and told the whole thing to the entire country? There wouldn't be any point in anyone killing me after that. Everything I know or suspect would be out in full public view."

Ryan shook his head. "Go to the press? Without any kind of proof? That would be the worst thing you could do."

"I don't see why." She put up her chin. "In fact, the more I think about it, that's just what I may do. I'm ready to end this."

He took the step needed to close the distance between them and caught her by the arm. Just like the rest of him, his hand was big. His fingers felt warm and strong curling into the soft skin just above her elbow. His grip was firm, almost hard.

She was very aware of it — and him. Whether she wanted to be or not.

"Don't even think about doing that." There was an intensity to his gaze that told her he meant every word. "If you go public with the stuff you told me, without any kind of proof to back you up, then it will be just you accusing some very dangerous people of murdering the First Lady of the United States and a bunch of other people, too. That would cause them a problem. What's the best way to take care of that problem?

Take care of you. No more witness? No more problem. Poof! The whole thing just goes away when you do."

"People would still investigate. . . ."

"They might, but you wouldn't know anything about it because you'd be dead." He must have realized that his grip on her was getting too hard, because he let go. "You do want to get out of this alive, don't you?"

The look she gave him was answer enough.

"Then just hang tight. I've got people looking into it. If we get some proof, then you can think about going public. But not until then."

"Fine."

He studied her. His expression softened fractionally. "Look, I'm handling this, okay? Everything's going to be all right."

"Are you going to pat me on the top of my head now?"

For a moment he looked surprised. Then he grinned. "I would, but you look like you might break my arm if I tried."

"Just so we're clear."

"Clear as glass. Go to bed, Jess." He walked past her, opened the door, and paused, looking back at her. "By the way, you look damned good in a towel."

Before she could react, he closed the door and was gone, leaving her heart to flutter like the poor foolish thing it was.

By the time she put on the fuzzy pink pajamas and crawled into bed, she was so tired her head was spinning, so tired she couldn't think straight.

Which was good. Because she didn't want to think at all.

Because if Ryan wasn't filling her head, worse things were: images of Davenport pointing the gun at her and firing, of the big window wall suddenly shattering so that the office was open to the night, of Davenport lying lifeless in the street below, of Marian flying up into the air.

Followed by memories of the crash itself.

Ryan wouldn't tell anyone that she had remembered. He'd promised, and anyway, he was on her side, and . . .

Annette Cooper was buried today.

Okay, enough. Jess started counting sheep, picturing the woolly little things leaping a fence in a spring-green meadow.

One little sheepie, two little sheepies . . .

The next thing she knew, she was waking up. Which meant, of course, that she had been asleep. So deeply asleep that it took her a minute to get reoriented, to recall whose bed she was sleeping in and where

302

she was.

The room was so dark that she knew where the door was only because of the thin line of light seeping beneath it. There was a clock beside the bed, the kind that glowed if you touched it, so she did. The glow happened, but the numbers were blurry. Putting on her glasses, she saw that it was four-forty-nine a.m. She'd been asleep for about five and a half hours.

She had to go to the bathroom.

Jess remembered the bottle of water she'd chugged before going to sleep and grimaced. She should have known better.

Getting up reluctantly, she headed for the bathroom without bothering to turn on the light.

The house was quiet. The upstairs was dark, while a glance down the stairs told her that below some lights were still on. The good Secret Service agents below were acting as her bodyguards, and thus had stayed awake all night to protect her. Or maybe they were sleeping in shifts.

Coming back out of the bathroom, she found herself looking toward the master bedroom at the far, dark end of the hall and wondering if Ryan was in there, asleep.

The picture that conjured up awoke a little pulse of heat deep inside her body.

You look damned good in a towel.

Just remembering him saying that made the flicker of heat get a whole lot hotter.

He . . .

Voices from below distracted her.

". . . feel like breakfast?" The voice was muffled so that she couldn't really identify the speaker, except that it wasn't Ryan. It was obvious that whoever it was had just walked into the living room, which was why she had heard only the last part of what was said.

"Kind of early for that, isn't it?" Jess thought that might be Wendell talking. It kind of sounded like a woman, but without seeing the speaker it was hard to be sure.

"It's never too early for breakfast, sugar."

Jess stopped walking, like she'd been poleaxed. She stood in the middle of the hall, with the pool of light from below ending just in front of her bare feet. Unable to help herself, she looked down the stairway toward the living room. She could see nothing but the newel post and a rectangle of wood floor at the bottom. The sudden tightness in her chest was accompanied by an awful sinking sensation in the pit of her stomach.

The roaring in her ears was so loud that if they were still talking, she couldn't hear it.

But she'd heard enough: that one word, *sugar.*

With a certainty so intense it was sickening, she knew where she had heard it before.

19

This will help you go back to sleep, sugar.

That's what the person in the too-small scrubs with the suit pants and shiny black shoes showing below them had said just moments before he tried to kill her.

She'd just heard the same endearment again, in the same voice with the same intonation.

As Jess faced the truth of that, her heart pounded so hard it felt like it was trying to beat its way out of her chest.

The person who wanted to kill her was here. He was, as she had suspected from the beginning, a Secret Service agent, one of Ryan's supposedly "good" Secret Service agents who were downstairs right now with a mandate to protect her.

The ringing in her ears subsided enough so that her hearing came back.

". . . two scrambled eggs, then. With sausage."

"If you're cooking, I'm eating. I'll have the same thing."

" 'Fraid I'm all out of sausage." That voice was Ryan's. She would recognize it anywhere. He was down there, too. With them.

One of them. He'd lied about the results of the testing on her IV bag. At least, until she had called him on it.

"You got bacon, then?"

"Should have." Ryan again. "Check the fridge and see."

There was a reply, but it was muffled so that she couldn't quite make out the words. Probably the speaker was heading for the kitchen.

Jess didn't wait to hear anything more. Moving very, very quietly, she headed back to the bedroom and shut the door. Curse the luck, it didn't have a lock.

For a long moment, she simply stood in the pitch dark with her back pressed to the door, trying to slow her breathing, trying to calm her pounding heart, processing what she'd heard while panic surged icy cold through her veins.

What do I do?

Going running to Ryan was obviously out. First, the scale had again dipped drastically in favor of not trusting him. And second, he was down there with the others.

Every instinct she possessed shrieked that she needed to get out of that house as soon as possible. Before Shiny Shoes, as she was going to call him, got a chance to try to kill her again.

Maybe they were all in on it. Even Ryan.

At the thought, she broke out in a cold sweat and her breathing grew ragged.

She didn't know. She had no way of knowing. All she knew was that she recognized that "sugar" — and that was enough.

I have to get out of here.

The thought brought another surge of panic with it.

The good news was, they all thought she was asleep. It would be an hour, maybe an hour and a half, until dawn, so she'd have darkness to cover her escape. Probably no one would even consider checking in on her before eight at the earliest. At the minimum, she had about three hours to put as much distance between herself and them as possible.

Where do I go?

Her mouth went dry as she realized she had no idea. She couldn't go back to her apartment: Even if Grace wasn't there, it was the first place anyone would look. She couldn't go to her mother's and put her family in danger. Friends and coworkers were out, too, and for the same reason: How awful would it be to visit on them the fate that seemed to befall everyone who got caught up in this?

I've got to find a place to hide out.

But where? Given everything that had happened, she had to assume that whoever this was could track her anywhere. That they *would* track her anywhere. That they would be relentless in trying to find her, and ruthless when they did.

The bottom line was that she needed to disappear. But how?

The window of darkness she would need to get away from the house unseen was rapidly shrinking. She was going to have to work out on the fly the details of what she was going to do once she was out of there.

Jess took a deep breath. First things first: She had to get dressed. She had to collect the belongings she meant to take with her. Then she had to get out of the house.

If I could get to my car . . .

She owned a gray Acura TL. It should still be in the parking garage next to her apartment. The keys were in her purse.

The car's in D.C.

Turning on a light was a bad idea. Probably everyone was inside the house. Probably they wouldn't notice. But she wasn't willing to take that chance, because the only advantages she had was that, one, they imagined she was sound asleep, and, two, they had no idea she had discovered that the person who had previously tried to kill her was in their midst.

Probably they'll be able to put some kind of all-points bulletin out on my car. Once they realize I've taken it.

There was a tiny flat flashlight attached to her key chain, the kind that's supposed to last forever. Jess remembered it, crossed to the night table where her purse rested, extracted her keys by feel, and pushed the flashlight's button.

Presto, a narrow beam of white light.

I should be able to get at least a few hundred miles away before they even know I'm missing. Then I can ditch the car, switch the license plates, something. Trade it in, maybe.

Her underwear hung from the windowsill weighted by a book. The silky nylon wasn't quite dry, but she gathered it up. Her suit was damp, too, and so was her shirt. And her shoes — she groaned when she remembered them.

Why did I have to wear heels?

There were possibly items she could use in Mark's daughter's closet, but there was no way to be sure, and she was afraid someone might hear her in there and come up to investigate. It wasn't worth the risk.

How to get to the car?

A quick check inside the closet in the room she was in came up empty. Not so much as a hanger.

Okay, then.

She got dressed as quickly as she could in her damp clothes, threw her purse over her shoulder, and, picking up her shoes so that the heels wouldn't clatter on the hardwood floor, padded barefoot over to the window. The curtains were some kind of thick slubby material lined in white, she saw as she shoved them aside. Immediately, pale moonlight flooded in through the multipaned, double-hung window. The rain had passed, which was both good and bad. Once outside, she would be able to see what she was doing without the flashlight. On the other hand, she would be easier to spot, too, if anyone happened to be looking.

Jess saw the lock, shined her flashlight on it. Surprisingly, it was bright brass and looked brand-new. Unlocking it was easy. The window itself, however, was old. The only encouraging sign was that the handles set into the bottom of the frame were, like the lock, bright new brass. Somebody had replaced the hardware in the recent past, which meant they had probably opened the window, too.

Stowing the flashlight in her purse, grasping the handles in the window frame, she pulled upward.

Please let the window open.

It did, with the most ear-splitting screech imaginable.

Her heart going wild, Jess froze with the thing only partway up, looking over her shoulder as if she expected a bad guy to pop up behind her instantly.

Did they hear?

Nothing happened. No shouts. No footsteps as someone came upstairs to check out the screech. Just the same hushed house sounds as before, plus the soft moaning of the wind outside. Through the open window, cold, damp air poured in around her, causing the curtains to billow, making her think about needing a coat. Which there was no way in hell she was going to take the time to look for.

Go. Now.

There was a screen in the window blocking her exit. Putting a cautious hand through the opening, Jess felt rather than saw it. She was afraid to use the flashlight now unless she absolutely had to. The bright beam could give her away. So she ran her

fingers over the cold roughness of the
screen, feeling it, testing it out. It was thin
wire mesh, designed to foil insects while letting air into the house. She tried to raise it.
It was stuck fast.

Cut it.

Pulling her keys from her purse, she did
just that, using her apartment key (she was
afraid of damaging her car key, because she
needed it so desperately) as a blade and
sawing through the screen from bottom
corner to bottom corner, then up on both
sides. The sound reminded her of ripping
cloth. Only if someone was right outside
would they hear.

By the time she finished, her nerves were
so on edge she felt ready to jump right out
of her skin.

Go.

The path was now clear. She had about
two feet of space between the sill and the
window frame. Given the sound it had made
the first time, she didn't dare try to raise
the window further. Taking a deep breath,
Jess stuck her head out and looked carefully
all around. It was a straight drop down, with
nothing beneath the window but grass. The
earthy scent in the aftermath of the rain was
strong. The wind blew past the house with
a soft whooshing sound, making the tops of

the nearby trees sway back and forth as if they were doing the wave. It was cold, maybe mid-forties. The bedroom was located at the back near the middle of the house, and the window looked out over a small, neat yard with some kind of patio to her right and woods encroaching on the unfenced lawn just a few feet beyond the patio's end. Her immediate goal was to make it to those woods.

I can see light from the kitchen.

Panic surged through her all over again as she spotted the square of yellowish light spilling out over the grass and realized what it was. It wasn't bright, which meant it was probably filtered through a thin curtain or something — she remembered the kitchen's unfortunate gold-and-red-checked curtains and nodded to herself — but it was definitely there.

All anybody in the kitchen would have to do is look out into the backyard . . .

They're probably in the kitchen right now. Cooking. Eating.

Jess visualized the kitchen, the placement of the table, the stove, the refrigerator. None of it was situated in such a way as to give anyone sitting, cooking, or opening the refrigerator a view of the backyard. She didn't think.

314

If she dropped straight down, she wouldn't land in the light. She would land right in the dense bank of shadows directly below. Even if they heard something and looked out, they shouldn't be able to see her. The bottom of the window was, perhaps, ten feet up. The ground beneath looked clear. If she held onto the windowsill with both hands, she would fall less than five feet. She hoped she wouldn't hurt herself, or make much noise.

Then she could run like hell.

Experimentally, Jess dropped her shoes, aiming them a little to the side so that she wouldn't land on them, and heard nothing as they hit. *Good.* Obviously the ground was soft from the rain. She had one final thought, and lightly touched the bottom of the screen's frame. It was, as she had feared, sharp and ragged enough to scratch her up pretty badly as she squeezed out.

The towel.

The orange one she had been wrapped in earlier. It now hung from the closet door-knob. Retracing her steps, she grabbed it, folded it over the ruined screen, pressed down to flatten the sharp edges as much as possible, then left it in place as a barrier between her skin and the wires.

This is as good as it's going to get.

Luckily, she was small. Hiking her skirt, throwing one leg over the windowsill and feeling the cold breath of the wind on her bare skin, she slithered out, then hung awkwardly from her hands before letting go. The towel fell with her — good thing; it was bright orange and to anyone looking at the rear of the house, it would have given her away as soon as dawn broke. She landed on her bare feet in smushy wet grass, the jolt of it shuddering through her, the towel fluttering down beside her. Her glasses were knocked askew. Shoving them back into place, she immediately went into a crouch, looking all around like a hunted small animal, heart pounding.

There were no shouts of discovery, no sounds other than the normal ones of a rural predawn. A quick glance at the lighted square on the grass, then up at the kitchen window itself, showed no change: The lights were still on in the kitchen, and as far as she could tell no one was looking out.

She reached for her shoes, picked them up, then grabbed the towel so its brightness wouldn't give her away.

Run.

Throwing herself forward, she made a dismal discovery: She couldn't. Running was beyond her.

But still she moved, lurching toward the questionable protection of the woods with an unsteady gait that sent needles of pain shooting up her spine. *Maybe I'm doing myself damage, maybe my injury's not healed enough for this. . . .* The thought brought a surge of panic with it. But what was the alternative? There was none, so she forced herself on, glancing wildly over her shoulder and all around as her bare feet sank into the icy wet grass and she clenched her teeth to keep them from chattering for fear someone might hear.

It was still night, still dark with thick, shifting shadows dancing across the ground from the clouds that played hide-and-seek with the pale sickle moon overhead. To her right she could see the parking area, Ryan's RAV4, and the outbuilding, which she could clearly tell now was a detached two-car garage. With a bicycle leaning against the side of it and another car — presumably having been used by the other agents — parked in another small paved area behind it.

Jess practically leaped into the blacker darkness at the base of the woods even as the presence of that bicycle imbedded itself in her mind. Already, her feet were so wet and cold that they were next to numb, which was probably a good thing because of the slippery leaves and sharp twigs and other debris piled beneath the trees. Small, prickly branches from the heavy under-growth scratched at her legs, and in the near distance a pair of round, golden eyes stared unblinkingly down from what had to be the lower limbs of a tree. She could hear rustling as if the owl — she hoped it was an owl — was ruffling its wings. The insect chorus was louder now that she was away from the house. The scent of wet earth was stronger. The air felt colder.

As she paused to quickly dry her feet on the towel and slip on her shoes — any protection from the cold, treacherous ground was better than none — she realized that she was shaking all over. Gritting her teeth, she tried to will the tremors away. Having finished with the towel, she dropped it and kicked leaves over it until she was as certain as it was possible to be that it would stay hidden from view once the sun came up.

Straightening, looking fearfully back at the house, she realized that her escape was tenuous at best. They could miss her at any moment. Then they would come look-ing. . . .

Her heart thundered at the thought.

318

I've got to get a plan. No way can I walk from here to my car. No way can I ride a bicycle that far. I can't steal Ryan's car. She distinctly remembered him taking the keys. *Or the other car, either. What am I going to do?*

Unless she could put miles between the people in that house and herself first, they would be on her like a pack of wolves on a doe as soon as they discovered she was gone. On her own, on foot, how far could she possibly get in just a few hours?

The answer clearly was, not to her car. Not even into D.C.

Her choices, then, came down to this: hide or find a ride.

The woods were out. They were too close. They would be searched. Jess had a hideous vision of herself running (lurching) away from pursuers following her trail with packs of baying bloodhounds. If she were caught, by whatever means, she had little doubt she would be killed. Shiny Shoes had tried it once before, and there would be nothing to stop him from trying again, and probably succeeding.

Nothing except Ryan. But she couldn't count on that. She couldn't count on him. To do so would be to risk her life.

The previous plan — which was, basically,

trust Ryan to get her out of this alive —
obviously had to be scrapped, too.

Which brought her back to the *previous*
previous plan. Go to the media. More
specifically, to the reporter she knew at the
Post. During the last year, she had dealt
with Marty Solomon on at least a dozen occasions when Davenport had met with him
to provide deep background on certain
stories, or had her call him with judicious,
client-favoring "leaks." Presented with the
scoop of a lifetime, Solomon would be
ecstatic. He would also be prepared to roll
instantly out of his warm bed and drive like
a bat out of hell to pick her up.

Did she remember his number? Jess
thought for a second, then felt a glimmer of
triumph. Yes, she did.

The back door opened. Just like that, with
no warning whatsoever. Jess jumped at the
suddenness of it, then took a couple of silent
steps back into the inky black protection of
the nearest tree as Ryan came out onto the
stoop. All she could see of him was his tall
form silhouetted by the light pouring out
around him, but she knew with no possibility of mistake who it was. She could hear
voices — whoever else was in the kitchen
talking — and as another gust of wind hit
her she could smell, just faintly, bacon. Eyes

widening, heart slamming against her ribs, Jess flattened herself against the rough bark of the tree trunk and watched as Ryan closed the door behind him and headed toward the RAV4.

He was alone.

I could run to him, tell him that the person who tried to kill me in the hospital is one of his friends in there. We could jump in the car and get out of here together. We could . . .

No.

She could not run to him, although she realized dismally that she wanted to with every fiber of her being. She realized, too, that the crush was alive and well and possibly in the process of morphing into something more.

Something dangerous, considering that Ryan had summoned to his house the person who had tried to kill her in the hospital. For the purpose, perhaps, of setting her up for another attempt on her life.

It would be stupid to assume he wasn't in on it, too.

Trusting him could cost her her life.

So she pressed closer against the tree and watched him open the door of the RAV4, watched the light inside the vehicle come on and illuminate his fair hair, his handsome face, his broad shoulders, watched him close the door again and start to walk away before clicking the lock shut over his shoulder. He was carrying something, she saw before the interior light in the car went out, something small that he could hold in one hand. Then he reached the stoop, knocked, and was let in by someone she couldn't see. The door closed and he was gone.

Alone again in the chilly darkness, still staring at the now closed door, Jess was disgusted to realize she felt totally bereft.

Get a grip.

Wasting time mooning over Ryan was nothing short of idiotic. Any one of them could go upstairs at any moment and discover that she was missing. The bedroom door didn't lock. The window was open. Figuring that she had gone out of it would not require much of a mental stretch. Then the chase would be on.

Icy prickles of fear raced over her skin at the thought.

I've got to get out of here.

She wasn't going to get far on foot. At this point, her legs were totally unreliable.

Her gaze went to the bicycle. Could she pedal? The driveway had a gentle downward slope. As far as she remembered, the road was pretty much downhill, too. Certainly there was no big hill she would have to pedal up that she could remember. Under those circumstances, yes, she thought she could.

Keeping a wary eye on the house — and mindful, too, that there might be danger from another source lurking unseen anywhere around, behind her, on the other side of the garage, crouched in any shadow or hidden behind any tree — she made her way through the woods until she was even with the garage. Then, heart pounding, she crept across the cursedly moonlit yard.

This was the most dangerous part, she realized as she reached the bicycle, which leaned in deep shadow against the garage's clapboard wall. If there was anyone at all around, anyone to see, she would be caught now. Pulling it out with clumsy haste, turning it to face down the driveway, trying to be as quiet as a little mouse, she slid her purse over the handlebars, hitched up her skirt, and hopped on, casting scared little glances around all the while. There was, simply, no place to hide.

It was a girl's bike, a ten-speed, presumably his daughter's. Taking a deep breath, knowing that anyone coming out the back door or who happened to be in the vicinity (what if one of them had gone out to check the perimeter again, for example?) would spot her instantly, she took off, her shoes slippery on the pedals as she forced her still-dodgy legs to pump as best they could.

It was enough to get her going.

There was no outcry, no rush to stop her, nothing. She rolled silently down the driveway with the crisp, rain-scented wind nipping at her cheeks and her hair flying behind her and her bare legs and hands already tingling with cold and threatening to quickly grow as numb as her feet. Her back ached. Her head throbbed. Her breathing came in short, frightened pants. Still she pedaled doggedly, hating the rattle of the chain, the whisper of the tires, battling the urge to look over her shoulder and thus possibly upset her balance. If anyone was back there, she would find out soon enough. The thought was terrifying.

Shoulder blades tensing, she leaned closer to the handlebars, half expecting to be stopped by a bullet in the back at any moment.

It didn't happen. Nothing happened. The night remained calm and cold, its peace undisturbed. The road, when she reached it, unfurled in front of her like a silver ribbon in the moonlight. On it, she discovered with a quick upsurge of fresh fear as she turned out of the driveway, she was hideously exposed. She could only pray that no one would come looking for her until she'd had time to meet up with Solomon and be whisked away.

Putting her head down, she coasted, occasionally pedaling to keep up her speed, thankful for the momentum the downward slope of the driveway had given her, concentrating on putting as much distance between herself and the house as she could.

Much as she hated to, though, as soon as she judged she had gone far enough to make immediate discovery unlikely, she braked, pulling over to the side of the road. She could not place the call she had to place while racing away. She had too much to lose if she crashed trying to juggle the phone and handlebars while keeping the bike on the road. Finding herself at the top of a gentle slope, she decided that this was the place. As she slid off the seat, straddling the bike and stretching her aching back, the woods on either side of the road suddenly seemed to close in. Darkness settled over her like an all-enveloping blanket. She felt very small, very alone. Very scared.

Aware of her surroundings with every nerve ending she possessed, pulse pounding so loud in her ears that she could barely hear the night sounds all around her, she fished her phone out of her purse, opened it, and punched in Solomon's number with shaking hands.

What if he doesn't answer? What if I get his voice mail?

The call seemed to take an inordinately long time to go through. She listened to it ringing with her heart in her throat. The glow from the phone unnerved her. It undoubtedly could be seen for a long way. Plus, she knew that using a cell phone was a risk in and of itself, that the signal could act as a tracking device, giving her position away. But she was counting on the fact that no one was looking for her yet, and by the time they started looking for her she would be so far away from here that the problem would be moot. The hard truth was that sooner or later Ryan and the others in the house were going to discover that she was gone. Then they were going to come after her. At least one, if not more of them, wanted to kill her. In her opinion, her best chance at survival lay in getting as far away as possible before they missed her. Calling Solomon and having him pick her up and drive her to her car was her best chance of making that happen.

After placing this one call, she would not

use her cell phone again. She would throw it away. She would . . .

"Jessica? Jessica Ford?"

Solomon's voice in her ear made Jess jump. Of course, her name had popped up on his caller ID. She was so rattled she hadn't thought of that. No wonder he'd answered so quickly. Right now she had to be the flavor of the month among journalists.

"Yes, Marty, it's me." Although there was no one around to hear, she kept her voice low, glancing around apprehensively. Overhead, the sky was vast and black and lightly sprinkled with stars. The woods rose up on either side of the narrow road like tall black walls. *Eerie* was a word that came to mind. *Terrifying* was another. "Listen, this is urgent. I need you to —"

"I don't fricking believe this. Where are you? Did you hear about Davenport?" he interrupted, sounding surprisingly alert considering that she must have woken him up. She pictured him, probably sitting up in bed, his bald head with its fringe of black hair shining in the light from a bedside lamp he'd switched on, thrusting his wire-rimmed glasses onto his beaky nose. He was maybe fifty, short and stocky, and she'd seen the outline of a wife-beater beneath his dress shirt on more than one occasion. He probably slept in that and — never mind. She didn't want to go there. "He killed himself last night. Jumped out his office window."

"Yes. I was there. That's why I'm calling. There's something —" she broke off, debating how much information she should give him over the phone. After all, once he had the story he would no longer need her. And every instinct she possessed screamed that she needed to get off this dark and potentially deadly road fast. What she had to do was entice him to come for her as quickly as he could. "Can you come and pick me up? Right now? I'll tell you everything then. An exclusive. About Mr. Davenport and the crash and everything. But you have to hurry."

"Baby girl, I'd come to the ends of the earth to pick you up right now." Jess could practically hear him salivating at the prospect of the story he was hoping to get. "Just give me directions."

Jess recalled the exit Ryan had taken and told him how to get there. Then she asked what kind of car he would be driving.

"A blue Saturn." He gave her the plate number: EGR-267.

"I'll be looking for it. Pull in at the 7-Eleven that's right there as you get off." It was maybe six miles from where she was at that moment, she guessed. How long did it take to bicycle six miles? She had no idea. "Park and wait. If I'm not at your car in five minutes or so, come looking for me. I'll be somewhere down a little two-lane road that's" — she tried again to recall the route she and Ryan had taken; coming up with the name of the road was impossible because she'd never known it — "to the left of the intersection. Head northeast."

"I'll find you," he promised, and she knew he would. Davenport had always said that Solomon was a pit bull in the pursuit of a story. "I can be at the 7-Eleven in, say, half an hour."

"Okay." Jess had a momentary qualm. Once he knew the story, his life might very well be in danger, too. Until it became public knowledge. Then they'd both be safe. "Marty, there's a lot going on here. Dangerous stuff. Be careful."

"I live for this shit," he said happily. "I'll be there as quick as I can."

He disconnected. Jess looked down at the still glowing phone, then turned it off and stuck it back in her purse. Time enough to throw it away once she connected with Solomon. Until then, there was no way to know if she might need to make another call. In case he didn't show, or — well, who knew.

They couldn't track her if they weren't looking for her, Jess reminded herself when her pulse started racing out of control as various horrifying scenarios of triangulating cell phones flashed through her mind. Deliberately dismissing them, she took a deep breath and climbed back on the bike again. Gripping the handlebars hard, she pushed off and started to pedal. Her legs felt weak, her back hurt like crazy, but she gritted her teeth and kept going.

Some ten minutes later, just as she was resting her aching legs, coasting as she sailed around a curve, something caused her to glance back over her shoulder. What she saw nearly caused her to run off the road.

A car was coming toward her fast, its headlights slashing through the dark like twin white laser beams.

Jess's blood ran cold.

Dear God, is it them?

20

Braking, practically falling off the bike, Jess realized she had no chance of making it to the woods. The car was coming too fast, swooping down toward her like a bird of prey, already at the top of the curve she'd just coasted around. Thank God for the tall grass! Half running, half stumbling, her heels catching in the soft ground, pushing the bike with her because she was afraid to leave it, afraid it might be spotted and give her away, she plunged into the nearly waist-high weeds, covering just a few measly yards before she realized, with a quick, terrified glance over her shoulder, that the car was almost upon her. Dropping the bike, throwing herself down in the grass, she covered her head with her arms so that the paleness of her face wouldn't give her away and peeked out as the headlights swept over the wheat-colored grass, over her, just a flash and then they moved on. The car itself —

the RAV4, Jess was almost sure — followed with a whoosh of tires. Then it was gone.

Jess wasn't aware she was holding her breath until she let it out. Her heart pounded so hard in her chest that she could actually feel it beating against her ribs. Her stomach had knotted tight.

It's okay. The car's gone.

Taking a deep breath in an effort to calm herself, trying to figure out just how far she was from the 7-Eleven — probably not more than two miles, a walkable distance if she could only walk properly — Jess realized that taking to the road again verged on suicidal. As much as she wanted to believe that the vehicle that had just passed wasn't the RAV4, she couldn't. The only smart thing to do was assume she had been missed far sooner than she had expected and they were now looking for her.

Oh God, what do I —

Jess never finished the thought. She was still staring dry-mouthed down the road after the SUV when she saw the red flash of its brake lights.

She froze.

The thing was stopping — turning, a wide, fast U-turn, its headlights sweeping the woods — and coming back.

Coming back for what?

Jess was horribly afraid she knew. Whoever was driving had seen something to tell them she was there.

What? It didn't matter.

Heart thumping, hands flattening on the cold, wet weeds on which she lay, she scrambled up into a crouch as the SUV barreled back toward her. Careful to keep below the top of the grass, bending almost double, she turned and scurried toward the woods, her shoes sliding on the slippery grass, her heels sinking in the mud, catching herself with her hands when it seemed she might fall. Wet stalks slapped her in the face. Insects rose buzzing around her. It was so dark she couldn't see anything except the pale curtain of grass directly in front of her eyes — and, in her peripheral vision, the bright blaze of headlights closing fast behind her.

A screech of brakes. The slam of a car door. Heart thundering, Jess dared a quick, hunted look back over her shoulder.

The SUV had pulled off onto the soft gravel shoulder just yards away, and was now stopped with its headlights still slicing through the dark, pointing back the way it had come. A man walked around the hood, a tall man, moving fast. The headlights gave her a glimpse of black dress pants and a blue shirt with the sleeves rolled up.

"Jess!"

Oh, God, she'd known it was Ryan as soon as she'd seen the car. Sucking in a quick gulp of air, she dropped to her knees, afraid that the movement of the grass as she plunged through it would give her away.

"Jess!"

Cringing, making herself as small as possible, she turned just enough so that she could watch him easily and then held very still, like a rabbit in the presence of a dog. What did he want with her? Her stupid heart urged her to run to him, to trust him, but her head told her she dared not. If she was wrong about him, it could cost her her life.

A small circle of white light appeared out of nowhere like an unblinking eye. A flashlight. He was holding it, looking around, scanning the area where she had left the road. How was he able to pinpoint it so precisely? She didn't know. It didn't matter. Somehow it seemed he just knew.

A moment later, her heart leaped into her throat as she realized he'd found the bicycle.

"Goddamn it, Jess! Answer me!" It was a roar that seemed to echo off the trees. He looked up again, scanning the darkness, the flashlight beam skimming the feathery tops of the grass. "Jess!"

The flashlight lowered, circled, paused, then moved in her direction with uncanny accuracy. Jess realized to her horror that he was following the trail she'd left through the grass. He would find her in a matter of minutes. If she ran, he would catch her. He was bigger and stronger and faster and in her present state she had no hope, no prayer, of getting away.

Plus, he had a gun.

At the thought, she broke out into a cold sweat.

Maybe you can trust him. . . .

"Jess!" He headed toward her unerringly, the flashlight beam leading the way. Her pulse thundered in her ears. Her chest tightened.

He's done everything he can to keep you alive so far. . . .

He was still coming and was now just a few yards away. She could hear the crunch of grass beneath his feet above the pounding in her ears.

"Ryan? Is that you?" She stood up on rubbery legs.

"Jess?"

He closed the distance between them in two long strides, caught her elbows, and pulled her against him, wrapping her tightly in his arms, hugging her close. She allowed herself to rest against him because there was no other choice, then found herself taking momentary insane comfort in the solid warmth of his body, in the muscular strength of his arms around her. If she hadn't been leery about trusting him, she realized she would have been so glad to see him she would be dizzy with it. Much as she hated to acknowledge it, his arms felt right around her. Despite everything, she discovered that in them was just exactly where she wanted to be.

"You scared the absolute shit out of me! Are you all right?"

Her heart still pounded like a trapped bird's. Her cheek nestled into his wide chest and her arms circled his firm waist while her mind raced a mile a minute, trying to decide what to do. His gun was in its holster at his waist; she could feel the hard protrusion of it hidden beneath his shirt. Comforting — or scary? She breathed in the scent of him — powder fresh, a hint of musk — as she realized that choice had been taken from her. Since she had no reasonable hope of getting away, she had to trust him . . . or at least pretend to.

God, she wanted to be able to trust him.

"Where are your friends?" she asked, her

voice only slightly unsteady.

Grasping her upper arms, Ryan pushed her away from him a little and looked down at her. If she hadn't been wearing her heels he would have towered over her, and she still had to tilt her head back to see up into his face. She couldn't read his expression: The night was too dark. She doubted that he was having any more success with hers.

"Where do you think? Out looking for you." There was a definite edge to his voice. "Wendell went upstairs to take a shower and felt cold air blowing out from under your door. She checked on you, and guess what? The window was open. You were gone. I take it you left voluntarily? Nobody dragged you out by your hair or anything?"

"Could we talk about this somewhere else, please?" He was alone in the car, she was almost positive. Still, she was having hideous visions of one of the others showing up at any second. Driving away in his car with him felt a whole lot safer than standing here in the great outdoors waiting for that to happen.

"That's probably the best idea you've had all night."

Grabbing her hand, he started walking back toward the RAV4. Considering that her legs felt about as sturdy as rubber bands and her back ached like a sore tooth and she was so tired she felt wilted, keeping up was hard to do.

"You okay?" He glanced back as she stumbled.

"Yeah. They're not, like, right behind you or anything, are they?" She kept walking even though it required a major effort of will, looking back up the road for any sign of another vehicle.

His grip on her hand tightened. "Something about that make you nervous?"

"I don't trust them."

"Is that why you . . . ? Never mind. We'll have this conversation in a minute. Get in the car."

They had reached the SUV by that time. He opened the passenger-side door and watched her sink into the seat with more relief than she hoped showed. She hurt in places she hadn't known she could hurt.

"Stay put." He shut the door on her. Shivering from some combination of cold and nerves, Jess cast a quick glance at the ignition — no keys. Not that she had expected to get that lucky. Would she really have driven away and left him there beside the road anyway? She didn't even have to think about that: Yes, she would.

Her life was on the line here. And just

whose side he was on was still very much up in the air. The question was, how much did she tell him when he got back in the car? If she went with the truth, the whole truth, told him how deeply she felt the Secret Service was implicated in this, would he openly turn into the bad guy she feared he secretly might be?

The interior light flashed on as he opened the back cargo door, making her jump. He lifted the bicycle inside and closed it again. A moment later the driver's-side door opened and he slid in beside her, tossing her purse into her lap. By the car's interior light, she could see that he was looking tired, stubbly, and decidedly grumpy. Angry, even.

"Thanks."

"So talk." He gave her an assessing look as he closed the door and thrust the key into the ignition.

"Like I said, I don't trust your friends."

"I kind of gathered that."

It was once again dark inside the car. That didn't stop her from admiring the clean, classical lines of his profile. She was just like her mother, she realized dismally: a fool for good-looking men. Getting a glimpse of herself in the sideview mirror, she was reminded that she was still wearing her glasses. *Well, so be it.*

"You didn't tell them what I told you?" Not that she supposed it mattered now. At least one of them clearly already wanted to kill her, and giving him an additional motive wouldn't make her any more dead. Ryan shot an unsmiling glance at her.

"Did you think I would?"

"I wasn't sure."

Hesitating, Jess thought frantically. Should she tell him the rest? Of course, if he was a bad guy, she had already talked way too much and he already knew enough about what she knew to seal her fate. But she felt the opposite of threatened by him. In fact, she realized that somewhere deep inside, she was glad he had found her. Whether it was foolish or not, she *felt* safe with him.

"Good to know." There was a definite edge to his voice. The RAV4 had already pulled back onto the pavement and was starting to pick up speed as it headed back around the curve. With another glance at her, he turned on the heat and cranked it up, and she realized he must have noticed the fine tremors that shook her. "So, you want to tell me what you were thinking to do something as stupid as climbing out a window and deliberately running away from a protected environment?"

"Just so you know, I wasn't feeling all that protected."

"You think you're safer out here? On your own? You've got to be nuts." He sounded like his patience was wearing thin. "Just for the record, I about had a heart attack when Wendell told me you were missing. You know why? Because there may very well be a killer out here somewhere who's just waiting his chance to take you out. If you're right about the First Lady's death, then you know what that makes you? The only thing standing in the way of somebody getting away with it." He glanced at her. It was too dark to see his expression, but his tone left no doubt that he was getting angrier by the minute. "Jesus, I thought somebody had gotten to you."

He was driving too fast, handling the car like a weapon. The distance that she had covered on the bicycle was, she realized as the tires ate it up, really ridiculously short. Her heart started to speed up as they passed the place where she had made the phone call to Solomon. Another few minutes and Ryan's driveway would come into view.

She wrapped her arms around herself in an effort to banish the shivering, and saw his mouth tighten. Maybe she was making a mistake, but she was going to go with her

gut and trust him. He'd had ample opportunity, after all, and she wasn't dead yet.
And he'd cranked the heat. You didn't crank
the heat for a woman you were preparing to
kill. She thought.

"Okay, you want to know why I went out
the window? Because I think one of the
agents you brought in might be the person
who attacked me in the hospital."

"What?" He cast an incredulous glance at
her. A shaft of moonlight spilling in through
the car window allowed her to see that he
was frowning, disbelieving, and, yes, angry
— but not suddenly self-conscious or guilty-
looking, as she would have expected him to
be if he had some kind of prior knowledge
that what she was telling him was the truth.

The hard knot in her stomach relaxed a
little. The shivers started to ease. Trusting
him just might have been the right thing to
do.

"I'll tell you the whole story, but you've
got to turn around first. I can't go back to
your house."

"You're not serious."

"Turn around."

There was a moment of silence during
which Jess could feel the issue hanging in
the balance. Then, thank God, he braked,
turning the car around in another wide

U-turn so that the tires crunched on the gravel berm. His driveway couldn't have been more than a few minutes ahead.

She let out a sigh of relief.

"Okay, cut the crap." He was still driving too fast, but at least it was in the right direction. This time Jess was thankful for the speed that ate up the distance. "Why would you think something like that?"

"Because in the hospital, just as he started to put whatever was in that needle in my IV line, the person who attacked me said, 'This will help you to go back to sleep, sugar.' And tonight I heard that same voice say 'sugar' again. I woke up, had to go to the bathroom, and when I came out I was standing at the top of the stairs and heard him downstairs saying something like 'It's not too early for breakfast, sugar.' "

"You heard a *man* saying that? We're talking Fielding or Matthews here?"

"I'm not clear on the names. It was somebody who was downstairs in your house about twenty minutes ago. And I'm almost positive it was a man."

"I didn't hear anybody say anything like that. Of course, I wasn't with them all the time."

"I know what I heard." Her tone dared him to doubt her.

"Fielding or Matthews, then." He paused, seeming to think it over, then shook his head. "That's not possible."

"What do you mean it's not possible? It's *true*."

"Do you know how many guys go around calling women 'sugar'?"

"It was exactly the same. Same voice, same intonation. What, do you think I'm imagining things again?" She put some bite into her voice on that last.

They had passed the place where she'd hidden from him now and were swooping on down in the direction of the 7-Eleven. Jess spared a passing thought for Solomon, who was undoubtedly barreling in their direction at that very moment. She still meant to give him his exclusive, although she was sure that Ryan was going to hit the roof when he found out she'd called a reporter despite his warning. Still, she had to rely on her own best judgment, and going public was the only thing she could think of that might have any chance of making this whole thing just go away. But maybe, after talking to Solomon, she would stay with Ryan until she felt safe again.

If he would let her, that is.

"If you believed that, why the hell didn't you come tell me?"

"Oh, I don't know, maybe because you were downstairs with the person I heard saying 'sugar' and you're a Secret Service agent, too?"

"You thought it was a better idea to jump out a window and run away into the dark?"

"I was kind of short on options."

"You should have come to me." They were rounding another bend, and Jess saw, just faintly, the lights of I-95 glimmering in the distance. Soon they would be off the dark country road and heading toward — where? Time to work that out when she'd convinced him of this. "You know, I've known those three back there for years. They're good people."

"One of them isn't." Jess realized she was no longer shivering. The heat was working — and so was the idea, however wrongheaded it might be, that she was safe with him. "Why are you having such a hard time believing me?"

"There's never been a traitor in the Secret Service. Never."

"So this is something new. Get your mind around it. I'm telling the truth."

"I'm not saying you're not. I'm just saying that maybe you're mistaken. If one of those guys tried to kill you in the hospital, the reason would have to be to perpetuate some kind of cover-up of the First Lady's death, which means they would have to be involved in that. I don't buy it. I can't."

To Jess's ears, it sounded like he was trying to convince himself.

"There's something else," she said. "After the crash, those people I told you about who went rushing down past me with flashlights? The ones who surrounded the car and either set it on fire or watched it burn?"

"Yeah?"

"I think they were Secret Service agents, too."

Dead silence greeted that. Jess looked at him, trying to read his expression in the shifting darkness. All she could see was his profile, and all of a sudden it looked like it had been carved from stone.

"Why would you think — ?"

Jess jumped as the "William Tell Overture" blared out of nowhere, interrupting. It took her a moment — and the sight of him digging his cell phone out of his pants pocket — to realize that it was his ringtone. It seemed to her that after looking at the caller ID he hesitated for a moment before he flipped the thing open and pressed the connect button.

"Yeah?" he said into the phone.

"You got your problem fixed yet?" The

voice on the other end belonged to a man. It was faint and crackly and unknown to her, but Jess could hear every word.

"Taken care of."

"You found her?"

"Yeah."

"She with you now?"

"Yeah."

Jess didn't need the glance Ryan slanted at her to realize that she was the topic of conversation. She stiffened, watching him intently. From the brevity of his responses, Jess gathered that he didn't realize she could hear both sides of the conversation.

The voice continued. "She's been talking. To a reporter."

Jess went cold with horror. How could anyone know that?

"I don't think so," Ryan replied. They were nosing into a sharp curve, and Ryan tapped the brakes, slowing the car. Now she could almost see the individual trunks of the tall pines as they whipped past the window. Pale gray moonlight filtered in through the windshield, dappling the interior of the car. The changing light made him look like a stranger.

"It's true. He's on his way to meet with her now."

The look Ryan directed at Jess was sharp.

"What?"

"Yep. There's more going on here than you know. It stinks, but we've got to take care of this."

"I am taking care of it."

There was a stop sign at the bottom of the curve. She remembered it now: Stop at that sign, cross an intersection, and then they were on the road that led to I-95 and the 7-Eleven.

The voice crackled again. "She can't talk to any reporters."

Another glance came her way from Ryan, this one unmistakably grim. "She won't. You have my word."

Jess thought she heard a sigh through the phone. "I'm afraid that's not good enough anymore. Why don't you go on and take her back to your house? I'll meet you there."

"How do you know I'm not at my house?" Ryan's voice suddenly had an edge to it.

There was the briefest of pauses. "I think you know the answer to that. You've always been a team player, Ryan. We appreciate it, too. Don't think we don't. And we'll remember this."

Jess watched Ryan's hand tighten on the phone.

"You have anything to do with what happened to Davenport and his secretary?" His tone had an ugly undernote now.

Jess couldn't help it. Her eyes widened on his face. She could feel her heart slamming against her rib cage. Her palms turned clammy and she wiped them on her skirt in response. They were almost at the stop sign, she saw out of the corner of her eye. The RAV4 was slowing down.

"No. Hell, no. Look, just bring the woman back to your house. I'll meet you there, and we'll talk this out."

Ryan glanced her way once more. His face was in shadow again, and she couldn't read his expression at all.

Oh, God, please let me be able to trust him. She was suddenly terrified that she'd made a mistake, that she couldn't, that she'd let her attraction to him cloud her judgment. Her mouth went dry at the thought.

"Yeah, okay." The ugliness was gone. He sounded perfectly normal again. "As long as we're both clear that talking is all we're going to do."

Jess took a deep breath. Her stomach plummeted clear down to her toes. She wasn't letting him take her back to his house. No way in hell. She would be killed. She was as certain of that as she was that the sun would come up in about forty-five minutes.

And Ryan was in on it. That thought was almost more horrifying than anything else.

"Absolutely." The man sounded relieved. "It'll take me maybe half an hour to get there."

"All right."

"Keep her with you. Don't let her out of your sight."

Ryan wasn't looking at her now, but the new tension she could feel emanating from him in waves spoke volumes. "You got it."

His answer struck fear into her soul. There was absolutely no emotion in his voice at all. Coupled with the suddenly fraught atmosphere in the car, that told her everything she needed to know. Swallowing, she pulled her gaze away from him to their surroundings with real effort. A four-way stop. A small slope leading to a strip of tall grass like the one she had just hidden in, leading to a strip of woods. The woods couldn't be very deep because of the road cutting through them that intersected this one in a T. Pass through the intersection, and you were on the road leading to the 7-Eleven. Solomon was waiting there, or would be soon. If she could just get to the 7-Eleven . . .

All that went through her mind in a flash as Ryan disconnected. At the same time, the RAV4 rocked to a halt at the stop sign — and she grabbed the door handle and shoved the door open.

"Jess!" Ryan grabbed at her and missed.

"Leave me alone!"

"Damn it to hell, Jess!"

This time his grab caught the tail end of her jacket. She just managed to yank it free as she catapulted from the car.

Her feet in the cursed high heels struck the gravel shoulder hard. She staggered and almost fell, barely managing to catch herself before she hit her knees. One shoe came loose, and she kicked it off, then kicked off the other to match and went plunging barefoot down the slope. Darkness immediately cloaked her, but she knew that wasn't going to be enough. Behind her the RAV4's interior light glowed yellow, lighting her path at the same time as it ruthlessly exposed her. Gravel cut into her soles. The straw-like grass was slippery underfoot and whipped around her legs. Her heart raced and adrenaline surged through her like rocket fuel as she launched herself through the waist-high grass, stumbling frantically toward the woods. Her legs felt as heavy as if she were wearing concrete boots, and she knew escaping from him was going to be all but impossible — but she had to try. The tone of the conversation had made it perfectly clear — Ryan was one of them after all. Maybe reluctantly, maybe halfheartedly, but still a team player just as the other man had said.

The hard truth was, she was a danger to them. A danger that could only be fully eliminated by her death.

Ryan had agreed to bring her back to his house. Even as she reeled at the knowledge that he was involved, that she was just as foolish as she had suspected, Jess shuddered at the thought of what they might be planning to do to her. An accident — would they want to make it look like an accident, like Marian's death? Or a suicide like Davenport? Or would they . . .

There was the smallest of sounds behind her, a funny little metallic click. It was such an insignificant sound that she didn't know what made her glance over her shoulder in an attempt to identify it.

But she did, and was just in time to watch as the RAV4 exploded with a hollow-sounding boom accompanied by a fireball the size of a house.

21

Jess whirled to face the explosion, both hands flying to cover her open mouth. For a moment she just stood there, dumbfounded, as a whoosh of heat blasted past her and a geyser of debris shot skyward. A split second later, car parts rattled down on the road and the area surrounding it, although none reached as far as where she stood frozen in the tall grass perhaps thirty feet away. The blaze completely engulfed the RAV4, lighting up the night like a giant bonfire. Black smoke billowed toward the sky. The smell of burning hit her, bringing back instant hideous memories of another burning car. . . .

"Mark!" she screamed, as the past was wiped out by a rush of brand-new horror. "Mark!"

He had been in that car.

Moving like she had never believed she would be able to move again, she raced toward it, adrenaline giving her dicey legs a strength and purpose that carried her back through the grass toward the car faster than she had run away from it. Heart thundering, pulse pounding, gasping with emotion, she watched the flames devouring the vehicle and knew already that there was nothing she could do, no help she could give.

Too late, too late, too late — the thought beat through her mind like the desperate pounding of a drum.

Scrambling up the slope, feeling the heat as intense as a furnace on her face and exposed skin, she heard the crackling of the fire, smelled burning rubber and gasoline and she refused to think what else, and saw that the asphalt on which the vehicle sat was already melting and bubbling from the intense heat of the flames.

Then she was on the road, running around the front of the RAV4 to the driver's side, her eyes stinging, her throat aching, knowing it was useless but . . .

Even as she tried to absorb the reality of the total conflagration that made any attempt at rescue both impossible and pointless, she spotted him. Her heart gave a great leap.

He wasn't in the car. He lay sprawled on his stomach on the pavement on the opposite side of the road. The leaping flames that lit up the night bathed him in a flickering orange glow so that the dark bulk of him was just visible against the glittering blacktop.

Oh, God, thank God, he'd been thrown clear.

"Mark!" She flew toward him. *Is he hurt? Is he dead?* "Mark!"

Dropping to her knees beside him, she ran her eyes over him, put her hands on his shoulders, and felt the solid, intact strength of them, slid her hand to the center of his back to see if she could detect the rise and fall of his rib cage that would indicate he was still breathing, checking the extent of his injuries as best she could by the uncertain light of the blazing fire behind them.

Please, God, please, God, please, God . . .

He groaned and rolled over, then sat up, blinking at her.

"Mark!"

Throwing her arms around him, she hugged him, pressed her face to his, kissed his warm, bristly cheek a couple of times, so glad he wasn't dead that she completely forgot everything else. One hard arm came around her, and she felt him clumsily patting her back. That brought her back to reality a little, and she let go of him, sinking back on her haunches to frown at him, her freezing toes curling into the rough pavement. He quit patting her, but his arm still curved loosely around her waist, casually intimate.

He was looking past her at the burning car, his expression as astounded as hers must have been moments earlier.

"Holy shit," he said.

"Are you hurt?" Her voice was sharp.

He frowned, then shook his head. "I don't think so. A little dazed, maybe. Jesus Christ, if you hadn't gone jumping out of the car like an idiot and I hadn't gotten out to go chasing after you, we'd both be toast right now."

That brought everything rushing back in a reorienting burst of memory. *He was going to take me back to his house to be killed.* Her widening eyes met his narrowing ones for a pregnant instant of shared knowledge, and then she pushed his arm aside and surged to her feet.

Lunging forward, he grabbed her wrist, his long fingers circling it like a manacle.

"Oh, no you don't."

She did her best to yank her arm free. "Let me go, you son-of-a . . ."

"What the hell is the matter with you, anyway?" He held on tight. "Are you *trying* to get yourself killed?"

"What, do you think I'm stupid? Do you think I'm deaf? I *heard* that phone call. I heard that man telling you to take me back to your house, and you agreeing to do it!"

Grimacing, he rolled to his feet without letting go of her wrist. "I was just agreeing with him to buy a little time. Jesus, we don't have time for this. I'm on your side, okay?"

Your side.

"You need convincing, take a look at my car. That bomb would have gotten me, too."

Bomb. That was the first time that exactly what had happened really registered with her. The RAV4 had been blown up with a *bomb.*

She stopped struggling to look at the burning husk of what had been his SUV. The fire was consuming the RAV4 at a furious clip. Hot and orange, it popped and crackled and hissed, putting out incinerator-like heat intense enough to shimmer in the air and warm the pavement beneath her feet. If either one of them had been inside, they would have been cremated by now.

"Give me your purse." Apparently feeling he had convinced her, or else figuring it just didn't matter because there wasn't any place she could run to that he couldn't catch her easily, Mark released her wrist, grabbed her purse off her arm, and opened the small zipper compartment at the side.

"What're you doing?" His action so completely surprised her that she actually felt indignation, and tried futilely to snatch her purse back without even thinking about attempting to get away.

"There's a homing device in here. How the hell do you think I found you?" He tore something from the zipper compartment and, taking a step forward, hurled it into the fire. Speechless, Jess watched the button-sized device arc into the flames. "Where's your phone?"

He was already pawing through the larger compartment.

"What? No . . ."

Too late. He tossed her phone into the fire, then followed it with his own.

"We can be tracked anywhere with those." He thrust her purse back at her. "Here. Let's go. We need to get out of here before they show up."

They. The word was even more galvanizing than the idea of a bomb. It made her heart jump.

He grabbed her hand and was pulling her across the pavement in the direction she had been going to begin with when she happened to glance past the flames up the road in the direction of his house.

What she saw sent a stab of terror through her.

Round white lights flickered through the trees, small because they were still distant but moving toward them far too quickly.

A car.

Jess stared, electrified.

Of course, it doesn't have to be them. . . .

At this time in the morning? Who are you kidding? Who else would it be?

"Headlights," she gasped, tugging on his hand and pointing. "A car's coming."

"Shit." His gaze followed hers. He was just starting down the slope while she still stood at road level close enough to the fire to feel its heat radiating through her jacket to warm the skin on her back. Plunging on, he pulled her down to the bottom of the slope with him. She barely felt the sharpness of the gravel on her cold, bare feet this time. With what she considered great presence of mind, she grabbed her shoes as she passed them. The heels were a problem, but she had already figured out the hard way that bare feet were worse. "Come on."

At the bottom she stumbled and would have fallen to her knees if he hadn't caught her. Making an impatient sound, he snatched her up in his arms and bolted toward the woods with her.

"You don't have to carry me."

"Baby, I want to live."

Okay, he had a point. Clearly, in this moment of emergency, he was going to be far faster at getting them both out of the reach of danger than if she tried to run on her own. Her shoes were useless, and the ground was tearing up her feet. Her legs already ached from her previous efforts, and her lower back throbbed. She spared a momentary longing thought for the pain pills in her purse, but there was no time. Tucking her shoes in close to his body, balancing her purse on her stomach, Jess gave in to expediency, twining her arms around his neck and curling close to his chest and hanging on for dear life, watching dry-mouthed over his shoulder as the approaching headlights closed in.

He was just bounding from the grass into the deeper darkness of the woods as the headlights slowed and then stopped a few yards behind the burning car.

An icy shiver of fear shot up her spine.

"Mark." It was an urgent whisper delivered almost into his ear. She could just see the denser outline of his profile against the backdrop of tree trunks and hanging vines. Glancing back, she saw a quick flash of light as the interior light came on, but then as he kept going more trees obscured her view before she could see anything else, like someone emerging from the stopped vehicle, which she guessed was what was happening. "There they are. At the car."

The tangle of undergrowth beneath the trees had caused him to slow down. He was no longer running but, rather, forcing a path through prickly branches that reached as high as her bent legs and hanging vines that occasionally smacked her face like cold, damp hands. The earthy smell of vegetation gone wild was strong. Here in the trees, the insect chorus was loud enough to all but block out the now-distant roar of the fire. Holding her higher against his chest in a near-futile attempt to protect her from the scratchy things all around them, turning to maneuver through a particularly dense patch of undergrowth, he cast a quick look back, but he didn't stop, or even slow down. He couldn't see anything anyway, she realized as she followed his gaze, except two frosty white beams of light pointing toward the bright orange glow that had been his SUV.

"If we're lucky, for the next fifteen minutes or so they'll think we're inside the car."

"What happens if we're not lucky?"

"They'll come looking sooner."

Jess's stomach knotted. She took a deep breath to try to stay calm.

Plan. Plan. What's the plan? Aha, she had one.

"Whoever you were talking to on the phone was right: I did call a reporter. Marty Solomon from the *Post*. I'm supposed to meet him at the 7-Eleven just up the road. He should be there now. If we can get to him before . . ."

She let her voice trail off, because the "before" was obvious. Before they were caught.

"Didn't I tell you going to the press was a bad idea?" He was starting to sound breathless. She could feel his body growing progressively warmer through the thin cotton of his shirt. Good thing the guy was muscular, because no matter how petite she was, she was still a solid armful under the circumstances. Her calves began to cramp, and she unobtrusively tried to stretch. "I bet you used your own phone, didn't you?"

"I sure wasn't going to use the phone in your house."

"Well, guess what? Your calls were being monitored. When you called this reporter, somebody was listening in. They heard every word you said."

"And you knew about this?" Jess's voice,

though still scarcely louder than a whisper, went shrill with indignation.

He didn't answer. Instead, his mouth twisted. And that, for her, was answer enough.

"You did. You knew!"

"Yeah, I knew."

"You put a tracking device in my purse! You knew they were listening to my phone calls! You lied about the results of the IV testing! You agreed to take me back to your house where you know as well as I do I was going to be killed! And I'm supposed to believe you're on my side?"

"In case it's escaped your notice, I'm also lugging your ass through a fucking jungle and my car just got blown up with me almost inside it. I think you're pretty safe in assuming I'm trying to keep you alive."

Okay. Good point.

"Anyway, I think you're missing the important thing here," he continued. "That being that if you made the arrangements to meet your reporter friend at the 7-Eleven on your cell phone, anybody listening in heard that, and if they have half a brain they'll guess that's where we're headed."

Jess felt her stomach tighten.

"I did," she said in a small voice.

"Figured." He sounded more disgusted

than alarmed. "The good news is, we've got a little time. Whoever's calling the shots is still hoping the bomb worked. When the people on the ground figure out it didn't, they still have to call the bad news in, and whoever's listening to your conversations has to remember about the 7-Eleven. So if the reporter's there and we're quick, we've got a shot at getting away before they put it all together."

Jess digested that.

"Who were you talking to, anyway?"

There was a pause, as if he were debating answering. "Harris Lowell."

Jess's jaw dropped. "The White House Chief of Staff?"

"That's the guy."

"Oh my God." Her world rocked on its axis. "At least tell me you believe me now about the Secret Service being involved."

"Looking that way."

"And one of your agent friends from the house attacking me in the hospital."

"That way, too."

It wasn't a ringing endorsement of everything she'd told him, but for the moment it would have to do, because just then they reached the outer edge of the woods. The terrain before them was awash in moonlight. It seemed hideously open compared to the

364

darkness and heavy cover they were leaving behind. Jess realized that she could see it all clearly: another strip of tall grass about thirty yards wide, a narrow ditch, and then the road that intersected the one the RAV4 was still burning on. On the other side of the road was more tall grass leading into more woods. The intersection was up to the left. Jess couldn't see it from where they stood. The road that led to the 7-Eleven — a continuation of the road the RAV4 was on — could be just glimpsed as a solid black strip cutting through the trees across the road.

Moonlight wasn't the reason she could see so much, Jess realized about as soon as Mark went plunging into the grass, and suddenly she had to work a little harder to breathe. Cold little curls of fear twisted through her insides. It was no longer quite as dark as it had been. The deep charcoal of night was slowly fading into a paler shade of gray. Dawn would break soon. . . .

Jess's breath caught as a terrible thought occurred.

"If they don't know it already, they'll know we're not in the car as soon as it gets light. They'll be able to see our trail through the grass."

"Yeah." Mark didn't sound like this revela-

365

tion came as a surprise. Clearly, it had already occurred to him. "As much as I think your little chat with the reporter was a bad idea in principle, that's what we're banking on now. You better pray he's there, because we're running out of time."

"What happens if he's not?" she asked, anxiety making her voice catch as he reached the ditch and, gathering himself, jumped across. She hung on, her arms tightening around his neck even as his grip tightened on her, then cast a scared glance back the way they had come. Through the trees, she realized she could still see the orange glow of the fire — but not the dark outline of the car parked behind it. Should she be able to see it? Had she ever been able to see it? God, she couldn't remember.

It was difficult to draw air into her suddenly constricted lungs.

"We go to plan B." Climbing the slope, he looked both ways, then sprinted across the road.

"Plan B?" The echo was surprised out of her. She hadn't known they had one.

"Yeah." His answer was short as he leaped another ditch, then forged through more tall grass. His body was growing warmer, the soap-tinged scent she was starting to associate with him more intense.

Her reply was polite. "I'd love to know what that is."

"Would you, now?" A fleeting grin accompanied the glance he gave her. Even as tense as she was, the sight of it warmed her. This guy — Mark, and as his given name came automatically to mind she realized that the attempt she had been making to mentally keep him at arm's length by continuing to think of him by his last name had just abysmally failed — was risking his life for her. It was kind of starting to make up for the fact that he had never so much as noticed her before the crash.

"Yes, I would."

"We wing it."

Jess gave him a withering look, which she doubted that he saw.

"You know, whoever that is back there might not have stayed with the RAV4," she pointed out as they cut catty-corner through the woods and emerged at another road. This one, she realized, was the one the 7-Eleven was on. The one the RAV4 was on. They were on the other side of the intersection now. "They could be driving around looking for us. They could come this way."

"They could." His tone told her that he'd already thought of that, too. "That's why I want you to keep a look out for their headlights. We'll make better time if we take the road."

Jess's heart lodged in her throat as he leaped the ditch and took to the pavement, his shoes slapping the asphalt loudly enough to make her cringe. Could anyone hear? Only if they were close enough, she told herself, which wasn't exactly comforting. But they had worse problems. While they were in the woods, she realized, it had been growing lighter by the minute. The trail they had left in the grass wouldn't be hidden by darkness much longer. Once it was seen, the hunt would be on for real. Clearly aware, Mark was moving faster, picking up the pace, jogging down the road toward the 7-Eleven, which, she judged, was just around the next bend. She kept a wary eye on the road behind them, but it remained deserted.

So far.

But they were getting close. If she listened hard she could hear the distant hum of traffic on 95 — and a siren. Yes, she could definitely hear a siren. Make that multiple sirens. Were they heading their way?

A sudden spurt of hope leaped inside her.

"Do you hear that siren?" She didn't wait for an answer. Clearly, if she could hear it he could, too, despite his heavy breathing. "Maybe somebody called the fire department. Or the police. About the burning car. If they come, we could —"

"No, we couldn't." He cut her off, his speech a little ragged now. The gloom had faded enough so that she could see the color infusing his face and the fine sheen of sweat popping out on his forehead. But his arms around her were still sturdy and strong, and he was moving at a surprisingly fast pace. Of course, he could see that dawn was breaking, too. Heart hammering, Jess cast another searching glance back down the road. Still nothing. Which didn't mean someone couldn't already be following their path through the trees . . . "I could flash my badge and demand protection, and they would probably do their best, but the truth is they can't protect you from these guys. They're lethal. They're playing for keeps, and they're serious about making you dead. Now that they know we know they're coming after us, they're going to go at it full-throttle. Our best chance — hell, just about our only chance — is to hide until we figure out who's involved. Then we'll know who isn't, and that will be who we go to for help."

Jess felt a quick upsurge of nausea. "What if we guess wrong?"

He didn't answer, but his expression did. They would be dead.

Jess looked at the tense, determined face so close to her own. "You know, they're not really after you. They're after me. You could leave me."

He gave a derisive huff. "Babe, I'm not leaving you. No way, no how. Put the thought out of your head."

"I'm just sayin'," she said. But, reassured and more thankful than she even wanted to think about, she tightened her grip on his neck and curled a little closer into his warm chest as they rounded the bend that brought the 7-Eleven into view at last.

"Did you happen to ask your reporter friend what kind of car he would be driving?"

"A blue Saturn." They were within shouting distance of the 7-Eleven now. Screaming distance, if it came to that.

Feeling a rush of relief so strong she nearly went limp with it, Jess eagerly scanned the mix of vehicles parked in front of the store and refueling at the gas pump.

It wasn't hard. There were only four of them.

"He's not here." Ryan had just completed the same visual scan she'd been engaged in.

Having already come to the same sickening conclusion, Jess looked around again.

"He'll be here," she promised a little desperately, casting another quick, precautionary look over his shoulder as she spoke. At what she saw, a thrill of pure fear shot through her.

A car swept up the road from the intersection they had just skirted around. It was still too dark to tell a lot about it at that distance, but she could see the approaching headlights clearly through the trees.

22

"Mark. *Mark.*" Jess's stiffening like a board and stuttering his name almost in his ear gave him a split second's warning that more bad news was headed his way even before she laid it on him. "A car's coming. I think it might be them. We've got to hide."

"Shit."

Casting a quick glance back, he took off, sprinting toward the store through the shadows blanketing the edge of the parking lot. Desperate to find an alternative solution, he scanned the parking lot as he ran. A 1990s maroon Escort, a gray '05 or '06 Jetta, and a green '08 PT Cruiser were parked in front of the store, an open-twenty-four-hours type with a well-lit interior that allowed him to see customers and a single bored male clerk at the cash register inside. A white '86 Silverado pickup with a long bed sat at the gas pumps. Just sat there, no gas hose connected to it. Nobody in any of the vehicles, nobody watching anywhere as far as he could tell. In a snap decision, he looked back at the Silverado. Already making the call in his mind, he veered toward the truck even as he continued to visually check it out. A couple of ladders bungeed together and some equipment sheltered by a blue tarpaulin were stowed in the back. The black plastic bed liner was worn and scarred. Clearly a work truck.

Bingo. Just what they needed: a way out.

The other choice, which involved hiding in the woods and waiting for the reporter to show up, had just gotten a whole lot riskier. As he'd told Jess, Lowell and company knew the guy was coming to the 7-Eleven, which might be why the car, if it was indeed a pursuing vehicle, was heading their way. Whoever was in it — much as he hated to think it, there was a good chance it was Fielding, Wendell, or Matthews, or some combination thereof — would park and wait for Jess and him to show up to meet the reporter. Letting Jess connect with a representative of the media was the very last thing they wanted to happen. They would stop it however they could.

Under those circumstances, the best-case scenario would be if he and Jess were nowhere in the vicinity when the reporter showed up.

"What are you *doing?*" Jess was trying to keep her cool, but her face was whiter than the truck in the purpling light of daybreak. She'd obviously expected to take shelter inside the store.

"Getting us out of here. Grab your stuff." Mark skidded to a stop at the back of the truck, cast a final searching look all around — clear — and heaved Jess, shoes, purse, and all, over the side of the bed. "Get under the tarpaulin. Fast."

"What?" She sounded stunned. The truck rocked slightly as she landed. Despite her question, Jess apparently got the idea, because as soon as he let her go she dropped out of sight. There was the smallest of clatters, as if she had dropped something, probably one of her stupid-ass shoes.

Mark sprang up himself. A foot on the bumper and a hop and then he was in, crouching low, glancing around. Just as he'd suspected, her stray shoe was almost at his feet. He grabbed it. Couldn't leave anything so obviously out of place to be found by the owner or anyone who might happen to look into the bed. The area around the pumps was relatively brightly lit, and a high-heeled shoe appearing out of nowhere was the kind of thing somebody might notice. Having already lifted the edge of the tarpaulin and currently in the process of scooting feetfirst beneath it, Jess looked at him wide-eyed. Her glasses were slightly askew, her lips were parted, her bare feet were pale against the black plastic, and the slim-cut skirt of her business-like suit was riding interestingly high on her slender, bare thighs. He was just noticing that when both of them saw the slice of headlights through the lightening gloom at the same time as a new vehicle — almost certainly the one they'd seen coming — bumped into the parking area. Mark felt his gut clench and forgot all about her skirt.

Innocents arriving by chance, his buddies from the house on a search-and-destroy mission with him and Jess as targets, or the far deadlier possibility of a team of unknown assassins on their trail: The car could contain any of the three.

"What happens if somebody looks in the truck?" Almost under cover now, Jess sounded panicky as the lights flashed over the truck bed before moving on toward the store.

"We deal."

Lips tightening at what he had to admit wasn't an especially helpful response, Jess slithered the rest of the way beneath the tarpaulin without another word.

Keeping his head low, Mark reached for his holster as he crawled to join Jess. Unsnapping his Glock, he thrust Jess's shoe at her, then shoved his legs under the tarpaulin, sliding in on his side beside her on the hard plastic so that they were lying chest-to-chest, the top of her head level with his chin, and her shoes and purse digging into his stomach. Pulling the tarpaulin over them both, breathing in the smell of paint — there were cans of house paint and various tools stored in an open plastic container behind Jess, and her back was pressed up tight against the container — he eased his pistol free. For the moment he kept it pressed against his thigh. The familiar smooth metal of the gun in his hand provided a modicum of reassurance. If push came to shove, he could shove back.

"What do you think they're doing?" she tilted her head back to ask. Her voice was a mere breath of sound.

"I don't know. Parking."

Hunting was the real answer, but no need to say that. The fact was, if the people looking for them found them, a firefight would ensue. Cornered now, with no place left to run, shooting it out with them was his only choice.

As he contemplated plugging a bullet into Fielding, or Wendell, or even Matthews, his mind reeled. Could he do it? He felt Jess shiver against him. For her? Oh, yeah. He could.

Just like they could plug a bullet into him.

The whoosh of tires on pavement as the arriving vehicle passed nearby made Mark go tense with anticipation. Whatever was going to happen would happen very soon. His hand tightened on the Glock.

Jess clearly heard the arriving vehicle, too. She shuddered and pressed so close against him that he could feel the pounding of her heart. Or maybe it was his own heart that was thumping away. Hard to tell.

Straining to hear, he listened carefully, trying to pick up any and all sounds beyond the truck bed. He'd rarely felt so helpless in his life. With his field of vision confined to the blue cocoon in which he and Jess were wrapped, his ears were all he had left to use.

The muffled one-two slam of car doors was his reward. The sound made Jess start. He could hear the hiss of her breath as she inhaled.

There were at least two of them, then.

He badly wanted to look out, to free himself from the damned constricting, blinding tarpaulin, to see what was going on with his own eyes. If this was one or more of the guys from his house, he wanted to confront them, to look them in the eye and ask them point-blank what the hell they thought they were doing, but he didn't. He couldn't. He had Jess to consider.

If they were here, they were no longer his friends. They were her enemies, and that's how he had to think of them.

A team of assassins was what he most feared. They would be black ops, under the radar, paid to handle problems like Jess, no fuckups, no mercy, cold as ice.

He'd made his choice, thrown his lot in with Jess, so whoever was out there was his problem, too. The bomb — and damn Lowell or whoever for blowing up his car, which still had two years' worth of payments to run on it — had made it clear they knew whose side he was now on. There was no going back for any of them: This was going to be a fight to the death.

"How are we going to know when Solomon — the reporter — gets here?" Jess whispered.

"We won't. Shh."

He heard — or thought he heard — something nearby. A shuffle of footsteps, a rustle of clothing . . .

Going still as a stone, barely breathing,

his senses so attuned to what was going on beyond the tarpaulin that he felt like a single exposed nerve, he moved the hand holding the Glock to rest, very lightly, on Jess's shoulder.

If he was fast, he could spring up and snap off a few shots, maybe take one or more of them out before they realized what was happening.

Yeah, and maybe he could walk on water, too.

Silently he watched as Jess spotted the gun with a downward flick of her lashes and froze. Then she wet her lips.

The gesture made his heart constrict. He knew she was terrified, knew by how still and stiff she was, by the rapid rise and fall of her chest against his, by the unevenness of her breathing, by the way her hand that was resting on his waist clenched into a fist. But she glanced up at him then and he saw that she was okay, keeping her head, keeping her composure, just as she had throughout this whole ordeal, and he realized he admired her a lot for that.

The girl definitely had game.

A click near at hand made them both quit breathing. The truck tilted and swayed. A door slammed.

The driver had returned to the truck. He

was in the cab. Even as Mark realized that, the sound of the engine turning over confirmed it.

His whole body slumped with relief.

"What about Solomon?" Jess's whisper was urgent as the truck, with a couple of sputters just to ratchet up his anxiety level, slowly got going, curving around the gas pumps.

"We can't hook up with him here. It's too late. They're already watching for us. That's why they showed up here so fast."

The ride came complete with so many rattles and squeaks and bangs that at least they no longer had to worry about being overheard. Jess acknowledged the probable truth of what he said with a silence that lasted until the truck left the parking lot with a hard bounce that made the tailgate drop open. Mark knew that was what the sudden loud clang was because he had lifted the edge of the tarpaulin just a couple of inches at about the same time to let in some badly needed air — and see if he could spot who was waiting at the 7-Eleven.

The newcomer to the parking lot was a black BMW, Virginia tag BCW-248. Not Fielding's Saab, which he had last seen parked behind his garage. Not a vehicle that he'd ever seen before. Which, he realized, didn't mean a thing.

First chance he got, he needed to check the tag. For now, speculating was all he could do.

The paint smell was suffocating. His eyes were already starting to water. He figured Jess had to be about ready to expire, since she was snuggled so close up against him that he could feel her warm breath on his neck as well as the sharp heel of one of her shoes digging into his stomach and every curve and hollow of her sweet little shape that wasn't displaced by the driver's equipment.

"At least no one's following us." Jess's whisper was reedy. She craned her face toward the opening, too, clearly welcoming the influx of oxygen. He made it as large as he dared, then tucked the edge of the tarpaulin beneath his body so he wouldn't have to hold it in place. The truck was on the ramp leading up to I-95 now. With the tailgate down, he could clearly see the road behind them almost all the way back to the 7-Eleven. The good news was, there was not a vehicle in sight.

"Where do you think we're going?" Jess was looking out, too.

The truck was heading north, picking up speed. The jolting was picking up, too. Mark plucked Jess's shoes and purse from between them after a particularly vicious stab in the gut and shoved them down behind his legs out of harm's way. "I don't know. Toward D.C. We'll see where we end up."

"They're not going to give up, are they?"

"No."

Restoring his gun to its holster now that, in his judgment, the immediate danger had passed, Mark did what he could to make himself and Jess as comfortable as possible. As soon as they were out of the truck, they would be on the run, probably on foot, and since he'd gotten no sleep at all, grabbing a few minutes' rest while he could would probably be wise. Not wanting to shift around too much lest the truck's driver should spy suspicious movement in his rear-view mirror and stop to check under his tarpaulin, or even call the police so they could check under his tarpaulin, he ended up whispering to Jess to roll over. Then when she complied he simply wrapped his arms around her so his body could maybe cushion her from the worst of the jarring ride, which he had no way to brace them against. With both their faces turned up toward the air, her back to his front, her head resting on his upper arm and her body plastered as close to his as peanut butter to jelly, he was surprised to find himself feeling any number of things. Comfortable, however, was not one of them. He had a quick flashback to how hot she had looked wearing nothing but a towel, then had to work hard to try to force the image from his head. She kept moving, kind of wriggling as if she was trying to get comfortable, which didn't help. He distinctly remembered her kissing him repeatedly right after she'd thought he'd been blown up. At the time, shell-shocked as he had been, the soft little pecks she had planted on his face had barely registered, but now, in retrospect, they registered.

"Mark." The husky quality of the whisper stirred his blood.

"Hmm." Her skirt was riding up again. He could feel it, feel the cloth bunching up high on her thighs. He was reminded of how sexy her legs looked with the skirt riding up on them. Then he caught himself taking it further, trying to imagine what kind of underwear she wore. Granny panties? A bikini? A thong?

No. He fought to banish the tantalizing images.

"My left leg is cramping. I have to turn over."

She wriggled against him again, and he

realized that what she was actually doing was trying to straighten her legs. With a wry inner grimace, he obligingly loosened his hold on her waist.

She turned over, sighing with relief as she stretched out her leg.

Discovering with some dismay that his body was acutely attuned to her now, he felt the small, soft globes of her breasts flattening against his chest, and tried to force his thoughts elsewhere — with, unfortunately, indifferent success, especially since the jolting of the truck kept bouncing her against him.

"We need to come up with a plan," she said, sliding her arm around his waist and squirming again, this time, he thought, to escape the ridges of the plastic bin that had to be cutting into her back. Her head was still on his arm, and he could feel the warm tickle of her breath against the underside of his chin. Glancing down, he saw that her face was turned up to his. The glasses made her look like a librarian, but when you looked past them you saw wide eyes the color of sweet tea, plus soft, full lips and creamy skin that he already knew was silky to the touch, and a tangle of chocolaty dark hair that looked damned sexy spilling across his arm.

Her glasses were crooked again. He straightened them out for her in a gesture that even he recognized was really kind of tender, took in the sudden surprise in her eyes, and put his itching-to-wander hand right back where it belonged: flat on her back.

"We've got a plan." If his voice was a little gruff, well, it was a small price to pay for exercising some self-control.

"Oh, yeah? What?"

"Survive."

He glanced away from her just to break the sexual tension, which as far as he could tell was all on his part. Dawn was breaking for real now, and the sky was slowly turning from deep purple to lavender. Visibility was improving by the minute, which under the circumstances wasn't a good thing. Even so early in the morning, traffic was heavy. Mindful of the snarl of traffic that the expressways became during rush hour, a great many people were already heading in to work. A swaying eighteen-wheeler cast a shadow over the truck bed as it rumbled past. The breeze of its passing rattled the tarpaulin and sent a blast of exhaust-scented wind swirling beneath it. Even that was better than the smell of paint. Mark realized to his dismay that he was starting to feel faintly nauseated.

The good news was, feeling sick to your stomach was a great way to get your mind off the woman in your arms. The bad news was, when you had a government-authorized death squad after you, wanting to barf could not be considered a plus.

"Not funny." Jess poked him in the ribs, which caused him to look back down at her. She was frowning censoriously at him. Either her stomach was stronger than his, or she was doing a better job of hiding what was going on with it. "I think the best thing to do is call Solomon from a pay phone the first chance we get."

Mark shook his head.

"You can't contact him again. They'll be watching him now, and if you call him they'll be on us like a duck on a june bug. See, they look for you where you've been. Rule number one of hiding out: You can't contact anybody you've ever known. That's how they find people."

He would have continued, but he needed air. Turning his head toward the opening and breathing deeply, he missed whatever she said in reply. All he knew was that it started with *"But . . ."*

Of course she was going to argue with him: That, he was learning, was Jess. But he was feeling too queasy to listen. He tried concentrating on the horizon — which, unfortunately for him, was obscured by moving cars that wove in and out and emitted a hell of a lot of exhaust.

". . . has to be the President," she said, her tone letting him know those were the concluding words of a lengthy statement.

"What?" He glanced back down at her. "Sorry, I missed that."

She gave him an impatient look. "We've got to seriously consider that the President himself might be behind this. Lowell's his Chief of Staff, and that's who phoned you to make sure we were both in the car right before it blew up. And who else could order the Secret Service around like this?"

Mark knew he wasn't quite hitting on all cylinders at the moment, but two things he was sure of even through the worsening waves of illness: David Cooper had loved his wife, and the Secret Service had never had a traitor.

"Assumptions are dangerous things." He spoke to himself as much as to her. "They can blind you to the truth. For example, just because Lowell called me right before my car blew up doesn't mean he blew it up. Necessarily."

He had to break for air again before he

could arrive at any more profound insights. Figuring out who was behind all this was a necessity, he knew, if they wanted to come out alive on the other side, but he just wasn't up to mental gymnastics right now. At the very least he required fresh air and terra firma. A double line of vehicles all barreling in the same direction clogged the road behind them for as far as he could see. They were weaving in and out like the line down the middle was some kind of maypole. The truck driver was booking it now. The old truck rattled and banged and shook like a hoochie dancer.

Jess said something he didn't hear.

Mark would have closed his eyes, but he had the feeling that doing so would prove fatal — to his stomach, not his life.

Then, suddenly, thankfully, traffic started slowing down.

The truck braked, lurched, and merged into the right lane, where other cars quickly joined it, and slowed to a crawl. An almost smooth crawl. As pleased as he was that they were now inching forward, Mark started to get a bad feeling that wasn't centered in his stomach, which was actually a good thing because it was an indication that his stomach might be starting to settle down. The traffic tie-up probably wasn't related to them at all, but still his thoughts ran along the lines of a driver with a cell phone reporting suspicious movement beneath a tarpaulin in the back of a pickup truck. Almost as bad would be a roadblock for drunk driver checks, or . . .

". . . something the matter? You've gone white as a sheet." Jess's whisper penetrated again at last, and he took a risk and looked down at her, pleased to discover that he no longer felt like upchucking the instant he inhaled paint smell. "Is there something you're not telling me?"

She was looking tired, anxious, and way too pale herself. With her face tilted toward his and her head resting on his upper arm, she was so close that he could have counted every tiny individual freckle on her nose and cheeks.

"Nope."

Frowning, she looked more anxious still. "I don't believe you. You haven't been listening and you haven't been talking. There has to be a reason." She wet her lips and her body tensed. He could feel the hand that had been resting on his back clenching. "So what don't I know? If there's something, please tell me. I don't care what it is, I would just rather know."

Apprehension radiated from her like heat.

Her eyes searched his, looking for some awful truth she seemed to suspect he was hiding.

"Look, don't worry about it."

"Mark, please."

His mouth twisted wryly.

"The paint smell and the motion haven't been bothering you at all?"

"What?" Her frown deepened as she stared at him in incomprehension. Then her eyes lit up with sudden understanding. "Are you saying you're carsick?"

"No," Mark said, revolted at the wimpy image that conjured up. "No, I am not saying that. I'm just saying that the paint smell was kind of getting to me for a minute there."

"You're *carsick.*" She grinned, then chuckled outright at the expression on his face.

"Maybe." Mark started to frown her down, but she looked so delighted, so bright-eyed and twinkly with amusement suddenly that he didn't have the heart. Smiling a little sourly at her instead, he realized that it was the first time he had ever seen her laugh. "Funny, huh?"

"Just a little."

Watching her enjoying the moment, he decided that making a fool of himself was worth it.

"You know something? You're beautiful when you laugh," he told her, and when that made her quit laughing and look suddenly serious and self-conscious and kind of shy, he was so struck by the way she was looking at him that he leaned forward the required six inches and kissed her.

23

Mark was kissing her.

Mark was kissing her.

It took Jess's stunned brain a second or two to absorb the fact, and by then her heart was pounding and her pulse was racing and her body had already caught fire. The warm, firm pressure of his mouth had caused her lips to part and her head to tilt so their mouths fit together perfectly, and the hand that wasn't trapped between them slid sensuously up his back, reveling in the feel of the taut muscles beneath his shirt — and that was before she even truly realized what was happening.

When she did, she went all light-headed and shivery inside. Closing her eyes, she kissed him back like he was the culmination of every erotic dream she'd ever had — which he was. Slanting her mouth across his, she took the previously gentle kiss to a whole new level, returning it with a heat and hunger that she'd never felt before, not even once in the whole twenty-eight years of her life.

I want you so much. But she didn't utter the shattering confession aloud. Instead, her body spoke for her, quaking and burning and yearning against him while her mouth explored his with a blistering urgency that made her bones dissolve. Her heart thumped so hard she could hear its fierce beat against her eardrums. Her blood turned to steam.

He tasted, faintly, of coffee. It suddenly became her favorite flavor in the world. She absolutely could not get enough. Pressing herself against him, she discovered proof positive that he was turned on, too — and the knowledge made her wild.

"Jesus God," he muttered against her lips when he pulled back a moment later to grab a quick breath.

"This is crazy." She saw that his eyes were dark and hot.

"So maybe crazy's good." His lips curved in the smallest of smiles, and then his mouth was on hers again. Sliding his hand around behind her nape, he shifted so that he was leaning over her. Pressing her head down into his hard-muscled triceps, he kissed her so expertly and so thoroughly that she forgot everything, the danger they were in, the rickety, rocking truck, the paint fumes and tarpaulin, all of it. Everything except Mark.

She was kissing *Mark.*

Dizzy at the knowledge, she wrapped her arms around his neck.

She could feel the heat of him, the hard strength of his body against hers, the weight of his chest pressing against her breasts, their urgent, swelling response. Her bare toes curled. Her fingers threaded up through the short, crisp hair at the back of his head. Deep inside, her body tightened into an intense rhythmic throbbing that was the most delicious thing she had ever felt.

I'm in love with Mark.

The truck stopped with a jolt.

It took a moment for that to register. Actually, it probably wouldn't have registered at all if Mark hadn't torn his mouth away from hers to, she presumed, check things out. For a moment she blinked up at him in befuddled incomprehension before she noticed that they were no longer moving. Although his mouth was still scant inches from hers, he wasn't looking at her. He was looking out through the opening at the back of the tarpaulin. And his face was, just briefly, tinted blue.

Revolving blue, she corrected herself, as the color came back, receded, and came back again in split-second rotations.

Jess's eyes widened, and with a quick indrawn breath she shifted so that she could look out.

What she saw was a police car parked in the passing lane, an empty police car with the siren off. Its flashing blue lights were going strong, though, lighting up the still-grayish dawn. As the truck started moving again, she saw that another police car was parked in front of it, empty and silent, but with its strobe lights going as well. Jess never even considered that they might be there on account of her and Mark.

What she thought, even before she saw the ambulance, before she saw the stretcher being lifted into its open rear doors with a white sheet covering the figure strapped to it, before she saw the crushed car that rested diagonally across the grassy median, was that there had been an accident.

The line of traffic was being waved forward past the accident site when she learned that she was right. Only one car was involved, as far as she could tell.

Jess barely saw the cop who was doing the waving, or the other police cars and the fire truck they rumbled past.

Her attention was all on the crushed car.

It was a blue Saturn. It was still too dark and the distance was too great to allow her to read the entire plate, but she was almost sure the first two letters were EG.

The realization felt like a blow to her solar plexus.

"Mark."

He was up on an elbow, looming above her, still taking in the scene. Even as the truck trundled clear of the accident site and started picking up speed again, she continued to stare back. Her heart beat in slow, thick strokes. The tinny taste of bile was bitter in her mouth.

"Yeah."

"That was Marty Solomon's car. The reporter."

"Yeah." His tone told her he'd already realized that.

Jess took a deep breath. "You were right: They were listening to my calls. They got to him. They *killed* him. Because of me."

Her voice shook at the end.

"*Not* because of you." Mark lowered himself down beside her and pulled her into his arms. When her gaze continued to seek the tarpaulin's opening in order to keep visual faith with that mangled car, drawn by guilt and shock and fear and a whole jumble of other churning emotions, he caught her chin and made her look at him instead. "Not because of you, do you hear? Because of whatever sick thing that's happening here. He's a victim just like Mrs. Cooper and the rest. Just like you."

Her eyes clung to his. He let go of her chin to stroke gentle fingers over her cheek.

"You hear?"

"Yes, okay, I know." She tried to get a grip, but she was too shaken. "Oh my God, I talked to him just a little while ago. He was asleep. He'd probably be waking up about now, getting ready to go into work. Instead he's *dead*."

She was breathing way too fast and too shallowly, maybe getting close to hyperventilating, and she tried to consciously deepen her breathing and slow it down.

"There's nothing we can do for him." Mark's jaw looked tight. His eyes were dark and hard in the uncertain light. "Except stay alive to figure this thing out, and bring these bastards down."

"I hate this." Despite its fierceness, her voice was a mere breath of sound.

"I know."

He pulled her close, wrapping his arms around her, silently offering what comfort he could. Resting her head against his chest, she soaked up his warmth and listened to the steady beat of his heart. Closing her eyes, clutching his shirt front with both hands and holding on as if for dear life, she tried to calm herself, to force her emotions back. *I should never have called Solomon.* That was the thought that kept running through her mind. But *should've*s and *would've*s and *could've*s were wasted: What was done was done, and there was no undoing it. If she hadn't overheard that "sugar," she would probably be dead now, too. Or if she hadn't leaped from Mark's car, or if Mark hadn't followed her to Davenport's office — there were a dozen *or*s. She — and Mark, too — could still die at any time. The killers on their trail were probably only a step or so behind. As she faced that, fear, cold and solid as a block of ice, settled in her stomach.

I don't want to die. I don't want Mark to die. Especially not now that I've figured out I'm in love with him.

The anguished thought was both ridiculous and true.

For God's sake, get a grip.

Holding on to Mark as if one of them would vanish if she let go, she did her best. Finally, her natural determination asserted itself. If the key to her survival — and

Mark's — lay in identifying who was behind all this, then that was just exactly what she was going to try to do.

Blocking out everything else, she started turning pieces of the puzzle over in her mind.

By the time the truck rattled over the skeleton-like scaffolding of the 14th Street Bridge into D.C., she was feeling calmer. She also had a plan.

"We need to check the phone records." Loosening her hold on Mark's shirt, resisting the urge to smooth out the wrinkles her desperate grip had made in the cloth, Jess tilted her head back to look up at him. If she felt self-conscious about the heated kiss they had so recently shared, well, she'd be damned if she would show it. *Hey, I kiss big, studly guys like you all the time.* That was the attitude she needed to cultivate. If she'd been stupid enough to fall head over heels for the hottest guy around, at least she was smart enough not to let him know it. Accordingly, the look she gave him was her lawyer look, businesslike and cool.

"Phone records?" He frowned slightly as his eyes slid over her face.

Jess nodded. "Mrs. Cooper's, Davenport's, maybe Harris Lowell's. We should be able to tell from them where Mrs. Cooper was heading that night and who the others were talking to. Maybe that'll give us a direction to start looking in."

"Great idea — except I've got a nasty feeling I've lost my clearance to access things like that."

The truck slowed slightly as it bounced around a downward sloping curve, and with a quick glance out the opening Jess realized they were on an access ramp.

"I can do it," she said.

He looked surprised. "For real?"

"I checked phone records for Mr. Davenport all the time. All I need is a computer."

Mark gave her a slow-dawning grin. "Baby, where've you been all my life?"

Before she could reply — the truthful answer was "For the last few months, I've been right under your nose" — their attention was distracted by the truck coming to a shuddering stop. Another glance out through the tarpaulin's opening confirmed that they were at the bottom of a ramp, presumably waiting at a traffic light.

"First thing we've got to do is get off this truck," Mark said as the truck started moving again, clattering through the intersection and picking up speed. "Sooner or later the driver's going to stop for real. Or someone is going to spot us."

Jess nodded.

They were in a mixed residential and commercial neighborhood, she saw as the truck stopped again, hopefully one with a number of stop signs. They probably wouldn't get a better opportunity. Apparently, Mark thought so as well, because he thrust her purse at her.

"I'm going to crawl to the back." He was holding her shoes, presumably intending to carry them himself. "You follow me. Next time the truck stops, we jump."

"What happens if the driver sees us?"

"That's a chance we'll just have to take. What's he going to do, call the police? By the time they get here we'll be long gone."

He extracted himself from under the tarpaulin and crept to the tailgate, crouching there at the corner, staying low, looking back at her. Jess realized that she could see him quite clearly even as she forced her increasingly stiff legs to work, and she crawled laboriously to join him. Dawn was breaking in earnest. Bright bands of pink and gold streaked the eastern sky, and the rising sun limned the roofs of the two- and three-story brick buildings, surrounding them with a shimmering gold. The air was crisp and cold, particularly after the stifling warmth under the tarpaulin. A quick glance around as she reached Mark told her that they were driving through a block of small restaurants and shops, none of which were open yet, as far as she could tell. The sidewalks were, thankfully, deserted. Even as she swept a nervous look around, the truck slowed again. Mark jumped off while it was still moving, then reached up for her as it shuddered to a halt, grabbed her under the armpits and lifted her down at the corner, where it was possible to avoid the tailgate.

Her knees were shaky and the concrete was cold as ice, but with his arm hard around her waist they made it onto the sidewalk. A wary glance back at the truck found the driver, a man in a baseball cap, still looking forward as he got under way again, pulling on through the intersection. If he had any idea he had been carrying stowaways, he gave no indication of it.

"I don't think he saw us," Jess said.

"Just in case, we're out of here."

Mark kept his arm around her as they hurried along the sidewalk before ducking into an alley.

"I need my shoes," Jess reminded him once they were out of sight of the street. Her poor bare feet were freezing.

"Oh, yeah." Stopping, he handed them to

her, waiting while she slid her feet into them. Glancing up once she had her shoes on, she saw that he was looking at them with disfavor.

"When I decided to wear heels, I didn't know I was going to be running for my life," she said defensively.

He snorted. "I'm surprised you can even walk in those things."

"My legs are a little unsteady," she admitted. Which was an understatement. They felt stiff and unwieldy and her knees were weak and her lower back throbbed.

"I'm not surprised." His eyes met hers. The smallest of smiles touched his mouth. "I can always carry you again."

"Not necessary. Come on, let's go." She started walking. She could feel him watching her critically.

"Let me know if you change your mind."

Catching up, he offered her his arm for support in a gesture that would have been almost courtly under different circumstances. Jess slid her hand into the crook of his elbow, grateful for the support. Leaning against him, moving carefully as she tried to work some of the stiffness out of her legs, she realized something: She would be perfectly happy to snuggle up against his side for the rest of her life.

I'm in love with him. The thought wasn't a joyous one. Rather it filled her with dismay. *Think it hurt when he didn't remember you in Mrs. Cooper's office? Wait till this is over and he gives you a chuck under the chin and walks away.*

Of course, that cheerful image was predicated on the idea that one day this *would* be over, that the two of them would come through it and survive, which was looking iffy at best. Reminded of how much danger they were in, Jess pushed the awful truth about her feelings for Mark to the back of her mind. Before it became a problem that she had to deal with, they had to get out of this alive.

"They have public-access computers at the library. That's where we need to go," she said. Jess spared a quick, longing thought for her own laptop, which would be waiting on the desk in her living room right where she had left it. More than anything else in the world, she wanted to go home to her apartment, which, she guessed, was not an option.

"Later. The first thing we want to do is get out of this area as fast as we can." Mark cast a quick, assessing glance back over his shoulder, and Jess felt a corresponding nervous chill.

"We weren't followed" — she was almost sure — "so how could they know where we are?"

"By now they've probably realized they missed us at the 7-Eleven. Sooner or later, I'm guessing they'll either remember the truck or check the store's security cameras and find it and have a eureka moment. There's lots of ways they can trace it, from something simple like running the tag and going to talk to the owner to zeroing in on the route it took this morning with satellite imagery."

"Satellite imagery?" Jess felt sick.

"Baby, we've got eyes in the sky that can spot a mosquito on the roof of a building. Whoever this is, you can bet they have access. The problem is knowing where to look. And in the District, there are a lot of people to look at."

They reached the end of the alley and emerged onto 2nd Street, according to the sign. She was vaguely familiar with the area, which was a mix of fifties-era boxy concrete rectangles and older restored brick buildings. It was home to a plethora of federal agencies, including the FAA, the Department of Education, and the Department of Health and Human Services. None of them were open to tourists, and, more important, none of them were open this early. Up the street, there was an old woman walking a dog. Just beyond her, a homeless man pushed his belongings in a shopping cart. The rattling of the wheels on the uneven pavement jangled Jess's nerves. Other than that, this street, too, was deserted.

So much for his assertion that because there were lots of people in D.C., finding them would be harder. There weren't lots of people *here*. And the idea that a satellite might be recording their every move right at that very moment gave her the willies.

Jess's toe caught on something and she stumbled.

"You okay?" Mark stopped to steady her. Regaining her balance, she nodded, and he added, "I vote we head for the metro and put some distance between us and where we got off the truck as quick as we can."

"Just a minute," she said. Mark was scruffy, but then he looked hot scruffy. She had a strong feeling that she was scruffy, too, and she knew from experience that she definitely did not look hot that way. Unzipping her purse, she dug into it even as she spoke. "It would be better if we looked as normal as possible. Let me brush my hair."

"Now?" He looked at her with disbelief, but she was already dragging a brush through her hair. Finishing, she ran her brush over his.

"Hey."

"Your hair was sticking up."

"Nobody's going to notice *me.*"

"They might."

"If people are gonna be looking at us that close, you probably ought to know that you have dirt on your face."

"Really?"

"I was kidding." He groaned as she dug through her purse for the wet wipes she carried and carefully wiped her face. Then she pulled out a tube of the neutral pink lipstick she always wore and slicked that over her lips. Since she never wore much makeup anyway, Jess calculated that she now probably looked pretty close to normal. Except for the bruises and stitches, of course.

"You all done?" he asked.

Jess ignored the too polite tone. "Yes."

"Good." Taking her arm, Mark started walking, and she, perforce, went with him. "Look, I know this area. There's a metro station two blocks over. It would be nice if we could get there before the people who want to kill us catch up."

The reminder made her shiver. A few minutes later Jess spotted the brown pole with the M sign on it that indicated a metro station. So close to the metro there were numerous people around. Nervously her gaze slid over a couple of college-age men in hoodies and jeans wearing backpacks, a blond middle-aged woman in the kind of bright polyester uniform that a dental assistant or pediatrician's assistant might wear, an older guy in a suit carrying a briefcase, a woman about her own age in a Denny's uniform. All were hurrying toward the metro. None spared so much as a glance for her or Mark. None looked like a threat.

Mark stopped dead. Glancing at him in surprise, she discovered that he was staring at the intersection directly ahead of them as if he'd seen a ghost. A red light was holding up cross traffic, while a taxi sped through to zoom past them with a rattle and a whoosh of air.

"What?" she demanded. His expression was enough to make her stomach tighten without his even having to say a word.

"See that black BMW?" His voice was very quiet. His hand tightened on her arm, and he started walking again, urging her toward the metro station. His eyes were on the intersection that was maybe a quarter of a block away.

Following his gaze, she saw that there were three vehicles lined up waiting for the light to change: a red Honda or something similar, a white Econoline van with some sort of writing on the side, and the black BMW. Shiny and new-looking, it had tinted windows and bright chrome wheels.

"What about it?" she asked, as the light changed and those vehicles got under way in turn, crossing in front of them.

"It was at the 7-Eleven." They were almost at the steps that led down to the station. "I think it's a Dark Car."

24

"A Dark Car? You want to tell me what that is?"

The answer was going to be bad news, Jess knew as she asked the question. She could tell from the rigidity of his jaw, the tightness of his mouth, and the sudden deepening of the lines around his eyes as he shot a look at her. She swallowed hard. Her heart, which was already beating too fast, began to race.

"It's a special-ops vehicle."

Jess hesitated at the top of the long flight of concrete steps that led to the metro platform, glancing down them with dismay. Making a sound under his breath, Mark scooped her up and started down with her. Jess grabbed his shoulders and hung on. The truth was, the stairs were a problem for her for the moment, and they both knew it.

"They always use black, foreign-made cars. The tags, registration, all that will turn out to be attached to some sham company. Untraceable."

"Does it belong to the Secret Service? The CIA? What?" It was all Jess could do to keep the squeak out of her voice. They were on the platform now, and he set her on her feet. While not crowded, it was fairly well populated even as early as it was. Her gaze shot around, looking for — what? Men in dark suits? If so, there were a few, but none who looked threatening. Jeez, was she making a possibly fatal mistake by assuming that all government operatives wore dark suits and were as big and buff as Mark? But he was scanning the crowd, too, and didn't appear to find any fresh cause for alarm. The ubiquitous smell of subways everywhere, the stale air and exhaust mixed with notes of body odor, urine, and alcohol, wasn't too bad. D.C. was known for its clean stations. Jess could see that the train was already rushing toward them. The roar echoed off the concrete walls.

"Way more off the grid than that. Black ops. We're basically talking government-authorized hit men."

"Oh my God."

The train pulled into the station with a wheeze. As far as Jess could tell, nobody was paying them the least bit of attention.

Just to be safe, she shot a nervous glance back toward the entrance: a college-age girl bumping a bicycle down the stairs, a middle-aged woman in a red dress in a hurry to catch the train. Nobody threatening.

"You good by yourself for a minute?" he asked.

That caught her attention.

"Where are you going?"

"Right over there. Don't move."

Giving the newcomers a once-over as they reached the bottom of the steps and joined the milling group of waiting riders, Mark wove through the swelling assemblage to a vending machine half a platform away. Shooting continual wary glances at the eddying tide of people around her, Jess watched as he put in a few dollars and procured two fare cards. Returning, he handed one to her.

"I have a fare card," she told him as she accepted the one he gave her. Most residents of D.C. did; the metro was the easiest, most economical way to move around inside the District.

"I have one, too, and neither of us can use ours." His expression turned flinty again. "They're hoping we'll do something that dumb. We can't use credit cards, or debit

412

cards, or anything else like that, either, without them pouncing on us. We're strictly cash-and-carry from here on out."

Jess ran a fingertip along the edge of the fare card. Her stomach was now knotted so tight it actually hurt.

"I have about twenty-four dollars in my purse." That was including the emergency twenty, which her mother had replaced, showing the folded bill to her before tucking it into the zippered compartment.

"Well, I have a hundred and twelve, so that gives us a kitty of . . ."

"A hundred and thirty-six dollars." Jess's tone was glum. That wouldn't last long. She faced the terrifying truth. "We can't run forever, Mark."

"We don't have to run forever. We just have to keep a step ahead of them until we come up with some way to bring them down."

"Oh, is that all?" Jess shot him a look. "If that was supposed to make me feel better, I should probably tell you it failed miserably."

He smiled.

"Keep your head down. You've been on the news a lot lately." His hand slid around her elbow, urging her into motion. "The last thing we need is somebody recognizing you."

A thrill of alarm shot out along her nerve endings at the thought as she obediently ducked her head. Probably because she'd watched almost none of the coverage, she'd forgotten she had just been all over TV in connection with Annette Cooper's death.

"Do you think they will?" Her shoulders rose defensively as her head sank between them. She moved closer to his side.

"I don't think so. The glasses are good. Every time I've seen you on TV, you haven't been wearing them."

"That's because I hate them."

"Do you?" He sounded surprised. "You look cute in them. Brainy. Hot."

If she hadn't been scared out of her mind, Jess thought she might have blushed. She flicked a quick sideways look up at him.

"If you're after my twenty-four dollars, you can just forget it," she said tartly.

He laughed. "I'm serious. Brainy *and* hot. The combination's killer."

She didn't answer. Instead, she secretly hugged his words close as they fell in with the queue of people boarding the train. Oh, God, how idiotic was it that even while she was running for her life, just getting a compliment from him could make her go all warm and fuzzy inside? Unbidden, she had a sudden flashback to that blazing kiss.

Mark . . .

"Careful." His hand tightened on her elbow as she reached the train and stepped aboard, and the necessity of quickly vetting all the people already sitting in the uphol-stered seats was as effective at banishing romantic yearnings as a bucket of cold water to the face.

Forget being in love. What you want to do here is survive.

Her legs were more unsteady than she'd hoped, and she was relieved to find a seat. Mark dropped down beside her, eyeing the people around them before apparently deciding they were all as harmless as they looked.

The train groaned and jerked as it got under way.

"So what you're telling me is that some-body's decided your Secret Service buddies aren't getting the job done, and now they've sent in the real professionals?" Jess asked under her breath. The situation was now so bad it was almost funny. *Not.*

"It's because of me." His eyes were harder and colder than she had ever imagined they could be. His mouth was tight, his expres-sion unreadable. She was reminded that he was a federal agent, with a gun holstered on his belt. *Thank God.* "Last night, or rather early this morning, whoever's behind this apparently realized that if they killed you I wasn't going to be fine with it, and they were going to have to deal with me. So now they're out to eliminate us both."

"The bomb," Jess said, appalled.

"Yeah."

She tried to think logically despite the panic that was welling up inside her as irrepressibly as fizz in a shaken soda bottle.

"You realize this means I've been right all along. Nobody would send out a government hit squad if they weren't trying to cover up something as big as" — her voice, which had been scarcely louder than a whisper before, dropped even lower, although an anxious glance around reconfirmed that no one seemed to be paying the least bit of attention — "the First Lady's murder."

"I got that."

"In other words, we're in trouble."

He gave a curt little nod.

"Bigger trouble than I was in before."

"Oh, yeah." His eyes cut toward her. There was a sudden glint of wry humor in them. "Of course, now they're trying to kill me, too. They probably feel the job's going to be a little harder."

"So call out the big guns, *hmm?*" As her

grip tightened convulsively on the armrest, Jess took a deep breath. Panicking was useless. What she needed to do was stay calm so she could think. "Who do you think is behind this? Who could order out a black ops team? To hunt people down and murder them?"

Despite her best efforts, her voice shook. To think that this could possibly be happening to *her,* in the United States of America, was mind-boggling.

Mark was slouched down in the seat, his arms crossed over his chest, his long legs sprawled out in front of him. To the ordinary observer, his posture would look casual, even careless. Until they got a good look at his eyes. There was a cold watchfulness in them that reminded her of steel. They were the eyes of a man who had been trained to protect the lives of those he shielded by dying — or killing. Whichever it took.

Jess took heart.

"Not more than a handful of people." He seemed unwilling to go on.

"The President?"

He nodded curtly. "Along with a small group of his top advisers. The Secretary of State. The Secretary of Defense. The Secretary of Homeland Security. People like that."

"Harris Lowell?"

"Not on his own. Only if it was presumed he was acting on the order of the President."

Mark's expression had grown increasingly thoughtful. By the time he finished that last sentence, he was frowning into space as if he were turning something over in his mind. Jess was just about to demand to know what that something was when the brakes squealed and the train shuddered into another station.

Mark immediately stood up. She looked at him questioningly. Unless there was something she was missing, this definitely wasn't their stop.

"Before we do anything else, we've got to muddy the waters." Mark reached for her hand and pulled her up beside him. The doors opened, and riders started exiting the car as more filed in. Glancing nervously out through the windows, she realized that this station was much busier than the last, so busy that after only a moment she gave up on trying to scan every face and hunt for every dark suit. Seven a.m. marked the start of rush hour and, according to the big clock on the opposite wall, it was twelve minutes after that now. Maneuvering her so that she stood in line in front of him, Mark rested his hands lightly on her waist to give her some support and spoke in her ear as they filed out of the car. "It's obvious that they were able to identify the truck and track it into town. We can't take a direct route anywhere anymore. It's too easy to follow."

The main branch of the library was a modern four-story glass-and-steel cube located on G Street NW at 9th. By the time Jess slid into a seat in front of one of its computers, it was after two p.m. She was wearing new-to-her jeans and a white Hanes T-shirt straight from a really new three-pack along with her own jacket, a pair of black Converse sneakers, and a D.C. United baseball cap. Mark was still in the blue dress shirt and black suit pants he'd been wearing all along. The only change was the addition of a newly acquired Redskins cap. At his insistence, they'd gone shopping at a Goodwill outlet that morning. Their purchases, which included a three-pack of cheap cotton panties for her and a pair of boxers for him, had mostly come from the clearance bin and had totaled seven dollars and twenty-two cents. Mark had insisted the wardrobe change was necessary to make them harder to spot, and Jess was glad for the fresh clothes, especially the sneakers, but she regretted spending the money. After eating lunch at Taco Bell, which had cost an alarming four dollars and ninety-eight cents for both of them, their kitty had shrunk to one hundred twenty-three dollars and eighty cents.

Just thinking about it gave her palpitations.

But at the moment, she'd filed it, along with a whole boatload of other terrifying things, under the category of something to worry about later. The first thing she did, upon sitting down at the computer, was e-mail her mother, who she knew would be frantic with worry as soon as she heard about Davenport's death, especially considering the fact that Jess was no longer answering her cell phone. Using Grace's account to make it less obvious in case anybody was monitoring her mother's incoming e-mails, Jess left a message that she was fine, under Secret Service protection, and would be in touch as soon as she could. Then, she checked out a license plate number Mark gave her — BCW-248. It was registered to a chain of local dental clinics, which made Mark snort, "Yeah, right," when she told him. After that, she concentrated on gaining access to the phone records that, she hoped, would provide the information they needed. Ordinarily something like this was a snap. She knew how to bypass the access codes and passwords, how to worm her way into the phone company's or the Internet service provider's or the IRS's or whoever's information systems, how to zero in on the individual in question and pull up the appropriate data: It was part of what had made her so valuable to Davenport.

But almost immediately she ran into a problem.

"What?" Mark whispered as she quit tapping and frowned. He was leaning on the back of the open, shoulder-height cubicle, scanning the screen along with her. The screen that was, unfortunately, blank except for a code that she'd seen only once before.

Not good.

"*Shh.* It looks like somebody's pulled the records." There were maybe a dozen other users scattered among the terminals that lined the room. All of them looked harmless and appeared to be totally engrossed in their own work, but the last thing they needed was to attract any attention.

"Whose?"

"*Shh.*"

Annette Cooper's, Davenport's, Marian's, Prescott's, the driver's — she hadn't known his name but Mark supplied it when asked.

As the pattern became alarmingly clear, she checked Marty Solomon's. Same code. Same blank screen.

She faced the truth with a thrill of fear. The speed of it, the thoroughness of it, the power it would take to do such a thing, was terrifying.

"They've pulled them all. Everybody who's been killed. There's nothing here."

"Shit."

"Shh."

Okay. The next step was to try to access the records of likely suspects. Like Harris Lowell. Jess wasn't optimistic, and her lack of optimism was rewarded: His records were unavailable, too. Ditto the President's, of course, and the Secretaries of State, Defense, and Homeland Security — those whom Mark had mentioned as having enough clout to send out a government hit squad — as well as a few random shots of her own, like the Vice President and the Speaker of the House.

All blanks.

Fingers poised on the keyboard, Jess stared at the blinking code on a screen that should have been crawling with phone numbers, and thought. With no way to determine who any of the victims had spoken to in their last hours, it seemed they were well and truly stymied. They would have to find some other means. . . .

Wait.

Just like hacking into computer files, the key to getting the information they needed was to go in through the back door.

The records of high-level officials clearly were too protected to be accessed by a skilled amateur at a public computer. And whoever was behind this was smart enough to have pulled the pertinent records for those who had been killed. No one was getting to those.

But had they pulled the records of the people still in the game? The minor players, the foot soldiers, the extras?

To start off with, how about the limo company? Aztec Limos: Jess knew the name because that was the company Davenport always used.

Jess smiled, a satisfied little curl of her lips brought on by a flash of, if she had to say so herself, absolutely brilliant insight.

"What?" Mark must have seen the smile, because he moved to stand beside her, thrusting his hands into his trouser pockets as he leaned forward to peer at the screen.

"I'm going to check the limo company."

Pulling up the records was a snap. No attempt had been made to make them inaccessible. Jess paged to the night in question and found Davenport's cell phone number. It was the calls that came in immediately afterward that interested her most.

"Anything?"

"Maybe. That's Davenport's number." She pointed. "See those calls that came in to the company after that? The three of them right after Davenport's are from the same number. I'm guessing they're from wherever the limo was heading, checking to see why it didn't arrive as scheduled. You notice they were all placed between one and one-fifteen, and then they stopped."

"Because word of the accident was getting out."

"Yes." She pointed to the calls that started arriving nearly every minute right after the last of the three. Hundreds of calls, one right after the other. "Those are probably reporters and news agencies. But we need to check them, too, just to be sure."

"Can you print that out?"

Jess hit print. The distant hum of the printer going to work sent Mark off to retrieve the papers.

Annette Cooper had accused Prescott of calling someone, presumably backup, right before the Lincoln had been forced from the road.

"Give me the full names of the Secret Service agents who were at your house last night." Jess scooted a pad and pencil, thoughtfully provided by the library and left in the cubicle for the use of its patrons, toward Mark when he returned. "Also their phone numbers and addresses, if you know them. And Prescott's, too."

"Why?"

"Mrs. Cooper accused Prescott of calling for backup. If he did, it's possible that whoever he called either was in the car behind us or sent the car."

"I know their names, partial addresses, and Fielding's number." He bent over, writing. "The other numbers were in my phone."

Which meant they were lost. But as long as she had the names, she could work it out.

Fielding's records came up beautifully. Scrolling quickly through them, working without Prescott's cell phone number, Jess realized that knowing the date and approximate time of the call would be enough.

Bingo.

Elated, she almost called out to Mark and stopped there. But then, just to make sure, she decided to check Matthews's phone records.

Another bingo. Same number, presumably

Prescott's, two minutes later.

Frowning, she went into Wendell's.

Bingo again. Same number again, four minutes earlier than Fielding's hit. And then a second one ninety seconds after Matthews's.

"So what've you got?"

"Prescott texted Fielding, Matthews, and Wendell separately in the ten minutes before the crash. Actually, he texted Wendell twice."

"He contacted all three? You're shitting me."

"Nope."

The problem was, the fact that Prescott had contacted all three agents made the information practically useless. It did nothing to pinpoint a traitor in the ranks. As they both silently absorbed that, Jess hit print so they could comb through the records more thoroughly later. Mark again went to fetch the printouts before anyone else could pick them up.

Prescott would have been in the Lincoln with them at the time. Jess realized that the picture of him frantically texting his fellow agents fit with what she remembered. That's why he had been so quiet in the front seat and had paid so little attention to the histrionics in the back. The First Lady had been right on the money: Prescott had contacted backup. Actually, when Jess thought about it, she had been right on the money about everything so far.

I'm a fucking prisoner. The words echoed through Jess's mind. Annette Cooper had been referring to her Secret Service detail, Jess was almost sure.

Of which Mark had been special agent in charge.

Just because of that, and because she was now a charter member of Paranoids-R-Us, and because she wanted to make absolutely certain that none of her really sick residual suspicions weren't so, Jess keyed in Mark's information.

His cell phone records popped right up. *No problemo.*

Jess's eyes widened and her heart started beating faster as she paged through them. Before the crash, nothing jumped out at her. But in the days after the crash, a familiar number occurred with increasing frequency: Davenport's.

In fact, Mark's last call to Davenport had been placed some two hours before he had fired a shot at Jess and then stepped out the window.

"Jess. We gotta go." Mark was back, thrusting the folded printouts into his pants pocket as he spoke. She barely had enough presence of mind to push the quit button to exit the file before she looked up at him.

Blindly.

"Get up. We're leaving." He hit the power button on the computer, turning it off as he grabbed her arm and pulled her to her feet. She must have looked as stunned as she felt, because he gave her arm a little shake. "Jess. They're here."

25

"What?" That got her adrenaline going. Whatever he may or may not have done, she discovered that at her core, she did not fear Mark. However, she feared those who were chasing them to the point of teeth-chattering terror.

"I checked out the window when I was coming back with the printouts." Mark grabbed her purse and the plastic bag with their old clothes and the new purchases from Goodwill as he spoke. "I saw the Dark Car drive past. If they're in the vicinity, you can bet your sweet life it's because they know we're here."

They were moving as he spoke, Jess managing to keep up with Mark's long strides because of the sheer juicing power of abject fear. Her heart pounded. Her pulse hammered in her ears. Her stomach — well, the poor thing had almost forgotten what if felt like *not* to be twisted into a pretzel.

"Somebody must have tagged the files." Jess had been afraid of that. Of course, if somebody went to all the trouble of pulling the information, tagging the files so they would be notified if someone tried to access them would be the next logical step. She had at least hoped to have a little more time before anybody noticed and took action. "When I tried to access them, it sent out an alert."

"Which they were able to trace back to the computers here." Mark's voice was grim. They were moving through the third floor's open center aisle as they spoke, heading, Jess realized, toward the far corner of the building, where, presumably, there was a staircase and elevator bank other than the central one. It was Friday afternoon, school had apparently just let out, and the rows of tall shelves were fairly well populated. A story session, complete with small chairs and a yellow-smocked librarian, was getting ready to get started in one corner, Jess saw as they reached a back hall, which held restrooms and an emergency exit.

"How did you know where the exit was?" Jess asked in a hurried whisper as Mark, holding her hand tightly, raced her toward it. Unspoken between them ran the knowledge that they had very little time; their pursuers would almost certainly come straight up to the computer room, realize immediately that their quarry had fled, and give chase. Remembering the open nature of the corner on which the library was situated, Jess realized they would be ridiculously easy to spot as soon as they left the building.

"I read the signs."

Before Jess could point out an alarm would probably sound if he opened the door — in her experience, emergency exits were like that — he flipped open the little plastic door on the small red rectangle set into the wall by the exit and pulled the fire alarm.

Immediately, loud, clanging peals filled the air. Jess's jaw dropped as he pulled open the door to the emergency exit — an alarm did sound, a tinny little one almost lost beneath the full-throated scream of the other — dragged her into the stairwell, picked her up, and ran down the stairs with her.

She didn't even protest.

"That was brilliant," she said, holding tight and regarding him with awe.

"Fuckin' A."

By the time they reached the ground floor, the stairwell behind them was clogged with people heading down. More people

431

streamed out the exit at the bottom of the stairs. Emerging into the crisp spring air, looking desperately all around, feeling hideously exposed in the bright sunshine that had burned off most of the morning's chill, Jess saw that there were swarms of people pouring out of the building, milling around on the sidewalks, coming out of nearby businesses to stop and stare. Librarians tried to herd the kids into a group and keep them out of the street at the same time, with scant success. Patrons holding books and magazines blended into the growing crowd. This was an area of three- and four-story buildings, mom-and-pop-type stores, lots of foot traffic, and lots of vehicular traffic, all of which was slowing down and gawking and honking. Jess could hear the wail of sirens rushing to the rescue.

Putting her down, taking her arm, Mark pulled her out into the middle of the street at a near run. Trailing behind, Jess nearly got mowed down by a startled-looking mom in a minivan at approximately the same time that she saw a tall, dark-haired, granite-faced man in a black suit thrusting through the swirl of bystanders at the corner.

He was obviously looking for something. Jess felt a jolt of terror as she realized what — or, rather, who.

"Mark," Jess squeaked, as her eyes stayed glued to the man, who continued to wade through throngs of people and head in their direction without, she was sure, having yet seen them. "There's one of them."

Jess heard the quick intake of Mark's breath as he looked — at the exact same instant as the black-suited man saw them. Throat tightening with alarm, Jess watched the bad guy's gaze sweep over them, freeze, and come back. His face registered surprised recognition, and then he stuck his hand beneath his suit jacket. One word popped into Jess's horrified mind: *gun.*

Her heart leaped.

"Mark," she moaned in warning, but he had already seen, or maybe not; maybe the plan was already in motion and she had missed it, because he grabbed her and thrust her ahead of him.

"Get in."

Even as she gasped and refocused to see what was happening, he was cramming her inside an open car door. As her butt landed on a cracked vinyl seat, she realized that Mark had just stuffed her in a taxi that was being vacated by someone else.

"Scoot," he barked, but she didn't need to be told. She scooted like a dog with its tail on fire, and he jumped in beside her, slammed the door, and said, "Union Station, fast" to the cabbie, who sped off.

Jess's mouth was still hanging open as she glanced back. The black-suited man ran through the crowd, pushing people out of the way as he came after them, his hand still hidden beneath his jacket. She grabbed Mark's arm and tried to stutter out a warning, but nothing coherent emerged. Then the cab turned a corner and he was lost to view.

Jess thought she was going to melt into a little puddle of reaction right there on the seat.

"Friend of yours?" she asked. Her eyes rolled around to Mark, who gave her a warning look. Clearly this was something that was not to be discussed within earshot of the cabbie. Oh, yeah, she got why. Probably because the idea that murderous goons were chasing his cab with the idea of riddling his passengers with bullets might not go over so well. In fact, if his thought processes were anything like hers, the cabbie might well slam on the brakes and order them out on the spot. Good for him. Bad for them.

Thanks to near gridlocked Friday-afternoon locals-get-out-of-town traffic, progress seemed glacially slow. But no Dark

Car appeared behind them, or beside them, or anywhere else. All vehicles moved in bumper-to-bumper unison.

As the Beaux Arts–style building that was Union Station came into view, Mark was already handing over a ten from their dwindling kitty. Jess spared no more than a passing thought for the money as the taxi stopped in front of the statue of Columbus and she scrambled out.

Some things were worth paying for. Like living.

Mark was right behind her. He grabbed her hand and towed her after him like a barge after a tugboat. Her legs and back had been bothering her earlier. Now, with the knowledge that a death squad was right behind them, the aches and pains were reduced to minor twinges that barely slowed her down.

"Did you recognize him?" she gasped out.

"No."

Hundreds of people were in and around the building. Jess barely registered the ornamental facade festooned with eagles, or the replica of the Liberty Bell. Instead, she concentrated on getting off the street and out of the sight of any arriving cars, and when they burst through the doors to join the teeming crowds inside the vast open space, she felt an overwhelming wave of relief.

"Unless they followed us" — she might be being overly optimistic here, but she was pretty sure the bad guys hadn't been able to get close enough to the cab to see where it went — "there's no way they can know where we are, right?"

Given the fact that Mark was still dragging her through the Main Hall, which seemed as long as a football field and boasted a 96-foot-high barrel-vaulted ceiling, she wasn't too surprised by the wry twist of his mouth, which told her that her optimism was sadly misplaced.

"Simple enough to find out where the taxi that just picked up passengers in front of the main library let them out. What we've got here is a few minutes' start." His eyes darted around, roaming over everything from the tourists munching pizza at the food court to the escalator that led to the movie theaters, with an occasional glance over Jess's head to survey the terrain behind her. As Jess had been casting frequent looks back herself, she knew what he saw: There were so many people that picking out black-suited goons with murderous intent would be impossible until the goons were practically upon them.

"This way," he said. Her pulse was now thundering so loud in her ears that she wouldn't have heard the words if she hadn't been looking right at him when he spoke. Pulling her with him onto an escalator, he looked like he wanted to push his way through the impassable lineup of people clogging the slow-moving thing. Instead, he stopped, seething with barely concealed impatience as the escalator leisurely chugged its way down.

Jess would have said something, but she was too busy catching her breath. After their life-or-death race from the library, she was sweating, she was exhausted, she was terrified, and her body ached like a losing prize fighter's. She'd swallowed a couple of pain pills along with her tacos earlier, but they were no match for the kind of day she was having.

Their destination, she discovered as they left the escalator and Mark dragged her through another set of doors, was the metro.

"Be right back." As soon as they were on the platform, he dropped her hand and strode away. Swallowed up in the milling crowd, she cast scared looks all around. Before she could totally succumb to panic he was back, thrusting a fare card into her hand. A moment after that, they were boarding a train.

Jess flopped down into one of the seats with relief. Taking a couple of deep breaths and straightening her glasses, which had gotten knocked crooked in their rush through the terminal, she cast a jaundiced eye at Mark, who dropped down beside her. She was glad to see that it wasn't just her — he was breathless and sweaty, too. He'd lost the baseball cap, and as she put a hand to her head in reaction she discovered she had lost hers, too. The bright sunlight streaming in through the windows showed up how bloodshot his eyes were, as well as the puffiness beneath them. More than a day's worth of stubble now darkened his cheeks and chin. His shirt was limp and had lost a couple of buttons, and he looked kind of like a bum. A sexy bum, which was the annoying thing, because she was fairly certain that sexy was one of the last words that anyone would use to describe her appearance at the moment. Questions about his calls to Davenport loomed large in her mind, but this was neither the time nor the place to confront him. Best not to upset the status quo with your protector until you were someplace safe.

"We can't just keep running," she pointed out between gulps of air as the train jolted

438

out of the station. The car was almost full, so her voice was just loud enough to reach his ears. "We need a plan."

"We've got one."

She seemed to remember hearing that before. "Oh, yeah? Do tell."

"Trust me."

Her expression must have been something to see, because he laughed, picked up her hand that was lying curled on her lap, brought it to his mouth, and kissed it.

The sight of his handsome head bent over her hand, the feel of his warm lips on her skin, would have been enough to stun her into dazzled compliance at any other time. Even under the circumstances, for a moment there her heart did a little tap dance, and she teetered on the brink.

Then she got a grip, snatched her hand back, folded her arms over her chest, and scowled at him. "No."

"Guess you'll just have to wait and see, then."

He was still smiling a little. Mindful of their fellow passengers, Jess restrained herself. They sat in silence through two stops. By the time the train chugged into a third, she was breathing normally and her heartbeat had resumed its usual constant, steady rhythm. Then Mark stood up, pull-

439

ing her up beside him, and her heart gave an automatic uneasy thump.

"Our stop," he said, and Jess almost groaned. She was worn-out, bone-tired, in pain, scared to death, and sick of it, filled with uneasiness and lack of trust toward her partner in flight, and in general ready for this to end.

Not that she said any of that. What was the point? Embracing her inner stiff upper lip, she left the station with Mark without saying anything at all. At least, she thought, as they hot-footed it across the street hand in hand, he was no longer walking as fast as he could, which seemed to argue that he felt they were relatively safe for the time being. Or maybe he was just being considerate of her still-much-less-than-optimum physical state. They were in Dupont Circle, the eclectic, primarily residential area with accommodations ranging from Civil War–era mansions, many of which had been turned into apartments or condos, to boxy new office buildings. There were numerous restaurants and quite a few art galleries and museums, and lots of people. Unfortunately, Jess was in no mood to appreciate the little bistros and boutiques that lined the streets. The people, however, she appreciated. Just in case the bad guys were using eye-in-the-sky technology to search for them right now, she wanted as many people around her as she could get.

She occasionally liked to try to solve the Waldo books when she babysat her nephews. Now, she realized, she and Mark were Waldo, and the game had become *Where're Mark and Jess?*

Trying to keep her breathing from going haywire at the thought, she looked at Mark. "Now what?"

They had turned onto a quieter residential street with far fewer fellow pedestrians to get lost among, and then he pulled her into a narrow, grassy alley that ran between two identical four-story brick rectangles with colonial-looking white pedimented doorways and green shutters out front. There were no people at all in the alley. Glancing up, Jess saw a bright blue strip of sky above them and shuddered.

"Congressmen fly home on the weekends to make nice with constituents and see their families. They're required to maintain homes in their districts. Most of them — the honest ones — don't make squat. Therefore, they rent relatively cheap apartments to live in during the week when they have to be in Washington."

They reached the end of the alley, which

opened out into a larger one with a lot more blue sky above it. A strip of blacktopped pavement ran down the middle and Dumpsters and trash cans lined either side. The slanting sunlight of late afternoon beamed down, but thanks to the buildings they were in deep shadow. She wrinkled her nose at the faint smell of garbage as she cast another worried glance up at the sky. Across the street, a calico cat watched them from inside a window two stories up. Other than that, there was no one around.

"Which means . . . ?" So far what she was hearing did not add up to anything helpful.

He pulled her around a brick retaining wall and let go of her hand. "We're going to borrow one for the night."

"What?" Jess's head snapped around. All thought of searching for bad guys was forgotten for the moment as her gaze riveted on Mark. He was standing on the stoop of the brownstone building beside the brick ones, punching numbers into a lock that hung from the back doorknob. He turned the knob and the door opened.

"The woman I was seeing is a realtor. She rents out apartments in these buildings all the time. I know her code." He pulled her into a gloomy, hardwood-floored central hall as he spoke, and she realized that the lock he'd punched numbers into had been a realtor's lock.

Glancing around as he closed the door behind them, Jess practically swallowed her tongue. A long row of flat brass mailboxes set into the wall lined the hall. She recognized some of the names as he pulled her past them and hit the elevator button: Sahlinger, Cristofoli, Urton, Guenther. Congressional representatives all.

"So we're going to let ourselves into an empty apartment?" Jess asked with a flicker of misgiving as they stepped into the elevator, the door closed, and it started its creaky ascent.

"I thought about that, but here's the thing: We've got to assume these guys know everything about us. So using an apartment she has access to is out. Sooner or later, when they can't find us, they'll probably think of that."

The elevator stopped on the fourth floor. Four doors, two on either side of the hall, bore the respective numbers 13, 14, 15, and 16. Beneath the numbers were affixed small brass plates with typewritten names inserted into the open centers.

"So . . . ?" Her voice trailed off as he stepped up to the door of apartment 14, knocked, and waited. Nothing.

"So we borrow one from Congressman Cristofoli."

Then he pulled a small Leatherman tool out of his pocket and applied one of the attachments to the lock.

Jess was still casting petrified glances all around in case somebody should come out of one of the other apartments and see what he was doing when he pushed open the door and grabbed her hand.

"Hurry up, I've got to turn off the alarm."

Still processing extreme dismay at the knowledge that they were breaking into a congressman's apartment as she scuttled in behind him, Jess felt her unease ratchet up to another level as she heard the warning beep leading to the earsplitting screech of a violated security alarm.

"This is so illegal. If we get caught, we could go to jail. I could lose my law license . . ."

"Baby, if we get caught that'll be the least of our problems."

Pushing the door shut behind her, Mark dropped her hand and disappeared into another room.

Facing the truth of what he'd said, Jess clasped her hands together and called after him in a wobbly voice, "Please tell me you know some way to shut off that damned alarm."

A moment later the ominous beeping ceased. Then Mark reappeared in the doorway between the two rooms and grinned at her.

"What did you do?" Wrapping her arms around herself, she was barely able to keep her teeth from chattering. And not from cold, either. From reaction. And fear. And way too much physical exertion. And exhaustion. And — everything. Her whole absolutely gone-to-hell-in-a-handbasket life.

"Took care of the alarm."

"How?" She asked the question before she realized she probably didn't want to know the answer.

"What can I say? I'm good." His gaze swept over her, and he frowned. "You look beat. Look, you can quit worrying for a while. I figure we've got a good twenty-four hours before we have to start thinking about moving on."

"Great." Which meant that a very uneasy day from now, they'd be on the run again — unless he was wrong and they got killed first. Still, as the prospect of even a nerve-racking respite began to seep through her system, she very slowly exhaled. She hadn't been aware of how tense she was until the worst of it started to ease.

"Are you hungry? Looks like there's food in the kitchen." He headed into the other room.

Jess was, indeed, hungry. She also realized that the solid core of trust she'd thought she'd established with her partner in flight was suddenly not so solid after all. They were all alone now in a place that was totally out of the public eye. What if he'd actually tipped somebody off to meet them here? What if . . . ?

She heard the sound of the refrigerator door opening and, as if in answer, her stomach growled. Firmly, she pushed all the terrifying *what if*s out of her head.

Unless something more concrete than suspicious phone numbers turned up, she wasn't about to rush back out into eye-in-the-sky-ville alone. Which meant she was on board with Mark.

She trailed after him through the small apartment. The front door they'd come in through opened directly into a living room, which connected to a single bedroom and a small kitchen in an open plan intended to make the place seem larger. The rooms were decorated in beiges and browns, and filled with furniture that she could only character-ize as "early hotel." Inexpensive-looking beige carpet extended through the living room and bedroom to the kitchen. There was apparently a big window in both the living room and bedroom, because the drapes in both rooms, which were drawn, covered the entire outside wall. The only bathroom — which was also the only room with an actual door — was located between the kitchen and bedroom. She made quick use of the facilities, washing her hands and face, and emerged minutes later feeling a little better.

Mark was seated in one of the two bentwood chairs at the small glass-topped bistro-style kitchen table that sat in the middle of the tiny kitchen. A long, narrow window with its mini-blinds open ran the length of the far wall, making the kitchen, with its white cabinets, appliances, walls, and tile floor, the brightest room in the house. There was a paper plate in front of Mark, what looked like a heap of coleslaw on the paper plate, and a sandwich, which he had just taken a big bite out of, in his hands. A juice box sat beside the paper plate. Jess saw that another paper plate, complete with sandwich, coleslaw, juice box, and fork, waited across the table for her.

Swallowing, he nodded at her plate. "Made you a sandwich."

Jess looked from the plate to him. He was already taking another huge bite. His blue eyes met hers guilelessly.

"Thanks." Crossing the kitchen, she pulled two paper towels from the roll by the sink — she saw no sign of any napkins — and offered him one as she sank down opposite him.

The sandwich, she discovered as she bit into it, was ham. The coleslaw was spicy. And the juice was orange. Her stomach gave a little hiccup of delight.

Waiting and wondering was not her style, Jess discovered as she responded to some enthusiastic comment of his about the amount of food the congressman had on hand. So she put down her sandwich, looked him in the eye, and came out with it.

"Why did you call Mr. Davenport just a couple of hours before he tried to shoot me?"

26

Mark choked on his ham sandwich. She knew right then she wasn't mistaken: Surprised guilt was there on his face, easy to read as a first-grade schoolbook.

He swallowed and coughed a little and drank some juice.

"What makes you think I did?" he asked at last.

Good try. Not working. "Mark."

He took another big bite out of his sandwich — a stall tactic if she'd ever seen one — chewed, and swallowed. Then he washed it down with a slurp from the juice box. All of which clearly gave him time to think.

She lifted her eyebrows at him, waiting.

He sighed and gave up. "I was authorized to make you a cash-settlement offer. Since it wasn't supposed to be known that it came through the Cooper family, we were funneling it through Davenport."

Jess's eyes widened as she remembered

Marian telling her she would be getting a settlement. She never had learned how much it was going to be, which was probably just as well. No point in tormenting herself about its loss.

"We?"

"Well, actually they. The Cooper family."

"Why would the Cooper family give me a settlement? They have no liability in the accident. The liability lies with the limousine company, its driver, and, to a lesser extent, Mr. Davenport and Davenport, Bascomb, and Kelly, because I was technically on the clock for them when the accident occurred."

"The settlement we were offering came with a secrecy agreement." He took another bite of sandwich.

"A secrecy agreement?"

"Would you eat?"

"Would you talk?"

Mark started in on the coleslaw. Before popping a forkful in his mouth, he said, "The President and his advisers thought you might have learned something detrimental to the First Lady during the course of your association with her. I was authorized to offer you enough money to make it worth your while to forget it."

Jess stared at him. "What did they think I might have learned? That she and her husband fought? That they'd had a fight?"

Mark's mouth twisted. "They fought, but that wasn't it. Mrs. Cooper had a drug problem, all right? The original feeling was that you might have been somehow connected with it, maybe somebody she was buying from. Certainly that you had learned of it."

"What?" Jess blinked at him. "She had a *drug problem? Annette Cooper?"*

"You know those pain pills you've been popping for the last week? It started out just like that for her, too. She broke her back in a horseback riding accident about eight years ago, had constant pain from then on, and started taking pills to deal with it. The whole thing just snowballed until she was a full-blown addict."

Jess goggled at him. "How do you know this?"

He shrugged. "I was head of her security detail."

"Wait. Hold on a minute. Are you saying that the whole time they've been in Washington, Annette Cooper has had a drug problem?" Jess thought back to when she had first become aware of the Coopers as the new vice president and his wife. That was almost five years ago. All she could remember of Annette Cooper from that period was stories featuring her working with children and charities. She'd seemed very much the traditional political wife, and completely devoted to her husband.

Mark nodded.

"*That's* why they killed her. Because of the potential embarrassment to her husband." Jess couldn't believe it. There it was, the motive. "If you knew she was addicted to drugs, you had to have suspected that was the reason she was killed. Why didn't you tell me?"

"You want me to talk, you're going to have to eat."

"Mark."

"Eat."

Jess realized he was right, realized she needed food, and took another bite out of her sandwich.

"At first I couldn't believe her death was anything but an accident," Mark said. "Even now that I know it wasn't, that it was murder, I'm finding it tough to believe that her drug problem was the reason. We were dealing with that. Dealing with it successfully."

"Dealing with it how?" Looking at him with fascination, Jess drank some juice.

"She was being weaned off them. We were keeping her away from her suppliers. In fact, we'd pretty much cut her off from the ones she'd always used, the ones she preferred. Occasionally, she would manage to meet with someone who wasn't on our radar and get some more. That's where Prescott and the others thought she might have been going when she slipped away from them the night of the accident. That's why no big alarm was raised and they just tried to round her up themselves. They were scared that the press might get wind of her buying drugs."

"Instead, she was running away from the White House." As Jess put them in context, the First Lady's words took on a whole new meaning. "We both saw Prescott looking for her. She didn't want me to wave to him and get his attention. She said, 'Don't you understand? I'm a fucking prisoner.' "

"Yeah, well." Mark polished off his sandwich. "It was for her own good."

Jess took another sip of juice. She couldn't eat another thing. Remembering the night of the accident had completely killed her appetite.

"So how long has this been going on?"

"The drug problem? I told you, pretty much the last eight years. It got gradually worse until the people around the President faced up to what was going on and came up with a plan to deal with it."

"What I meant was, how long had you been trying to keep the First Lady away from drugs?"

"They brought me on board last August. Up until then I'd been working on the outgoing President's detail, but I was asked to make the switch to Mrs. Cooper, and I did."

Jess frowned. "Why you?"

"I knew them. I'm from Texas, too, you know. Abilene. Actually, Lowell, Davenport, quite a few others that make up the inner circle — I know them, too. Known them for years. We're all from the same place. It was a tricky situation, and they felt they could trust me."

"You mean you knew the Coopers before you came to Washington?"

He nodded. "My mom worked as the elder Coopers' — Wayne and his late wife, Virginia's — housekeeper after my dad was killed on an oil rig when I was four. I pretty much grew up on their ranch in Abilene. David and his sister were gone by then — grown, with David working as a lawyer in Houston before he got into politics — but he came back to visit a couple of times a month. I got to know them all pretty well."

Jess looked at him with fascination mixed with more than a little bit of anxiety. This involvement with the Coopers — did it make him less trustworthy? If his ties to them were strong . . .

"Does your mother still work for them?"

He shook his head. "She remarried and moved to Florida. I go see her when I can. I'm her only child."

"Are you . . . close to them? The President and his family?"

"Depends on what you mean by 'close.' I know them. They know me. They knew they could trust me to do what I could to help with the situation they had." His gaze sharpened on her face. "If you're asking me would I conspire to commit murder for them, no. Would I keep my mouth shut if I knew they had conspired to commit murder? No. They know it, too. You need proof, all you got to do is cast your mind back to the bomb in my car."

Again with the bomb. But she had to admit, it was definitely reassuring.

"So how did you become a Secret Service agent? Was it because of the Coopers?"

"In a roundabout way, I guess. I played football in high school and college. Actually, that's all I ever wanted to do. I was good, too. Good enough to go pro. I got drafted by the Cowboys out of college and played for them for almost one full season.

Second-to-last game, I got hit below the knee and something snapped: worst pain I ever felt in my life, and then I was on the injured list. At first I thought I was going to be able to come back. I had surgery, did physical therapy, the whole bit, but my knee was never the same. My speed was gone, and my agility was limited. It took me about a year to admit it, but then I knew I wasn't ever going to be able to play pro ball anymore. No matter how hard I worked at it, I wasn't going to be able to come back."

His tone revealed nothing but wry acceptance, but there was a flicker of pain in his eyes that told her how difficult it had been for him.

"That must have been terrible."

"Life happens."

Jess thought of his daughter. "You were married then, weren't you?"

He nodded. "Heather and I met in college. We got married our senior year, and Taylor came along soon after that. Heather was pretty, ambitious, loved the idea of being a pro football player's wife. When my career ended, so did our marriage. Of course, it took me a while to see that, too. Once everybody figured out I wasn't going to be playing pro ball anymore, Mr. Cooper — the old man, Wayne — helped me get on with the Secret Service. Knowing what I know now, it seems likely that he already had it in mind that David — he was in the Texas Senate at that time — would be going to Washington one day. So I moved up here with Heather and Taylor, worked round the clock trying to suck it up and get my new career on track, and in the process lost my marriage."

Jess looked at him questioningly. She didn't want to pry, didn't want to ask it outright, but she very much wanted to know what had led to the breakup. He must have seen the question in her eyes, because he grimaced.

"You want to know how it ended? It was classic, and I guess I should have seen it coming, but I didn't. I found out that Heather was sleeping around. With a guy I knew, Ted Parks, an FBI agent. A guy I thought was a friend. I couldn't get past that. Not even for Taylor, although I swear I tried my best. To be fair — and it's only in the last couple of years I've been able to be that fair — I was no piece of cake to live with after I figured out I was never going to be able to play football again. I had some down times. I drank too much. I spent a couple of years kind of cursing at fate, you know. Then I was working too much. The

Secret Service is pretty much a twenty-four-hour-a-day, seven-day-a-week gig, and Heather was always the kind of woman who needed attention. Lots of attention. There were some rocky moments between us during and right after the divorce, but we're on good terms now. For Taylor's sake. Of course, Taylor plays us off against each other, which causes the occasional dustup. I just took her to Florida to see my mother for spring break. You know what she did while we were there? She got a tattoo on her butt. A butterfly, so I hear. I take her to the mall, she does it while she's supposed to be shopping, and then I don't know a thing about it until Heather calls me to blast me for letting her do it. A tattoo. At fifteen. Can you believe it?"

Mark looked so aggrieved, Jess had to smile. She hadn't even met his daughter, and she was liking her more and more. "It's the style. A lot of teenage girls have them."

Mark's eyes showed an unmistakable flare of interest. "Do you? No."

"No," Jess replied firmly. "I don't. And just for the record, I'm not a teenage girl. I'm twenty-eight years old, remember? But Maddie does."

Mark's eyes widened. "Jesus, that's just what I needed to hear. No worries there.

First a tattoo, then she's pregnant. I'm going to have to lock her up till she's thirty."

Jess narrowed her eyes at him. She might not be thrilled to pieces about Maddie's pregnancy, but Maddie was her sister, and criticism of her from anybody outside the family was not allowed.

"You know what? Life happens." She threw his own words back at him with bite.

"I know, I know." Mark held up his hands in apology. "It's just — Taylor's my daughter. I don't want to even think about going there. She doesn't even date yet" — he frowned suddenly, looking uncertain — "I don't think."

That blatant manifestation of male cluelessness was so adorable Jess had to smile again.

"Anyway," Mark continued, with the air of someone getting back to the subject at hand, "I spent a good bit of time talking to Davenport about your settlement. Even though I never did think having you sign a secrecy agreement was a good idea. Almost as soon as you and I started talking, I realized you didn't know a thing about the First Lady and drugs."

"No, I didn't," Jess agreed.

"That's why I couldn't believe somebody was trying to kill you. There didn't seem to be any motive until you told me you thought the First Lady's death was murder. If you were right, and clearly you are, but hindsight's always twenty-twenty, the fact that you're the only witness to something that big would do it." He frowned. "But I'm willing to bet almost anything I own that Annette Cooper was not killed to keep her drug problem quiet. There's another reason. I guarantee it."

Jess was thinking about that when she realized he was looking at her intently.

"Back there in the library, you looked at my phone records, didn't you?"

Gulp. But there was nothing to do but fess up. "Yes."

"You know, you have some real trust issues."

That was so unfair, Jess could only blink at him in disbelief.

"I have trust issues? Well, gee, I wonder why. Let's see: Someone kills the First Lady in a car crash, which was also meant to kill me; then when they realized I survived, I was attacked in my hospital room; I try to tell people, including you, what's going on; you don't believe me, nobody believes me. I try to tell my boss, and he tries to kill me. I start trusting you, sort of, enough to let you take me to your house, where you promise

I'll be safe, and while I'm there I hear the voice of the person who tried to kill me in the hospital. The person you called in, mind you. Your friend and fellow Secret Service agent. Not being stupid, I run, and you chase me down. I trust you again, sort of, until you start talking to another of your friends about bringing me in, which, we both know, means to be killed. I jump out, and your car blows up. Then I start trusting you again, sort of, because I really don't have a choice, and I find out, not because you told me but because I checked your phone records, that you have a prior relationship with my boss, the one who tried to kill me. You have an even stronger relationship with the President and his associates, one or several of whom are almost certainly behind the ongoing efforts to try to kill me." She took a deep breath and glared at him. "So if I have trust issues, is it any wonder why?"

Their eyes met. Then he smiled at her.

"Okay, point taken."

"*Point taken?* Is that all you can say?"

"What do you want me to say?"

"Something else."

"You're beautiful?"

Her eyes narrowed at him. That was the second time he had called her beautiful, and

461

it made her feel as vulnerable this time as it had the first.

"Wrong answer." She stood up abruptly, gathering the remains of her meal and stalking away to dump them in the trash can.

"Jess. I'm teasing." He shoved back from the table, picked up his garbage, deposited it in the trash, and followed her into the living room, where she was in the process of sinking down on the couch. "Although you are. Beautiful, I mean. Actually, I think I'm developing kind of a thing here for petite girls with big greenish eyes and glasses."

He stopped walking, leaned a shoulder against the doorjamb, crossed his arms over his chest, and smiled at her. Smiled *dazzlingly* at her.

The look she sent him could have fried an egg in midair.

"If you're trying to distract me from everything you *didn't* tell me, you might as well give up," she said. She was suddenly supremely conscious of her disheveled state, her unstyled hair, her bruised, stitched and makeup-less face, her ill-fitting, ill-matched, sexless clothes, her damned glasses. The problem was that she did not feel beautiful, never had, probably never would, and that, she discovered, was what was really ticking her off. "So you can just cut out the crap,

462

pretty boy, because it isn't working."

His eyes widened. His smile widened. He straightened away from the doorjamb to grin at her.

" 'Pretty boy'?" Instead of being stung, as she had intended, he was, she was incensed to see, starting to chuckle. *" 'Pretty boy'?"*

"Oh, go away." She barely managed to control the impulse to chuck something at him. With studied indifference, she turned her attention to the coffee table in front of the couch, where today's paper lay folded and ready for reading.

"Fine," he said. She could feel him studying her, but she didn't look up. She picked up the paper and snapped it open, perusing the headlines, ostentatiously ignoring him. "I didn't get any sleep last night, and I'm starting to feel a little groggy. I'm going to go take a shower and see if that doesn't perk me up."

"Fine."

"Keep the TV on low if you want to watch it. And don't answer the door. And stay off the damned computer. And the phone."

With that, he left her alone. A moment later Jess heard the click of the bathroom door closing. She thumbed through the paper — the front section was almost entirely devoted to coverage of the First

Lady, and the luminaries who came in for the funeral, the size of the crowds, and the reactions of ordinary citizens, none of which she could bring herself to read — and listened to the muffled rush of the shower. Her skin tingled in atavistic response. She really, really wanted a shower. A long, steaming hot shower . . .

With Mark in it.

Do not go there, she chastised herself fiercely.

Scowling, she was scanning the pages for some mention of what had happened to Davenport or Marian — nothing, and no obituaries yet, either, and it would be too soon to even look for anything about Marty Solomon — when she heard the shower shut off. A couple of minutes passed before the bathroom door opened. That sound was followed by the soft pat of bare feet on carpet. Mark was heading for the bedroom. Probably wearing nothing but a towel . . .

She gritted her teeth, staring doggedly at the newsprint in front of her. And never mind that she was no longer taking in a word.

"You want to take a shower, it's all yours," he called.

She heard more footsteps followed by a rustle of plastic — the bag their clothes were in, she was guessing — followed a moment later by a long creak. Then nothing.

Finally, Jess couldn't stand it anymore. Folding the paper, she got up and went to check on him.

He was in bed, sprawled on his stomach with a white down comforter covering him to the waist. Thanks to the heavy drapes, the room was gloomy-dark, but she could see enough of him to know that his broad, bare shoulders and wide, muscular back and brawny arms were — the only word that came to mind was *fine.*

She was already mentally backing out when a snore told her that he was sound asleep.

It was the only bed in the place. Right now, she was tired but not particularly sleepy, certainly not ready for bed. But later, sometime tonight, she had the option of crawling into that supremely comfortable-looking bed with him or grabbing a pillow, scrounging up some kind of cover, and sacking out on the couch.

Couch, Jess told herself firmly. The other choice was so dumb it bordered on self-destructive.

While Mark slept she took a shower, washed her hair and blew it dry, brushed her teeth, smoothed on ChapStick and a little face cream — thank God for the supplies in her purse — and popped a single pain pill. Mark's recounting of the First Lady's troubles made her wary of taking more than she absolutely had to. But the ones she had swallowed earlier were wearing off, and her legs and back were really starting to ache. So she compromised on one and hoped for the best.

By ten o'clock Mark still hadn't awakened. His snores, ragged but blissful-sounding, continually reminded her that he was sacked out one thin wall away. She was on the couch, dressed for sleeping in one of Mark's T-shirts, so big on her it hit her at mid-thigh, and a pair of the plain white cotton panties. Having stolen a pillow from the bed and found a quilt folded on the bedroom closet shelf, she had made herself as comfortable as possible.

To keep herself from dwelling on the possibility that the black-ops death squad had discovered their hideaway and was even now creeping up on it with guns drawn, she turned the TV on. Low. So low, in fact, that she had to strain to hear the *CSI* episode that wasn't really all that interesting anyway. Once she heard footsteps in the hall outside and her heart went haywire and she almost ran for Mark, but whoever it was went into another apartment, and after that silence reigned. Too nervous to turn on a lamp, Jess tried to read selected sections of the paper by the faint light of the TV. The comics, Ann Landers, and sports all provided a welcome distraction from the fear that seemed to have taken up permanent residence in her gut.

She was even starting to get sleepy until she turned a page and found a picture of herself in the paper. Actually, two. One as a little girl. Soaking wet, wrapped in a blanket, and staring big-eyed at the camera. The other as she was now. With contacts, not glasses, taken from her driver's license.

Death Car Survivor Had Previous Brush with Death, the headline read.

27

Jess didn't have to read the accompanying story to know what it said. Even as the paper fell from her fingers, she felt impossibly familiar waves of grief and pain. It had been so long now — she never thought of it anymore. Never, except maybe in the most secret depths of her deepest dreams. It was a tragedy of her past, long over. Long put behind her.

It could not make her feel this way anymore.

Standing up, she started to head for the bathroom and stubbed her toe hard on the coffee table.

"Ow! Shit! Damn it!" Clutching her injured foot, she hopped a couple of times, then sank back down on the couch, displacing more of the paper, which fluttered to the floor. Cradling her foot in her lap, rocking back and forth as she cursed under her breath now, she glanced down and saw the picture of herself looking up at her. Kicking at it with her uninjured foot, she closed her eyes.

She did not need this on top of everything else.

"Hey. I heard you yell. You all right?" Mark's voice made her jump. Her eyes flew open, her head jerked around, and she saw him standing there in the doorway, frowning at her, wearing only his boxers, with his gun in his hand. It was an indication of her state of mind that her gaze slid over him exactly once, and she didn't even flinch from the gun.

"Fine."

"Are you crying?"

To her horror, Jess realized she was: She could feel the warm, wet slide of tears trickling down her cheeks.

Turning her head away, she swiped at her cheeks with both hands. "No."

"What the hell?" Padding toward her, he put the gun down on the table at her elbow, then stopped in front of her. By dint of much blinking and sheer force of will, she got the tears under control. With her peripheral vision, she saw a very masculine-looking bare foot and a long, powerful-looking leg. A section of muscular stomach. A sliver of wide chest. A buff arm. "Did something happen?"

She wasn't quite ready to look at him again yet. "I stubbed my toe, okay?"

"Hard enough to make you cry? Let me see."

"It's fine. Don't worry about it."

She heard him sigh. Then he sank down beside her on the couch. Feeling the brush of warm, bare male flesh and realizing she couldn't order him to scoot over because of the pillow and blanket now piled on the rest of the couch, she looked at him with a forbidding frown. A well-muscled naked shoulder and a sculpted chest filled her vision as he reached for her foot, the one that rested in her lap. His hand slid around her instep, holding her foot still, his fingers long and strong. He leaned closer, peering at her toes.

"No blood. Can you move them?"

She jerked her foot from his grasp, put it on the carpet, and shot him a "back off" look. "I told you. It's fine."

But he wasn't looking at her. He was looking down.

"Is that you?"

She already knew what he was reaching for even as he bent forward. The light from the TV played over the rippling muscles of his bare back, and she watched it as if mesmerized, trying her best to hold off the moment she knew was coming. The rustle of the paper being picked up made her grit her teeth and look away. She realized in that split second that he was going to read the article and they were going to talk about it, nothing she could do to stop it at all, and she needed a moment to steel herself.

"It's too dark in here for me to read anything but the headline," he said a moment later, and Jess felt a tiny frisson of relief until he continued, "so we can do one of two things: You can tell me what it says, or I can turn on a light and read it for myself."

The idea of turning on a light, a light that would certainly be visible around the edges of the drapes and through the kitchen blinds and under the door, a light that could possibly lead to the killers that were certainly still hunting them finding them, made her shiver.

He was still holding the paper with the two photos topmost. She couldn't look at them.

"My father took my sister and me to the beach when we were little." Since there was clearly no help for it, she gave him the bare bones, her tone expressionless. "We got caught up in an undertow. He came out to try to save us. Courtney — my sister's name was Courtney — and my father drowned. I managed to make it back to shore."

For a moment her voice just seemed to hang in the air while the memories — the water closing over her head, her sister's tiny hands dragging at hers, the punishing waves forcing them apart — hit her.

"Jesus. I'm sorry, baby." Another rattle as he set the paper down on the coffee table. Then his arm came around her, bringing with it the smell of soap and warm male flesh. Jess felt the solid heaviness of it circling her shoulders, the comforting grip of his hand on her arm, the squeeze of a hug, and tensed. Until she got the memories corralled again, sympathy was the last thing she needed. She had to stay tough, stay strong, force them back. "I remember now. They ran all kinds of stories about you on TV this past week, and one of them said something about that. To tell you the truth, it kind of tore my heart out."

"It was on . . . TV?" Jess could hardly breathe at the thought of the whole world watching something so personal. He was looking at her. She could feel his gaze on her face, but she couldn't look back at him. She could only stare straight ahead, braced against the pain she knew would come if she didn't armor herself against it.

"Yeah."

Suddenly Jess remembered, while she was in the hospital, Grace saying something about the press wanting to talk to her because she was "the survivor." With an emphasis, like it had a special significance. And her mother saying, "Grace, don't worry your sister." This was what they must have been talking about. Grace, like Sarah and Maddie, the children of Judy's second husband, hadn't even been born at the time of the accident, so it wasn't much more than a curiosity to her, but their mother knew how deeply the tragedy was seared into Jess's soul.

She and Courtney had been inseparable.

"I don't ever even think about it anymore. It was a long time ago."

"You were five, weren't you? That's a tough age to lose people you love."

She remembered that he'd said his father had died when he was four.

"Were you close to your father?" she asked, barely breathing. It felt as if there was an iron band around her chest limiting the amount of air she could take in.

"Not really. From what I've been told, he was gone all the time, working." His hand tightened on her arm and he pulled her more firmly against his side. Jess refused to allow herself to relax against him. She was too intent on keeping the pain away. "To tell you the truth, I don't remember him at all. He's just somebody standing there with my mother and me in old pictures."

It wasn't so much sadness in his voice but regret, she realized. As if he wanted to remember and was sorry he couldn't. Jess took a careful breath.

"I can't really remember my father, either. My parents had split up, and he wasn't around a lot, so I guess that's why. But I can remember my sister."

"She was younger, right? Three, wasn't it?"

Jess nodded, surprised he remembered the details so well. He must have been watching the program closely, and the knowledge both touched and comforted her. What had he said? That watching had just about torn his heart out?

The thought made her dizzy. Some of the stiffness left her body. Hardly aware of her own softening, she let herself rest against him.

"Want to tell me about it?" His voice was almost unbearably gentle.

Her automatic answer, the answer she'd always given to anybody who had ever tried to probe her memories of the tragedy, was "no." But this was Mark. And, well, suddenly she just wanted him to know. For whatever reason.

She took another, deeper breath, and this time her lungs actually expanded to let in sufficient air.

"We were wading in the surf. My dad and his girlfriend were lying on towels on the sand, and I was supposed to be watching Courtney. She had those little floaty things on her arms, and she kept sitting down in the water and letting the waves carry her in. Only one of them pulled her out. She was laughing; she thought it was great because she was riding the wave. I was trying to catch her — I could swim a little — and I couldn't. Then one of her floaty things came off. I can still see it; it was clear with yellow-and-white fish on it, bobbing toward me. She went under, and I started screaming for help and dog-paddling toward her as fast as I could, only I couldn't see her anymore. Then she popped up right beside me and I caught her, caught her hands, and we both got dragged under again, and then she got pulled away from me. I came up and I saw her come up, too far away for me to grab her this time, but I saw her looking at me. She'd lost her other floaty thing by then and her eyes — she had blue eyes, like Mom, and dark hair like me — were big and wide and scared, and she was opening her mouth — I always thought it was to call to me, but I don't know for sure — when another wave broke over her. I think my dad went rushing past me about that time, but I don't really remember that. What I remember is Courtney's eyes, and then a wave breaking over her and over me and me somehow winding up near the beach where somebody pulled me to shore." She broke off and closed her eyes. "The next time I saw her, she was lying in a little white coffin at the front of our church. I touched her — I thought if I touched her she would wake up — and she was cold. And still. And she didn't wake up."

The pain that engulfed her as she finished was so intense that it made her shudder. Bracing against it, refusing to cry, she did what she had learned to do over the years: endure it until it ebbed.

"Jess." Both Mark's arms were around her now. He must have felt her violent quiver because he shifted his grip on her, lifting her onto his lap, holding her close. She felt something brush the top of her head, and thought it might have been his lips. "That's a hell of a thing. I'm so sorry you had to go through that."

Jess took a moment to just breathe. Sure enough, the sharpness of the pain, the hard edges of it that cut like knives, went away. What was left was a dull ache that would recede, too, if left alone, burying itself deep within her subconscious until something called it forth again.

"It was a long time before I would babysit any of the others. My mom used to get so mad at me." She tried to smile, but it didn't quite work. Judy's steely determination not to let grief disable either of them had been hard on her until she had gotten old enough to recognize it for the courage it was.

"Baby, it wasn't your fault. You were five years old."

It was twenty-three years in the past, and the guilt was still there. Buried under layers of time and reason but still there. He'd gone right to the heart of what had tormented her most over all the intervening years.

"I know." Silently she added, *but still.* "I actually don't ever think about it anymore. Unless something reminds me."

"Like seeing an article about it in the damned paper." His hand rubbed up and down her arm in rough comfort. Relaxing as the pain slipped away just as she had known it would, Jess rested her head against his shoulder. "Jesus, I wish you hadn't gotten caught up in this."

That almost made her smile. She slanted a look up at him. "You and me both, believe me."

" 'Course, we wouldn't have met."

Her brows twitched together. Her head came up again. Straightening her glasses, she gave him a severe look. "For the record, we met months ago. When you brought the First Lady to Mr. Davenport's office. You smiled at me. We talked. We talked several times after that, too."

"I don't remember."

"That's not exactly flattering, you know."

The look he gave her was almost surprised. Then he smiled.

"When I'm working I don't see anything except my principal and threats to my principal. Angelina Jolie could dance naked in front of me and I wouldn't notice."

Jess suddenly found herself looking at the history of their acquaintance in a whole new light.

"Really?"

"Yeah, really."

"That's good to know."

"Is it?"

She nodded thoughtfully. "You didn't see me — which is what I thought — but it was

478

for a reason. That makes it much better."

"I'm not following you."

Jess smiled. "Never mind. It's not important."

She was suddenly acutely aware that she was sitting on his lap with his arms around her, and all he was wearing was a pair of boxers. Unbelievable that she'd registered the broad strokes of it but missed all the tiny details until now. The shirt she was wearing had ridden up, and her new panties were on the substantial side, but still she could feel the heat of him burning through them, and the solid muscularity of his thighs. Her bare legs lay on top of his so that the silkiness of her skin slid over the hair-roughened firmness of his every time one of them moved. Her shoulder butted into naked male chest. It was wide and buff and, she noticed with interest now that she was capable of noticing such things, sported a wedge of ash-brown hair that stretched from one flat male nipple to the other and tapered down over a trim abdomen and out of sight.

She glanced up to discover that he was looking at her. Looking at her looking at him, to be precise. There was something in his expression, a sudden sensuous glint to his eyes, a curve to his mouth that made

479

her heart beat faster. His thighs felt harder, his arms around her more tense.

I want you so much. That's the thought that ran through her head as their eyes met, just as it had once before. Only this time, his eyes widened and blazed in response, and Jess realized to her horror that she hadn't just thought it but *said it aloud.*

It was all she could do not to clap a hand over her own mouth.

Her dismay must have been apparent in her face, because he smiled, a slow sexy curve of his mouth that made her stomach clench and her blood heat and her heart turn over.

"Good to know," he said.

Then he bent his head and touched his lips to hers.

28

It was a gentle kiss, not hard or demanding at all, but the heat and thoroughness of it made her dizzy. Her lips parted. Her eyes closed. Her hands found his chest as her heart began to pound — and then he lifted his head.

"Mmm." She made an involuntary sound of protest. Her lids rose to find that he was studying her face, his eyes dark and hot, his mouth almost tender.

"Talk about your coincidences." His face was still so close she could feel his breath on her lips. Her parted, damp, yearning lips. Her hands splayed over his rib cage in silent supplication. *Kiss me again. . . .* But this time she didn't say it out loud; she did have, she was thankful to discover, some control. "See, here I was thinking pretty much the same thing: I want you like hell."

"That *is* a coincidence," she managed, trying to keep some perspective, trying to keep from totally losing her head, and he smiled that sexy smile again.

Then he kissed her again, tilting her so that her head was tipped back against his hard-muscled upper arm, brushing his lips over hers, licking between them, tantalizing her until she shivered and closed her eyes and surged against him and put a stop to the teasing. Her mouth clung to his, greedily prolonging the contact, deepening it with a building urgency that sent fire shooting through her veins and melted her bones and made her pulse go crazy.

Forget perspective. Forget not losing my head — it's too late. Jeez, I'm in so much trouble here.

She knew it, recognized the future pain she was almost certainly storing up for herself, and she didn't care. Her hands slid up over his chest, luxuriating in the freedom to touch him, taking sudden intense pleasure in the warmth of his skin, the firmness of his muscles. His shoulders were broad and thickly muscled, and she loved touching them, too, loved sliding her hands along the brawny smoothness of them before surrendering to the need to wrap her arms around his neck and kiss him like she burned for him — which she did.

His arms around her tightened as he

kissed her back with a torrid eroticism that sent her senses spinning. He was holding her so close now that she could feel every taut muscle and sinew of his chest and arms, feel the heat of him radiating through her shirt, feel the racing of his heart. Her breasts swelled and tightened and tingled at the contact. With a tiny, pleasure-filled sound, she undulated instinctively against him as the hot, rhythmic quickening in her loins intensified and spread, making her go almost mindless with anticipation, with need. Pressing her breasts harder against him, she squirmed deliberately in his lap, feeling his instant response with an upsurge of desire that made her shake.

"Jess." His mouth slid across her cheek to plant hot kisses down the side of her neck. His hand found her breast, fondling her, warm and strong as he tested the size and weight of the tender globe through the soft cotton before his thumb searched out her nipple, rubbing over it, pressing and playing.

Her lids lifted. Her gaze focused on how big and unmistakably masculine his hand looked against the white T-shirt as it covered her breast. The sight was unbelievably sexy. Her tongue came out to wet her lips because her mouth went suddenly dry.

"That's . . . so good."

"Is it?" His voice was thick.

"Mmm."

He didn't stop, rubbing her nipples and caressing her breasts and tracing a burning path around the loose neckline of the too-big shirt with his mouth all at the same time. She clung to him, dizzy with wanting, pressing hungry, distracted kisses of her own along his bristly jaw, nibbling at the soft lobe of his ear. Then his mouth slid down the front of her shirt to close over the tip of her breast, suck at it, the sensation hot and wet and so unbelievably erotic that she moaned and tightened her grip on him and forgot all about his ear as her heart threatened to beat its way out of her chest. His tongue found her nipple through the cloth and played with it, teasing it until she was gasping and arching her back and basically doing everything except begging him to make love to her, which she was damned if she was going to do. Then he moved to the other one and did the same.

"Mark." When he lifted his head at last, though, she couldn't regain control quick enough to keep herself from clutching at his shoulders and breathing that small, instinctive protest.

"Hmm?"

More was what she wanted to say but she didn't; she bit it back even as it trembled on her lips. She didn't need more; what she needed, as any smart woman would surely recognize even at this, the eleventh hour, was less.

"Maybe this . . ."

Isn't such a good idea were the words that the tiny sliver of her brain that was still moderately cool and dispassionate tried to force her to say. But the rest of her rebelled. This was what she wanted. *He* was what she wanted.

"What?"

She was lying back in his arms, woozy with pleasure, breathing hard, flushed and quaking and dying to feel his mouth on her again, his hands on her again. She could feel him looking at her, feel the heat of his gaze touching her everywhere, she thought, so she opened her eyes to find that she was right, his eyes were all over her, taking in the slender length of her bare legs that were curled now toward the back of the couch, the curve of her body as she lay across his lap, the jut of her nipples against the T-shirt, the wet circles where his mouth had recently been.

He must have felt her looking at him, too, because suddenly their eyes met. His were dark and intent. His face was hard with desire.

"Kiss me," she said. Because it was just exactly what she wanted to say.

His eyes blazed. "How about we get you naked first?"

The hoarse undertone to his voice was enough by itself to make her heart lurch. The idea of getting naked for him — *for Mark* — sent a thousand fiery tremors racing over her skin. Her breathing got ragged and her pulse raced and the delicious throbbing that he had brought to life deep inside her body suddenly got a whole lot hotter and more intense.

She was *dying* to get naked for him. But that didn't seem like the thing to say, and given that her heart was beating like a jackhammer now and she was breathing way too fast to make intelligent conversation anything but a remote possibility and she was afraid to talk anyway, for fear she would blurt out something that was better left unsaid, she just didn't say anything at all.

What she did was sit up in his lap, trying to look several degrees less turned-on than she felt, trying to keep a modicum of cool, and took off her glasses and put them on the table behind her.

"Hey, I like those."

She shook her head at him. Not that she didn't feel sexy with her glasses on — with Mark, she now kind of, sort of, sometimes did — but she definitely felt sexier without them.

"They'll just get knocked off." At least, if she had anything to say about it they would.

The sudden gleam in his eyes made her go weak at the knees. "You think?"

"Yes."

His head rested against the back of the couch now, and his grip on her had loosened enough to allow her freedom of movement although his arms still encircled her waist. He watched her with what looked like lazy interest, and if she hadn't been close enough to see the hard restlessness in his eyes and the carnal set of his mouth, she might have started feeling a little uncertain, even shy. But she did see them, did feel the rock-hardness of his body beneath her legs, and so took his stillness for what she was almost certain it was: the calm before the storm.

"Let me see you, baby." His voice was low and husky. His eyes ate her up.

Taking a deep, shaky breath, she took hold of the hem of the T-shirt and lifted it over her head, then dropped it on the floor beside the couch. Even as the garment fell she had a flash of clarity in which she saw

487

herself, sitting upright in his lap, naked except for a pair of plain white cotton underpants, the bluish light from the silent TV flickering over her small pert breasts with her nipples, already aroused, dark and erect and wanton-looking against the creaminess of her skin. She was small-boned and slender, with a narrow waist and slim hips. More boyish than voluptuous, actually, but in that moment, with his eyes on her, she felt incredibly female.

"Jesus, you're beautiful," he murmured. This time, when he said it, the look in his eyes made her believe it, too. Her heart slammed against her ribs. Her breath caught. Then his gaze slid down her body. Even as she leaned toward him, even as his head lifted and his back straightened and his arms tightened around her and he pulled her into an embrace, his hands moved down her back to slide over the smooth cotton of her underwear.

"Ah, granny panties. My favorite."

"What?" She almost frowned. The husky, sensuous-yet-satisfied-sounding murmur made no sense, but she was so dizzy with longing that she couldn't quite care.

"Forget about it."

By then his mouth was on hers and his hands were inside her panties, cupping her cheeks and squeezing and stroking and then pulling her astride him, so she did — forget about it, that is. She melted against him, her breasts burning and swelling against his chest, shuddering because his hands on her felt so good, kissing him back with a fierceness that shook her to her core. Rocking against him, feeling the heat and hardness of him pressing into her with only that thin layer of cotton between them, she felt as if her bones had turned to lava and her insides to flame.

He moved against her deliberately, holding her still for it, making her feel him, dropping his mouth to her breast and suckling it at the same time, and the sensation was so incredibly arousing she cried out.

"That's it. I'm going out of my mind here." His voice was so thick it was hardly recognizable. Then he stood up with her, kissing her with a hungry intensity that rocked her world as he carried her toward the bedroom. Curled against him, her arms around his neck, her mouth locked to his, she kissed him back, so hot for him she could have sworn the very air around them sizzled.

More than she had ever wanted anything in her life, she wanted this.

When he pulled his mouth away from

hers, she made a tiny sound of protest and opened her eyes. Without her glasses the world was more of a blur, and the bedroom was dark except for the faint illumination provided by the distant glow of the television, but she could see him, see how heavy-lidded and hot his eyes were as they moved over her, see the chiseled planes and angles of his face set hard now as if he was trying to maintain control, see the sensuous line of his mouth.

Then he looked away and juggled her a little awkwardly. About the time she realized what he was doing — yanking the covers down — her back was making contact with the cool smoothness of the fitted sheet. But instead of coming down on top of her, which she wanted so badly now her teeth were clenched in anticipation and her hands clung to his shoulders, reluctant to let go, he pulled away from her, standing over her, looking down at her. With his back to the only source of light he suddenly looked very tall and strong. Very broad-shouldered above narrow hips and long, powerful-looking legs. Very big and fit, like the pro football player he had once been. Intimidating, even.

Except he wasn't, not to her.

"Mark . . ."

But his name died in her throat as he hooked his fingers in her waistband and pulled her panties down her legs, pulled them off and threw them on the floor. Suddenly she was naked and he was looking at her and she loved that he was, loved it so much that her breath caught and her nails dug into the mattress and her heart thundered.

Their eyes met. Electricity surged between them as powerfully as a lightning bolt. She felt a rush of desire so intense that she shivered.

He was already shucking his boxers when she sat up, rolled onto her knees, and took him in her mouth.

She heard him inhale sharply. He stood stock-still for a moment. Then his hands found her head. His fingers threaded through her hair.

"Jess." It was almost a groan. She heard the shock in his voice, the deep pleasure, the mounting urgency.

His butt was high and round and tight, an athlete's butt. The feel of it in her hands made her insides melt, made the pulsing deep within spiral tighter. She was dizzy at the idea of what she was doing to him, at the intimacy of it, at the searing response she could feel radiating from him in waves.

When he pulled away from her she could do nothing but blink up at him, still dazed with sensation. Her hands slid down his thighs. Muscular, hair-roughened thighs . . .

"Mark . . ."

"Easy, baby. Wait."

She got the impression he was talking through his teeth, but she didn't really have time to think about it because he was already tumbling her onto her back and coming down on top of her, his weight and hardness heavenly against her, but only for a moment.

Pressing scalding wet kisses over every inch of her skin, he slid down her body until he reached the velvety delta between her legs. When he kissed her there, she moaned and writhed against him and went totally mindless with sensation. He knew just what to do, how to turn her on, how to make her shiver and pant and burn.

When he slid back up her body at last she was trembling like her insides were made of jelly, so hot and hungry for him that all she could do was clutch him and breathe, arching her back and moving in silent, compulsive invitation as he pressed lingering kisses to her breasts before claiming her mouth. Kissing him back as if she would die if she didn't, she wrapped her arms around his neck and surged against him, needy and wanting and absolutely on fire for him. He came inside her then, hard and fast and filling her to capacity, and it felt so good, so incredibly, mind-blowingly good, that she cried out. Murmuring something thick and throaty that she didn't catch, he pulled back, then plunged inside, deeper and harder than before, and she cried out again.

Wrapping her legs around his hips, drawing him in, she matched his movements with her own, lost in an urgent maelstrom of desire.

"Mark, oh, Mark," she gasped, burning higher and hotter as their tongues met with greedy passion and he pushed her down into the mattress, coming into her with such fierce need that she was driven to the brink, quaking inside, building . . .

"Oh, God, Jess," he groaned, and seemed to lose control, taking her higher and hotter with furious pounding thrusts that drove her out of her mind with passion, winding her tighter and tighter, making her wild.

Making her come.

In a shattering series of fiery explosions that was exactly what she wanted, what she craved.

"Mark, Mark, Mark, I love you so much, *Mark*," she cried at the end, breaking hard, shaking, clinging to him as she was swept away.

"Jess." He buried his face in the tender hollow between her neck and shoulder and drove into her one last time and held himself deep inside her and found his own release.

Lost in bliss for a good minute or so afterward, Jess came crashing down from the heights of ecstasy to face the terrible reality of what she had said.

Maybe he hadn't noticed.

It had been so hot between them, so incredibly, indescribably good, and, like her, he'd been so caught up in it that maybe . . .

She remembered every word he'd said. Every groan and growl and indrawn breath, too.

What were the chances that he'd been so blissed out that he had missed her declaration of love?

In two words, not good.

Opening her eyes, she assessed the situation. Mark lay sprawled on top of her, deadweight and sweaty and heavy as a load of wet sandbags, his face still buried against her neck, his arms still wrapped around her, his legs still stretched between hers. Her hands rested on his back. His skin was hot and damp, and she could feel the rise and fall of his rib cage. His breath felt warm against her throat.

Much as she wanted to, she couldn't quite convince herself that he was asleep.

She quit breathing as he stirred.

A moment later he was propped up on his elbows, looking down at her. His eyes were sleepy-looking, and a smile just touched his mouth.

Their gazes met.

"Hey," she managed feebly, and felt color flood her face.

His eyes narrowed. His smile widened.

Then a sound — a metallic-sounding click — from the other room made him sharply turn his head.

29

Before Jess could say anything, before she could do anything, Mark clapped a hand over her mouth and shook his head warningly at her. Their eyes met, and she saw that his had suddenly gone diamond-hard.

Shh, he mouthed. When she nodded, he placed his mouth against her ear. "Get down behind the bed. Be as quiet as you can."

Then he slipped silently from the bed.

There was another sound — the faintest of rustles, like clothing brushing against something — from the living room.

Her heart gave a great leap. Her blood ran cold.

Somebody was out there, in the living room. She might be wrong — maybe the congressman was back — but the first thought that popped into her head was *bad guy with a gun.*

Oh, God, had they been found?

Holding her breath, watching Mark move soundlessly toward the door, she slithered off the far side of the bed, which — wouldn't you know it? — gave a slight creak. Her eyes widened. Her stomach clenched. As her knees hit the carpet, she shot a fearful glance toward Mark, toward the door, but nothing changed. Mark kept going. He didn't even glance around.

He was flattened against the wall by the door from the living room, his back pressed against it, his head turned toward the doorway, she saw an instant later, having scuttled on her hands and knees to the foot of the bed and peeped around the corner of it. Despite the darkness of the room, she could see the shape of him outlined against the white wall. Her hand touched crumpled cloth — the blue shirt he'd been wearing all day, she realized, as her fingers explored further. Hastily pulling it to her, pulling it on, fastening just a couple of buttons — naked was no way to confront a killer — she had a sudden flash of terrible memory: Mark had left his gun in the living room, on the table by the couch.

He was unarmed.

Oh, God, please let this be the congress-man.

Without warning, a small white light —

the beam of a flashlight, Jess realized with horror — shone into the short hall between the kitchen and the bedroom, moving from side to side, checking out the space.

A man appeared. Holding a gun. This she saw in an instant, as a dark silhouette against faint light, before he turned toward the bedroom and played his flashlight over the bed.

Light-headed with terror, heart pounding so hard and fast it sounded like a drumroll in her ears, she shrank back — and Mark exploded from the shadows, launching himself onto the man in a low, fast dive. The flashlight hit the carpet and rolled. The gun fired. There was no *bang* — it must have been equipped with a silencer, which made the sound more like a whistle — but Jess knew for sure because the bullet buried itself in the wall with a *thunk* just an inch or so past her head.

She yelped and ate carpet.

"Jess?" There was real fear for her in Mark's voice. The question was flung over his shoulder as he fought for his life, Jess saw as she looked up. He was in a desperate struggle with the gunman. They were cursing and grunting and bouncing off the walls, careering through the doorway, through the hall, and into the living room.

"I'm okay." Scrambling to her feet, she raced to help, meaning to grab Mark's gun off the table and hand it to him. Or something.

The sound of blows came thick and fast. As she rounded the corner she saw that they were on the floor. Mark was on top — no, on the bottom — they were rolling around, trading punches, grappling for possession of the gun in the bad guy's hand. With the blue glow from the television flickering over them, it was like watching outtakes from an old movie — a violent and scary movie.

"You're a dead man, you son of a bitch," the stranger grunted as he locked an arm around Mark's neck and yanked him sideways.

"Eat shit, asshole." That was Mark, pounding his fist into the other's stomach with a sound like a pumpkin hitting pavement, and then rolling back on top.

"I have a gun! I'll shoot!" she cried, snatching Mark's gun off the table and dancing around the struggling men like she knew what she was doing.

"Damn it, Jess, no!" Mark punched the other man in the face while at the same time trying to rip his gun away.

Even with her glasses, she probably wouldn't have tried it: She had never fired a gun in her life. Without her glasses, both men were blurred. She could tell which one was Mark — he was naked, which helped — but where he ended and the other man began was a little fuzzy.

If she pulled the trigger, she might hit Mark. Clearly, clobbering the bad guy over the head with the handle was the way to go.

She had her back to the front door, the gun reversed (but carefully not pointed at herself) and her eyes on her target, still circling them, when the front door opened.

Just like that, no warning at all. There was a click, the sensation of air swooshing in behind her, a wedge of yellow light spilling over her.

Then somebody grabbed her from behind.

A man. In a dark suit. With a gun.

Jess squealed. She would have screamed, but the choke hold he instantly put on her was too tight. She dropped Mark's gun.

"Give it up, Ryan," the man holding her ordered. Writhing, fighting, Jess clawed at his arm — his jacket-protected arm — with her nails. Smacking her in the side of the head with his gun — she saw stars and her knees went wobbly — he pointed the gun at Mark.

Who shot him in the head.

Of course, it took a few seconds for Jess

to realize exactly what had happened. One moment she was on her tiptoes seeing stars while a thug choked the life out of her and threatened Mark. The next there was a sharp *smack* — kind of like the sound of a hand slapping flesh — and then the man crumpled. Just crumpled like a discarded towel.

He didn't even make much of a thud.

Jess would have crumpled right along with him except, finding herself suddenly freed, she was too desperate to get away. She leaped out of reach, whirling to look at her attacker, who was lying on his side with a dime-size black hole in the left side of his forehead from which a trickle of black liquid — blood, she realized with growing comprehension — meandered toward his eye. She recognized him with a sense of shock: He was the man who'd chased them outside the library. Then she remembered the other bad guy, and leaped around to get a visual on him, too.

He was lying flat on his back on the carpet with his arms splayed out beside him. Unmoving. His eyes were wide open and staring at the ceiling. She was pretty sure he wasn't breathing.

Mark was getting to his feet beside him, the gun in his hand.

"You okay?" He sounded slightly winded.

"Yes. You?"

"Never better." His tone was grim.

"Is he dead?" She was referring to the man Mark had been fighting with, because there was no doubt in her mind about the guy with the hole in his forehead. Her eyes were still on Mark, running over him, checking to make sure he was in one piece. Now that it was past, she realized that as much as she had been terrified for herself, she had been equally terrified for him.

"Yeah." He sounded disgusted. "I was hoping to keep him alive. It would have been helpful if we could've asked him who he was taking his orders from. But when his partner showed up and grabbed you, I had to act fast. We would have been dead in another five seconds."

He had moved around her and was in the process of shutting the door as he spoke. The wedge of light vanished. The lock clicked shut.

They were left alone in the TV-lit living room with two freshly killed corpses. The smell of death hung in the air, thick and horrible.

She suddenly felt woozy. Her heart was slowing down, but her leg muscles were acting up. Or rather, giving up. She sank down abruptly in the nearest chair.

"That guy — he was at the library — knew your name. Do you know who he is?"

"Never saw either one of them before in my life."

"So what do we do now?" She meant about the bodies. Actually, the gore, too. On the wall by the door, a circle of black dots had appeared, the result of the gunshot that had killed the man holding her. The back of his head must have — she couldn't go further without wanting to gag.

"Get dressed. We're out of here. We've bought ourselves a little time, but when whoever sent these guys realizes they've gone offline, they'll come looking." Mark was bent over the dead men, going through their pockets.

"Oh, God." Forget being woozy. Forget spaghetti legs. Jess got up and stumbled toward the bedroom, grabbing her glasses off the table and putting them on as she went. Snatching up her clothes, she headed for the bathroom. She absolutely had to splash cold water on her face or pass out. Shedding Mark's shirt, she ended up giving herself what amounted to a quick, icy sponge bath, which helped a lot in banishing the wooziness, before dressing and snagging her purse from the shelf where she had left it. Mark was in the bedroom fastening his holster on over his pants as she emerged. Silently noting in passing how powerful his chest and arms were, she handed his shirt to him.

"Thanks." He pulled it on, buttoning it, then picked up the gun that lay beside him on the bed and thrust it into the back waistband of his pants. His other gun — Jess realized that he had taken one from their attackers — was in his hand.

Feeling the need for two guns was not a good sign.

"Find anything in their pockets?" She was gathering up their belongings and cramming them into the plastic bag that held their discarded clothes.

"Cash. ID — supposedly they're employees of Countrywide Exterminating — pretty funny, when you think about it." He was on the move, grabbing her hand as he went past, pulling her after him. "Car keys. Nothing useful."

They skirted the bodies, which, now that Jess could actually see them in focus, were really kind of pitiful-looking, in a terrifying way.

"Are we going to just . . . leave them?" She cast a haunted look back as he opened the door.

His voice dropped as they stepped into the hall. "Whoever sent them will send along a cleanup crew as soon as they find out what happened. By the time the good congressman gets back, I guarantee you the bodies will be gone and there won't be a trace of this left." Dropping her hand, he closed the door quietly and they moved toward the far end of the hall, where the elevator and fire stairs were located. The light from the overhead fixture in the hall unnerved Jess. It made her feel horribly exposed. She glanced around anxiously. "His apartment will be good as new."

"You're kidding," Jess whispered, appalled. The elevator was on their floor, so they decided to, in Mark's words, "chance it," riding it down and exiting the building without incident. Mark kept his gun in his hand, which was both nerve-racking and comforting, and they both cast wary glances around the alley as the cold night air hit their faces.

Remembering the whole eye-in-the-sky thing, Jess drew her head into her shoulders like a turtle as they hurried through the alley. Fortunately, it was a dark night, with only a few stars and the smallest sliver of a moon. All she could do was pray that satellites didn't come equipped with night-vision goggles.

That spirit of optimism was dashed as soon as they were back on the street. Dupont Circle was hopping, so busy Mark immediately holstered his gun to avoid attracting attention. The restaurants were full, and the bars and social clubs were overflowing. Pedestrians crowded the sidewalks. Parked cars lined the streets. Music, talk, and laughter, plus the occasional honk from a car horn, filled the air.

"Oh my God, it's Friday night," Jess said under her breath. Weekend nights were big with tourists and college students alike.

"Saturday morning, technically. It's seventeen minutes past midnight."

They reached Massachusetts Avenue, which was even busier and more crowded. Jess cast anxious glances all around. The horror of the scene they had left behind stayed with her. The prospect of being dropped by a bullet where she stood had suddenly become horribly real. Mark was moving fast, but the massive doses of adrenaline that had to be pumping through her veins had given her legs new strength, and she was able to keep up.

"You see a cab, you let me know," he said.

"A cab? Not the metro?"

"We need to get out of here as quickly as possible. Time is what we don't have."

Jess felt her stomach plummet as she once again came face-to-face with the hideous truth that the hunters were closing in. Her heart picked up the pace. She rolled an eye at him. "Plan?"

He smiled. "Oh, yeah. We . . ." A yellow cab coming toward them caught both their eyes at the same time, interrupting. "Taxi!"

Once they were inside, Mark said, "The Hay-Adams," and the driver nodded and took off, swerving out into traffic. The bright lights and picturesque buildings of the area rolled past.

Jess turned to him. "We're going to a *hotel?*" she mouthed incredulously. Not that she didn't have faith in Mark's judgment, but taking a cab to the very public Hay-Adams, where one had to register and produce a credit card and jump through all kinds of hoops to rent a room, did not sound like a plan. At least, not a good one.

He shook his head at her. Clearly, carrying on any kind of substantive discussion with the driver listening in was impossible, so she let it drop, at least until they got out of the cab.

Mark picked up her hand and held it. He held her hand a lot, because dragging her from place to place required a lot of hand-holding, but this had a different feel to it. A little of her tension eased as her eyes met his. There was a warmth for her in his eyes that made her feel almost shy.

"Just for the record, that blew me away back there." His voice was low. She could tell from the way he said it that he wasn't talking about the epic battle with the dead men.

"Me, too." Okay, maybe as a response that was feeble. And maybe this wasn't exactly the best time and place for romance. But now was the only time and this was the only place they could be sure of, and that changed everything. Her eyes clung to his and her heart beat faster. The memory of how they had been together sizzled in the air between them, unspoken but as tangible as steam. He carried her hand to his mouth, kissed the back of it — jeez, just the touch of his lips on her skin was now enough to make her dizzy — then lifted his head again to look at her.

"That last thing you said — was it for real?"

Asking "What last thing?" was clearly not going to work. She knew exactly what he was talking about, and she could tell from the way he watched her that he was perfectly aware she knew.

She took a deep breath. "Kind of. Maybe."

His eyebrows lifted. His mouth curved with sudden amusement. "Way to lay it all on the line."

Still holding her hand, he leaned over and kissed her. A lush, deep, hot kiss that was nevertheless quick. Jess's head was still spinning and she was just getting enough of her senses back to glance away before he could read the embarrassing naked truth about how she felt about him in her bedazzled eyes, when her gaze hit on an advertisement pasted to the back of the seat.

Under a picture of a Learjet lifting off from a runway and the tagline *Remember when the skies were friendly?* was the advertiser's name, *YourJets of Virginia.* Under the name was a phone number. It was the phone number that caught Jess's eye and caused her jaw to drop, but she recognized the company name, too.

"Mark." Her attention refocused just like that, she gave his hand an urgent tug and pointed to the ad, and never mind that he was still looking at her with heat in his eyes. "Do you still have those printouts?"

He followed her gaze. Frowning, he stuck a hand in his pants pocket and came up with the folded papers from the library. Jess scooted closer as he unfolded them, then took them out of his hands altogether, flipped through to the Aztec Limo sheets, and pointed wordlessly.

The three calls to the limo company immediately after Davenport's had been made from the YourJets number.

"Jesus," Mark said.

Mindful of the driver, Jess tried to keep her response cryptic. "That's where she was going. They operate out of a private airport in Richmond. Mr. Davenport used them all the time."

The cab pulled to the curb. A bright glow lit the inside of the vehicle, and Jess realized that they had reached the Hay-Adams.

Mark tucked the pages back into his pocket, handed over money, and they got out.

The doorman at the hotel eyed them with disfavor, and Jess realized that both she and Mark must be starting to look pretty seamy. A well-dressed couple walked past them into the hotel and a limo pulled slowly away from the front as Mark slipped a hand beneath her elbow and steered her away, into the safer shadows farther along the block.

"She really was running away. That explains the credit cards, too." Mark's tone was thoughtful.

"What?"

"Nothing."

He was looking across the street, toward the dark acres of Lafayette Park. It was much quieter here than in Dupont Circle. During the day, the area teemed with tourists. After dark, the homeless, druggies, hookers, thugs, and those locals attracted to such things, as well as the occasional too-brave or too-clueless tourist, mixed and mingled in the park. On the streets around it, at this time of night, a few pedestrians walked, a few cars glided by, and the hotels and a few bars were open. During the day, it was safe. At night it was one of those places Jess wouldn't want to visit by herself.

"Back to the plan," Jess said firmly, looking up at him. "Want to let me in on what it is now?"

"You don't think I have one, do you?"

"I'm hoping."

"Oh, ye of little faith." Mark stopped walking, turned her to face him, cupped her face in his hands, and kissed her again. A brief, hard kiss that nonetheless made her breath catch and her heart beat faster.

"Mark . . ." She curled her hands around his wrists.

"That conversation about whether you

meant it about being in love with me? We're going to finish it. Later."

Then, taking her hand, looking both ways, he hurried her across the street and into the dark environs of the park.

30

"So what are we doing here?" Jess's voice was low.

It was stupid, she knew, considering that she had an armed federal agent by her side who had just proved himself lethal in the extreme when conditions warranted, and ordinary criminals were the least of her problems anyway, but the dimly lit paths and shadowy areas beyond them gave her the shivers. They weren't alone by any means, but only a few others — a trio of goths with black everything, a hulking teenager with a blue mohawk and a chain hanging from his jeans, a man in tattered clothing who was shuffling out of the light toward the tent city for the homeless that sprang up each night at the far end of the park — were visible. The rest lurked in the shadows, conducting their business under the trees, behind the bushes, in the lee of almost forgotten statues and monuments.

Drunks sprawled on the grass, swigging from open bottles. A few teenagers made out. The heavy, sweet scent of pot wafted past in occasional drifts. The fact that the White House could be seen glowing like the proverbial beacon on a hill in the near distance didn't seem to discourage anybody from anything. It was there, a fact of D.C. life, and it was ignored.

"I thought of somebody who might've seen the First Lady after she snuck out of the White House and before you picked her up at the hotel. Somebody she might have talked to."

"Who?"

"A woman she met when she was touring a halfway house. Her name is Dawn Turney. A real sad case, was an accountant before she got addicted to crack and crystal meth. She got arrested, lost everything, went to jail, then went into the halfway house, supposedly cured. She and Mrs. Cooper used to meet privately sometimes to talk about the woman's progress — one of her charity cases. Only we found out a few months ago that Dawn was also supplying her with drugs. We put a stop to the meetings — we thought — and then we found out that Dawn was hanging out here in the park, dealing and doing drugs. The First

Lady found out, too, before we did. She would 'accidentally' run into her sometimes while she was out jogging at night and they'd do a drug deal with her detail looking on. Of course, they didn't know what the hell they were seeing. They just thought it was a harmless chat with some fringe person she somehow knew."

"You think she met this woman before going on to the hotel?"

Mark shrugged. "It's possible. She had drugs in her purse that night. I checked. We'd been weaning her off oxy, but when I looked inside the bottle she hid her pills in I saw she had some. Where'd she get them? My gut says here."

Jess felt like a thousand unseen eyes were watching them through the dark. Her skin crawled at the thought. Two members of the hit-man contingent were dead. That didn't mean there weren't more. In fact, the hard truth was that of course there were more. She tightened her grip on his hand.

"Mark. I think we need to get out of D.C. I think we need to run away from here as hard and fast and far as we can."

"Yeah, I think so, too." The fact that he agreed with her scared her almost more than anything else had done. It told her that *he* thought the net was closing in, the situation was getting out of control, the odds of them being caught were ratcheting ever higher. "I want to talk to this woman first, see if she saw the First Lady that night and if she can shed any light on what was going on with her before somebody else tumbles to the fact that she might know something and gets rid of her. Then we'll get the hell out of Dodge while we try to figure out what to do." He hesitated, but from the expression on his face Jess didn't have any trouble divining the rest.

"I know that doesn't mean they'll quit coming after us." Her voice was flat. A deep tiredness that she recognized as the forerunner of despair was creeping over her, making her suddenly conscious of the renewed ache in her legs and back, her growing headache, her need for sleep. "They'll never quit, will they?"

"Not as long as they think we're a threat. The good news is, we're doing a helluva job outrunning them."

Jess shivered. "For now."

"Now's all we've got. It's really all anybody's got."

They had reached the statue of Andrew Jackson on horseback that dominated this section of the park. It was set in a concrete circle that was barely visible as a pale ring around the monument. The lights surrounding it were out, either from lack of maintenance or, more likely, from deliberate vandalism. Benches leading up to it were mostly occupied. People milled around the circle, moving in and out of the nearby bushes and trees. Jess couldn't see anyone clearly. They were dark wraiths weaving through darker shadows.

"Stay close," Mark breathed as they left the path for the concrete circle, and Jess did.

They were accosted immediately.

"You got a twenty you can give me, man?" The punk was one of a group that had been smoking dope near the bronze horse's raised forelegs. All Jess could see of him through the darkness was that he was under six feet tall and stocky, with long, stringy hair. He planted himself in front of Mark, still holding his joint, the tip of which glowed red. The smell of weed was strong.

"I'm looking for Dawn. She around?"

"You want to buy some shit, man? I got shit."

"I want Dawn."

"Who's that looking for me?" A woman pushed through the group and came toward them. Reed-thin, with teased black hair that fell down past her shoulders and a face so pale it seemed to float through the darkness like an oval moon, she was wearing skinny pants and an oversized sweatshirt. "Who wants Dawn?"

Mark didn't say anything, just turned his head to watch her approach. A few steps away, some of the swagger left her gait.

"Oh, it's you." It was clear from her tone that she recognized Mark and didn't like him. "What do *you* want?" Then in an aside to her stringy-haired friend, she added, "Get out of here, Daryl, he's a Fed."

"Oh, shit," Daryl said, and disappeared into the shadows.

"I want to talk to you," Mark said.

"About what?"

"Mrs. Cooper. Did you happen to see her a couple of hours before she died?"

Dawn crossed her arms over her chest and glanced away without saying anything. Jess could see the sudden tension in her body.

"I'm not looking to bust you or get you into any trouble. I just need some information."

Dawn's gaze fastened on Jess.

"Who's that?" Her voice was heavy with suspicion.

"Nobody you need to worry about."

"I ain't talking about nothin' in front of

somebody I don't know." Her eyes rested on Jess.

"I'll just go wait for you over there," Jess said to Mark, nodding toward the nearby base of the statue. When he squeezed her hand, then let go, she took it to mean that he agreed with her assessment as to the best course of action and moved off. None of the shifting clumps of people eddying around them seemed to be paying her the least bit of attention, but still she didn't go as far as the statue's base, because that was where everybody seemed to be hanging out and because it was really dark there and it would be easy to lose sight of Mark. Instead, she stopped just a few paces away, out of Dawn's sight but close enough that when she turned around, she could still clearly see Mark. And, she thought, he could see her.

"So you saw Mrs. Cooper that night."

Folding her arms over her chest and doing her best to fight off the shivers that assailed her, Jess realized she could still hear their conversation. Mark's tone had made it a statement rather than a question.

"Maybe she bought some 'killers from me, I don't know." Dawn sounded sulky.

"Was she by herself?"

"If she was here, she was."

"She say anything or do anything to make you think she might be upset?"

Dawn hesitated.

"She was good to you, Dawn," Mark said. "It would mean a lot to her memory if you could help us out with this."

"Yeah, okay. She was real jumpy, said she needed the 'killers to help her calm down. Her hands were shaking when she paid me, you know? And she kept looking around, like she was expecting *you* to jump out of the bushes." She said that last with a touch of venom.

"She say anything about why she was upset?"

Dawn shook her head. "Only other thing she said was she asked me about e-mail. She asked me if I knew how to e-mail something. A video that was on her phone. I said, hell, no."

"A video —" Mark began, but broke off as the sound of footsteps pounding through the grass in front of the statue caused him to look sharply around. Pulse leaping, Jess took an automatic step back, her eyes widening as her gaze shot past him.

To discover what looked like an onrushing wall of men.

"Mark Ryan?" one of them called.

"Run," Mark barked in her direction as he

whipped around, his hand diving for his gun.

Mark.

Jess screamed it in her head as she was almost knocked off her feet by Dawn's sudden dash away. Even as she regained her balance, even as her eyes found Mark again, there was a whistling sound and he groaned and staggered and then dropped, just dropped like a stone, falling to the concrete like he'd been shot.

A sudden unwanted vision of how the man Mark had shot dropped flashed into her head.

Mark had crumpled just like that.

Oh, no. Please, God, no.

Her heart gave a great thump. Her feet rooted to the spot. Her mouth opened to shriek, but her throat had closed up so tight no sound could escape. Then, without warning, she was hit by a wall of people, borne backward by the stampede of cursing, shouting bystanders fleeing the scene, and for a moment she could no longer see Mark.

Please, God, please.

She got knocked on her butt, and by the time she managed to scramble to her hands and knees and look again, there was a quartet of men in suits standing over Mark, three of them with guns drawn, one reaching down as though to check his vital signs.

Mark didn't move. Didn't make a sound. Just lay there facedown on the pale concrete around the statue. It was too dark and she was too far away to tell if he was breathing, to see if his chest rose and fell.

Everything in her wanted to go to him, run to him, fling herself down on top of him and do what she could to save him.

But there was nothing she could do.

Even as she faced that terrible truth, one of the suited men started glancing around, scanning the dark. As if he were looking for — what? Her?

They knew who Mark was — they had called him by name. That meant they almost certainly knew about her.

Jess rolled onto her hands and knees and started crawling away. The short, crisp grass was cold and damp beneath her palms. The scent of earth was strong. Bottles, cans, still-smoldering cigarette butts, all kinds of assorted trash that had been flung down in the mass exodus created what was basically an obstacle course in her path, and she did her best to dodge them. As soon as she judged she was far enough away so that they couldn't see her, she reeled to her feet and stumbled rubbery-legged into the dark.

It was only as her vision blurred that she felt the tears that were pouring thick and fast down her cheeks.

31

Jess had never been so cold in her life. Her teeth chattered. She shivered like she would never stop. She felt like she was freezing to death from the inside out. Her throat ached. Tears rolled down her cheeks. Sobs racked her.

Please, God, don't let Mark be dead.

She was running, lurching, staggering, scrambling away from him as fast as she could go. Leaving him lying there like that was tearing out her heart. But to go back, to let herself be taken as well, would do him no good. If they succeeded in killing her, too, they would get away with it. The truth of who they were and the terrible things they had done would never be known.

And if Mark wasn't dead — please, God, please — maybe there was a chance that she could still save him.

If she could just come up with a plan in time. She latched onto the thought with a feverish urgency. It was all that kept her from going to pieces.

What she needed was proof that the First Lady had been murdered. Proof that she had been running from something and they had killed her before she could get away. Proof she could take to, say, the *Post*. She would go to their headquarters and tell everyone there what was happening, what she suspected, what had happened to Mark, to their own Marty Solomon, Davenport, Marian — all of them. And show the proof.

Which she didn't have.

Without proof, would anyone listen? Yes. Would they believe? Hmm. Would they print her words, her claims, and at least get them out there for the public to judge for themselves? She thought so, given her status as "the survivor," but she couldn't be sure. Washington was a company town, and whoever was behind this had the kind of power and influence that could maybe find a way of making the story disappear. Just like they could make her disappear.

Maybe she should run straight to the police. The FBI. Somebody like that. But that might be an even faster route to disappearing. Unless she chose the right agency, the right cop or agent, she could be whisked away easily, never to be heard from again.

No, she should go to the *Post,* tell her story, and have them call both the police and the FBI. Even if they took her away, even if they made her disappear, at least there would be witnesses. Lots of witnesses. Not even killers as ruthless as these could take out a whole newsroom, plus assorted innocent, uninvolved cops and FBI agents, too. Because there had to be more who weren't involved than who were. The trick lay in knowing which was which.

But whatever happened, whatever she did, it was probably going to be too late for Mark.

That conversation about whether you meant it about being in love with me? We're going to finish it. Later.

She could almost hear him saying it. The memory stabbed her like a knife to the heart.

Please, God, let there be a later.

The image of him dropping to the concrete replayed again in her mind, and even as she tried to block it out — to get anything done she needed a clear head, needed to be able to think — she found herself gasping for air. Her insides twisted into a knot. Her heart gave a great aching throb. The pain almost brought her to her knees.

Then she had a thought that galvanized

her, that brought a blessed flood of adrenaline with it: They had to have known Mark was talking to someone, there at the statue. It probably wouldn't take them long to find out about Dawn. To find Dawn. Who, voluntarily or not, would tell them what questions Mark had asked, and about the video on the First Lady's phone.

Grieving, if grieving it had to be, would have to wait. Staggering through tent city, glad that there were now people around her even though they were paying her no attention, even though she knew they provided her with no protection at all, she realized that the thing she needed to do first was go get that phone.

She had an instant vision of the First Lady in the car, trying to make calls that wouldn't go through. Of her throwing the thing in frustration. Of herself on her hands and knees trying to retrieve it from under the seat.

Then thrusting it deep in her pants pocket as the accident went down. Where she thought there was a good chance it still was.

When her mother had returned her purse and phone to her in the hospital, she would have mentioned a second phone if one had turned up. Therefore, it probably hadn't. It was probably still in the pocket of her good

527

black pants, which had been cut off her in the ambulance, wadded up with everything else she'd been wearing, and given to her mother later.

To be stored in a bag in the laundry room until Jess told her what she wanted done with them. Her mother had told her that, too.

The first order of business was to retrieve that phone, see what if anything was on it, and then, if it provided anything like the proof she desperately needed, convey it personally and at warp speed to the *Post.* Or even if it didn't. While calling a lawyer — George Kelly, Davenport's partner, sprang immediately to mind, but she hesitated even as she had the thought because of what had happened to Marty Solomon. But she needed an ally, lots of allies, as many as possible. Frowning, she thought of Davenport. Davenport had tried to kill her. Would Kelly be in the pocket of whoever was orchestrating this, too?

The bottom line was, now that Mark was gone, except for her immediate family, there was no longer anyone she felt certain she could trust. That left her with the old adage about there being safety in numbers.

She would pick up the phone and head straight for the *Post,* and ask them to summon every law-enforcement agency she or they had ever heard of after she told them her story.

As a plan, it was rough around the edges. And in the middle, and everywhere else. But it was the only plan she had. Even if she wanted to save only herself. Because just running wasn't going to work. They would catch her, just like they had caught Mark tonight.

Now's . . . really all anybody's got.

His words whispered through her mind. Suddenly they seemed terrifyingly prophetic. Oh, God, had he had some kind of premonition that he would die tonight?

Her heart bled.

Blocking him out of her thoughts wasn't possible, although for the sake of her ability to do what she needed to do, she had to try. Gritting her teeth, she focused on putting one foot in front of the other and getting safely away. She was so stunned she was having trouble getting her brain to function beyond that.

People were leaving the park like cockroaches fleeing a fire, she saw as she pushed through a low hedge at the shadowy corner of East Executive Drive and K Street. Punks and hookers and thugs and druggies and the homeless and everybody else with something to fear from the suits who had invaded the park were hotfooting it along the sidewalks and disappearing down side streets, making tracks for somewhere else. Nobody wanted to be involved. If asked, nobody would have seen a thing.

Didn't happen, wasn't there, don't know: It was the code of the streets.

Mark had been shot in front of at least a dozen witnesses, and it was almost a sure bet that not one of them would say a thing.

Jess pulled herself up sharply. She couldn't think of Mark again. Every time she did, she could feel herself falling apart inside.

A cab — she needed a cab. Her mother lived on Laundry Street, down at the very end of 16th Street, the part of the city that spilled over into Maryland. How much would it cost to get there? Jess realized she still had her purse, which meant she had some money. How much? Her share of the kitty: twenty-four dollars. They had never gotten around to actually pooling it.

At the thought, Jess's heart gave another of those horrible aching throbs. More tears leaked from her eyes. Wiping them away with determination, she sent one more heartfelt prayer winging skyward.

Please take care of him, Lord. Please.

Then she saw a cab coming toward her,

and hailed it.

The ride to her mother's house was uneventful. Just to be on the safe side, she had the driver let her out on the next block over, and she cut through the alley. It was late now, well past one a.m. The chances that there would be anyone out and about in this slightly run-down residential neighborhood were slim. What worried her was that they — they, they, how she hated that terrifying, amorphous they — might have the place staked out, might be watching her even now.

Her steps slowed as she neared the two-story white house with its aging aluminum siding and black shingled roof. The family had moved here when Jess was a senior in high school, so her mother could be closer to her job. They'd all lived here until the last few years, when one by one they had started moving out. It was a working-class house, narrow and a little shabby, three bedrooms and a bath upstairs, living room, dining room, kitchen, and a half bath downstairs, and it had been crowded when they had all lived there together. Currently, depending on whether or not Sarah was still in residence with the kids, just her mother and Maddie lived there.

Jess stopped beside some garbage cans behind the house across the alley. Huddling against one of the rickety privacy fences that separated the tiny backyards from one another, she looked around — nothing out of the ordinary, nothing moving — and then back at her mother's house. Not a light on in the place. No cars in the graveled parking area that, when they were home, usually held her mother's Mazda and Maddie's Jeep.

Shivering, clenching her teeth to keep them from chattering, she hesitated, eyeing the house, almost ready to turn and walk away.

The very last thing she wanted to do was endanger her family. But it was the weekend, and Judy could often be found babysitting her grandsons while Sarah and her husband went out and then, if they got home late, just spending the night at Sarah's. (This was presuming Sarah's marriage was back on.) And Maddie might well be with Grace, or at a girlfriend's, or, more likely, with her boyfriend.

There was a good chance, then, that the house was empty. And it would take her only five minutes, tops, to slip inside, go down to the laundry room in the basement, and recover that phone if it was there.

If there was any chance, any chance at all, that Mark was still alive, for her to find evidence that the First Lady's death was murder and get it out to the public as fast as possible might be the only hope he had. After all, once the truth was out there, what was the point of killing anybody else? Of killing Mark?

She was probably kidding herself, and she knew it. There was no reason she could see that they would have kept Mark alive.

But she had to keep that slim hope. Otherwise, she was afraid she would just curl up in a little ball where she stood and cry and cry and cry.

Making up her mind, Jess took a deep breath and quickly crossed the alley. The familiar smell of home greeted her as she pulled her key from the lock and quietly closed and locked the back door. Something about just being inside the house was comforting. Her bedroom had been in the basement — as a teen, she'd made herself a whole lair down there — and knowing that her old bed and her old computer and everything else she'd left behind were still right where she had left them made her throat tighten with longing. But she couldn't stay. She couldn't even linger.

Holding her breath, listening hard as she crossed the well-worn linoleum floor, she heard nothing but the hum of appliances.

The glowing numbers over the microwave announced the time: one twenty-three. She'd been wrong, she discovered as she glanced into the hall. The light was on in the half bath at the bottom of the stairs. It had no windows, so she hadn't been able to see the glow from outside. Now it showed her that there were no shoes kicked off in the hall — something that her whole family tended to do as soon as they entered the house — and so reinforced her belief that no one was home. And it was enough to light her way down the basement stairs.

Once away from the dim pool of light at the bottom of the stairs, the basement itself was dark as pitch. Fortunately, she knew her way like the back of her hand. The basement was separated by thin plasterboard walls into three rooms: the laundry room, which was in the far corner of the poured concrete rectangle; the utility-junk area, which the stairs led down into and which she was moving through at that moment; and her own former bedroom, which took up the entire area to the left of the stairs.

There were no windows, which had bothered Judy when Jess had insisted on moving down there. But Jess had liked the privacy and had compensated for the lack of daylight by plastering her walls with fluorescent posters.

The door to the laundry room opened with a creak. A faint mustiness and the scent of fabric softener hit her as soon as she stepped over the threshold. Once inside, with the door closed behind her, Jess turned on the light, blinking in the sudden brightness.

The washer and dryer were located against the far wall, a drying rack to the right. The ironing board and iron nestled in a corner. To the left were shelves that held everything from detergent to bug spray.

A brown paper grocery bag with the top folded over sat on one of the shelves. Jess was almost sure that it was the bag she was looking for as soon as she set eyes on it, and when she opened it she discovered that she was right. Thrusting her hand down into the jumble of clothes and finding her pants, she pulled them out. They had been slit up both legs, but that didn't bother her. Checking the right pocket, she drew out a phone.

Yes.

Her hand tightened around it. Then, frowning, she realized that it didn't look like her memory of the phone the First Lady had had with her in the hotel bar. It had been too dark inside the Lincoln to see the phone Mrs. Cooper had tried to use without success just before the wreck, but Jess had assumed it had been the same one.

Now she saw that it wasn't.

Opening it, she pressed the button to turn it on, praying it still had power. It did. The Sprint logo flickered to life with a melodious beep that made her flinch. Quickly, Jess went to the menu, pressed another button, looked at the screen, and felt her stomach tighten as she realized that what she was holding in her hand was the President of the United States's personal cell phone.

His wife had obviously taken it. Why? Jess's heart knocked against her rib cage as she went to videos. Clicking on it, she watched what filled the tiny screen with stunned disbelief.

David Cooper had filmed himself in full bondage regalia being serviced by a leather-clad woman who was not his wife.

There were six similar videos.

The quality was not good. The film was grainy. But what she was seeing was unmistakable, as was the identity of the person she was watching.

Jess realized that she held the proverbial smoking gun in her hand.

Clearly, Mrs. Cooper had discovered the videos. Just as clearly, someone else had found out she had them and had been determined to stop her from showing them to anybody. They must have been going crazy searching for the phone ever since the accident. Or maybe they assumed it had burned up in the wreckage.

Now that she thought about it, Jess realized that Mrs. Cooper might have been trying to e-mail those videos in the final few minutes before the crash. That would explain why nothing was going through. That would explain her frustration.

Phone in hand, Jess was just turning toward the door when it opened.

She jumped a foot in the air before she realized that it was Maddie who was standing in the doorway staring at her.

"Jess? What are you doing here?" Maddie's hair was in braids and she was wearing a blue tank top, ratty sweatpants, and fuzzy pink socks, her typical sleepwear. Her pregnancy was only just beginning to show.

"I stopped by to get something." Jess brushed past her sister, already on the way to the stairs. Now that she knew somebody was home, she wanted to get out of there fast.

"Oh, my God, Mom's been so worried about you! When she heard that your boss killed himself, she started calling everybody she could think of, trying to track you down."

"I sent her an e-mail."

Maddie snorted. "That didn't even slow her down."

"So tell her you saw me and I'm fine, okay? I'll call her in a few days." Jess sought to turn the subject. "How did you know I was down here?"

"I was asleep on the couch upstairs. I thought I heard somebody in the basement." Maddie trailed her. "Are you leaving?"

"Yeah, I . . ." Jess had a thought and stopped dead. Her head swivelled toward her old bedroom, and then she changed course and hurried toward it. "Is anybody else here?"

"No, just me. Mom's at Sarah's and —"

"I want you to get out of here." Jess pushed through her bedroom door and went straight to her computer. She still used it sometimes, and kept it up to date. Turning it on, she glanced back at her sister, who was just a few steps behind her. "Where's your Jeep?"

"Out front. What's going on?" Maddie's comprehensive glance turned to a frown. "Have you been crying?"

Mark was shot. . . .

But she didn't say it. Jess swallowed to try to dislodge the lump in her throat, and ignored Maddie's question.

"Go get in your Jeep and drive away. Go to Sarah's. Do you hear me? Right now."

She had turned on the small lamp beside the computer and was fishing in her desk drawer for the cable she needed as she spoke.

"Something's wrong, isn't it?"

"Yes. And I'm not going to tell you what." She found the cable and sat down in her chair to hook it up. "Go."

"Jess . . ."

Blood pounding in her temples, her eyes still blurry from the tears she had shed, working as fast as she could with fingers that were clumsy and cold from shock and grief, Jess didn't look around. "Go to Sarah's. Right this minute. Please, Maddie, I'm begging you. You know I wouldn't tell you to do it if it wasn't urgent."

"Okay." A lifetime of trust was in Maddie's reply. Without another word, she turned and left the room.

"Don't tell anybody you saw me until tomorrow at the earliest. Whatever you do, don't bring Mom or anybody back over here tonight," Jess called after her sister. Knowing how her family worked, she needed to be sure that was understood. "Promise me."

"I promise." Maddie's now frightened-sounding voice floated back to her.

"Hurry. Don't take anything. Just go."

She could hear Maddie's footsteps on the stairs. A moment later, as she listened to the front door open and close, she heaved a sigh of relief. At least her sister would be safe.

Then she got down to work. The process took a few minutes, but it wasn't hard, and it was helped along because she knew all the shortcuts. In fact, she was so engrossed in what she was doing that she didn't even realize she had company until she saw a shadow of movement in the still-open door and heard Maddie say, "J-jess."

She was just registering the wobbly tone of Maddie's voice when she glanced over her shoulder to see Maddie standing there watching her.

One of the dark-suited goons had an arm around her neck and a gun pressed to her temple.

32

Jess's heart went into overdrive. Her blood ran cold. Her eyes collided with her sister's. Maddie looked scared to death.

Oh, God, what have I done?

"Hello, Ms. Ford." The goon flipped on the overhead light. He was maybe six feet tall, broad rather than lean, with buzzed black hair and an olive-skinned, harsh-featured face. Black suit, white shirt, black tie. One of *them.*

With nervous fingers, Jess immediately pressed a button on the computer and scooted her chair back a little to get out of the way.

"I had to . . . he made me . . ." Maddie stuttered. The arm around her neck tightened, cutting off her words, making her claw at his arm and gasp for air.

Jess knew she didn't have time to waste giving a useless command for him to let Maddie go.

"You're on a webcam. Millions of people are watching you right now," she said crisply, as the gun left Maddie's temple to point at her. Remembering how quickly Mark had been shot, how fast Mark had shot the guy in the apartment, her worst fear was that he would blow her and Maddie away before he even realized that he was on *Candid Camera.* Her heart hammered. Her pulse raced. But it was terror for her sister even more than for herself that helped her project an outward calm.

She could not bear to see another sister die before her eyes. She had lost so much tonight: the man she loved. She couldn't lose Maddie, too.

"What?" He frowned, looking from her to the computer. The camera mounted on it was small but unmistakable.

Smile, asshole.

"You heard me. You — and me and my sister, all of us — are on the Web right now. Live. Everybody out there is listening to this conversation. If you shoot us, they'll be watching. All those people will be witnesses."

"What?" He stared at the monitor, then looked closer, as if he suddenly realized that he, Maddie, Jess, the whole scene he was part of, was there on the screen for him to see, just like he was watching them as part of a TV show.

"Turn it off. I'll kill her." The threat was directed to Jess. The gun was once again pressed to Maddie's head.

"Jess." Mortal fear clouded Maddie's eyes. Jess watched her sister's face whiten until it was the color of chalk, and felt her stomach turn inside out. *I'm sorry, so sorry . . .* Maddie's hands were on her captor's arm, just resting there as if she was scared to try to pull it loose, scared to move. She looked like she was ready to faint. Jess felt herself breaking into a cold sweat.

"Too late, everyone already saw. It's already all over the Internet." She knew she had to lay all her cards on the table fast. Palms clammy, she clutched the armrests of her chair and projected confidence like she had never projected anything before. "Do you understand what I'm telling you? They've already seen you. They can identify you. They'll know you killed us. Everybody out there who's watching this right now."

His gun hand jerked. The computer exploded with a bang as a bullet hit it. Jess jumped and squeaked as shards of glass and plastic flew past her to rain down everywhere in a shower of debris. Her heart lodged in her throat. Maddie's scream was immediately cut off, and Jess realized he had tightened his hold on her neck again.

A smoky, burning smell wafted beneath her nostrils.

"Fuck your camera, bitch." The gun pointed at Jess. In a split second her heart hit what felt like a thousand beats a minute. Trying not to cringe in terror, she tensed, feeling cold sweat pour over her in waves as she braced for the bullet that any second now was going to blast through her flesh.

Oh, God, would it hurt?

Desperately, she kept talking. "You can't erase what's already out there. Plus, you should probably know I found the phone. The President's phone. You need to call whoever you're working for and tell them that. Tell them I posted all those dirty videos of the President all over the Web. They're on YouTube. CNN's iReport. iWatch. Everywhere. If they haven't gone viral already, you can bet they will any minute. That means they'll be all over the world. Millions of people will see. There's no stopping it. Nothing anybody can do. It's over. You need to call and tell them that."

"She's t-telling the truth." Maddie wet her lips. "She's good at stuff like that."

Jess pointed at the phone that was now lying beside the shattered remains of her computer. The cable was still attached to it.

"See?" she said. "That's the President's phone. See the cable? I uploaded his videos to the Internet."

The goon stared at the phone.

"Nobody else home," a man's voice called from what sounded like the top of the stairs. "We got cleaners on the way, so hurry up."

Jess realized there was a second goon, and didn't know why she was even surprised. She should have learned by this time that they traveled in pairs.

"There's a problem," the goon called back. "Come down here."

Listening to the sounds of heavy footsteps on the stairs, Jess cast a cautious eye over the desktop, looking for anything she could use as a weapon. There was nothing. These guys were big, strong, well-trained professional killers. What was she going to do, staple them to death?

"What kind of problem?" The second goon was maybe an inch taller, twenty pounds lighter, and a little better-looking than the first. But in dress and manner, they could have been twins.

"Tell him." The first goon nodded at Jess. His gun was still aimed right at her. One squeeze of his finger and . . . even as the tiny hairs at the back of her neck prickled to life at the thought, she forced her mind away from it. But at least his grip on Maddie had eased. His arm was more around her collarbone than her throat now. Maddie still looked terrified, with her eyes big as plates and sweat beading her upper lip, but at least she could breathe. Jess could see her chest heaving from where she sat.

Heart hammering, doing her best to keep up a brave front, Jess told the second goon what she had done.

He walked over, looked at the President's phone, looked at the cable, looked at the dead computer, then looked back at the first goon.

"You better call," the second one said.

The first goon's lips compressed. Letting go of Maddie, he gave her a shove toward Jess.

"Get over there and behave."

Maddie stumbled toward her. Jess rose on unsteady legs to wrap her arms around her sister, whose breathing was ragged and who shook from head to toe. Maddie was several inches taller than she was and quite a bit bigger, but it didn't matter: In this time of extremis, her little sister looked to her for comfort and protection. Knowing that she had pretty much provided what protection she could by employing the webcam and the Internet, Jess tried to keep her own physical responses under control as she registered with an icy thrill of fear how both men watched them with nearly identical expressions: not hate, not even dislike, but cold indifference, which was more terrifying than either. They would clearly have no more trouble shooting her and Maddie than they would disposing of a piece of trash. Jess's insides churned at the thought, but she tried not to let it show. Seeing how terrified she was would only scare Maddie more.

Keeping his gun on them, his thick body blocking the door, the first goon pulled a cell phone out of his pocket and punched in some numbers.

"There's a problem," he said into the phone. Then he told whoever was on the other end what Jess had told him, said a few *uh-huh*s and *yeah*s and concluded with a terse, "Got it."

Then he hung up and waved his gun at her.

"You. Glasses. Get the phone. We're going for a ride. All of us. And if you give us any trouble, the first person we'll kill is baby sister."

They were heading northeast.

Maddie rode in the front seat beside the second goon, who was driving. Jess sat in the back beside the first one, whose gun rested casually on his thigh. Both women had their hands fastened behind them with plastic ties; seat belts secured them in place. The car was a black Lexus, comfortable and roomy, smelling of new leather — and fear. As the lights of the city gave way to the quiet rushing darkness of back roads that wound through the countryside, Jess's stomach cramped and her throat went dry at the thought of what might be waiting for them at the end of the journey. Having been ordered not to talk when she'd first asked where they were going, and having that order reinforced by a casual aiming of her seatmate's gun at Maddie, she sat silently behind the driver, watching her sister's pale face in profile. Maddie's lips trembled, and her breathing was ragged. Her shoulders slumped, and she kept glancing around and licking her lips.

My fault. I got Maddie into this.

Her already lacerated and raw heart felt like it was being shredded anew every time she looked at her sister's despairing face.

Their only hope was that someone had seen what was happening via the webcam and notified the police. Of course, it would take the police some time to track the broadcast to its source, and even when they did, they would have no idea where she and Maddie were being taken. She didn't even know that.

So her only hope wasn't a hope at all. It was more like wishful thinking. If she and Maddie were to survive, they needed something more concrete.

But before she could think of anything, the Lexus slowed, turned into a winding lane, and purred uphill.

Jess's heart began to pound as she realized their destination was at hand. The car slowed still more as it approached a wrought-iron fence that had to be at least ten feet tall. Equally tall bushes behind it formed a hedge that prevented Jess from seeing anything beyond it but curving treetops swaying against an inky-dark sky. They braked, and Jess saw that they had reached a tall gate complete with a small stone guardhouse and uniformed guard. The driver rolled down the window and waved. The guard, clearly recognizing him, nodded back and said something into a headset he wore. The gate opened inward. The Lexus rolled through.

"Where are we?" The question escaped her. There was no answer except the increasingly loud gasps of Maddie's breathing. The goon beside Jess gave her a single contemptuous glance then turned his attention forward. Jess was left to look out the tinted windows to try to make sense out of what was happening.

Acres of large trees; grass smooth and, so late at night, dark as black velvet; perfectly matched stones lining the driveway; then, finally, a glimpse of an imposing stone mansion — they were pulling up the driveway of an estate. An awesome estate, the kind that had to cost millions of dollars.

Jess's mouth went dry as she thought about who might own such a place.

Then she had no more time for speculation, because they had reached a large underground garage and a door was opening for them. As soon as the Lexus pulled inside, the door closed behind them.

Trapped. The word echoed through Jess's brain, chilling her to the bone.

A moment later they were out of the car and walking through a small door into the house. There was a tension in the air now; Jess could feel it, and her nerves stretched taut as piano wire. Her scalp prickled. Her pulse surged.

"Who lives here?" she asked, not because she expected an answer — she didn't. It was to break the increasingly oppressive atmosphere, to give Maddie, who was looking increasingly wild-eyed and terrified, a bit of heart.

"Shut up" was the growled response. The second thug, who was walking behind her sister, who was leading the way, gave Maddie a shove.

Maddie stumbled, regained her balance, and seemed to shrink. Feeling the welcome heat of building anger — welcome because it was an antidote to fear — Jess shut up.

As they were herded along a hall, Jess got the impression that they were still underground. The floor was stone, the walls seemed to be the real old-fashioned kind of plaster, and the air was quiet and cool. At the end of the hall was an elevator. They rode it up three floors in silence. The tension in that elevator was so thick it could have been cut with a knife.

When the door opened, Jess was pushed out first with a rough hand in the middle of her back. She found herself stumbling into what seemed to be an extremely large office, maybe thirty by forty feet, with a slate floor and bookshelves fashioned from some fine dark wood lining three of the four walls. The fourth wall, the one to the right of the elevator, had deep blue floor-to-ceiling curtains drawn over a pair of windows that flanked a white marble fireplace with a portrait of a woman over it. Scattered about were a number of gold-upholstered wing chairs positioned in pairs with a table between them. Jess could smell, just faintly, a mix of cigar smoke and lemon-tinged furniture polish in the air. A quartet of black-suited men, two on either side of the room, stood with their legs apart and their hands clasped behind their backs in the classic military at-ease position, their expressions impassive as they stared straight ahead, clearly on guard duty. Jess's heart pounded as she spotted them. *They, them* — those were the names she knew them by, and just the sight of them made her go all light-headed. A huge mahogany desk sat catty-corner across the far corner of the room. Two men were behind it, one standing, the other sitting. The sitting man rose as Jess stopped just beyond the elevator, looking at them.

Her breathing suspended as she recognized him: Wayne Cooper, the First Father.

"You've got yourself into a bad situation, I'm afraid, Ms. Ford." He sounded perfectly normal, if a little severe. He looked just like he did on TV, which was the only place Jess had ever seen him. But there was something about him, about the expression on his face, about the way his fingers tapped impatiently on the desktop, about the aura of power he exuded, that sent a chill racing down Jess's spine. "I need you to come over here, give me that phone of my son's, and tell me exactly what you've done."

He turned and pointed a bony forefinger accusingly at a computer monitor. The man behind him was absolutely ashen-faced as he looked at it, too. The reason was obvious: It was running one of the videos she had so recently uploaded.

"Free her hands," Cooper ordered over his shoulder. One of the goons must have had a knife, because he sliced through the plastic tie. Jess shook her hands, chafed her wrists, and glanced at Maddie, who had just been pushed down into one of the wing chairs.

Maddie's eyes clung to hers. Jess could see tears swimming in them. Her chest went tight.

"My sister?"

Cooper snorted. "Get the hell over here and give me that phone."

A goon pushed her forward. With her peripheral vision, Jess saw Maddie let her head drop against the back of the chair and close her eyes. She could feel her sister's terror, reaching out like icy fingers to clutch at her own heart. As she moved toward the desk, Jess swallowed, the taste of fear sour in her mouth.

She was horribly afraid they were just about out of time; even if she wanted to, even if they ordered her to at gunpoint, or with a gun to Maddie's head, what was done could not be undone.

Once they figured that out, would they kill them both?

Bubbling anger trumped the sick fear that threatened to turn her bones to water and her muscles to mush. These people were terrorizing and threatening her sister. They had ripped her own life completely apart. They had killed so many people. They had shot Mark.

She was caught, with no way to escape them that she could see. And thanks to her, poor, innocent Maddie was caught along with her. But she refused to cower. No way would she give them the satisfaction of seeing how very frightened she was, of how helpless she felt.

Her head came up. Squaring her shoulders, she walked to the desk.

"Hand over that phone." He held out his hand. Jess pulled the President's phone from her pocket and put it in his palm. She had no further use for it, anyway. She'd taken what she needed from it.

"Now I want you to tell me just exactly what you did."

Ignoring her pounding heart, Jess looked Cooper in the eye.

"I uploaded those videos to every media outlet I could think of. I put them on You-Tube. iReport. iWatch. Everywhere. They're all over the Web. And those goons of yours who broke into my mother's house and kidnapped my sister and me? That was captured on my webcam, too. It's all out there now. Millions of people are probably watching it as we speak."

His eyes bulged. His face slowly purpled with anger.

"God in heaven, young woman, you've done a bad day's work. A bad thing for your country. You —"

The phone on his desk rang, interrupting. Breaking off, fixing her with a fulminating stare, he snatched up the receiver.

"Yes," he said into it. Then, "It's about time. Send them on up."

Then he hung up.

"There's no fixing this, Mr. Cooper," the man at his side said. He looked absolutely ill as he glanced at the screen then away again. Jess thought there was something familiar about his round face and blond hair, but she couldn't quite place him and wasn't inclined to try. Instead, she was busy trying to think of anything, any sliver of a plan, that might save them. "Once it's out there on the Internet like this, there's no calling it back."

"There has to be."

A barely audible click and the whisper of the doors opening announced the arrival of the elevator.

Automatically, Jess glanced over her shoulder. Her eyes widened. Her heart wobbled. Her breath stopped. She turned, leaning back against the desk for support.

Mark walked into the room, a new, barely congealed gash in the left side of his forehead, his face tight with stress, tension apparent in the controlled way he moved, but very much alive. Their eyes met. Her soul sang hosannas. The icy grief that she'd been keeping so carefully isolated suddenly melted and turned into a rush of thanksgiving that surged through her veins.

It was only then, as her world righted itself on its axis and she drew a deep, cleansing breath, that she registered the identity of the man right behind Mark: Fielding. He was pointing a gun at Mark's back.

33

"Mr. Cooper. Lowell." Mark nodded grimly at the two men behind the desk. Only then did Jess realize who the second man was: Harris Lowell, the President's Chief of Staff. With Fielding still behind him, Mark walked toward them. Guards and goons alike watched him carefully, but with Fielding's gun on him and outnumbered seven to one, he apparently wasn't considered a threat, because they let him come. Jess saw the sideways glance with which he took in Maddie's presence, as well as the subsequent narrowing of his eyes and thinning of his mouth. Maddie was sitting up now, tear stains on her face, looking at Mark with renewed hope.

Hoping was foolish, Jess told herself sternly as she caught herself hoping, too. The odds were so high — too high. Mark was still alive, yes, but he was in no better case than Maddie and herself: He was a captive, almost certainly slated to die.

"Mark." Cooper's eyes pinned him. His expression was unfriendly, to say the least. "If you'd kept a lid on Annette like I asked, none of this would have happened. How the hell are we gonna fix this?"

"Ms. Ford posted videos of the President all over the Web," Lowell said, gesturing unhappily at the monitor, where one of the films was playing. "It's bad. As bad as can be."

Mark reached the desk. He was so close his sleeve brushed hers, so close she could see how very raw and painful-looking the gash in his forehead was. It looked like the kind of thing that could have been gouged out of his flesh by a bullet. Had he been shot, as she'd thought, and that was the result? Even with Fielding and his gun behind him, Jess was so glad to see him that a warm little glow filled her. It must have shown in her eyes, because his eyes warmed in turn and he gave her a quick, intimate smile.

"It was the President's phone that I picked up right before the car wrecked," she told him. "Mrs. Cooper must have found it that night before she ran away from the White House. There were videos on it. . . ." She gestured at the monitor. The graphic images spoke for themselves.

"My question is, how did you know Annette had it?" Mark asked Cooper. He was very calm, but she could feel his stress. He was wound tight, his edginess apparent in the hardness of his eyes and jaw, the tautness of his shoulders. Behind him, Fielding's face could have been carved out of stone.

"David called me and told me. He realized his phone was missing as soon as he got up to the residence from that damned dinner for whoever it was. He was panicking, because he knew what was on it and that she must have took it. She'd been threatening him with divorce, you know. He guessed she was going to use those damned pictures against him. That boy always was a fool when it came to women."

"So you had Annette killed to stop her from using the videos against David in a divorce?"

Cooper grimaced. "Hell, no. I had her killed to save his Presidency. If they'd got out it would've been over. Now that I've seen 'em, I know he wasn't exaggerating one bit about that."

"They are out," Jess pointed out. "They're everywhere. It's over, Mr. Cooper."

"Nothing's ever over, Ms. Ford." Cooper's eyes met hers. "If you'd died in that wreck like everybody else, none of the rest of this would've been necessary. But you didn't, you lived and you remembered and you talked and you put these damned pictures on the Internet, so that's where we are."

"You'll be charged with murder, Mr. Cooper." Lowell sounded like a man in shock. "Hell, they'll charge me as an accessory after the fact, even though I had nothing to do with killing the First Lady and just got on board later to try to clean up the mess. The President . . ."

"He was out of the loop," Cooper said. "He suspects some, but he doesn't know."

"He'll have to resign just on account of these videos, if nothing else," Lowell said.

"No." Cooper shook his head. "I've been thinking. We can claim the pictures are fakes — claim it's a look-alike and not David at all. There'll be some talk, maybe some things printed in rags like the *National Enquirer,* but they can't prove it's David, and we can face it down. There's no proof of anybody murdering anybody. Annette died in a car accident, pure and simple. Davenport committed suicide without anybody threatening to reveal that he'd been embezzling from his firm for ten years or more if he didn't kill himself and take this young lady with him — which the damned drunk failed to do. His secretary — hit and run. That reporter — car accident. It's all nothing. It can all be explained away. The only people who know otherwise are right here in this room." Jess knew what was coming. A thrill of fear shot down her spine even as Cooper looked around at his guards. "I want you — all of you — to take these three people here away and shoot 'em, then hide their bodies where they won't ever be found. Hennessey, I'm putting you in charge of that. We can't afford any screwups on this, you understand?"

"Yes, sir." Hennessey — the second goon — nodded and drew his gun.

"Oh, please, I'm having a baby! I don't want to die!" Maddie cried, bolting up from the chair and darting toward Jess. Jess's gaze shot to her. Her heart clutched. Her stomach turned over. Her arms reached out for her sister. . . .

Horror grabbed Jess by the throat as she realized Hennessey's gun was tracking Maddie.

"Maddie!" she screamed, lunging toward her.

"Please, please . . ."

"Get down!"

Mark dived on top of both of them. Even as she hit the stone floor hard, Jess realized

Mark had a gun. He was rolling, coming to his feet, aiming . . .

And screaming into his sleeve, "Where the hell are you guys?"

A split second later a dozen armed men burst from the elevator, yelling, "Freeze, Federal agents!"

An hour later. it was all over. Having taken Mr. Cooper and Lowell away first, the FBI was now loading the last of Cooper's private security personnel into vans. Put together from former federal agents, Cooper's team had all the skills of the real thing with none of the legal restrictions. Mark had been glad to learn that the men who had been trying to kill Jess and, later, both of them, had been Cooper's employees rather than Feds. The thought that he had killed two fellow agents had bothered him. Knowing that they were basically thugs for hire eased his conscience. It also saved him from the scrutiny, hearings, etc., associated with the killing, no matter how justified, of another operative.

"I'm so glad you came." Wrapped in a blanket, her hands freed, Maddie was in the backseat of Fielding's car, which Mark had "borrowed," if one wanted to use the term loosely, which he did. He was driving them — her and Maddie — back to D.C. Maddie to be dropped off at her sister's, and Jess — well, he had other plans for Jess. "I was *so* scared."

"So was I." Jess sat in the passenger seat beside him, smiling at him. She'd been smiling at him basically ever since he'd hauled her up off the stone floor in Cooper's house, with the occasional hug thrown in, and as soon as they got somewhere private he was going to demonstrate in a big way just how much he appreciated that. She shivered, looking at him. "I thought you were dead."

"Is that what was scaring you?" Maddie sounded indignant. "You thought *he* was dead? I thought *we* were going to die. That's what was scaring me."

Mark smiled at Jess. "Yeah, well, when I heard that Hennessey and Smith had caught up with you at your mom's house, my whole life flashed in front of my eyes. Their MO is to kill people on the spot."

"Jess talked them out of it," Maddie said. "With her computer stuff. It was probably the webcam that did it."

"So what happened after you were shot?" Jess asked. He had already told her that, just as she thought, the crease in his skull had been opened up by a bullet, which fortunately had ricocheted off his thick skull.

"I was knocked unconscious for a little while. When I woke up, two guys were carrying me through the park. I guess the other two had gone for the car or something. That made getting away from them fairly easy. I circled back to see if I could find you, but you were gone. Not knowing where you were or what was happening to you took a few years off my life there, I have to tell you, because I knew they would be coming after you hard. So I tried to think how to wrap this thing up before they got to you. I was desperate, so I called Harvey Brooks — he's a lab guy I know. I had him run some tests on the Lincoln to see if some kind of impact had caused the crash, and lo and behold, when I called him he told me there was evidence that a bullet had been fired into the right rear tire, blowing the tire and probably causing the crash. Anyway, he came and picked me up, and while I was waiting for him I took the opportunity to go over those phone number printouts again. Know what I found?"

He looked at Jess, who lifted her eyebrows at him. "What?"

"Remember how Prescott called Fielding, Wendell, and Matthews right before the crash?"

"Yeah?"

"Right after Prescott called Fielding, Fielding placed a call to Wayne Cooper. To his private cell phone. I happen to have that number, too, so I recognized it. So much as I hated to think it, I knew from that Fielding had to be the one." He had already told Jess that Fielding was the man who had attacked her in the hospital, the man who'd said "sugar" downstairs in his house.

"Then what?"

"I had Brooks call Fielding and tell him he had some real sensitive information on the death car, as everybody was calling it, and could he come over so he could tell him personally. I knew that if Fielding was involved, that would get him, and it did. When he got there, I tackled him and, uh, basically got him to confess the whole thing." No need to tell Jess and Maddie that he'd been so terrified for Jess's life that he'd put a gun to his old friend's head and threatened to blow out his brains unless he told everything he knew. The thing was, he would have done it, too. By then he'd been sweating bullets worrying about Jess. If anything had happened to her, he had realized, it would have been a blow from which he would never have recovered.

"I'm sorry Fielding was involved." Jess's smile turned sympathetic. She reached over and patted his leg. Mark had to fight the urge to stop the car and take her in his arms. With her teenage sister in the back-seat, though, he refrained.

"During the course of our conversation, I reminded him that there had never been a traitor in the Secret Service. You know what he said?" He glanced at Jess, who looked questioningly at him. "He said he wasn't a traitor. He said he was doing his job, protecting the President and the presidency. Of course, he was conveniently overlooking the fact that he was on Wayne Cooper's payroll, too."

"I guess he had to justify what he was do-ing some way," Jess said.

"I guess." Mark frowned out the wind-shield. They were back in D.C. now, cruis-ing along the Beltway, which was thin of traffic at this time in the morning. "Once I knew the whole story, knew he was the only agent involved, I called up the chain. Ar-rangements were made, and Fielding was offered a sweetheart deal if he cooperated. See, by that time Fielding had gotten a buzz on his radio to let him know that Hennes-sey and Smith had captured you." He cast a glance back at Maddie. "And a sister. I didn't know which one it was until I got there."

"Glad to know I'm important," Maddie muttered. Jess threw her a quick grin.

"After that, we had to move fast." No need to mention how sick with fear he'd been that he'd get there, get to Cooper's house where they were taking Jess, and it would be too late. It had been at right about that time that he had realized just how crazy about her he really was. But that was something to go into with her later. In private. "The deal was, Fielding was going to get me in there so you'd have some protection. The others were going to wait until Fielding and I were inside before storming the place, just in case one or more of the guards managed to get off an alarm. What everybody wanted" — him most of all — "was to get you two out of there safely."

"Which you did." Jess's smile was bright enough to light up the inside of the car.

"I was never so glad to see anybody in my life," Maddie said. "Oh, wait, get off here, Sarah's house is two streets over. On Clay."

Mark pulled off the next exit. The streets of the quiet residential area in which he found himself were dark and deserted. Even the trees looked lonely. He looked for Clay.

"There's no chance Wayne Cooper can buy his way out of this or something, is there?" Jess asked.

Mark shook his head, found Clay, and turned onto it. "I was wearing a wire, so everything Cooper said — which was pretty much a thorough-going confession — is on tape. Add to that what you put on the Internet, and the whole gang is going down. Wayne Cooper is looking at spending the rest of his life in prison, and David will have to resign. Vice President Sears will wake up this morning to the happy news that he's going to be the new president."

"You know, Mrs. Cooper might not even have released those videos to the public," Jess said, as Maddie directed him to the third house on the left. It was a single-story brick ranch house with a bike lying in the driveway. Mark was glad he saw it before he ran over it. "She might just have used them to get what she wanted in the divorce."

"Clearly, that was a chance Wayne Cooper wasn't willing to take." Mark cut the lights and killed the engine. The house was completely dark, and he didn't want to wake everybody inside. "Having his son be president meant the world to him. He worked toward that his whole life."

"I have a key." Maddie unfastened her seat belt. "You all don't have to come in with me if you don't want to. In fact, if we're not supposed to talk about this to anybody, it'll be better if you don't."

In the interests of national security, Jess and Maddie had been asked to keep quiet about what had happened until the story could be officially released. They had agreed.

"I really don't feel like facing Mom and Sarah right now," Jess confessed. Mark didn't say anything, but he absolutely agreed with her there.

Maddie slid out. "This has been fun, guys, but . . ."

"I'll walk you in." Jess got out, too. They closed the doors, and Mark watched as the two of them walked side by side to the front door. They hugged, Maddie let herself in, and Jess headed back. She was small, he registered, watching her, and boyishly slim, and her beauty was the quiet kind. But it was definitely there. Along with so much more. Brains. Guts. A loyal, loving, kind heart.

She was, in fact, the kind of woman he'd been looking for all his life. Who knew he'd find her right under his nose?

She got back in the car then, and before he turned the motor on he leaned over and kissed her. Hard and long.

When he drew back at last he said, "Remember that conversation we were meaning to have later?"

"Yeah?"

"I'm crazy in love with you," he said, and kissed her again. Kissed her until he saw a light come on in one of the bedrooms inside the house.

Then he drew back, turned on the engine and lights, and started backing out of the driveway. This was a moment he didn't feel like sharing with anyone but her, much less her whole clan.

She was looking at him with absolute stars in her eyes. Mark felt his heart kick into overdrive.

"Oh, yeah?" she said.

"Yeah." He backed into the street, shifted into drive, and headed toward the intersection. "If you want, I could take you home with me and prove it."

"Sounds like a plan," she said, and smiled at him.

34

"To my daughter. And the young man she's going to marry." Judy was on her feet, glass in hand, delivering the toast with a broad smile.

The young man in question, the father of Maddie's baby and her new fiancé, turned bright red. Maddie glowed. Jess and Sarah and Grace beamed at her. Seated farther down the table in Pat's Steakhouse, where Jess's family had gathered en masse to celebrate Maddie's engagement, Mark saluted with everyone else and took a sip of wine. Beside him, Jess was looking lovely and so happy that her sisters had teasingly asked if she was sure she wasn't the one who was getting married, while casting sly looks at Mark.

"Don't be silly," she'd answered. But her flushing cheeks had told the real story: They were in love. Like Jess, Mark was happier than he'd ever been in his life, and he was sure it showed. The icing on the cake was that Jess liked Taylor and Taylor liked Jess. In fact, they got along so well that Mark suspected they would start ganging up on him any day now. For the present, though, he and Jess were taking it slow and just enjoying each other. After all, they had all the time in the world.

A month had passed since the night in Wayne Cooper's mansion. For the good of the country, no public question had been raised about the accidental nature of Annette Cooper's death, and the few who knew the truth had been asked to keep silent. David Cooper had been allowed to quietly resign, and President Sears and his family now occupied the White House. Wayne Cooper, Harris Lowell, and a number of Cooper's private security personnel had been killed in the crash of a private plane less than twenty-four hours after Mark had last seen them alive. Officially, the terrible accident had dealt the final blow to David Cooper's ability to govern. Unofficially, Mark was sure it hadn't been an accident at all. The shadowy forces whose job it was to make things that were bad for the country go away had once again performed with impressive efficiency. The videos that Jess had uploaded to the Internet had even been rendered harmless. The originals had been impossible to recall, but damage control had begun immediately. Mark had heard through the grapevine that they had copied the videos, digitally replaced David Cooper's face with that of the leaders of all the major nations, and uploaded those as well. The resulting uproar had been considerable, but all the videos, including David Cooper's, were subsequently proclaimed fakes and the public's attention had shifted elsewhere.

The wheels of government continued to turn without a hitch.

"So are you and Mark coming by the house?" Judy asked Jess when the meal was over and the group was saying their good-byes before leaving the restaurant.

"Not tonight. I start my new job tomorrow, remember?" It was a Sunday night, and Jess had to be in her new office at a law firm that had done business with her previous one by eight a.m. Monday. She'd been excited when the position had been offered to her, and since she was excited, Mark was excited for her. Just like she was happy for him when he got the transfer he wanted into the investigative arm of the Secret Service.

"You won't be so busy working you'll forget you're going with me to try on dresses Saturday, will you?" Maddie asked Jess as she came up to them, pulling her bashful fiancé by the hand. "I have to have my maid of honor with me."

"Wait a minute. I thought I was your maid of honor," Grace objected.

"You're all going to be my maids of honor. I'm having three," Maddie said, as Sarah, holding her sons by the hand and followed by her husband, joined them. "And you're all helping me choose my dress this Saturday. And so is Mom."

"Technically, I'll be your matron of honor," Sarah pointed out. "Your *only* matron of honor."

"Unless Jess . . ." Grace turned twinkling eyes on Jess.

"Not happening," Jess said firmly, and tucked her hand in Mark's arm. "Come on," she said to him. "We're going home now."

They were living together in his house. Jess had gone home with him that night a month ago and basically had never left.

"Sounds good to me," he answered, smiling.

"I'll see you Saturday," she called over her shoulder to her mother and sisters as she and Mark left the restaurant. It was dark, with a full moon just beginning to climb the sky, and the area around the restaurant was busy. Mark found himself struck by the exchange he and Jess had just had, and thought it over as he opened the door of his new car for Jess and she got in.

A moment later, he slid behind the wheel and looked at her.

"Just so you know, for a long time my house was just a house, a place where I slept and changed clothes. It wasn't a home."

"Are you saying it is now?"

"Yeah," he said. "Because you're in it. That's the difference."

He leaned over and kissed her. Then he drove her home.

ABOUT THE AUTHOR

Karen Robards is the author of more than thirty novels, most recently the *New York Times* bestseller *Guilty.* She lives in Louisville, Kentucky.

The employees of Thorndike Press hope you have enjoyed this Large Print book. All our Thorndike, Wheeler, and Kennebec Large Print titles are designed for easy reading, and all our books are made to last. Other Thorndike Press Large Print books are available at your library, through selected bookstores, or directly from us.

For information about titles, please call:
(800) 223-1244

or visit our Web site at:
http://gale.cengage.com/thorndike

To share your comments, please write:
Publisher
Thorndike Press
295 Kennedy Memorial Drive
Waterville, ME 04901